ACCLAIM

Wish Me Joy West Virginia

"Valerie Banfield has cleverly woven and captured the spirit of the Charleston Ballet's early history in her book *Wish Me Joy West Virginia*."

—KIM R. PAULEY, Artistic Director and CEO of the Charleston Ballet

Wish Me Home West Virginia

"From the moment I set foot in Bigler's General Store, I felt like I was home. Valerie Banfield paints the hills and the people from them with gentle grace. I can hear the whippoorwill and feel the breeze through the sycamores. As they say from my neck of the woods, 'You done good.'"

—CHRIS FABRY, author of the *Dogwood* series

While I Count the Stars
CASCADE AWARD WINNER

"The presentation of the Costa Rican involvement in WWII was fascinating. It's a new perspective that I suspect few people have and it deserves a wider audience. This is a book I will recommend to those who love historical fiction, especially WWII enthusiasts."

—JANE KIRKPATRICK, *New York Times* and *CBA* bestselling author

While I Count the Stars

"Banfield accomplished the difficult task of finding a little-known fact of history and bringing it to life. Well done! She carefully, successfully, balanced two stories and made them work—alone and together."
—KAY MARSHALL STROM, author and speaker

Playing Carnegie

"No collection of historical fiction is complete without this Korean War-era gem by Cascade Award-winning author, Valerie Banfield."
—LISA GRACE, author of *The 15th Star*

Deceived: A Case of Mistaken Identity

"Banfield's unique and different voice allows the reader some *oohs* and *ahs* throughout her writing. Her book includes suspense and romance, and is storytelling in its truest form."
—LINDA K. RODANTE, author of the *Dangerous* series

Signs of Life

"Banfield takes us on a journey with Zach Hoyt who is Caucasian; his wife, Juanita, who is American Indian; Stan Benton, who is African American, and a diverse cast of secondary characters. I would have loved this book alone for that reason, but Ms. Banfield added another element: Juanita is deaf, a condition that ties the stories together. I also loved the faith element found in this realistic and captivating book."
—TONI SHILOH, author of the *Maple Run* and *Freedom Lake* series

wish me joy
West Virginia

ALSO BY VALERIE BANFIELD

Deluge: When Yesterdays Collide

Checkered: A Story of Triumph and Redemption

Deceived: A Case of Mistaken Identity

Gifted: A Basket Weaver's Tale

Sidetracked: If Yesterday Steals Tomorrow

Signs of Life

Beneath the Healing Rain

~

HISTORICAL FICTION

Anchored: A Lamp in the Storm

While I Count the Stars

Playing Carnegie

Wish Me Home West Virginia

~

BY VALERIE BANFIELD AND SUE COPELAND

West Virginia Crude

West Virginia Still

West Virginia High

wish me joy West Virginia

All the best,
Valerie Banfield

Valerie Banfield

Copyright © 2019 by Valerie Banfield

ISBN: 978 1 0884 4528 0

Cover artwork used under license from Shutterstock.com.

Scripture taken from The Scriptures, Copyright by Institute for Scripture Research. Used by permission.

All rights reserved. No part of this publication may be reproduced, stored in a retrieval system, or transmitted in any form or by any means, without the prior written permission of the copyright owner.

This book is a work of fiction. Where real people, events, establishments, organizations, entities, or locales appear, they are used fictitiously. All other elements are the product of the author's imagination.

For Karen and Joyce

*As the Father has loved Me,
I have also loved you.
Stay in My love.*

John 15:9

Prologue

August 1943
Brussels, Belgium

Andre wrapped his clammy hand around the Walther PPK grip, pressed the weapon deep into the hay bale, and waited for Maggy's permission. As soon as she stepped outside and closed the stable door, he pulled the trigger, keeping his thumb clear of the hammer as it engaged the firing pin and discharged the round. The hay muffled the sound, and the scent of damp feed absorbed the gunpowder's distinct odor, but Andre didn't dare exhale until his recognized that the bullet had swept through the barrel without vibrating against the metal. He still had all of his fingers, and he had a match.

Maggy crept back inside but didn't venture toward the empty horse stall until he gave the signal. While Andre concealed the firearm beneath his shirt, she retrieved the small canvas bag filled with bullets and slipped it into the side pocket of her skirt.

"Mark those as 7.65 millimeters," Andre told her as they walked the short distance to their temporary residence, the home the mayor used to occupy. The mild breeze that drifted across the grounds did little to alleviate Andre's heightened wariness. Brussels was a sea of uniforms and the mayor's house was located in the center of it. Some would consider the frequent events in the stable foolhardy. Andre preferred the terms *brazen* and *obligatory* to describe their participation in the chaos. Each time they paired a smuggled gun with the proper caliber ammunition, they forced the German itinerary back a step, be it miniscule in nature or with effects that might ripple all the way to the Führer.

When it was time to leave, Maggy ran her fingers through Andre's longish, dark hair. She smoothed his shirt collar before planting a short, but tender kiss to his lips. "Do you have everything?" she asked before they began their walk to the opera house.

Andre lifted one hand, which held a pair of ballet slippers. "Always."

German flags hung limply from windows and street lamps, the black swastika, a symbol of evil and darkness, twisting and swirling into white, intent on ravishing innocence and degrading truth. The air was as reluctant to furl the banners as the townspeople were indignant at having to display them.

They rounded a corner where two German soldiers were examining a young woman's paperwork. While one continued to question her, the other approached Andre and Maggy.

"Papers," he demanded as he stretched out his hand. His visual inspection of Andre was anything but cursory. Few men Andre's age remained in the occupied city.

From out of his back pocket, Andre pulled a photograph in which he was on stage, wearing his dance attire. He handed it to his inquisitor.

"What's this? I asked for your papers."

Andre raised his ballet slippers, but the unspoken message escaped the soldier. While his heart raced fast enough to burst,

Andre donned his practiced stage mask and willed his body to relax. Maggy stood silently, her hands clasped at her waist and her gaze fastened to the ground.

The soldier's gruff voice drew the attention of his cohort, who gestured for the young woman to be on her way. The two men mumbled in German, one pointing to the photograph and shoes while the other stared, wide-eyed, at Andre.

The first soldier returned the photograph and said, "You go."

Andre pulled Maggy's hand into his own and moved quickly toward their destination, the heft of the pistol and ammunition weighing heavier on his understanding than it did in his knapsack.

"We should be grateful we are playing host to soldiers who appreciate art, and you, in particular." Although Maggy's comment was true, her tone was derisive, and rightly so. They'd just escaped apprehension because those military officers who oversaw the occupation in Brussels thought well of Andre's dancing. Had any of their underlings harmed him, their punishment might be as hideous as what they would ordain for Andre and Maggy.

Andre did not reply, nor did they engage in conversation. He gulped air when the neo classical Théâtre Royal de la Monnaie came into view. Stretched above eight columns was a pediment filled with Eugène Simonis' bas-relief entitled, "The Harmony of Human Passions." The figure of Harmony stood at the center, flanked by those representing Murder, Remorse, Discord, Love, Pleasure, Desire, and more. Andre's focus rested on the trio that occupied the lower right side of the triangular space. For the duration of the German occupation, they would Hope and they would surely Suffer. They would pray for Consolation. Had Monsieur Simonis lived to see the war-torn city, he might have sculpted an image for Justice.

After they entered the building, Maggy accompanied Andre

to his personal dressing room. She sat on a chair and forced herself to slow her anxious, rapid inhalations. The color returned to her pallid complexion, and as she gathered another round of composure, she stood and gave him a peck on the cheek. "I'll go to my seat now."

"Don't disappear during the performance," Andre replied. His comment was not a joke, for if the Third Reich suspected either of them of participation in the resistance, one, and then the other, would disappear.

After he dressed for the performance, Andre took a last glance at the boots he'd worn to the opera house. While the theater overflowed with Nazis who would enjoy the ballet, an unknown Belgian resister would empty Andre's boots and transport the goods to the next destination. As soon as they received another delivery, Andre, Maggy, and another invisible accomplice would repeat the precarious routine.

Andre waited in the wings as the members of the orchestra tuned their instruments and stagehands prepared to raise the curtain. After he took his place, front and center, he held his body as still as one of Simonis' bas-relief sculptures, but his eyes canvassed the audience until they found Maggy. Only then was he free to take his first step.

Elizabeth, West Virginia

The wind captured a sound, a trace as thin as a whisper, and carried it through the sycamores. Fern ought to clear her throat or otherwise announce her arrival. At the least, she should retrace her steps and leave the woman to herself. Instead, like the doctor's wife who made everybody's business her own, she craned her neck, straining to catch the conversation, and tiptoed forward. When Nettie turned her face and pushed a loose strand of hair out of her eyes, Fern hunched her shoulders, making herself smaller, although she needn't have bothered. Her mother-in-law wallowed in sorrow so deep that she paid no heed to her surroundings.

"It's as if someone reached down and stole the music out of the world," Nettie said. "I can't hear a melody anymore. What's left is strident, out of tune, cymbals crashing and drums thumping an endless war chant. This is madness, Gordon. I worry about the boys fighting overseas, but we've got troubles here too, especially where Muriel is concerned."

Fern winced at the mention of her sister-in-law. She never could make sense of her brother Leland falling for the educated city gal, but he did, and the two of them made a pretty good go of it. But that was before.

"She reminds me of a wounded rabbit hiding in its nest, and I don't know how to help." Nettie's torso trembled as she pressed her hands against her face.

Nettie was right to worry, but it seemed to Fern that nothing would get better until Leland came home. Despite the number of times Fern and Nettie tried to sooth Muriel's melancholy, the woman was bent on retreating from love, from family, and from the folks who lived in Elizabeth. Her being was as hollow as the old moss-covered log that rested alongside the creek.

"I am powerless to fix things," Nettie said.

When the caw of a crow greeted Nettie's confession, she scanned the treetop and lifted her hand to shield her eyes. The bird perched in the lower branches where it preened its blue-black feathers. When its companion squawked, both took to the air.

Fern was about to step into the clearing when Nettie spoke

again. "I love Muriel. Don't get me wrong. But she's different from most folks, and I can't relate to her. I've tried." Nettie's voice faltered when she said, "I've tried so hard."

Fern hung her head. Nettie would not find a remedy here, no matter how many times she put forth her plea. Fern studied the ground while dank air flitted over the grass, too listless to do anything more than make its presence known. Nettie couldn't fix Muriel. Neither could Fern. On the other hand, Fern could comfort Nettie.

"Nettie?" Fern kept her voice low and made as much of a ruckus as she could as she plodded up the rise and closed the distance between them.

Nettie made a vain effort to hide her tear-stained face and to gather a feeble smile. "I didn't hear you."

"I didn't mean to startle you, but are you all right?"

"Right as rain."

"Right as rain that's raising the creek to flood level." Fern tipped her chin toward the object of Nettie's conversation. "Do you really think he can help you sort things out—you know—talking to him like you do?"

"Not really. It's just my way of thinking things through. Talking out loud."

"Instead of waiting here for an answer that won't come, why don't you follow me back to the house? Supper's about ready."

Nettie pressed her lips together and forced the edges upward. "Did you manage to get Muriel to give you a hand?"

"No, ma'am, but Ellie helped set the table while Becca wrastled with Wayne and Roy. So, we're all set. We just need you to take your place at the head of the table."

"Right where old granny belongs," Nettie said as the anxious lines in her face softened. "I don't know what I'd do without that tribe of yours. It's remarkable, Fern, the way grandbabies can warm a woman's soul."

"Those babies do the same for me, filling their momma to overflowing."

Fern linked her arm in the crook of Nettie's elbow, but cast a glance over her shoulder as they started toward the house. Her breathing hitched at the sight of the stone markers where loved ones rested in peace while the living struggled to contend with the mayhem inflicted by men with evil intentions. Things would be better as soon as the war ended. The Good Father willing, Leland would fill the empty places in Muriel's heart, and Percy would return to Fern and the children, and to his mother, too. Iffen He were willing.

Chapter 1

April 1955

Leland Dugan settled the ax on the tree stump, wiped his face and neck with his damp handkerchief, and massaged his aching ribs. A gust of wind, a remnant of yesterday's wicked storm, flitted through a strand of sycamores, lifting the jagged edges of the leaves and twirling them like pinwheels. The sight was as spectacular as a fine-tuned dance, the type Muriel could appreciate, providing the entertainment originated on a stage in a grand auditorium where performers wore dazzling costumes for their hoity-toity audience.

The pine tree that tumbled during the night had to have been close to seventy feet tall, but by a miracle it fell short of the Bigler's barn. Leland watched Percy Bigler drag another scraggly limb toward the growing burn pile. When he caught Leland loafing, he dropped his load.

"Something wrong?" Percy asked.

"No."

"Is your back bothering you again?"

Leland shrugged. "No more'n usual." Shrapnel lodged in his

chest and ribs, not his back. Regardless of the location of the damage, work that taxed his upper-body muscles tended to mimic a backache. Sure enough, his body suffered after a full day of work at the lumber mill, but his gratitude at coming back from the war in one piece, such as it was, ran deeper than his complaints.

"Then why the perturbed look?"

Leland opened his mouth, ready to deny the accusation, but clamped it shut again. He *was* perturbed. Up on the ridge, pair of rust-breasted bluebirds lit on a branch before they dashed from one tree to another. Their playful display induced a pang of longing. If only his marriage could reflect that carefree harmony. When a blue jay swooped into the mix and announced its arrival with much ado, the bluebirds vanished into the woods. Leland released a weary sigh. Muriel, with her soft, pleasant appearance, resembled the bluebird. Her personality, however, related more toward the blue jay's harsh jeers.

"Do you ever think we got it wrong?" Leland asked.

"Got what wrong?"

"You know. You . . . me . . . Muriel."

"What did we get wrong?"

"Did you ever wonder how things might have turned out if you'd ended up with Muriel instead of me?"

One side of Percy's mouth went cockeyed and deep furrows streaked across his forehead. He glanced toward the house, something Leland should have done before he said what he did.

"Aren't you about twenty years late with that question?" Percy bent over and reached for the severed tree limb.

"It's an honest question."

"It's a stupid question."

"Think about it. Muriel gets a hankering for city life more often than not, especially since her father died." That was the honest truth. Since 1943, when Gordon Levy died, nothing pleased Muriel. Or maybe it was the version of the husband who came home from the war that frustrated her. Seemed to Leland that he added to his wife's troubles.

"So she takes a trip to Charleston every now and again. Why would that bother you?"

"What I'm saying is, well, here you are, all these years later, working for Anders Oil instead of writing for the *Charleston Gazette*."

"I still write for the *Gazette*."

"One article a week. How many times have they asked you to come full time?"

"A few."

"More'n a few. I just got to thinking that if Muriel had chosen you, the both of you would be happy living in Charleston. That's all."

"That's all? Did you forget about my wife, my children, my mother, and everything in Elizabeth that makes this my home? What's wrong with you?"

"Nothin'."

"I'm serious. What's got you all het up?"

"I'm a mite het up about Muriel, her being depressed all the time. No matter how I try, I can't do anything right. I always figured she'd be happy if we'd had children . . ."

It came as no surprise when Percy kept his mouth shut at that remark. Percy, like everyone else in the family, knew it was true, knew it was probably the crux of Muriel's despair. Leland's sister Fern had gifted Percy four children, one right after the other. The fourth one arrived in 1942, just before Percy went off to war. Muriel accepted her lot, never speaking of their lack after Leland returned from the front, until Fern found herself expecting her fifth baby in 1950. It was plain to see that baby June's arrival awakened a deep-rooted jealousy in Muriel that no one had the means to rectify.

"Muriel has been a second mother to your nieces and nephews," Percy replied. "They adore her. Especially Ellie."

"Ellie has a city girl's makeup."

"Don't remind me. After her last trip to Charleston, Ellie couldn't quit talking about an advertisement she saw for dance lessons. You know how she loves to dance." Percy wagged his head, his face reflecting a father's misgivings, or maybe his fears. "Fern doesn't object to Ellie tagging along when Muriel visits Charleston, but losing her to the city would tear her mother apart. It might inflict permanent harm to her father too."

"See. You know what I'm talking about," Leland replied. "Muriel's itching for more, and I'm pretty sure she thinks she'll find what's missing wherever street lights glow all night long, where sophisticated folks live."

Percy's pinched expression was unexpected. "I thought she liked running the store."

"She'd like it a lot more if she sold evening gowns and high heeled shoes instead of molasses and chicken feed."

"Go to Charleston with her. Take her to the opera."

Leland had to clutch his belly when his laughing got out of control. "Me? Sit through a musical production? Why would I do that?"

"Because it would please Muriel. It would show her that you care about things that mean something to her. Life isn't just about hours working behind a store counter or sweating at a lumberyard, eating, and sleeping. It's about sharing things that are important to your wife."

"You're serious," Leland said.

Percy's nod was almost imperceptible. "Yes, I am."

"I wouldn't know how to act."

A wide grin bloomed on Percy's face. "You remember your first date with Muriel?"

"How could I forget? I remember her cowgirl clothes, her boots, and her turquoise belt buckle, but it was her eyes that drew me like a magnet." Leland took a long gander at Percy and asked, "You ever miss those days in Hawthorne?"

"No. Nevada wasn't home. Never could be. I miss the Civilian Conservation Corps in some ways, and I can't forget that it turned both of us into genuine adults."

"That, it did."

"Back to my question. You remember that Muriel insisted on a chaperone, don't you?"

Leland hooted. "She made me drag *you* along, but you did get to meet that little Hawthorne girl who sat beside you during the movie."

"The one who was about thirteen? I'd rather forget. Anyway, my point is that maybe you should take a chaperone along for your first visit to the opera."

"Why?"

"Take Ellie. Let her tag along. She'll tell you everything you need to know about Charleston, the rich folks who live over in South Hills, and the location of the best shops and restaurants. Better than that, she'll prattle about every single thing related to the opera, and while most folks would tune out the better part of it, you can grab hold of the information and make the best of your date with Muriel." Percy hefted a shoulder. "Wouldn't hurt to give it a try."

"Maybe I would if you and Fern would go too."

Percy choked and coughed. "No, thank you."

"Fern might like a night on the town."

"She'd just as soon sit in front of a bonfire and listen to owls hooting. Be brave, Leland. Go."

Chapter 2

"Haven't you heard the saying, 'If it ain't bothering you, let it be'? None of us ought to be into Leland and Muriel's business." Fern yanked a knot of weeds out of the ground and tapped the loose soil around her wilted tomato plant. She moved on down the row, plucking interlopers from among her tender seedlings. The earth needed a good, soaking rain.

Percy kept his face to the ground as he worked the next row. "I wasn't interfering. Leland was frustrated. I gave him a suggestion. That's all."

"A suggestion that included Ellie going to Charleston. Again." Fern stood upright, slipped a hand out of her glove, and wiped her eyes.

"Why are you crying?"

"I ain't. It's just dirt."

"Fern?"

"What?"

"Don't you think it would do Muriel good if Leland took an interest in what she likes? Leland will suffer through the ordeal and Ellie—"

"Will love every moment of the performance and find ten

more reasons to move to Charleston when she finishes school."

"She's just dreaming," Percy replied. His expression, though, told Fern otherwise. Ellie's daddy was as worried about losing his girl to the big city as her momma was.

"No, she's not," Fern said. "She's talking about it. Don't you remember the rules about courting? The proper sequence?"

Percy's Adam's apple bobbed at the same time his troubled eyes met Fern's judgmental stare. He pert 'near stuttered when he answered. "Well, first there's sparking, then courting, followed by talking, and then marrying."

"Muriel introduced Ellie to the sparking phase the first time she took our daughter to Charleston. The city's been courting Ellie ever since. Now the girl's talking, Percy. *Talking*. You know what's next. Those shiny lights and the bustle of industry and commerce are just waiting for Ellie to reach out and grasp the invitation to settle down." Fern rubbed her eyes again, but this time her fingers nudged moisture, not dirt.

Percy straddled the tomato plants, put his arm around Fern's shoulder, and pulled her toward him. "It's just a musical. Maybe she'll find it as dull as it sounds to you and me. One thing's for certain. You and I want all of our children to be happy. If we try to control them, we'll lose them whether they're in Elizabeth, West Virginia or out in a faraway desert like Hawthorne, Nevada."

"I know, but I can't find it in myself to accept it. Charleston is just a short drive from here, but I know how life gets in the way of doing what we want. We have enough of doing what we have to do. No matter how often we'd like to visit, or she'd like to come home, I know it won't be enough."

Percy pressed a gentle kiss to Fern's lips and said, "One day, though not for a long while, all of our children will be on their own, and we'll spend the better part of our days with just the two of us. Will that be enough?"

Tears dribbled down Fern's cheeks as her husband's soft, hazel eyes met her own. "I reckon you were enough before those babies came, so I 'spect I can revert to my old ways. You'll be more'n enough, Percy Bigler. Don't you dare think otherwise. You hear?"

Percy took Fern's hand and pressed her palm to his chest where she found solace in the steady pulse of his heart. "I don't just hear you. I know. Come on, let's go see what Becca and Ellie put together for supper. Afterwards, I think I'd like to sit on the porch and listen to the Bigler Bluegrass Orchestra. Think we can talk them into a concert?"

"Only if you and I offer to do their chores," Fern replied. "I've got dibs on milking the cows. Hope you don't mind doing the dishes."

Percy's smile lit up the vegetable garden and at least a hundred acres beyond. "If it would make you happy, darlin', I'd put on my retired boxing gloves and go a round or two with Leland."

Fern's mouth fell open. "I've got a better idea. Why don't you teach me how to box? Leland can teach Muriel. Then she and I can go toe-to-toe. Loser has to quit taking Ellie to Charleston."

"Please tell me you're joking," Percy said. He looked more than a mite worried.

"Well, I was just teasing, but now that I think about it, I like the idea." Fern finished her statement with a playful one-two jab to Percy's midsection. He didn't laugh.

More than once Leland waggled his head with the same fervor as a hound dog shaking a bee from the underside of his floppy ear.

His mind was a-buzzin', but it wasn't from an incessant insect searching for a soft target, an action meant to make the intruder move along. In this case, the relentless nuisance came in the form of a seventeen-year-old who couldn't get her victim to move fast enough to partake of every sight the city of Charleston had to offer.

Leland took care to dress his best for the occasion, but he hadn't given much thought to Muriel's request to arrive at a particular time. He ought to have checked the theater's schedule. The women had allocated three long hours to walking every street and avenue, but with regular stops in front of store windows, particularly those displaying the latest fashions and footwear, they had to hustle from one awe-inspiring attraction to the next. Ellie's jabbering, coupled with her exhausting enthusiasm, would lay him waste long before the theater's curtain would rise.

"This is it," Ellie exclaimed as she jerked to a halt.

Leland regarded the contents in the shop window. "Haven't you seen enough shoes today?"

"This is the place where I saw the ad for dance lessons. Shh. Listen."

Listen? Leland didn't mind driving to Charleston every now and again. Didn't mind heading north to Parkersburg either, but it was the noise of the city that always nudged him back into his car and to the road that led back home. Cities were loud, with people gabbing while they walked down the sidewalk or yelling at each other from across the street. Buses, delivery trucks, and countless cars filled the air with exhaust fumes while their noisy engines and occasional horns added to the unpleasant mix. Listen?

When a young woman entered the building, the sound of a piano lilted into the air. A few moments later, a second woman approached. Like the first, she was slender and carried herself with confidence and purpose. As she reached the door, she studied Ellie from head to toe. A warm smile prefaced her question. "Are you here to sign up?"

"Sign up?"

"For Mr. Van Damme's class? He doesn't have openings often, so if you want to enroll, you'd better go on upstairs while you can."

Ellie glanced at Muriel. "I'm just—"

"Would you mind letting us watch for a while?" Muriel asked. She rested her palm on Ellie's shoulder. "We need to see if this is the right place for our girl."

Leland clamped his mouth shut, certain that if he said a word his wife would do more harm than an irritated honeybee.

"Come on up."

They climbed the steps to the third floor where a small sign identified the tenants:

AMERICAN ACADEMY BALLET
Andre Van Damme

PIANO LESSONS
John Hiersoux

FRENCH LESSONS
Mrs. A. Van Damme

Their hostess escorted them inside, and when she led them to several empty chairs, Muriel, Ellie, and Leland sat, although Ellie's posterior hovered over her chair more than it rested upon it. She floated on air, her awareness captured by the dozen dancers swaying this way and that. They followed the directions of a dark-haired man who, despite his slight form, dominated the room. After each unfamiliar command, which he delivered with a heavy accent, the students responded with identical movements, their synchronized limbs displaying an unexpected agility and elegance.

Leland swallowed hard. Percy and Fern would never forgive him for this. He could place the blame on Muriel, flat where it belonged, but his West Virginia male pride reminded him that he was the leader of the house. And he would be . . . if not for his wife. Then again, this excursion to Charleston was Percy's doing. Supposing he could air his defense before Percy lit into him, Leland would still have to contend with his sister. Fern would have his hide. Percy's too.

A blond-haired woman stepped into the room and when she saw the visitors, she walked over to them. In a quiet voice, she asked, "May I help you?" She was in her mid-thirties and spoke with the same accent as the instructor did.

Leland started to rise from his chair. "We were just curious."

"About the classes," Muriel added.

By the time the three left the dance studio, Leland wanted to throttle his wife. How could she do what she'd done? The weightier concern was how he might undo it.

When Muriel accepted Leland's invitation for a night out in Charleston and chose to attend a musical rather than an opera, the prospect had eased Leland's apprehension, as had the plan to let Ellie accompany them. Now, seated in the theater where the Kanawha Players were about to perform *Girl Crazy*, Leland stared at the curtain, dazed.

What were the odds that Ellie would find herself on the sidewalk in front of the ballet school at the very moment an opportunity awaited inside? Probably about the same odds as Leland Dugan had when he courted an educated woman like Muriel Levy, daughter of the Civilian Conservation Corps company commander in Hawthorne, Nevada. Leland had counted himself lucky, although his marriage to Muriel was as inexplicable and unexpected then as it was today.

Maybe Percy and Fern needed to see the potential in Ellie with the same open eyes that Muriel had used to see the soul of a backwards mountain boy. Muriel wasn't easy-going, and a few folks considered her uppity, but her dogged determination and her need to push everyone to exceed their perception of potential, had made Leland a better man. If Muriel thought she could help Ellie make the most of her talents and her passions, who was he to argue with his wife? As the lights in the theater dimmed, Leland emptied his lungs with a slow, steady exhale. Neither Percy nor Fern would have qualms about arguing with Muriel.

Despite the setting, his preconceived notions, and the earlier events at the dance studio, Leland laughed hard enough to draw tears to his eyes. It wasn't just the fun of sharing the performance with a crowd of equally amused people or the quality of the musicians and actors. The stage set brought back memories of the naïve youth that he was when he first arrived at the CCC camp in Hawthorne.

While Hawthorne didn't resemble *Girl Crazy's* dude ranch setting, the cast, their dress, and their mannerisms generated a heap of familiarity. Scenes depicting the actress who played the part of Molly Gray, the local postmistress, reminded Leland of his first date with Muriel. He'd never forget how Muriel looked in her embroidered blouse, her denim skirt, and those fancy western boots. Granted, the similarities between Molly Gray and Muriel ended with the western garb, but they stirred emotions that drew him to the edge of his seat.

As the musical progressed and the plot unfolded, Leland stared at the action, his mouth dangling open. He didn't identify with the pleasure-seeking Danny Churchill, who turned his family's farmstead into a dude ranch with entertainment of questionable repute, but that was before the character fell for Molly Gray. Danny's quest to lasso Molly's affections hit Leland square in the chest. He reached over and squeezed Muriel's hand. When she squeezed back, she nestled against his shoulder. He didn't let go of her hand until the curtain fell.

Muriel and Ellie dozed while Leland drove home. He'd enjoyed the day despite himself. Muriel was joking when she suggested that Leland could get a job at one of Charleston's glass factories, and that Ellie could live with the two of them while she took dance classes from the famous Andre Van Damme. At least Leland hoped she was joking.

A fine mist gathered across the land and drifted upwards as the temperature fell and the humidity rose. The car's headlights reflected against intermittent patches of fog as Leland navigated hairpin curves, pressed the gas pedal to ascend a hill, or tapped the brakes when the road wandered down the other side of the slope. Used to be, when he and Muriel bought their first vehicle, it didn't take driving more than thirty miles an hour along Route 14 to turn Muriel's face green. After their first excursion, he learned to carry a couple of paper bags and a few old towels with him, but she got used to the jostling and swaying eventually, her motivation being the outings to Charleston.

By the time Leland pulled into the driveway next to Bigler's General Store, a dazzling moon and a host of flickering stars filled the clear night sky. The two-story homestead attached to the rear of the store was dark. Nettie hadn't waited up for them. Toward the back of the property, in the home Percy and Fern built after the birth of their firstborn, lace curtains muted the light coming from the sitting room window.

Some may have considered it odd that Leland and Muriel lived in the place where Nettie and Noah Bigler reared Percy, but when Captain Levy took ill after he married Noah's widow, Muriel and Leland moved into the old house so they could help Nettie tend to her husband. After all, the captain was Muriel's father, and it was her relocation to Elizabeth that brought Nettie and Captain Levy together in the first place. After he passed away, no one gave any thought to Muriel and Leland moving elsewhere.

Before he turned the key in the ignition, Leland considered how he might draw the family tree, but a simple rendering did not materialize. Because the intertwining of the families was something of a jumbled knot, an artist's depiction might require something as intricate and unique as an unruly morning glory vine. He found that image rather satisfying.

Leland walked around the car and nudged his two sleepy passengers awake. While they yawned and stretched, and climbed out, he surveyed the store and the house. Never in his wildest imaginations had he considered leaving Elizabeth, but when Muriel suggested they move to Charleston, what had she said? *No matter the location of the house, home is where you find the people you love.*

Chapter 3

Fern drew a damp cloth across the counter, collecting puddles of water and food crumbs. She didn't mind cooking, serving, or cleaning after the meal, but when the ragtag ensemble began picking and strumming without waiting for her to join them, she had to shove her annoyance out the back door. Why all of her children neglected their chores the moment Aunt Muriel and Uncle Leland stepped inside the front door was beyond Fern, but it had become a habit. Nor was it unusual for the after-dinner Bigler bluegrass session to become a Bigler Dugan production, but couldn't they, just once, wait for Fern to join them? Since it wasn't worth stirring trouble, Fern bit her lip while she hung the dishrag on a hook, turned out the kitchen light, and wandered outside. She had to shoo the neighbor boy away so she could drop into the chair next to Nettie.

Muriel was already into the second verse of "I Love You Truly," which was Leland's favorite tune, leastways when his wife did the singing. She looked up from her accordion and greeted Fern with a nod, which wasn't as welcome as helping hands in the kitchen, but it was better than nothing.

Leland sat with his shoulders hunched, strumming Fern's

guitar. Instead of handing the instrument to her, he offered her a toothy grin and tapped his foot to the gentle beat of the old song. She regarded her brother's contented expression, taking in his green eyes and coarse red hair. Strands of silver collected at his sideburns and invaded the rusty edges of his day-old beard. Forty was far too early for Leland's hair to give way to age, but maybe it had to do with surviving a world war.

People used to joke that their parents, Harold and Vera Dugan, had learned how to manipulate nature. Out of nine children, each boy wore his father's red hair and green eyes, and every one of the girls inherited her mother's blond hair and vivid blue eyes. When Percy and Fern produced offspring with a wide variety of physical characters, the townsfolk considered that to be fodder for a different sort of teasing.

Becca plucked her guitar strings, drawing a soothing harmony into the mix, while her warm alto blended with Muriel's sweet soprano. The sight of her eldest, who had immersed herself in the offering, touched Fern. Becca was the easy child, the gentle, soft-spoken big sister whose character was the spitting image of her grandmother Nettie. She stole her hazel eyes and honey-blond hair from her father, but in reality, Nettie had passed those traits to Percy so that he could gift them to Becca.

Fourteen-year-old Wayne, who slipped a few soft tones from the harmonica into the rendering, took after Percy's father. He and five-year-old June were brown-haired, brown-eyed, and slight in stature, but big on attracting attention. In the end, June always won that award. Right now, the girl was a whirlwind, dancing and twirling in the yard. With each revolution, she paused when she faced her audience, making sure everyone kept their eyes on her.

Roy, who arrived just twelve months after Wayne was born, tapped a rhythm on an upturned barrel. Except for songs that required the foot-stomping swish of a washboard, Roy stayed in the shadows. Given his druthers, the boy would retreat to the river where he'd fish for hours. Other times he'd hike into the woods where the wonder and mystery of wildlife would spark his curiosity.

Like Roy, Ellie inherited Fern's flaxen tresses and dark blue eyes. Ellie sat on a chair near the steps where Percy picked the strings of his father's old banjo, her interest drifting between the folks on the porch and her twirling baby sister.

As soon as Muriel ended her song, Leland bobbed his head and ran through a couple of chords. Muriel recognized the selection and started playing a melody while Leland commenced to croon. He sounded just like Gene Autry as the lyrics to "Red River Valley" rolled off his tongue. When Muriel's voice joined his, goosebumps tingled Fern's neck and arms. The pairing of the two never ceased to amaze her, but at times like this, she accepted that Percy was right all along. Leland and Muriel, different as they were, complemented each other.

When the others found their instrument's place in the tune, Ellie stepped off the porch and extended her hands toward June. The two barefoot girls pranced in the carpet of grass, clover, and lemon-yellow dandelions. They stood opposite each other, hands clasped and arms stretched, and began to spin in a circle. Ellie tilted her face toward the sky where the waning sun glinted against her hair.

How could such a touching sight inflict intense despair? Ellie's figure was lithe, and each step, each movement displayed a gracefulness so natural it defied explanation. Hers was not a talent learned, but a gift endowed.

June released Ellie's hands and spun like a top, shrieking and laughing until she tumbled to a stop. When she righted herself, she hiccupped. Instead of clambering to her feet and picking up where she and Ellie left off, June stared at her sister, enrapt by her unrehearsed performance. Ellie's motions were fluid and captivating, but unlike previous dances, she stretched until she balanced on her tiptoes, elongating her form. The action only magnified her elegance and poise.

The scene, and all of its implications, seared Fern's heart. She shuddered at the knowing. It was obvious that Ellie was already a dancer. Fern covered her mouth with her hand and blinked away tears.

Leland caught the heat of Fern's perturbed frown as her eyes shifted from her daughter and back to him. His neck warmed, although he pretended not to notice where Fern placed the blame. Her expression demanded an accounting of Muriel's influence on Ellie, but it wasn't as if he could tamp down his wife's indomitable personality, as Fern was quite aware. He wasn't the ringleader in this new predicament, and he aimed to make Percy take his place among the accused. The worst part was that Fern, who was already peeved about Ellie gushing over everything in Charleston, hadn't heard the half of it.

"Wayne, I'm turning the singin' over to you." Leland stood, handed Fern's guitar to her, and set his sights on Percy. "Time to whet your whistle, partner."

When Percy didn't respond, Leland arched his brows and tipped his chin toward Ellie. The girl continued to dance, stepping side to side while she held June's hand, all the while she glued her eyes to the scene on the porch. Muriel had sworn the young woman to silence. If Leland didn't do as he promised soon—meaning now—Ellie might burst. Muriel too.

Percy lowered his banjo to his seat as Fern started to rise.

"Just me and Percy," Leland said. The infrequent glower that heightened the color of Fern's cheeks seared his backside as he escorted Percy into the house and to the kitchen table.

Leland walked to the sink and turned on the faucet. "Glass of water?"

"Just get on with it. It's plain to see that you, Muriel, and Ellie are in cahoots."

"It's like this," Leland said as he turned toward the table where Percy had taken a seat.

When Percy motioned for Leland to join him, Leland ignored the invitation.

"Are you trying to hold the upper hand, or are you preparing to flee?" Percy asked.

"Little of both, I suspect."

"Just get on with it."

"This never would have happened if you hadn't forced me to take Ellie to the musical."

"I didn't force anything. I strongly recommended. I thought y'all enjoyed the show."

"We did. If we're still friends after this conversation, I'll tell you all about it. *Girl Crazy* reminded me of Hawthorne. You'd a liked it too."

Percy pushed his chair back. "If you have something I need to hear, would you just say it?"

Leland pulled out a chair, spun it around, straddled the seat, and rested his forearms across the back frame. "While the women window shopped, they stopped in front of a building on Quarrier Street where they heard piano music. The place turned out to be a dance studio." Leland's exaggerated grin, meant to convey a warning of things to come, was lost on Percy.

"And?"

"One of the students saw us standing there, listening, and she invited us to watch for a while." Leland would skip the part about

Muriel asking for a preview of the classes.

"Watch what?"

"Dance classes."

Percy looked like he had to bite his tongue, but so far he hadn't lost his temper.

"It wasn't what I expected," Leland said. "Not at all."

"You've imagined what goes on in dance classes?" Percy crossing his arms wasn't a good sign.

"It wasn't anything like the square dance lessons Miss Kimble gave us back in grade school. You remember them, don't you?"

"Yes, I remember." Percy's patience was traveling to the exasperated level.

"The instructor's wife called it ballet. That's *b-a-l-l-e-t*."

"You don't have to spell it for me."

"That's right. I forgot you worked for that big city newspaper. I'm sure you know all about it," Leland replied, his tone a bit harsh, considering the circumstances.

"I heard the Society Page editor mention it a couple of times. Get on with the rest of it, would you?"

"These dancers wore odd-looking slippers with stuffing in the toes."

"*S-l-i-p-p-e-r-s?*" Percy asked as he rolled his eyes.

"I thought you wanted to hear this."

"Not really."

"Those shoes let the dancers prance around on their tiptoes. What a sight it was, I'm telling you. The way they moved their arms was impressive, too. I was flabbergasted, to tell the truth. The other truth is that they reminded me of Ellie, the way she moves when she dances."

"Why are you telling me this?"

"On account of Ellie signing up for classes."

If Fern had thought to grab Percy's double-barreled shotgun

before she commenced her eavesdropping, Leland would already be sporting a spray of buckshot. As it was, the situation resembled more of a standoff.

Leland didn't know whether the sudden appearance of two reinforcements would bolster his defense or seal his doom, but there they stood, Muriel and Ellie, one rolling up her battle sleeves, the other prepared to pirouette across the floor to plead her case.

Chapter 4

"Let me explain." Ellie walked across the room and sat at the head of the table. She waved her hand, summoning Muriel and Fern. "Y'all are making me nervous. Would you please sit down?"

Fern kept quiet as she slid into the chair opposite Ellie. A mother's facial expressions went a long way toward communicating with her child. If Ellie wanted to assume the place of authority at the bargaining table, Fern would use her position to unravel each of her daughter's misguided dreams. For that's what they were. Dancing was a pastime, whether for a teenage girl with a vivid imagination of stardom or a lass who relished stomping her boots at a bluegrass festival. Where had her daughter caught the notion that dancing would define her future?

"You might want to ask Nettie to join us," Leland said. "Hard telling how this chat might affect her."

"She already declined," Muriel said. "Said she'd rather enjoy the entertainment on the porch."

Fern didn't need to hear the earlier conversation between Percy and Leland to know that she wanted to throttle both of them. When she finally caught Percy's wavering gaze, a shade of unease drifted across his face. That expression usually prefaced an apology on Percy's part.

Ellie shrank in her chair as she examined the adults who held power over her. After she dared a glimpse at her mother, she sucked in her breath and focused on her primary champion. A boxing match with Muriel sounded a heap more realistic tonight than it did when Percy had talked Fern into letting Ellie go to Charleston. Maybe Fern ought to go a round with her spouse, and her brother too.

While Fern fumed, Muriel bent forward a tad and coaxed her niece. "Just tell them what happened when you met Norma."

Confidence buoyed, Ellie lifted her shoulders and began. "Before the musical started, Aunt Muriel and I wanted to show Uncle Leland the sights."

"Mostly they wanted to shop," Leland said. Fern's glower kept him from adding another uninvited comment.

"We stopped when we heard piano music coming from one of the buildings. Norma, a girl about my age, came along and invited us up."

"Up to where?" Fern asked.

"The third floor," Ellie replied. Her volume and the speed of her speech increased as a sheen of excitement glimmered in her eyes. "It was a dance school. The American Academy Ballet."

"Ballet?" Fern asked.

"B-a-l-l-e-t," Leland interjected. Percy's vicious glare prevented Leland from offering any further explanation.

"I've heard of it," Fern said. "It's a type of dance they do over in Europe. Isn't that right?"

"Mostly," Ellie replied. "Ballet companies are still new to America, but you can find them in places like New York City and Boston. Mr. Van Damme—he's the director of the school—is from Europe. He immigrated after the war, and he brought ballet to Charleston. We're so lucky." The girl acted as if she might swoon. Fern wanted to slap a handful of sense into the lot of them.

"Tell them about the class," Muriel said.

"This is the best part." Ellie leaned forward as eagerness lit up her face. Her eyes held as many twinkles as a clear night sky. "To hear people talk, Mr. Van Damme was famous in Belgium. Taking classes from him is an honor and—you won't believe this—he has two openings in his class and his wife promised one of them to me."

The girl all but jumped out of her seat. She might have danced on the table had she not, finally, looked at her mother. During that miniscule passage of time, Ellie's eyes brimmed. "Mom? Please say you'll let me go."

"Let you go?" Percy asked. "Dreams and reality aside, how do you expect to take classes in Charleston? Let me start with a list of considerations." He lifted a finger. "One. Classes imply that the instructor expects to be paid for his lessons."

Instead of watching her girl back down, Fern saw Ellie's spine stiffen.

Percy raised another finger. "Two. The studio is too far away for you to commute, whether classes are once a week or five times a week."

Ellie pursed her lips and shared a weighty exchange with Muriel. Fern gritted her teeth as the word *conspiracy* came to mind.

"Three," Percy continued as he wagged yet one more objection in Ellie's face. "You have a commitment here, working at the store with your Aunt Muriel, not to mention chores around the house."

That one garnered an eyeball roll and an impatient huff. Fern bristled at the girl's audacity. Did Ellie dare act that way because Muriel had already promised her a haven if things with Fern and Percy didn't turn out the way she wanted?

When Percy got to objection number four, Ellie thrust out her hand, her action reminiscent of a sentry ordering an interloper to halt. "Stop. Please. Let me tell you how this would work."

"No." Fern shoved her chair back. "We're finished here. This is your home, Ellie. This is where you belong, whether you can see that today or not."

"I think she deserves a fair hearing," Muriel said.

If Leland hadn't put his hand on Fern's shoulder, his voice offering a soft, sincere appeal, Fern would have walked out the door and taken an extended, aimless hike. She'd climb the rise behind the house and lose herself in the woods until the beauty and wonder of it all calmed the war that raged within her.

"After the musical," Leland said, "we met Norma, the dancer who invited us to the studio, and another student named Kay. We went to Three Squares Diner where they both work. It's just two blocks from the ballet school, where Dickinson Street ends at Quarrier."

Ellie picked up when Leland paused. "They said I could move into their apartment with them. One of the dancers who left the class used to be their roommate. She got married, which opened a space in the class and a place for me to live."

"Classes and apartments take money," Percy said.

"I know. Norma and Kay introduced me to their boss, and he said he'd be happy to let me make a go of waiting tables."

"If you wait tables, when will you have time to take classes?" Percy asked.

Fern sat back, hiding her fists under the table. She had a long, long fuse, but if anyone lit it, her temper would give way to saying things she couldn't take back. She'd just as soon turn the table on its end than to sit still while Ellie's future drifted away to a place that didn't include her mother, but the vision of Ellie twirling in the yard brought a lump to Fern's throat. Fern couldn't move, neither could she speak.

"I'll follow the same schedule as Norma and Kay. We'll work in the early morning, doing the breakfast shift, and come back after class and cover suppertime."

"They make enough money for rent, food, clothes, and the academy's fees?" Percy asked.

"Not alone. It will take all three of us to make it work. See, Dad? I need to do this for me, but they need me too. Please? At least let me try." Ellie lifted her face and redirected her aim. "Mom?"

"Uh, Sis, may I remind you of a particular situation?"

"No."

Leland brushed off Fern's glower as if it were a bothersome gnat. "Now, hold on a minute. This is worth saying."

"What?"

"I think you ought to recall your Sonny Carter dilemma."

"It has nothing to do with this."

"It has everything to do with parents choosing what they think is best."

Ellie grabbed onto hope's lifeline before Fern could protest. "Who's Sonny Carter?"

Fern stared at Leland while his uninvited interference took her back to an incident that saved her as much as it cost her. Hers was the right decision, but it created a rift with her parents that never fully healed. "I was a mite younger than you when your Grandma Vera and Grandpa Harold had my future all worked out."

"Your marrying Dad?" Ellie asked.

Fern replied with a *pfft*. "They had other plans."

Leland interrupted with, "Times were hard back then. They meant the best."

"I know, but if I'd allowed them to choose for me, I would

have been miserable."

"Why?" Ellie asked.

"They wanted me to marry a man who was as old as my father."

"Why would they want that?"

"I think they were being practical. They didn't have the means to feed all of us, and I'd reached an age where they could marry me off. Your grandma Nettie saved me from a life I didn't want."

"You defied them?"

"I never thought of it that way, but I reckon I did."

"So, are your objections to me becoming a ballerina mostly about being practical? Shouldn't I follow my heart?"

"My objections are plenty," Fern replied. "And they are selfish. I want you here. I'll worry every minute you're away."

The comment seemed to catch Ellie off guard. "Did you just give me your blessing?" Her shoulders shuddered while she waited for Fern's reply.

"Why would you think your mother just approved?" Percy asked.

"Because she said that she *will* worry, not that she *would* worry."

Percy's mouth hung partway open as he digested Ellie's reasoning. It wasn't Ellie's persuasive argument that redirected Fern's objections, but Fern's recollection of the mundane and empty life that had awaited her had she acquiesced to her parents' bidding and married the old widower.

Fern had harbored dreams, many of which had come true. Eventually, five of those precious blessings would make their own way in a world that existed both within and beyond the boundaries of Elizabeth, West Virginia. It was Fern's place to nurture and guide. Percy's too. It wasn't their place to censure their dreams, and no one could argue that Ellie's talent, a gift bequeathed by her Maker, brought her unspeakable joy.

Fern reached under the table and grasped Percy's hand. Only when she was certain he agreed did she turn her attention back to Ellie. "We will miss you, and we will worry."

Chapter 5

"Dang, Muriel. Would you just pull over?" Fern was ready to thrash her.

Nettie, who sat in the middle of the bench seat, reached over and patted Fern's fist. Her mother-in-law, as tight-lipped as a toddler refusing a spoonful of castor oil, gripped her other hand around her pocketbook.

"I have just as much right as everyone else to be on this road." Muriel glanced in the rearview mirror before she tossed her dark hair away from her face. To validate her claim, she eased up on the gas.

Fern listened to the grumble of the engine behind them as the driver of the old farm truck hit the gas, backed off for a spell, and hit it again. Each time he closed the distance between his truck and the car, the crunch of his tires on the gravelly pavement served as a warning that Muriel ignored. His was just one in a long line of vehicles driven by antsy, annoyed drivers. Any one of them might disregard the danger, pull out, and take a blind curve so he could get past the slowpoke and get on with his business.

"Those men would just as soon shoot out your tires as spend one more minute behind this car," Fern said. "If you won't pull over, would you at least drive fast enough to get out of first gear?"

Muriel scoffed when she replied, "I am in second gear, silly."

Fern wanted to bang her against the side of the door. Twenty years in West Virginia and Muriel still drove like a city girl, crawling along the roadway as if she were sitting in four lanes of stalled traffic.

When a short—very short—stretch of straight road came into view, the driver behind them stomped on his gas pedal, gathering gravel and spewing it across the pavement. He dared take his eyes off the road long enough to leer at Muriel while he veered around the car and pulled back into the lane. The pooch sitting in the truck bed struggled to stay upright, but let the wind tug his muzzle into a doggy grin as they drove out of sight.

Many miles, a simmering headache, and five rotations around the block later, Muriel spied a vacated parking spot that didn't require parallel parking skills. She inched into the space, if one were to measure the two-foot gap between the car and the curb by inches, cut the motor, and declared, "We're here."

Fern slid out of her seat and gave Nettie a hand while she exited the car and stepped to the sidewalk. Muriel rounded the car and shrugged at the vehicle's proximity to the curb, or lack thereof.

"If I weren't dizzy from circling the block, I'd stretch my muscles with a mile-long run along the river," Fern whispered to Nettie.

Nettie, a woman of unwavering grace, cleared her throat and said, "A wise man once told me that anytime one reached his destination in once piece and unscathed, he should consider the voyage a success."

Muriel's eyes widened. "That's uncanny. Those were the same words my father used to say to me when he taught me how to drive." She started to say more, but wrenched her neck sideways and peered into the automobile. "Oh, dear, I left the keys in the ignition."

When Muriel swooped around the car, Fern leaned into Nettie and asked, "That wise man you mentioned? I assume you quoted Captain Levy, father to Muriel Levy Dugan."

Nettie pressed her finger to her lips, not only calling Fern to secrecy, but to hide her glee. "Shh. Let's try to behave."

Fern inspected the two-story building that filled a good part of the busy city block. An attorney occupied an office at one end, and a bookstore filled the adjacent space. Next to the bookstore was a small awning that marked the entrance to a narrow passageway that led to steps. The sign hanging beneath the awning confirmed they'd reached their destination.

Beyond the residential entrance was Egan Appliance Mart, a massive retail shop that extended to the far end of the building. Behind four expansive windows, the proprietor displayed an impressive selection of modern appliances. Fern bent sideways as a matching washer and dryer caught her eye. "Are those pink?"

Nettie wagged her finger in a different direction and said, "I don't like the sound of that."

Fern followed Nettie's finger and read the sign a second time. Egan Apartments. "Ellie said the owner of the appliance store owned the whole building."

"I'm talking about the fine print."

Fern squinted as she read the rest. Reasonable Rates. Monthly, Weekly, and Daily. A hefty supply of adrenaline awakened her protective momma instinct. She spun on her heels, stretched to her full height, and leveled her unspoken accusation into Muriel's startled gray eyes. "You said this was a safe place."

Muriel took a step backwards. "It *is* a safe place."

"With a landlord who rents rooms on a daily basis? Did they run out of space on the sign to mention their reasonable *hourly* rates, or it that simply implied?"

Muriel blinked and slid her fingertips along her cheek, as if she needed to inspect the aftermath of a stinging slap. "The owners have a waiting list," she replied. "This is hardly a seedy hotel."

Fern gestured to the sign. "I can read, Muriel."

"The sign is probably as old as the building. Honestly, Fern, do you think I'd let my niece live in a place that wasn't safe? If you'd like, I can introduce you to Mr. Egan. He and his wife are sweet as can be. They'd probably open their business ledgers to prove to you that their tenants rent their rooms for long periods of time."

"What makes you think they'd do that?"

Muriel rolled her eyes. "Because I made them show me their books before I gave the place my blessing."

Fern memorized every inch of the building's exterior while she considered the depth of her blunder. What was that old saying? *If you've dug yourself into a hole, quit digging.* Well, she'd quit digging, but what was the saying for pulling oneself *out* of that hole? When clever words failed to materialize, she sucked in her pride. "I hope you can forgive me. I apologize."

"It's all right," Muriel said. "I know you're nervous about Ellie being here, but you ought to know you can trust me."

"One would think," Fern mumbled.

"Well, I needed to hear your explanation," Nettie said. "I was worried too."

"Let's go on over to the dance studio while there's still time to watch Ellie's class," Muriel said.

As they passed the pink washer and dryer, Nettie stopped. "Oh, my stars. When I heard you mention the color pink, I didn't know you were talking about appliances."

"Can you see the sign on top of the dryer?" Muriel asked. "It says you can also order them in canary yellow, cobalt blue, brown, and turquoise."

"Well, I don't know about the two of you," Nettie said as she moved along, "but I'll wait until they manufacture one that's pea soup green."

※

They reached the building that housed the studio, where the sound of a piano drifted into the air. Fern hoped she'd glimpse a ballerina gliding by the third story window, but from the sidewalk she couldn't see more than an occasional shadow pass in front of the glass. When one of the city buses jolted to a stop nearby, Fern inspected each of the riders as they disembarked. Their outward appearances offered a level of relief—not that dress and carriage revealed the inner person—but the tidy and professional clothing implied this was a decent part of town.

The bus driver held the door open while a woman with two young children stepped inside the vehicle, and as soon as they'd lowered themselves to a seat, he pulled the door closed and swooshed by. A city ran on unyielding schedules, forcing its inhabitants to do likewise. Fern snuck a peek at her wristwatch. They, too, had a timetable.

As the three women ascended the stairs, the unease that accompanied Fern to Charleston shifted from first gear to full throttle. Here, her hopes for Ellie collided with her protective character.

The young woman who waited for them in the hallway introduced herself as Kay Palmer, one of Ellie's two roommates. Kay's tights and leotard revealed long, slender legs and a willowy form. Her hair, which she'd gathered into a tight bun, was a rich shade of chestnut brown. Long, dark lashes framed light brown eyes. Her flushed cheeks may have been a byproduct of the heat that hovered in the third floor landing, or from her having just stepped out of her class.

"Are we interrupting your lesson?" Fern asked.

"No. I finished a while ago."

"You're not in Ellie's class?" Nettie asked.

"She's in the beginners' class. I've been studying under Mr. Van Damme for two years now, so my classes are more advanced."

"Of course," Nettie replied.

"You've received instruction for two years?" Fern asked. "How long does it usually take a student to graduate from ballet school?"

"It's not like that." Kay's amber eyes shimmered with enthusiasm as she offered an explanation. "It's a lifelong endeavor. Dancers always have room for improvement, and between classical ballet and the introduction of modern elements, the choreography and the skills needed to perform the routines are ever changing."

"Will you always be a student?" Fern asked.

"Only for as long as I dance. Why, Mr. Van Damme still studies. In fact, at about the same time he started the ballet academy, he traveled across the United States, and while he was in New Mexico, he visited Indian reservations and helped them improve their native dance presentations. The Pueblos and the Navajos, the Apaches and the Zunis. Can you imagine? I can only guess what deer, buffalo, turtle, and powwow dances might look like, but to see them in person? That would be so cool."

Kay lowered her voice, as if she had a valuable secret to share. Her excitement and her awe of Mr. Van Damme echoed the tone Ellie used when she spoke of her instructor.

"Mr. Van Damme studied with some of the most famous

dancers in Europe, including Victor Gsovsky, and Volinine, who was one of Anna Pavlova's dance partners. Both men were Russian, but taught in Paris. In Brussels, he studied under Leonide Katchourowsky and others."

Fern couldn't keep her brow from knitting together. She had no idea who these people were and couldn't begin to pronounce their names. Kay must have noted her confusion.

"While in America, he studied under George Balanchine and Pierre Vladimiroff. Besides dancing and choreography, Mr. Van Damme learned from Arturo Toscanini, the famous conductor. Are you familiar with any of them?"

"Toscanini, of course," Muriel said.

When Nettie replied, "That's quite a pedigree," Fern had to press her lips together to hide her smile. Nettie was as clueless about the names as Fern was.

"Before we go inside, let me tell you just a smidgeon more about Mr. Van Damme's motor trip." Kay must have realized she'd been jawin' a mite too long, and to make up for it, she spoke faster. "He also spent time in Hollywood. While he was there, he had an opportunity to study with Adolph Bolm."

When no one responded to the news, Kay appended the sentence. "He was associated with the Russian Imperial and Diaghilev Ballets. Mr. Van Damme also studied under Kathryn Charisse Etienne, who teaches motion picture stars how to dance."

"Charisse?" Muriel asked. "Is she related to Cyd Charisse, the famous actress and dancer?"

"While Cyd Charisse was married to her first husband Nico, she was Madame Etienne's sister-in-law."

Fern blinked at what Nettie had referred to as Mr. Van Damme's pedigree. It was apparent Kay retained the mass of information because she revered her instructor. She'd put the man on a pedestal, and for Ellie's sake Fern hoped he didn't take a tumble.

"So, you see," Kay said as she finally wrapped her hand around the doorknob, "I'll be a student as long as I dance. Eventually, some of us hope to join a dance company."

"How is that different?" Fern asked. When Kay pulled her hand back, Fern regretted the question. She wanted to see Ellie.

"A company is for professional dancers," Kay said as she arched her brows. "Dancers who earn wages."

Fern mulled over the *eventually, some of us*, phrase. The more she learned, the more she fretted over Ellie's dreams. When it came to performing and making a living, her ambitions promised a heap more *iffens* than *whens*.

"Does Charleston have a dance company?" Nettie asked.

"No, ma'am. Not yet."

"So all of this might be for nothing?" Fern asked. Did Ellie know this?

"In another year or two I might be good enough to try out for a company in New York, or maybe San Francisco." Kay drew her eyes heavenward and expelled a dreamy sigh. "Can you imagine?"

Fern, thunderstruck to the point of losing her ability to speak, grabbed Nettie's hand, just as much to steady her mother-in-law as to keep her own legs from failing her. Did Ellie have any idea how much her dancing could cost her? Fern shook her head at her own imagination. Ellie wouldn't trade ballet over a husband, a home, and children. Would she?

Kay, oblivious to the visitors' reactions to her report, reached for the door. "We'll sit in the corner and watch the class. I'll have to whisper, but I'll explain everything . . . one lovely dance step at a time."

Chapter 6

Leland slid the tip of the paintbrush into the corner, taking care not to let the bristles touch the ceiling. Satisfied he'd covered every speck of the pale blue paint with the color Nettie called lemony yellow, he descended the ladder and stretched. The stubborn hitch in his get-along drew out an inflated *oof*.

"Don't you think we'd finish this chore in double-time if your two boys lent a hand?" Leland asked.

Percy tilted the gallon container and poured more paint into his tray. He picked up his roller and walked toward the spot Leland had finished edging. "No, I think having helpers aged thirteen and fourteen would require double the time."

"Don't they need to learn how to do this?"

"They do, but this is my mother's kitchen. She spends a good part of her day here baking bread for the store, and I think she'd find satisfaction in carrying out her work in a place that's pleasing to her. Wayne and Roy are not fit for the task. I need to teach them how to put a coat of whitewash on the barn before I let them paint indoors. Besides, I sent them to the garden to give Becca a hand."

"Don't you need an adult to keep an eye on them, seeing how

they're not fit for work?" Leland made an effort to convey his question in the form of a joke, but it was his opinion that those two boys needed to take on more responsibility. If Leland's father had assigned similar chores to Leland and his brother Calvin, they'd have done as he demanded, no question. Then again, since their father hadn't bothered, neither of the boys did much of anything until they'd run face-first into adulthood.

"I assigned a supervisor," Percy replied.

"They don't listen to Becca."

"I meant June. She'll keep them in line."

Percy's little joke drew a chuckle, which set off a spasm under Leland's ribcage. He managed to hold back a groan, but Percy saw his grimace.

"You all right?"

"As right as any other day. Those fragments, small as they are, make me feel like an eighty-year-old man, especially when it's damp outside. Like today. Can't complain, though. Too many men came home with injuries bad enough to turn their lives upside down. Too many more didn't make it back. Feeling eighty is still living, still feeling, still loving. So, I'm doing fine, and I thank you for asking."

"I think every able-bodied boy in America should serve his country. It's no secret our stint with the Civilian Conservation Corps forced us to grow up, and although we didn't know it at the time, it prepared us for war."

"Sure did. In boot camp, it was plain as day which of us had served in the CCC. Those drill sergeants didn't have to teach us respect, or discipline, or how to get along. If not for the shooting part, we were battle ready, don't you think?"

"I agree. The CCC turned us into better men. The military does too. That's why I think every man should serve."

"I don't like the draft, though," Leland said. "At the back of my mind, I always wondered about those who didn't want to be at the front, wondered if they'd honor their obligations when the time came, or if they'd hightail it out of harm's way."

"No doubt, character and integrity come into play. You can't force a man to fulfill his part of a mission just because he wears a uniform."

Leland moved the ladder to the next wall, picked up his small pail, and climbed two rungs. He dipped the tip of his brush into the pale yellow paint and steadied his hand before he touched the brush to the wall.

"Being a soldier wasn't like serving in the CCC," Leland said. "Duty called both times, but the CCC was for building up while the war attempted to keep evil folks from tearing down. Both objectives were honorable, but one was a heap more satisfying than the other was. The CCC puffed my chest with pride, but with the war, memories of pain, suffering, and losses take me back to the foxhole. I don't like to talk about it."

"No one does. I don't think I've heard anyone brag about military heroics. Same as you, I believe we ought to leave those stories, whether about battles lost or won, buried as deep in our minds as we can put them."

Leland reached for the damp rag he'd hung on one of the ladder's spreaders and dabbed at a smudge of yellow that had found its way to the ceiling. "Let's move on to a different topic. Did you hear the rumor about the supermarket?"

"Mrs. Anders asked me about it last week."

"Her husband knows all the bigwigs in town. Is it true? Is a big grocery chain planning to build here?"

Percy gave his roller a quick turn through the paint in his tray and leaned toward the wall as he worked the roller up and down and side to side. "I'm just one of his clerks, Leland. Aside from chatting about the weather and polite conversation one might have at a church picnic, Mr. Anders and I limit our communication to gas and oil well leases, royalties, and such."

"Well, if he didn't say anything, what did his wife have to say?"

"She just asked if I knew anything. Wanted to know if Muriel had talked with the butcher or the greengrocer."

"When Muriel gets back from Charleston, I'll make sure she visits both of them. All three businesses might go under if a supermarket comes to town. The locals ought to band together. Prepare to protest."

"So far, it's just talk. Like the last two times. You know as well as I do, Elizabeth is too small and too far away from other towns for a big company to swoop in and take over selling everything. Besides, who wants to carry around a wire basket and search a dozen shelves to find what they need to buy when they can hand their list to the grocer and let him take care of things? And, what about loyalty? Don't you think the folks in Elizabeth would stay true to the business owners who have operated here for decades?"

"Loyalty takes a back seat to saving money, Percy, and you know it."

"Listen to me. We don't need to worry."

"I wonder if it's A and P. Maybe Kroger. Or how about those IGA stores?" Leland asked.

Leland almost fell off the ladder when the back door flew open and slammed against the doorstop. Roy and Wayne, red-faced and out of breath, raced into the kitchen.

"You gotta come see," Wayne yelled as he pivoted and ran back outside.

Roy hunched over, panting, and sucked in air. When he lifted his gaze, his wide blue eyes settled on Percy. "Hurry!"

Leland cringed when his pail teetered off the top of the ladder and plummeted to the floor, spewing rivulets of yellow down the front of the cabinets and across the floor tiles. Percy bounded over the mess and tore after the boys, Leland fast on his heels.

Outside, Roy stood at the corner of the barn, waving his arm. "This way."

Wayne waited at the edge of the clearing, urging Percy and Leland forward. Both men had to sprint to keep from losing sight of the boys when they darted into the woods where towering trees, showing off their summertime splendor, captured the humid air and obscured the sun's penetrating rays. Moisture-fed moss, ferns, and all manner of flowering plants blanketed the forest floor, muffling the sound of their footfalls.

A good hundred yards into the woods, June and Becca came into view. The girls were kneeling, their concentration fixed on the ground in front of them. Neither appeared the worse for wear, and as the men approached the boys, Roy pressed his finger to his mouth. "Shh."

When Percy continued forward at a fast clip, Wayne reached for his elbow, but missed. Keeping the volume low, he called after his father. "Slow down."

Roy was a mite faster latching onto Leland's arm and when the boy snagged his target, the jostling sent Leland sprawling. While his boots slipped out from under him, his backside promised to encounter dirt, rocks, or roots, or maybe a bit of each. His rear end hit first, cushioning the blow to his head, so it came as a surprise when searing pain originated from his foot.

"Uncle Leland, are you all right?" Roy asked.

His was a good question. "I don't rightly know, but help me up, will you?"

Before he inspected his body, Leland regarded Percy and his daughters. Nothing seemed amiss, but Percy had squatted down to their level. Whatever the reason for the alarm, it didn't appear to include blood and broken bones, which might not hold true of the rescue team.

Leland pressed his fingers against the back of his skull. It was tender to the touch, but didn't have a hint of swelling. His posterior was in fine shape too, except for the wet spot working its way past his undershorts and to his skin. When he put weight on his right foot, however, his brain told him he'd been struck by lightning. He'd use those words to describe it to the doctor, assuming he survived the trek out of the woods and to the physician's office.

Ray, wearing guilt all over his adolescent face, offered his shoulder and helped Leland limp over to the scene of the ruckus, which wasn't an appropriate description, because Percy, Becca, June, and Wayne were as quiet as church mice.

When June directed his attention to a pile of leaves, Leland had to squint pretty hard before he saw the culprit responsible for his injury. A newborn fawn lay still as a statue, its muzzle peeking out of the leafy covering her mother meant to protect her fragile offspring. Brown eyes, as dark and shiny as a buckeye nut, stared at the intruders. A foamy line of white milk around her mouth suggested the Bigler clan had interrupted feeding time.

"I wish I had a camera," Becca said.

"You'll have to fit this into your memories, all of you," Percy replied. "Right now, I think we need to leave. The longer we're in the doe's way, the less likely she is to return to her fawn."

The reluctant children took in the sight one last time before they started back toward the house. Roy, who lagged behind, offered Leland an apologetic grimace, but when the boy started to speak, Leland waved him off. Percy, who'd been too busy being a father to see his painting partner's distress, finally took note.

"What did you do?"

"I had a little help slowing down, that's all." When Leland shrugged, the motion sent another flash of pain up his leg.

"Can you walk?"

"If I can lean on one of your shoulders."

"You want me to fetch the horse?"

"Naw, just help me limp back."

"I'm sorry you hurt yourself."

"If you compared my sore foot to the visions I had when Roy and Wayne came screaming into the kitchen, you'd choose this over any of the alternatives."

"I don't know what they were thinking, scaring the daylights out of both of us."

"They weren't thinking. They were excited."

"Still, I think they need to understand the difference between the two."

"So you learned yourself a lesson out of this," Leland said as he hobbled forward on one leg.

"What lesson?"

"This is what happens, Bigler, when you put a five-year-old in charge."

Chapter 7

The ride home felt longer than their visit with Ellie, despite the fact that Fern was behind the wheel instead of Muriel. Fern needed to quit recollecting the dance class and the quick meal they'd shared at the corner diner, and pay heed to the road and the traffic.

"You might want to get out of first gear," Muriel said as she wrenched her neck and peered out the rear window. "If all those drivers were in the saddle, they'd resemble a posse." Muriel faced forward again, pushed her shoulders against the seat, and let out a rude *pfft*. "They could probably outrun you if they were on horseback."

Nettie angled forward, probably in an effort to block eye contact between the driver and the woman who sat beside the passenger door. "I think we're all tired. Let's just get home safely, shall we?"

"I'm not tired." Fern's snippy tone added fuel to Muriel's mocking attitude, but she couldn't help herself. "I'm distracted by all those French words swimming in my brain and all of Ellie's talk about her classes."

"You want me to drive?" Muriel asked.

When Fern and Nettie's, "No" rang out at the same time, Fern couldn't rein in her giggles. The annoyance on the face of the driver who took all of their lives into his hands when he sped by should have sobered Fern right up. Instead, she laughed harder. Opening the window helped clear her head, and applying more pressure to the accelerator appeased the folks who were tailing her.

"It's been a long day," Nettie said.

"Can you imagine how Ellie feels by the time she hits the hay?" Fern asked. "What a schedule."

"She's young, dear," Nettie replied.

"And highly motivated," came the quip from the far side of the front seat.

The unwelcome comment, delivered in Muriel-like fashion, provoked another round of resentment. Fern loved her brother's wife. That was the honest truth, but time spent with Muriel tended to drain every last drop of Fern's good will. It wasn't Muriel's fault—not Fern's driving, the short visit, nor Ellie's dogged determination—but it was hard not to begrudge her sister-in-law's delight in seeing Ellie stretch her wings and venture down a path that might cost more than it rewarded.

Nettie pressed her palm to her mouth, covering a yawn. "Excuse me. If you ask me, Ellie is as much in awe of Mr. Van Damme as she is fearful of him. Just watching those girls trying to keep up as he counted out the exercise steps wore me out. Considering Ellie's is a beginner's class, you'd think he'd let them pause for a few seconds between first position, second position, third position, and those *plea hays*, or whatever he called them. Couldn't understand the half of what he said. Aren't immigrants required to learn how to speak English?"

Muriel chuckled. "He spoke English and the term is *plié,* as in the word *plea* and the letter *a*. *Plié.*"

Fern pressed her lips together, all the while her tongue begged for freedom. It was always a question of when—never if—Muriel would put on her briggity, educated airs and share her brilliance with the common folk. Fern was not in the mood to suffer through a French lesson.

"Do you think all of Kay's talk about Mr. Van Damme being part of the underground resistance during the war is true?" Fern asked.

"Why would you doubt it?" Muriel asked.

"Because Kay said he brings it up all the time. The men around here don't talk about their time in the service. The pain runs too deep."

"Operating in the underground had to be a lot different from fighting in the trenches," Muriel said. "His story about running guns and ammunition is heroic, but his experiences wouldn't call to mind the death and destruction that came after those weapons made their way to the battlefields."

"The story intrigued me," Nettie said. "I like to hear about good people outsmarting evil. Who would have thought a ballet dancer, of all people, would transport contraband to the theater?"

Muriel stretched forward until she could see Fern. "It tells like a good suspense story, especially the part where an unidentified courier slipped away with the goods during a performance. Very mysterious." Muriel pressed a tad closer to the dashboard. "Percy says he's content with his editorial bylines at the *Charleston Gazette*, but Mr. Van Damme's story has the makings of a novel. You ought to tell your husband to give the idea some thought."

Fern bit her tongue hard enough to make her eyes water. Nettie, bless her peacemaker's heart, sensed Fern's angst.

"I don't know anything about ballet," Nettie said, "but hearing he was a principal dancer with the Royal Opera of

Brussels impressed me. Risking his position in order to support the underground says a lot about his character, his wife's too. Gruff teacher or not, I like him."

The conversation waned as Fern negotiated the winding road. When they arrived home, traces of an earlier rain marked the edges of the drive and loitered in uneven spots in the front yard. Fern stepped out of the car, stretched her arms, and inhaled the scent of moist clay and the perfume of flowers. As she passed the rose bush that edged the walkway to Nettie's front porch, tiny droplets resting on crimson petals collected the remnant of the setting sun, offering a magnificent performance of color and light.

At the sound of the screen door opening, muffled voices carried from the kitchen, followed by the sound of chair legs scraping the floor, and a multitude of footsteps moving around the room. Fern's gratitude brimmed. The noise belonged to her multitude.

"Oh my goodness, I have a new kitchen," Nettie exclaimed as she walked into the room and dropped her pocketbook on the table.

Percy, June, Roy, Wayne, and Becca stood in a line that stretched from one side of the back wall to the other. Leland sat at the table, his foot resting on the seat of another chair. When Fern gave him the eye, he drew back the edges of his mouth. Her shoulders drooped. She hated the surprises that oft accompanied that grin.

Nettie turned in a circle, examining every angle of the transformation and giving particular notice to the meeting of the yellow walls with the white ceiling. While her mother-in-law studied the scene above her, the unexpected trappings down below caught Fern's eye. This time, she cast a questioning glance in Percy's direction. He answered with an expression more akin to guilt than pride. Oh boy.

"It's as bright and cheerful as morning sunshine in here. Y'all did a beautiful job." Nettie's face depicted her approval, but her bearing froze during the last downward tip of her chin. "I don't rightly know what to say. I've never seen anything like this. Leastways, not in a kitchen."

"Do you like it?" Becca asked as she stepped forward and waved her hand toward the cupboards where an array of bright yellow sunflowers adorned the doors. "I did my best."

"They're lovely. Truly," Nettie said as she made a more thorough inspection of her kitchen. She fixed her attention to another collection of bright yellow blooms that trailed away from the cabinets. "I have to wonder, though, how those sunflowers will hold up to shoes scuffing the surface. I reckon I'll have to watch my step and walk around them as best as I can."

"Oh, you don't need to worry none," Leland said. "I guarantee those petals won't fade away during our lifetime. No, ma'am, those flowers are there to stay."

Although Nettie noticed Leland's elevated foot, she pretended not to see a thing, turned around, and addressed her next statement to Fern and Muriel. "Well, next time we go to Charleston, I reckon I ought to order a brand new General Electric oven to go in my new kitchen."

"What's wrong with the one you have?" Percy asked.

"It's not canary yellow."

Chapter 8

Muriel turned down Court Street, pulled the car to the curb, and helped Leland hobble to the front door of the Theatre Restaurant. She had a spring in her step when she retraced her path and drove to a side street where she hoped to find an empty parking spot.

Next door was the Elizabeth Theatre, namesake for the restaurant. Patrons, mostly high school students with an occasional baby sister or brother tagging along, stood in line to purchase tickets for the movie.

School would start right soon, and for the first time since 1931, the Wirt High School football team was the talk of the town. Rumor had it Coach Watson had trained every athlete until he'd reached his highest potential. Words like *undefeated season* and *playoffs* filtered into everyday conversations. The fervor that accompanied the gossip rumbled through the crowd, most of whom showed their solidarity by wearing the school's orange and black colors. As far as Leland was concerned, the season couldn't begin soon enough. *Go Tigers!*

Muriel rounded the corner and gave Leland a splendid smile as she walked toward the restaurant. Her flushed cheeks and rose-colored lipstick drew his awareness to her pale gray eyes. As she approached, she scanned his form with enough intensity to threaten his precarious balance. For a brief moment, he considered putting off what he had to tell her. Otherwise, the come-hither invitation she tendered might disappear altogether. Leland let Muriel play the part of the gentleman while she opened the door and helped him inside.

The restaurant was a nice place when it opened in 1947, but after the owners renovated and enlarged the space, the property equaled what they'd find in Charleston or a highfalutin place like New York City. The Theatre Restaurant was Muriel's favorite eating-out place.

Bright white walls framed the large black and white floor tiles, but it was the red and chrome accents that turned the place into a classy joint. Chrome edged the booths and red-topped tables, and red leather topped the stools sitting in front of the counter. Fluorescent bulbs brightened the space, and tunes played by a jukebox livened the place even more.

Dinner was better than expected, as was Leland's appetite. All day he anticipated he'd suffer from acute indigestion, as he was still absorbing unsettling news, but Muriel was so pleased with their date, he'd all but forgotten the unpleasant business. Their talk had been light and easy, and had conjured an occasional sweet brush with romance.

"Would you like a slice of pie before we leave?" Leland asked.

"I'll split a piece of blueberry with you, but I'd like my own cup of coffee to go with it."

"Want ice cream on top?"

"Sure."

After the waitress took their order, Muriel asked, "Are you all right? This has been lovely, spending an evening out with you, but something's weighing heavy on your mind."

In less time than it took Leland to summon a response, the waitress lowered two cups of steaming coffee to the table. She scurried back to the counter and returned with an extra plate, one piece of pie, and a knife. "Y'all need anything else?"

"No, thank you," Leland replied. He didn't need to check the menu to know it didn't include a serving of courage. He'd best get on with it . . . right after they finished eating pie.

Muriel forgot all about her inquiry as she divided the blueberry confection and commenced to gobble down her share. Leland cut a bite-sized piece with his fork, but didn't have the appetite nor the inclination to raise the utensil to his mouth. After Muriel cleared her plate, he nudged his to her side of the table.

"I ate too much. You go ahead."

"You sure?"

"Go on."

Muriel's eyes reflected her delight. Such a simple thing, eating out. Why had he been too stingy to do this more often? Or, had he just not bothered to make the effort? Either way, he couldn't repeat this invitation anytime soon.

He sipped his coffee before resting the cup on the tabletop. "Lester McKinney paid a call to the house this afternoon while you were working in the store."

"He's just now paying you a visit? It's been four weeks since you broke your foot."

"His wasn't a social call, Muriel. His father sent him on a different sort of errand."

She lowered her fork to her plate and dabbed her napkin to her lips. Her unrelenting stare burned him, not that it bore any accusation, but for what he had to tell.

"He wanted to know when the doctor thought I might be able to go back to work."

"Why? Aren't the other men working your hours while you're

healing? You told me most of them jump at the chance for overtime."

"They have, and they will, or at least they would if McKinney Senior asked them."

"Why wouldn't he ask?"

"They acquired new customers, a lot of new contracts. Those men who were working overtime to fill my shoes will have to work those extra hours just to meet the new contract. McKinney plans to hire more workers."

"And?"

"And since I can't work for at least four or six more weeks, which might be too soon to be putting weight and pressure on the broken bone, McKinney needs to replace me now."

"Surely he'll give you a spot when you're ready. You've worked for him for years."

"Lester didn't say as much, but his message was clear. His father doesn't think I'd be up to task again."

"Well, why not?"

"Lumber mill work is grueling. It was already hard to put in a full day's work. When I think about the shrapnel and a bum foot, I can't say I disagree with him."

"So, what will you do? What will we do?"

"For now, I think you need to take a tad more of the earnings from the general store so that we don't have to spend the money we've set aside."

"Take out more earnings? That's your answer?" Muriel's eyes brimmed, a rare occasion that caught Leland unprepared.

"It's the obvious solution. What aren't you telling me?"

Muriel closed her eyes and massaged her temple, but looked up long enough to acknowledge the waitress when she offered to refill their coffee cups.

"Things are rather convoluted where the store and the Bigler house are concerned. After the Depression ended, Nettie longed to reopen the store, and when my father came to town for our wedding, he was thrilled at the prospect of doing so. It made sense at the time. He paid rent to Nettie, I managed his store, and the boarders—including Fern—had a place to call home."

"Captain Levy moving to West Virginia and marrying Nettie did add some legal layers to operating the store, but it all worked out fine."

"Up until now. Hear me out," Muriel said. "When my father left the store to me, he knew I'd watch after Nettie, and I still pay rent to her."

"I know."

"You don't know everything. The store doesn't make but a few dollars from the sale of Nettie's bread and her brood's eggs. After my father died, I increased my rent payments to her. She's a widow, Leland, and we didn't need the money as much as she did."

Muriel's use of past tense where their money needs were concerned was disturbing. The present and short-term outlooks didn't hold much promise.

"I reckon we'll have to tighten our belts since the wiggle room isn't as big as I thought it was." When the waitress dropped the bill on the table, Leland reached into his back pocket and pulled out his wallet. The contents were already thin. If he'd known about the rent payment, he'd have taken Muriel for a walk instead of a night on the town, never mind that he couldn't walk right then.

After he pulled out his cash, Muriel locked her eyes on him and said, "I have more to tell you."

Leland's worries followed the greenbacks as the waitress took them to the cash register. Parting with them was, indeed, sweet sorrow.

"I'm listening."

"A while back, I started paying Fern higher wages."

Leland swallowed two, three times, trying to dislodge the lump wedged in his throat.

"They have five children, Leland."

"And you thought they needed the money more than we did."

"And it was true. Think about it. We have two incomes, no children, and a tidy savings." She turned away. "Or, we did. I put us in a worse position when I gave Ellie money to tide her over when she moved to Charleston."

The tension that accompanied the revelations related to Muriel's generous deeds was hard to ignore. She'd acquired an unfair reputation for being aloof, but she was always cordial and attentive, and considerate too. While she lacked outward warmth, she outdid herself in terms of generosity, whether it was her time, her teaching skills, or, apparently, their money. Leland couldn't criticize her actions, but neither could he ignore the consequences.

"So what you're saying is the wiggle room is a tad sparse."

"It's not sparse, Leland. It's . . . well . . . we don't have any room to wiggle."

Chapter 9

"Muriel, you can't keep putting me off. We have to talk about this. We need a plan."

"I'm working on one."

It didn't come as a surprise when Fern corralled Leland for a talking-to about his wife. Muriel didn't lash out when she was angry or upset, but she didn't do a good job of holding it all inside. It festered, and the longer she dealt with it—or refused to deal with it—alone and on her own terms, the more painful the ordeal became for the lot of them.

"Like what?" he asked.

"Maybe I'll put an advertisement in the Parkersburg paper and try to sell the piano."

"I won't let you." He wouldn't. The piano had belonged to Muriel's grandmother, and then her mother. It was an heirloom, not a disposable asset. Muriel sounded serious, but she had to be bluffing.

"I'm not asking for permission. We have to do something."

"I'm trying." Leland shifted his leg, grateful for the freedom to rest his cast-free foot on his other knee. A familiar twinge snaked around his ankle, a reminder that during the time the bone in his foot healed, the cast had immobilized his ankle. Working the kinks out of it was about as easy as wringing water out of dried cement. When the doctor removed the cast, it did not render Leland capable of manual labor.

"I don't understand why you can't find work. Elizabeth is doing well. Huffman Chevrolet's lot is overflowing with new models, FE Fint and Sons keeps adding new lines of televisions and appliances, and Chambers Furniture has more goods coming and going than would fill half of the houses in the county. If business is booming, why can't you find a job that doesn't require physical exertion?"

"I reckon I have a couple of answers. Stanley's Barber Shop had a Help Wanted sign in the window a couple of weeks ago, but I don't think he's searching for an employee who has experience laying dynamite, planting seedlings, or milling wood."

"Are you mocking me?"

"I don't mean to. Fact is, I'm not fit for the work. The bigger obstacle is that most business owners keep to their own. All those companies selling goods and counting their profits hire their kin. Folks around here take care of their own first. Ain't nothing left to trickle down to outsiders."

"You're not an outsider." Muriel's tone reminded Leland that she still considered herself a foreigner, and in some respects and by certain folks, she would always remain so. Wasn't anything he could do to change prevailing attitudes. Certain folks were clannish. It was part of their culture. Had been for generations.

"I may not be an outsider as far as the community is concerned," Leland replied, "but I am when it comes to families."

"Even if it's true, it doesn't make it right."

"We do the same thing here."

"What do you mean?"

"Who owns Bigler's General Store?" Leland asked.

"I do."

"Who owns the building?"

"Nettie."

"Nettie happens to be your step-mother." Leland arched his brows when understanding washed over Muriel's face. "Who do you employ?" he asked.

Muriel blew out a frustrated breath. "My sister-in-law and my niece." She pressed her lips together, and when she closed her eyes, the lamplight glistened on her damp eyelashes.

Leland didn't mean to summon tears. He needed to get on with what he had to say.

"Things are different in the cities," Muriel said. "Maybe you ought to find work in Charleston."

Leland sucked in a roomful of searing hot air. Muriel played her hand when she suggested Charleston over Parkersburg. It was his intention to suggest he find work in Parkersburg. The question was whether he could rightly call it a temporary arrangement. Parkersburg was just a piece down the road. Charleston, a longer trek in the opposite direction, was the path to what Muriel imagined would finally give her peace.

"I could come along and get a good paying job," she said. "With both of us working, we could build our savings back up."

"What about the store?" He'd follow along, see where she was leading.

"Fern and Becca can do everything except the bookkeeping. I could get Percy to mail the paperwork to me every week."

"I don't know."

"It would work."

"It might," Leland said, "but it would make it nigh impossible to come back home."

Muriel didn't respond, but a memory tugged and Leland's countenance hit bottom. Words can etch themselves deep into one's soul, and Muriel's comment, which he considered wise and true at the time, drifted to the surface, its appearance as unsightly as a jagged scar. *No matter the location of the house, home is where you find the people you love.*

If he abided by her counsel, and they both relocated to Charleston, they'd never call Elizabeth home again. How could Muriel suggest such a thing? The people he loved lived in Elizabeth.

❦

"You ought to be driving that truck instead of Fern," Leland said as the pickup rounded a curve and disappeared again. He pushed his car along the snaking path at a fast clip, but when blinding sunlight dipped into the hollow and cut through the windshield, he eased up on the gas pedal.

Percy gasped, and in a futile attempt to help slow the vehicle, he shoved his right foot against the floorboard. "I'll get the keys from her before it's time to drive home."

"You know it was Calvin who taught her how to drive."

"Your brother? No, I didn't know."

"No? Probably because she didn't want to spill the family secret."

"What's her driving got to do with secrets?"

Leland chanced a sideways glimpse at his passenger. It wasn't his place to tell, but after all this time, what could it hurt? Calvin wasn't one to worry about his reputation. Never had been.

"After the CCC rejected him on account of his heart murmur, he started running moonshine for a thriving enterprise over in Roane County."

"Calvin was a bootlegger?"

"Sure enough. It was the summer of 1934, after the folks in

Washington lifted the nationwide prohibition, and before West Virginia voters repealed the state's ban on the drink. That's when Calvin ran hooch a couple of times a week."

"How? He didn't own a car."

"That's true. When one of his friends got laid up, he had Calvin drive his route for a spell. As it turned out, Calvin was one fast driver, and the astute proprietors," Leland said with an air meant to convey the high standards of the not-quite-legal operators, "let him drive one of their cars. They'd already tinkered with the engine and the interior, so as to speed up the deliveries and increase the loads."

"Well, how about that. Turns out my in-laws include an outlaw."

"His career was pretty short. The way he tells it, a pair of fancy-suited revenuers almost caught him one night. They boxed him in, but before they could get out of their cars, Calvin opened his door and rolled onto the ground. He inched his way to the woods and hightailed it home. After Calvin lost the vehicle and the drink to the law, his bosses didn't have need for him any longer."

"Why did he do it? Why take the chance?"

"It was the only work he could find. The part of my CCC pay that went to my family didn't go far to feed all ten of them. Calvin was just doing his duty."

"I reckon I never considered bootlegging a duty, but when you put it that way, it's a mite easier to overlook."

"Getting back to Fern's driving. While Calvin had loan of the car, he taught Fern how to drive, so you can see where her bad habits came from."

"You have any more secrets you want to share?"

"Can't say as I do."

"Can't say or won't say?"

"Same thing." Leland hadn't enjoyed a lighthearted moment since money troubles came a-courtin', but the welcome banter and the lift in his mood fizzled into a recollection that was as distasteful as a day-old soda. "Ain't a secret. Muriel and I have a dispute to settle."

"Ma said she heard you arguing this morning."

If not for having to keep his eye on the road, Leland would have squeezed his eyes shut. Humiliation distributed a stinging sensation to his chest, a stranglehold to his throat, and heat to his collar. "How much did she hear?"

"You know Ma. If she heard every single word you exchanged, she wouldn't have shared it. Just so you know, she's the one who suggested Fern and June ride together in the truck."

"She tell you to give me a talking-to?" Leland asked.

"I don't aim to talk. If you want to talk, I'm here to listen. It's not my place to interfere."

As they neared Charleston, the bends in the road gave way to straight stretches of pavement at the same time the volume of traffic multiplied. Leland lowered the sun visor when the truck's chrome bumper grabbed hold of a shaft of sunlight and redirected it to his face.

"Muriel says she likes living in Elizabeth just fine, but she says most of the folks who welcomed her with open arms kept her at arms length when it came to treating her like family, and I don't have an answer for that. You tell me. Does she look happy to you?"

Percy averted his eyes and fidgeted with the handle to the passenger window as the city and its imposing gold capitol dome came into view. Leland followed Fern's truck as she wove through the city center's congested, narrow streets.

"I think she's content," Percy finally replied.

"She's always riled about one thing or another."

"You want an honest opinion?" Percy asked.

"That's why I'm talking. It's not as if you don't have a means to return to Elizabeth if you make me mad."

"I think Muriel's bluster conceals her insecurities."

"That's funny, Bigler. Muriel insecure? She's the smartest woman I ever met and she's as beautiful today as she was when I met her in 1934. If I made a list of all of her talents and her skills, it would be nigh twenty miles long."

"She hides behind those things."

"Why would you say that?"

"Because I don't think that *she* thinks anyone loves her unconditionally."

"Well, sure as shootin', I do."

"I'm not saying you don't, but I think she considers herself unworthy of unconditional love." Percy raised his hands and flicked his fingers, a sure sign something flustered him. "I can't believe what I just said. Unworthy of unconditional love. What an oxymoron."

"Huh?"

"Never mind. You need to remember that Muriel misunderstood the circumstances of her mother's death, for one thing, and spent years believing that her mother abandoned her marriage. Later, Muriel blamed her father for everything else. She came to forgive him, but don't you wonder if she's forgiven herself for the way she responded?"

"I thought she'd put the past behind her."

"That's where her bluster comes in, pal."

Leland pulled the car to the curb, parked behind Fern's truck, and switched off the engine.

"So, you don't think her wanting to come to Charleston has anything to do with being unhappy in Elizabeth?"

"I think she'll carry her search for self worth with her

wherever she is."

"After what I said, it might be too late for me to help her find it."

"It's never too late. Just open the door to conversation and tap lightly until she's willing to expose the hungry space in her heart."

"Have a conversation with her? How? How can I erase the last comment I spit out of my mouth before I stomped out the front door?"

"How bad was it?"

"You tell me. It went like this, 'Truth is, Muriel, I don't want to be around you right now.' "

"That's how you left things?"

"Sure enough. That makes me pretty stupid, doesn't it?"

Chapter 10

June ran past Leland as soon as he opened the apartment door, her forward momentum capable of propelling her farther than the room was wide. She skidded to a stop and whirled in a circle while she inspected the place. Two seconds later, she scrambled to the only interior door, took a peek inside, and promptly did an about-face. She folded her arms and scowled at Leland.

"Where's the rest of it?"

"The rest of what?"

"Your house."

"This is it."

"Where's the kitchen?"

"Just over there," Fern said as she pointed to an electric burner sitting on top of an abbreviated countertop. Next to the burner was a pint-sized sink. The hum of a tiny refrigerator equaled that of a window air conditioner, which was not among the amenities, and given its size, it might hold a pound of butter, a dozen eggs, and a quart of milk.

"That's not a kitchen."

"It's all your old uncle needs," Leland said as he scooped June off her feet and gave her a squeeze. Her silky brown pigtails were askew and her cheeks flushed from running up the stairs. June's unsullied nature, her easily summoned giggles, and the glee reflected in her sparkling brown eyes summoned a lump to Fern's throat.

This was not an event to celebrate, not that she expected June to have an inkling as to what this little trip to Charleston meant. Fern tried to act encouraging when she caught Leland's eye, but his attempt at cheerfulness was as trite as hers was. One of her children was responsible for the broken foot that created this mess, and by the downward pull of Leland's mouth, the conversation he and Percy shared along the route hadn't soothed her brother's misgivings about the remedy.

"Where's your porch?" June asked when Leland lowered her to the floor.

"I reckon I left it back in Elizabeth."

"Where you gonna sit while you play your guitar?"

"I didn't bring it with me, girl. I don't have room for it."

"Is that why you didn't bring Aunt Muriel? 'Cause you don't have any place to keep her?"

"She needs to mind the store," Leland replied, all the while his eyes probed Percy's face, as if he were begging him to interrupt the child's inquisition.

"Won't you miss her?"

"Sure, I will. And you too, but don't you worry none. I'll come visit."

June's curious, bright eyes lost their luster and the edges of her mouth dipped into a cavernous frown. She stared at the floor when she said, "That's what Ellie said, and she ain't come to see me since she started her lessons."

Fern's composure tumbled down the same slope that stole June's effervescent joy. If Ellie's absence had dismantled part of Fern's existence, how much more had it broken the trusting, innocent soul of her youngest child?

Before Fern lost what was left of her motherly bearing, Percy dropped down on one knee and clasped June's hand. He smoothed her hair, tucking a loose strand behind her ear. When she wouldn't look at him, he nudged her chin upwards with the tip of his finger. Fern had to choke back a sob when June's watery brown eyes focused on Percy's face.

"Since Ellie's been too busy working and dancing to come for a visit, we came here instead," he said softly. "I know it's a long ride and you'll have to make do with a hamburger and soda instead of your grandma's cooking, but we don't mind doing that for Ellie, do we?"

Simple, sweet assurances, delivered in Percy's easy-going, loving tone, drew a pair of tiny arms around his neck. "I don't mind," June said as she nuzzled her face to his chest.

Fern's distress melted as she witnessed the tender moment between father and child. How she loved that man.

Before he stood, Percy tapped the tip of June's nose. "No hard feelings about Ellie. Right?"

"Right."

༄

As Fern rested against the back of the sofa and watched Ellie move about the room, contentment set aside the worry that oft accompanied the unknown. Ellie's demeanor was pleasant and poised, traits one would expect of a person who felt at home.

"Why's everything so little here?" June asked as she inspected the apartment that Ellie shared with Kay and Norma. She splayed her little hands, one directed toward the combined kitchen and dining area, the other turned toward the bedroom where two twin-size beds filled the space. "Iffen you live here with two girls, do you have to take turns sleeping?"

"No, silly. Why would you think that?" Ellie handed the last glass of lemonade to Leland before she took a seat on the floor, next to the sofa.

"You sure you don't want this chair?" Percy asked.

"I'm fine. You sit still."

The apartment was small, but it was tidy. Violets in vibrant shades of amethyst, rose, and purple spilled over the edges of terra-cotta pots resting on the narrow windowsill. A smattering of framed photographs, lace doilies, and hand-embroidered coverings presented a welcome, homey appeal.

When a burp interrupted the conversation, June cupped her hand over her mouth. "That's from the Co-cola."

"Did you like your lunch?" Ellie asked.

"Sure enough." June turned sideways and studied the interior of the bedroom again. "Where's the other bed?"

"My bed's right here," Ellie said as she patted the sofa cushion.

"Why don't you get a bed?"

"We don't have room for one," Ellie replied. "Don't you worry, this works just fine."

June pouted before turning her attention elsewhere. Fern swallowed her opinion. No sense voicing criticism over things that didn't meet her parental standards. Because her previous visit to Charleston didn't include a tour of Ellie's apartment, this was Fern's first glimpse of her daughter's living arrangements. The crux of the situation was that Ellie looked good. Cheerful.

"What are these?" June asked. In her hand was a pair of satin shoes, the type worn by a ballerina.

"Those are called *pointe* shoes." Ellie lifted her face to her parents and uncle, and said, "That's *point* with an *e* on the end. Everything's French, you know."

"Those aren't shoes," June said. "You can't walk in them things."

"They're not for walking. They're for dancing." Ellie tapped the floor next to her. "Sit down and I'll show you."

Ellie unbuckled the strap on June's Buster Brown shoes and slipped them off her feet. She eased June's toes into the *pointe* shoes, wrapped the loose ribbons around her ankle, and tied a bow.

June pressed both palms against the floor, preparing to stand.

"Oh, no you don't. Kay would have me by my ears if I let you try to walk in her shoes."

"Those aren't yours?" Fern asked.

"I don't have any yet."

"Why? Are they expensive?" Percy asked.

"It's not about money. I'm not ready to dance *en pointe* yet. I need to be able to show Mr. Van Damme that I can do the dance steps and movements in my bare feet before he has to worry about me tottering around in a pair of those."

Ellie stood, situated herself behind June, grasped her under her arms, and eased her up until her toes dangled over the floor. "*Oof*, when did you get so big?"

"It's from hamburgers and soda," Percy replied.

"Now," Ellie said, "I'm going to ease you down to the floor, just for a second, but long enough for you to see how it feels to stand on your tiptoes."

Junes' eyes widened when her weight caught up with her feet. "That pinches."

"What would happen if I let go?"

"I'd keel over like a tired spinning top."

Ellie eased June back to the floor. "What did you think?"

"I think I like dancing barefoot better than standing on my tippy toes."

"I thought dance lessons would come easy to you," Fern said. "Did you know this ballet undertaking would be so hard?"

Ellie chewed her lower lip as she helped June out of the *pointe* shoes. "I underestimated pert 'near all of it. It's hard. Mr. Van Damme is difficult to please, but if he weren't, those ballerinas who prance around in those shoes wouldn't look as lovely as they do. You should see them when they're practicing a piece. They leave me spellbound. Hard as it is, I want to be one of them."

"I have no doubt that you will," Fern said.

"When you say the more experienced dancers practice a piece, what do you mean?" Percy probably pulled the question out of his ear. He wanted to be part of Ellie's dream and wanted to convey his support, but how many men knew enough about this art form to pose a question? By the same token, how many Americans had heard of ballet?

"Ballet has five basic positions." Ellie took to her feet again and demonstrated each one. "And there are various jumps and pirouettes, and a multitude of bending movements."

"Show me," June said.

"I'd need more room for that, kiddo. Anyway, Mr. Van Damme chooses a piece of music and choreographs the dance."

"Choreographs?" Leland asked.

"It's similar to what a composer does. Instead of writing musical scores, he composes the sequence of dance steps for each of the dancers who are performing on stage at any one time. Everything has to be perfectly synchronized. The body movements, the height of a jump, the extension and motion of the arms. It's an incredible sight that never fails to give me goosebumps."

"So, you have no regrets?" Percy asked.

"None. I'm grateful to be here, and I'm beholden to all of you for trusting me to do my best. I aim to make you proud."

Fern didn't need to get all emotional, not now. Ellie had to ready herself for work at Three Squares Diner. It was time to drop Leland off at his apartment and for Fern, Percy, and June to drive back to Elizabeth.

"Do you need anything?" Percy asked.

"I think you fixed that today. I was getting homesick, so I am tickled pink that Uncle Leland is just a few blocks away." Ellie turned to Leland and said, "Soon as you settle into your work schedule, let me know. I plan to fix you a home cooked meal at least once every week."

Leland's neck reddened at her unexpected offer, and when she scribbled her phone number on a piece of paper, the hue darkened. As she placed it into his palm, he said, "Guess I'd better get a telephone."

"Why don't you stop here after your first day at the glass plant? I'll have supper waiting."

Leland tucked Ellie's number into his pocket. "I don't know what to say except thank you. I'll see you then."

After they returned to Leland's apartment, Fern followed him inside to collect June's favorite dolly. Fern clutched the toy in her arm and slipped a wad of folded bills into Leland's pocket, but he yanked them out faster than a deer fleeing a forest fire.

"I don't want your money," he said as he tried to shove it into her fist.

"You listen up, Leland Dugan. You turned our money down after Roy helped you break your foot, wouldn't even take a dollar toward the doctor's bill. You were out of work for more'n three months."

"I don't want your money," he repeated through clenched teeth. "I've still got my pride."

"Well that pride of yours needs to take a back seat to your empty stomach. You probably don't have two dimes to rub together right now, and you won't see your first paycheck from the glass company for at least a week after you start working. You stuff those bills back into your pocket right this minute, you hear?"

Leland worked his jaw back and forth while he stewed. "Call it a loan," he said.

"Call it whatever you want. The money isn't taking a return trip to Elizabeth."

Leland looked Fern hard in the eyes. "I thank you. Percy too."

"You're welcome. They're waiting for me. I have to go. Iffen you need anything, you call."

June, who'd tucked her doll into the crook of her arm, lost the last of her energy about five minutes into the ride home. She sat in the seat between Percy and Fern, her head in her mother's lap. Except for the rumble of the tires on the pavement and the purr of the engine, they road in silence.

When Percy pulled to a stop and turned onto Route 14, June stirred. She rubbed her eyes and sat up. The sun was giving way to twilight, but it wasn't hard to see the worry etched across the child's face.

"What's the trouble, girl? Did you eat too much? Do you have a tummy ache?"

"Not my tummy. It hurts higher than that."

When Fern twisted sideways, Percy glanced at her, eyes wide. "You hurt?" Fern asked. "Where?"

June lifted her hand and held it to her chest.

Alarm wasn't a strong enough word to describe the body blow that accompanied June's answer. Panic gushed with the force of a roiling river as it breached the dam.

Percy took his right hand off the steering wheel and pressed it to his daughter's shoulder. "Does it hurt like someone pinched you, or does it hurt like you're sad?"

June sniffled and wiped her eyes. "Why is everybody breaking my little heart, Daddy?"

Fern sucked in air, the first to fill her lungs since June said she was in pain. It would take a while for Fern's heart to find its normal rhythm.

"Who's making you sad?" Percy asked.

"First Ellie, then Uncle Leland. How come they moved away?"

"Honey, you know Ellie wants to dance more than anything," Fern replied.

"More'n me?"

"Ellie loves you, always will. Comes a time when children grow up and go their own way. It was the same for your daddy and me."

" 'Cept you didn't move away."

"Elizabeth doesn't have ballet classes," Percy said, "and it doesn't have the right job for your Uncle Leland. That's why they went to Charleston."

"But if everyone goes where they don't have room for anyone else, who'll watch after me when I'm all alone?"

Fern turned away and stared into the shadows as they widened and lengthened. June's perspective promised a future as fearful and murky as the darkness that was about to envelop the hills. Tears slid down Fern's cheeks. Her voice failed her. More than anything, she needed Percy to find a response that would soothe her baby's soul. This time, it would take something a lot more promising than a hamburger and soda.

Chapter II

Leland lowered the small frying pan to the sink and let the water run long enough to cover the stuck-on mess of eggs that should have comprised the better part of his breakfast instead of his after-work scrubbing task. How was he to know the little dab of butter at the bottom of the pan was a requirement and not an option? Butter. One more thing to add to his growing list of necessities.

He walked to the window, which was as wide open as it could get, reluctant to close off the room to the unwelcome fragrance of burnt egg. Four- and five-story buildings obstructed his view of the eastern horizon, where the sun wasn't making much of an effort to roust the city's population. The straggly gray clouds that hovered overhead, apparently sympathetic to the sun's ambivalence, were too lethargic to threaten rain. Leland lowered the window, but left a two-inch gap where fresh air might sneak inside while he was off to his first day on the job.

He grabbed his lunch bag, which held a peanut butter and honey sandwich—less the honey, because it was not a necessity—and a golden delicious apple. When he picked up his key ring, the metal jangled against the key to his apartment door. No one locked their doors back home, just one more reminder that he was not where he belonged.

Leland took his time, having given himself an extra half hour to arrive at his destination. As he headed east, he passed through the part of Charleston known as Kanawha City. The manager at the glass company suggested Leland find a house to rent in that borough, where scores of the company's employees lived with their families, but Leland couldn't picture Muriel paying him more than a first visit if he tried to make her comfortable in a house that was smaller than the Bigler chicken coop. He wrinkled his nose as fetid air curled its way into the open window. The coop and the city stank about the same.

He crossed over the Kanawha River and turned onto MacCorkle Avenue where smokestacks on both sides of the street loomed over gargantuan factories. Like pieces on a chessboard, the row of brick shafts delineating the Libbey-Owens-Ford Glass Company plant looked ready to do battle with those of the Owens-Illinois Bottle Company plant.

Charleston was rife with industrial manufacturers, including the Carbide and Carbon Chemicals Corporation plant, which occupied more than one hundred fifty acres of land adjacent to the Kanawha River, as well as all of Blaine Island, a thin strip of land situated in the middle of the river. With that expansive site, and nearby brick-making companies and storage tanks comprising a good part of the land to the west of the city, on days when the air was stagnant, like this one, a metallic, eye-watering stench enveloped the metropolitan area. When Leland turned off the car's engine and stepped into the parking lot of the Libbey-Owens-Ford plant, it was hard to decide which were more offensive, burnt eggs or the pungent by-products of commerce.

Scores of workers walked toward the plant, a staggering sight for a man who lived in a town of around seven hundred people.

Leland ventured that the number of workers employed by the two factories had to total at least two thousand. This was as unfamiliar to him as his introduction to the CCC camp in Hawthorne, Nevada. Unlike those old times, Percy wasn't here to fulfill his sidekick role.

Leland completed the forms in the new employee packet and scanned the multi-colored product information sheets that accompanied the paperwork. During the ensuing lull, he compared his white button-down shirt and freshly pressed trousers, which he'd sandwiched between his box springs and mattress just for the occasion, to the attire worn by two other men who also reported for their first day of work.

In addition to well-made trousers and shirts, both men sported ties and blazers. They parted their hair on one side, and judging by the scent in the room, smoothed it into place with Vitalis hair tonic. Leland scratched at the back of his neck. Muriel was pretty good at cutting hair, except for the last time, when she let her temper wield the scissors. Maybe Ellie would stand in next time he needed a barber.

"Where will you be working?" Sophisticated Man Number One asked Sophisticated Man Number Two.

"Accounting. How about you?"

"Engineering."

The accountant tipped his chin, or maybe it was his nose, in Leland's direction. "You?"

"I'll be doing quality control."

"Probably easier than working on the line, but I'll take an office with air conditioning," the engineer said. His educated co-worker concurred with a nasal huff.

Next was a tour of the facility. Their guide, a young man who'd recently graduated from West Virginia University, relayed every detail of the plant's history, starting with its construction in

1917 and its claim to being the largest plate glass plant in the world just six years later. The sophisticated new hires talked casually between themselves instead of giving the college graduate his due. They acted as if they knew it all, probably because they did.

When their tour took them into the plant, Leland couldn't quit gawping. Every step of the manufacturing process added to the temperature in the factory, and by the time the group exited the building, Leland's shirt was as damp as a chamois cloth after a car wash. The engineer's previous comment about air conditioning made a heap more sense now than it had before Leland's in-person introduction to the art of glass making.

Although he wouldn't be working on the line, he'd spend a considerable amount of time in the confines of the factory. The heat, the noise, and the potential for harm called to mind his CCC days in Hawthorne, where the desert heat was as fierce as a furnace, the noise of jackhammers assaulted the air, and the mishandling of TNT used to build the road could wreak havoc over the entire crew.

At the close of his first day at Libbey-Owens-Ford, Leland climbed into his car and rolled down the window. It wasn't until he pulled out of the parking lot and sped back toward the apartment that the air moved around him. He filled his lungs with the life-giving element, although it was none too fragrant, and swallowed the wave of homesickness that was reminiscent of his CCC days.

≈

"I hope you don't mind, but I bought hamburgers instead of cooking dinner. I was plumb wore out by the time class was over." Ellie pulled two rumpled paper napkins out of the bag and handed one of them to Leland as she took her seat at the table.

"This is right nice of you." Leland reached for his wallet.

"Oh, no you don't. These are from Three Squares, and I didn't have to pay full price."

"Well, you had to pay something."

"Next time I'll let you buy, but not today." Ellie unwrapped her burger, used her teeth to snatch a pickle from under the bun, and grinned as she chewed and swallowed. "Tell me about your new job. Do you think you'll like it?"

"I didn't exactly do any work today, but the factory dazed me. I probably wore the same blank stare as Dorothy did when she walked into the Emerald City and came face-to-face with the Wizard of Oz."

"Was it intimidating?"

"Sure enough. I expected the plant to be big, but I didn't know how important a place it is."

"Important how?"

"I knew the company made windshield glass and windows, but it came as a surprise to hear that Libbey-Owens-Ford made the windows for the Empire State Building."

"They did?"

"That's what they said. And the Waldorf Astoria Hotel, too."

"Maybe you should take Aunt Muriel to New York City and show off your employer's products."

Ellie's carefree suggestion packed a punch she didn't intend to inflict. The girl didn't have any knowledge of the events that transpired between his broken foot and his collecting the key to his new living quarters.

"Wouldn't it be grand? Staying at the Waldorf Astoria?" Ellie tapped her index finger alongside her chin. "Hmm, I wonder if Mr. Van Damme has stayed there. He lived in New York before he came to West Virginia."

"Muriel said he was part of the resistance during the Second World War."

"He was, back when he lived in Brussels." Ellie dabbed her mouth with her napkin, and when she put it back into her lap, she said, "You and Aunt Muriel have something in common with Mr. Van Damme and his wife."

"We do?"

"First off, his parents didn't want him to dance. They expected him to join the military, just like the rest of the men in his family. It's just me thinking, but maybe his family let him join the ballet company because they knew he would eventually have to complete mandatory military service. Maybe they thought he'd change his mind after he served for a while. Obviously, that's not what happened. Instead of exchanging one for the other, he managed to be a soldier and a dancer at the same time."

"What does his career have to do with Muriel and me?"

"Well, you married the daughter of the CCC camp commander, and Mr. Van Damme married the daughter of the officer who ran his military unit. In fact, when he expressed his desire to marry Maggy, her father *invited* him to get moving because he could see a time coming, on account of the fighting in Europe, when they wouldn't be able to wed."

"I can't say Captain Levy *invited* me to marry Muriel." Leland wadded his wrapper into a ball and lobbed it into the small trashcan sitting on the floor near the kitchen sink. While the captain didn't oppose the marriage, he was probably as surprised as Leland had been when Muriel accepted Leland's proposal. "He was an all right father-in-law, though, and after he retired and settled in Elizabeth, we started acting like kin. When he married Percy's mother, we became a bona fide family."

"I was only six years old when he died, but I remember him. I have a hard time picturing him in a military uniform, barking orders to a bunch of soldiers or CCC recruits. He would pretend he was a big ol' bear, and would run after us with his arms wide and a deep growl coming out of his mouth, threatening to give us a papaw bear squeeze."

"I remember. I miss him." Leland missed Muriel too.

"You have another thing in common with the Van Dammes."

"What?"

"The war separated them for a time, just like this job has taken you away from Aunt Muriel. The Germans apprehended Mr. Van Damme and put him to work in a hospital. Later, he found himself aboard a train, supposedly taking him and other prisoners back to Brussels where the Nazis would assign them to jobs that supported Germany's war effort. After he realized they were traveling in a different direction, he managed to jump the train. He didn't know where he was, but it wasn't anywhere near Brussels. His walk back wasn't easy, but he made it."

"He returned to a city occupied by German soldiers?"

"That's true. And he went right back to dancing."

"They performed during the occupation?"

Ellie shrugged. "Turned out the Germans liked the ballet."

Leland missed his target when he tossed Ellie's wrapper toward the trashcan. He stood and stretched, retrieved the paper, and dropped it into the container.

"I ought to get back to my apartment. Give your old uncle a hug." Leland kissed Ellie on the forehead and said, "Thank you for dinner and for genuine, home-grown company."

Moths circled the overhead light on the landing as Leland unlocked his door. Once inside, streetlights pressed shadows against the walls and over the meager furnishings. He turned on a lamp just long enough to scrub his frying pan, and readied for bed in the dim, secondhand light. Instead of climbing between the sheets, he sat on the bed, rested his elbows on his knees, and lowered his face into his uplifted hands.

Andre Van Damme's story captivated Ellie. The way she talked, her dance instructor was a hero. Heroes have aspirations and display perseverance despite conflict. They don't take people for granted. They rescue them. They value them.

At what moment in time had Leland decided Muriel wasn't worthy of his company if it couldn't be in the place of his choosing? He'd walk every hill and hollow for his wife, but with the way he'd turned on her, the things he'd said, well, they sounded more like the words of a villain than those of a hero. How much more hurtful were his accusations, coming from the man who loved her?

He couldn't call because he didn't have a telephone. Besides, it would be too easy to add to the quarrel if one or the other of them mistook the tone of voice for something neither intended. Driving back home wasn't possible. He had to work in the morning, and until he had his first paycheck in his hand a long two weeks from now, he didn't have the money for gasoline.

Leland scrounged through one of the boxes he'd brought from home, needing a writing tablet and knowing he hadn't packed one. His eyes wandered toward the packet from the glass company. He'd make do. He pulled out the ballpoint pen his manager had given to him earlier in the day, the one with Libbey-Owens-Ford printed on the case, and reached for the collection of forms, advertising pamphlets, and pages printed with rules and regulations. If he kept his message to a minimum, and if he wrote in tiny lettering, he could use the back of the brochure that touted the benefits of the company's glare-reducing, E-Z-Eye Safety Plate Glass for automobile windshields.

Leland closed his eyes and offered a prayer, one in which he sought for words capable of taking the glare off his selfish, stupid mouth and redirecting the light to the deepest parts of his heart, the place that belonged to his wife.

Chapter 12

"We need to leave now," Wayne said for the third time. His impatience had his feet scuffing out a cadence on the old porch boards that rivaled a tap dancer's spirited shuffle. Becca sat in a rocker, reading a book. Beyond the house, the car door hung open, and Roy's feet dangled from one of the back windows. That boy could drop into a nap in less than five minutes. Considering the length of the delay, he was probably deep into dreamland.

Fern leaned toward the screen door and called after June. "We're waiting, girl."

Soft footsteps padded down the steps moments before the child raced onto the porch and the door hit the frame with a resounding thwack. June's chipper voice announced she was ready, but her impish expression gave Fern pause. When her inspection landed on June's feet, she rolled her eyes.

"Where's your other shoe?"

June hefted both shoulders.

"Where's your other boot?"

When June raised her shoulders a second time, a mischievous air accompanied her response.

"Can we just go?" Wayne asked.

"I'm not taking your sister anywhere while she's wearing one shoe and one boot."

"Aw, nobody will notice. If we don't go now, we won't get a seat." Wayne turned his begging toward his father. "Please, can we go now?"

Percy scratched his chin. "I reckon the boy's right. Let's drive separately. We'll save you a spot in the bleachers. What about you, Muriel? You want to ride with the boys or wait for the girls?"

"I'll help find the shoe. Or the boot."

Fern opened the screen door and directed her youngest child toward the stairs. "With any luck we'll be right behind you."

Twenty minutes later, June strode into the living room where Fern was on her hands and knees, searching under every piece of furniture. "Let's go, Mommy. I want to see the marching band."

"Where'd you find your boot?"

"In the laundry hamper."

"How'd it end up there?"

"Prob'ly Roy. He likes to joke."

"Prob'ly not, but at least you're wearing a matching pair on your feet. Go find Muriel and meet me outside."

"Yes'm." June tore off toward the kitchen and hollered, "Muriel."

"Are you sure you don't want to go?" Fern asked Becca.

"I watched my share of football games while I was still in school."

"I know you did, but you've heard about this year's team."

"Sure. Last week Wirt beat Williamstown fifty-nine to nothing. I'd be bored after the first quarter and embarrassed for the other team. That's downright humiliating."

"I can't say, as I didn't go last week, but in the first game of the season Sistersville put up a decent fight. As I recall, they scored thirteen points to Wirt's twenty-seven."

"You know I don't get much time to myself, so I thought I'd take advantage of it. Grandma Nettie and I will have the place to ourselves while y'all watch the game and take a trip to the ice cream shop afterwards. If the Tigers keep their winning streak, I'll go next time they play at home. Fair enough?"

"Fair enough."

Judging by the crowd jamming the bleachers, the better part of Wirt County did not have an itch for Friday night solitude. The fans who cheered for the home team stood on their feet more than they sat in their seats, and each time the football players' zeal overpowered their best intentions to play by the rules, multiple whistles interrupted the revelry. Seconds later, as yellow or red flags fell beside a yard-line marker, the announcer would call out, "Flag on the play. Personal foul. Fifteen-yard penalty for the home team," or whatever punishment suited the infraction.

The spectators took a short break from hooting and hollering during halftime, which was June's favorite stand-on-her-tiptoes event. As much as she enjoyed the high-stepping band members with their military-style uniforms, complete with shako hats and shoulder cords, and the majorettes with their short pleated skirts and white boots, June kept her attention glued to the cheerleaders during game time. Her apparent yearning to be one of them wasn't likely to fade before she joined the high school ranks. Fern would worry about that when the time came.

Muriel, who hadn't said much on the ride to the school or during the second quarter, hadn't quit wiggling her foot in tiny circles since she sat in the stands. Fern didn't mind the crowd's gusto, but the tension that accompanied Muriel's fidgeting was about to pass from annoying to exasperating.

When the band took to the field, Fern stood, stretched her arms, and asked Muriel, "Would you like to take a walk? Get away from the noise for a spell?"

"Um. Sure."

Fern tapped Percy's elbow, inclined her head slightly in Muriel's direction, and said, "We'll be back in a bit."

Percy didn't need a translator to understand that Fern and Muriel might be gone for a while. In fact, he'd be pleased if Fern could talk some calm into Muriel.

As dozens of spat-clad feet took to the field, the clash of symbols punctuated the rhythm commanded by the drum line. Soon, horns blared into the atmosphere and wind instruments trilled along. Fern led Muriel toward the school building so they could talk, assuming Muriel wanted to get things off her chest. When it came to emotions, she was better at kicking dirt over the weed than excavating the roots.

"Can you believe it hit close to ninety degrees today?" Fern asked. "You'd never know it now. It feels like it's seventy or so." The evening was sublime, the humidity low, the scent of fresh-mown grass and trees laden with their lush summer splendor anointing the air.

"Autumn is right around the corner." Muriel's voice held about as much enthusiasm as a punctured tire.

"You make it sound like a bad thing."

"Everything dies."

"Why do you always see the negative? The earth doesn't die. It prepares for its rest. Autumn is when the bears eat like pigs so they can sleep like babies until springtime. It's when families bring in the last of the season's bounty so they can gather in front of the warm fire and play banjos and guitars, and tell stories when winter comes. Fall is a time to prepare for a well-deserved rest."

"What about the ice, the wind, and the cold?"

"By the time winter sets in, you've squandered autumn's splendor. All we can do is prepare. Regardless of the season, we're not in control. You know that. We pray for mercy, for protection, and for provision, and we give thanks regardless of what happens, storms or otherwise."

When Muriel turned her face away, she wrapped her arms around her middle, as if she were cold. Much as Fern didn't want to interfere, Muriel's pessimistic focus was reaching an intolerable level.

"Why didn't you go visit Leland this weekend? He invited you, didn't he?"

Anger flashed in Muriel's eyes. "He wanted time away from me."

"That's not true. I talked to him when he called the other day. He said he'd asked you every week since he started working in Charleston, except for the first one."

"Before he left, he said he didn't want to be around me. I'm just obliging him."

"Muriel Dugan, you need to stop, right now, despite the hurtful words you said to one another. We all say and do things we want to take back, but what you're doing is downright spiteful."

"If he wants to see me, maybe he ought to get in the car and come here. Besides, he knows I have to borrow one of yours to make the trip to Charleston."

"And you know Percy and I would lend you the truck or the car. You're just excusing your decision. It ain't right."

"You needed both vehicles tonight, didn't you?"

Fern clenched her teeth before the huff escaped. Here she was, trying to get Muriel to get over speaking unkindly to Leland, when Fern was in a tizzy while she fought to keep her nasty comments from spewing out of her own mouth. No wonder Leland lashed out at his wife. Muriel could wipe the smile clean off the *Mona Lisa*.

"We did not need both vehicles," Fern replied. "Either

Wayne would have whined until we all arrived late, or June would be wearing mismatched footwear right now. Before we go off on another rabbit trail, I need to say one thing because it hurts me to see you so upset and hear my brother's brokenness over the telephone."

"Get on with it. Spit it out."

"You might want to call to mind the scripture that warns against letting the sun go down on our anger."

A sarcastic chuckle prefaced Muriel's response. "Many moons have risen since that first sun-setting."

"Too many. Every day you let another one slip by makes it harder to settle what caused the quarrel in the first place. Back peddling is about as easy as rowing a canoe against the current." Or painting the grin back on Da Vinci's *Lisa*.

"He's mad because I suggested he search for a job in Charleston. Why was that so awful?"

"It's not awful. He knew he had to find work."

"When I told him I'd move to Charleston too, get a job there, and help put our finances back together, one might think I'd hit him with a cattle prod."

Until now, Fern hadn't known what had driven the wedge between her brother and her sister-in-law. When Fern exhaled, it probably sounded like the punctured tire she'd envisioned.

"I reckon he thought you wanted to take advantage of the situation and finally get your wish to move to Charleston."

Muriel blinked, lowered her gaze, blinked again, and stared into the darkness beyond the school building. When she swallowed, it appeared as if all of her worries settled in her throat.

"Muriel? I'm sorry if you think I spoke out of turn."

"Is that what he thinks? That all I've ever wanted was to leave Elizabeth and move to Charleston?"

"Maybe not Charleston, but a city bigger than Elizabeth."

Fern back stepped when Muriel clutched her stomach and moaned.

"He thinks I want to leave here?" Pain flooded Muriel's gray eyes and sorrow bowed her lips. "Is that what you think?"

Fern flinched. It was hardly a secret that Muriel was as assertive, hard-nosed, and stubborn as she was beautiful, generous, and intelligent. For her to display such self-loathing at the same time she sought to dismember everyone who opposed her or who didn't understand the person she thought herself to be, stymied Fern. How was she to respond?

"Is that what *everyone* thinks?"

"Uh, I guess so. Maybe. I mean, you talk about how much you like the city. The cultural things. You like dance and opera, and nice department stores. In Elizabeth, we're happy to have a movie theater and performances put on by the high school students. No one blames you for wanting more."

"More? Everyone thinks I want *more?* Isn't there one single person in this family or in this town who knows me? Who I am?"

"Come on," Fern said as she pressed her hand against Muriel's shoulder. "You know we all love you."

"Do you?"

"Absolutely. You have to admit you don't share your feelings with us, not your deep ones."

"Obviously. I'm sure I'd offend everyone if I did."

"Sarcasm isn't going to help. You don't need to get defensive."

"I'm not defensive, Fern. I'm angry. None of you has a clue as to the person I am, what I cherish, or who I yearn to be."

Leland would tan Fern's hide if he knew how upset she'd made his wife.

"Listen—"

A voluminous roar from the bleachers drowned out Fern's

reply. The commentator, too excited to need the amplification boosting his microphone, announced, "Another touchdown, folks. That puts the Tigers at thirty-five points. Walton's still sitting at zero. These boys are on fire, though, so don't none of you leave before the clock ticks down to nothing."

Silence loomed between Fern and Muriel while the enthusiasm in the stands heightened. Minutes later, the masses began the final countdown, "Seven, six, five, four, three, two, one." The band accompanied the jubilant rumpus that followed.

Fern studied Muriel's broken countenance. So much for trying to soothe her sister-in-law or encouraging her to work out things with her brother. "We better get back."

The announcer blew air into the microphone, as one might do if he wanted to see if it was working. Which it already was. "Paging Fern Bigler. Fern Bigler, please report to the concession stand."

"Great, now we're both in trouble," Muriel said as the two women strode back toward the bleachers.

"Muriel?"

"What?"

"I'm sorry. Every one of us loves you. You have to hold onto that. But, please understand. When you keep your feelings to yourself, you leave us to guess how everything affects you. If we've hurt you, please forgive us."

Muriel's answer was lost in a sea of people pouring through the exits. Talk about rowing against the tide. The path to the concession stand was against the flow, and Fern and Muriel were like two sticks with paper sails pushing through the Spanish Armada. Fern finally spied Percy, who looked more worried than impatient.

"Where'd you go?" he asked as he wrapped his arm around her shoulder and examined Muriel's bloodshot eyes. The bright lights were none too kind. "Are you both all right?"

"As Leland would say, 'Right as rain.'" A glower accompanied Muriel's sarcastic reply.

Before Percy could respond, Wayne and Roy ran to Fern. Wayne pumped his arm in the air. "Did you see the last touchdown? It was spectacular."

Percy leaned around the boys. "Where's your sister?"

"Right behind me," Roy said as he turned around and called out, "June?" He turned back to Percy. "Well, she was right there a second ago."

As a group, they turned and pushed against the exodus, each of them yelling June's name. Ten minutes later, Percy went to ask the announcer to page June, but all those who were responsible for the equipment were already gone.

A good thirty minutes later, after combing the parking lot and the grounds between the playing field and the school, Percy asked one of the departing fans to call the sheriff.

An hour after three deputies joined in the search, stars studded the inky black sky while clouds flirted with the moonlight. Fern fastened her eyes on the celestial covering and offered another silent petition to the Designer of it all. She swayed as a wave of vertigo seized her, and grappled for Percy's arm.

"Fern!" Percy's arms came around her torso as the parking lot lights spun in circles. "What's wrong?"

"I . . . I c-c-can't breathe."

Chapter 13

"Inhale, Fern. Look at me. Inhale through your nose. That's right. Now, exhale through your mouth, slow and easy. Again. Good. Do it again." Percy's voice was familiar, but it took effort for Fern to shove the fog away and recognize that he cradled her head while she lay on the ground.

"Where is she?" A man's deep voice called from the shadows. As the figure approached and peered down at her, Fern recognized the face of Deputy Taggart. "This the lady who fainted?"

As memory surfaced, Fern struggled to right herself. Alarm squeezed her chest.

"Relax," Percy said. "Easy does it. Breathe in, breathe out."

"Where's June?"

"We're still searching, but don't worry. She can't have gone far," Deputy Taggart said as he checked her pulse. When he saw Fern's creased brow, he said, "I was a medic in the war. I suspect you're just a mite anxious, but thought I'd check you over before you tried to get up."

"I'll be fine once we find my daughter."

"Sit still just a minute longer. The others are combing the

area. We're checking the ice cream parlor, in case someone gave her a ride."

Gave June a ride? That's what kidnappers did. They offered ice cream, complete with transportation. If the medic-turned-law-enforcer meant to test Fern's reaction to dread, he'd chosen the words to do so.

"I think you're all right, Mrs. Bigler." Deputy Taggart offered a hand to Fern and helped her to her feet. "I think you ought to go on home and leave the searching to us."

"I can't leave." She couldn't. Wouldn't. When Fern caught Percy passing off an unspoken command to Muriel, Fern folded her arms across her chest and clenched her jaw.

"He's right. Let's get you home." Muriel extended an open palm to Percy. "I'd rather drive the car than the truck."

"I can't leave until we find her. Percy, please."

He was apologetic when he said, "If you pass out again, your emergency will slow the search."

Guilt buried Fern. What if *this* mishap, *this* delay put her child in deep jeopardy? A tremor inched up her spine at the thought, but . . . but if Percy and the sheriff's men didn't find June right this minute, she'd die, utterly mortified and eternally inconsolable. How could she go home without knowing her baby was safe? Tears came so fast they accumulated in wide blotches on her blouse.

Despite the passage of precious minutes, Percy lifted Fern's face until he captured her attention. Confidence and hope rested in those hazel eyes. "I know you're praying, and so is everyone else. You trust in Him," he said as he looked heavenward, "and you need to trust in those He brought together for this purpose tonight."

Fern handed the truck keys to Percy, but her resolve faltered with every step she took toward the parking lot.

When they reached the car, Muriel walked to the driver's door while Wayne and Roy fretted, their faces reflecting layers of confusion, guilt, and fear.

Percy reached for the passenger door handle at the same time Muriel's door opened far enough to trigger the overhead lamp. The sight inside the car took Fern's legs out from under her again. Curled up in the back seat was Fern's dozing cherub, her baby, her child. When Muriel gasped, June's dark brown eyes fluttered. She squinted at the blinding light and pulled herself into a sitting position. One of her rosy cheeks bore wrinkled stripes where she'd made a pillow out of Roy's scrunched jacket.

"Is it time for ice cream?" June asked before her mouth stretched into a yawn.

Fern pushed past Percy, scrambled into the back seat, and hugged her beloved child as if she'd just gone missing for two hours. It was the vision of a lifetime without June that prevented Fern from letting go.

"Mommy," June mumbled against Fern's chest, "If you don't quit squeezing me, I'm a-goin' wet my pants."

A giddy, grateful, overwhelmed-to-the-point-of-delirium laugh escaped Fern's lips. The prayer she offered toward the One who created the skies, the earth, and every being in it, had it been audible, would have transcended a heavenly choir.

It was midnight before June climbed into bed and Fern gathered the blanket up to her daughter's chin.

June patted her belly. "I'm full."

"I reckon you are. You liked your pudding all right?"

"Yes'm. Almost as much as ice cream."

"Next time we'll have to get to the parlor before they turn out the lights. And next time, don't you let anyone walk away from you in a crowd. You hold on to someone's hand. Tight. You hear?"

"Yes'm. I was watching the cheerleaders when I was s'posed to stay with Wayne and Roy. That's why I got lost."

"You worried us, honey, but it turned out all right. Were you frightened?"

June blinked a misty sheen from her eyes. "Worse than a scaredy cat."

"If you get lost at the football game again, what will you do?"

"Find the deputy who stands by the gate."

"What if you're in a store?"

"Talk to the worker who takes the money."

"What if—"

"Mommy, that's too many questions."

"I have one more. What if a stranger wants to buy you ice cream and they even offer to give you a ride to the parlor?"

"I'll run away as fast as three blind mice what's being chased by the farmer's wife."

"That's exactly right. It's good you were listening to us while you ate your pudding."

" 'Night, Mommy."

"Goodnight, precious. I love you."

A yawn cut short June's, "Love you too."

Fern whispered a prayer of thanksgiving. Their precious child was safe, in her own bed, and drifting off to sleep knowing that those who loved her would do anything in their power to nurture her, to protect her, and to love her. How much more was the unfathomable, perfect love of the Father who promises that nothing, not death or life, will separate us from His love?

"Come on, sport, what'll it be?" Wally spoke out of the side of his mouth while the cigar he'd clamped between his teeth flapped up and down. While he waited for a reply, Carl pulled out a cigarette, flicked a match, and drew air between his lips until the tobacco caught fire.

Leland dropped his cards facedown. "Fold."

"Again?" Wally asked.

George, who was holding his pair close to his chest, lifted his free hand and took a slug of drink from the bottle. "Either you've got the worst luck of anyone I ever met, or you don't like the game. You want to play something other than Texas Hold'em?"

"It don't matter to me," Leland replied.

Wally tapped the ashes off his cigar and reclined in his folding chair. How the metal frame supported the man's bulk was a feat in itself. That the four men managed to find room for the proffered game table in the studio apartment was near miraculous, not that any part of the event bore a relationship to spiritual things.

Leland grimaced as he tallied the price of his stupidity. The evidence was unmistakable, whether visible or unseen. He knew better, could tell from the way his co-workers eyeballed each other as they tried to convince him to get on board. It would be easy to blame Muriel for the mess, but what good would it do? She'd let her *maybe* hang in the air until late Thursday night when she called and turned it into another *not this weekend*. Just in case she'd follow through with a visit, he'd already tidied the apartment and bought the fixings needed to produce a few right nice meals.

After Carl won the hand, Wally commenced to shuffle the deck, but paused when he heard a knock on the door. Leland didn't like the smirk that attended the card dealer's reaction.

Wally's stogie wobbled when he asked, "You wanna get that, Carl?"

Carl's mouth responded in the same manner as Wally's had.

"Why, sure."

Leland choked when two women who worked in Libbey's payroll department stumbled into the room. Their girl-next-door images had given way to overzealous applications of lipstick, eye shadow, and rouge, all of which emphasized their glazed eyes and lopsided smiles.

"Thelma," Wally called out. "Come on over and have a seat."

While Leland searched for a place that might accommodate the two women, the redhead sauntered over and plopped herself into Wally's lap. The metal shifted, but it held. Another miracle.

Carl returned to his place at the table, but when he tapped his hand to his thigh, offering the spot to Violet, the gal demurred, and with obvious reluctance, she lowered herself to the edge of Leland's mattress. When Leland's eyes widened at her brashness, her cheeks took on the color of a red-hot coal. Judging from her needing to fan her face, heat joined forces with the hue.

Sure enough, Leland knew better, but when one of the Friday night card players had to go out of town with his wife, and when the other three pals heard Leland was on his own for another weekend, they were more'n pleased to have him take the empty seat. Trouble was, the out-of-towner was supposed to be the host. Therefore, the task fell upon Leland's shoulders, but only after he'd accepted their card playing invitation.

"You in?" George asked.

Leland slid his addition to the pot.

"Call," Carl said.

The pile of chips sitting at Leland's elbow didn't grow to any remarkable size, nor did it diminish to any measurable degree. He could hold his own, apparently, but if he had his druthers, he'd empty his living quarters of his guests, invited and otherwise.

The familiar sound of knocking made Leland groan. When none of the others showed signs of expectation, he strode to the door. On the other side was the elderly Mrs. Graber who lived in the adjacent apartment. She wore a flowered housecoat over her nightgown and pink slippers on her feet. A hairnet gathered the long silver hair that normally rested in a bun at the back of her neck.

"It's past my bedtime. If you won't send everybody home, would you at least keep it down?"

"Yes, ma'am. I apologize."

When she twisted sideways so she could see inside the apartment, Leland backed into the space and pulled the door against his body. The sight behind him would not endear him to his neighbors.

"Sorry, Mrs. Graber. Goodnight."

Leland didn't have a hankering to play cards, didn't care to gamble, and never made an effort to participate in a night out with the boys. But—and this was where it was *her* fault—he'd spent too many nights lolling in the apartment, and the solitude and claustrophobia left him with an itch he needed to scratch. So card playing it was. Except for the part that wasn't.

It was running well past two o'clock when Leland wiped down the little countertop and slung the dishtowel over the edge of the sink. Two dozen rinsed-out beer bottles rested upside down in the sink. Wally expected him to haul every last piece of glassware to work on Monday so he could collect the deposit.

Leland tiptoed down the stairs and carried his garbage to the alley. He held the disgusting collection of onion-laced hamburger wrappers and cigar and cigarette butts at arm's length, but the stink assaulted his nose and made his eyes water. When a driver turned the corner, the car's headlamps flooded the narrow passageway, captured Leland's silhouette, and cast it along the pavement and up the brick walls. Leland froze until the eerie apparition disappeared. He scanned his surroundings as he retreated to his apartment.

Buildings eclipsed the moon and obscured every trace of the constellations that graced the firmament. It wasn't until he moved to Charleston, where the stars retreated behind the glare of the city lights, that Leland realized he'd taken their nightly sojourns for granted. Although he knew the glittering orbs were right where they belonged, their concealment discouraged him. Likewise, he found no solace in Muriel's absence. Unlike the stars, it seemed as if neither of them knew where they ought to be.

He'd left the window open while he cleaned, but when he crossed back over the threshold, the odor in the room was what one might expect if he blended skunk oil with a gallon of sickly sweet cologne. The latter was a gift imparted by the two payroll clerks, both of whom wore enough perfume to ward off a vampire. Adding to the stink was the effect of stuffing too many people into a room meant to accommodate one.

The guys, being serious gamblers, had shooed the women out of the apartment after about half an hour, but Leland had to pinch his nose when both girls gave him a thanks-for-entertaining-us kiss on the cheek. His thoughts weren't kindly, but those females reeked.

Leland squatted in front of the window frame, pressed his face against the screen, and prayed for a tornado to spin through the streets of Charleston with enough force to clear the air. Instead, a passing city bus rewarded him with a plume of exhaust. The faint throbbing across his forehead escalated with every pulse. *Stupid, stupid, stupid.*

He brushed his teeth in the dark, swallowed a couple of aspirin, and hit the hay. Never again would he participate in a social engagement with his coworkers, even if he had to spend every non-working hour alone. Leland stared at the ceiling, waiting for the little white pills to calm his headache. Why was he spending another weekend alone anyway? He'd apologized more than once. Why hadn't Muriel come to visit? Probably for the same reason she told him he'd be wasting his time if he decided to spend the weekend in Elizabeth.

A rapping noise startled Leland awake. He sat up on the edge of the bed, rubbed the sleep out of his eyes, and listened. When another series of knocks punctuated the air, he clambered out of bed and opened the door. His visitor's eyes blinked repeatedly, as if they couldn't focus, and her nose crinkled while she inspected his bare feet and legs, his drawers, and his undershirt. When her gaze lit on his face, her gray eyes blazed.

Despite knowing better, Leland grinned. How about that? Muriel had come to Charleston after all. Too bad the flame he inspired wasn't of the I've-missed-you-my-darling sort.

Chapter 14

Leland opened the door wide and stepped to the side, an overt invitation Muriel chose to ignore. Despite the fire in her eyes and smoke spilling out of her ears, the sight of his wife delighted him. He'd missed her something awful. "Come on in."

"I don't think so."

"Well, you can't stay out here. We'll wake the neighbors." Leland didn't find it necessary to add the word *again*.

Muriel shook her head. "I made a mistake." She pivoted so fast that when Leland grabbed her and spun her back around, his movement almost toppled both of them down the stairs.

It was plain to see that when Muriel opened her mouth to protest, she'd use the same volume as if she were staring down a rattlesnake and daring it to make its move. Leland was none too gentle when he grabbed her arm and yanked her into his apartment, but at least he managed to close the door before she started spewing. When she bit the fat of his hand, which was the only thing holding back her pent-up rejoinder, it brought to mind the last time Leland tried to silence a member of the opposite sex. It was Fern who'd been mouthing off, back when she was about twelve years old. The memory and the scar on his pinkie were significant enough that he should have thought twice about repeating the action.

Leland gritted his teeth when he said, "I'm doing my best not to yelp, and my neighbors would be obliged if you'd hold your tongue when I let go. Shake your head if you promise you'll keep your voice down."

He had reservations, but since questioning her nodded agreement wasn't a smart way to initiate a long-awaited conversation, he uncovered her mouth.

"I'm not staying." Muriel inspected the hand encircling her arm. "Let go now and I'll leave quietly."

"Muriel, it's the middle of the night. You just drove all the way from Elizabeth. I won't let you turn around and drive back tonight."

"That's not for you to decide. I'll go to Ellie's apartment. She'll let me stay there."

"You'll drag three girls out of bed at three o'clock in the morning? You'll scare them half to death."

"I'll find a hotel."

"No, you'll stay right here."

"Haven't you had enough company tonight?" Muriel stared at Leland while she worked her jaw back and forth, daring him to reply.

"What?"

"Come here," Muriel said as she walked into the tiny bathroom. "Stand in front of the mirror."

Leland did as she commanded, and when she flicked the switch for the overhead light, his face turned beet red. The color was a pretty fair match to the lip imprint left on his cheek by either Violet or Thelma, not that it made a difference which of the two wore the smeary makeup.

"Muriel, it's not what you—"

"Oh, of course it isn't. And your apartment doesn't smell like a gin joint. And those bottles crammed into your sink? You're working overtime this weekend, running quality control tests on Libbey's bottles."

"We don't make bottles down at the plant. Those are made at the factory across the street."

"Really? How ignorant of me." Her voice ratcheted up a notch.

"Muriel, please hear me out." Leland motioned her toward a chair. "Please."

She sat, but all at once, she looked ready to fall to pieces, fatigue overtaking her ire and resignation subduing her quarrelsome bearing. Leland's chest constricted at her apparent despair. They'd let things simmer far too long.

"Can I give you a real quick explanation for the state of my apartment and my face so we can get to talking about what's really wrong between us?"

"Until you explain away this mess, I won't hear a word of the rest."

Muriel's expression didn't soften into anything akin to forgiveness as Leland shared what had to sound like one lame excuse after another. She bristled at the mention of Thelma and Violet, but she let him finish explaining and apologizing without making another attempt to flee.

"The whole thing was stupid, stupid, stupid. I'm sorry it happened and I'm sorry this is how I greeted you tonight—or this morning—whichever you want to call it."

Muriel closed her eyes for so long that Leland thought she'd fallen asleep sitting in the chair. Her eyes flashed open wide, but a moment later, her eyelids retreated to half-mast. "Now we need to talk," she mumbled.

"No, right now we both need to sleep." Leland offered his

hand and helped Muriel to her feet. "You take the bed. I'll sleep on the floor."

"I thought you were finished being stupid."

Those words pushed Leland's shoulders back against the wall. She may as well have ripped his flesh by firing squad. Since when did Muriel equate kindness with stupidity?

Muriel pinched her mouth and narrowed her eyes. "What? I'm just saying, you don't have to sleep on the floor. There's plenty of room for two of us on the bed."

After she exchanged her slacks and blouse for one of Leland's shirts, she slid between the bed covers and wriggled close to the wall. When Leland took his place beside her familiar form, regret and yearning overwhelmed his spirit. In scripture, the Father affirmed that when a supplicant called upon Him in distress, He rescued him. It was the answer to Leland's plea regarding the as-yet-to-be-spoken exchange between husband and wife that kept him from falling back to sleep. He relished a distinct reply, one he couldn't misinterpret, and it would be right nice if it came in the form of a soft whisper. In that particular psalm, however, the Father had answered the petitioner in "the covering of thunder." How might Leland brace himself for that?

*

The distant whine of a siren carried through the open window and nudged Leland awake. He listened to the familiar sound of a city bus as its brakes squealed to a halt. The motor rumbled while passengers climbed aboard or disembarked, and a split second after the air brake hissed, the driver revved the engine and continued on his early morning route.

Leland started to roll from his side to his back, attempting to stretch his arms in the process, but he tensed in alarm while his brain cut through the fog and the headache. The lingering scent inside the room brought his senses to the present. Card game. Beer. Cigars. Gals. Lipstick. Muriel.

Leland froze, not wanting to disturb the soft breaths that grazed his neck or to interrupt the steady rise and fall of Muriel's chest against his back. A sense of gratification emerged when he considered that his wife had snuggled next to him, curving her body into his. That's what love does. Things were going to work out fine.

His nose sniffed out the faint aroma of baking bread, a fragrant morning amenity contributed by the bakery situated in a cubbyhole of a building on the next block. When his belly growled for grub, he snuck out of bed and went into the bathroom to shower.

Goosebumps crawled over his body, but when the pipes managed to send warm water his way, shampoo and soapsuds swirled around the drain while the heat fogged the mirror. He shivered while he brushed his teeth and shaved, and when he stepped into the living area wearing only a damp towel snugged around his waist, his lovely wife was not waiting for him between the sheets. Her curling up next to him might have had more to do with the air temperature than wanting to take her rightful place alongside her man.

The aroma of coffee, while a measurable disappointment considering where he'd placed his wishes, was a welcome greeting initiated by the raven-haired beauty standing in front of him. His bathrobe hung loosely on her svelte frame, and her hair needed a comb, but her pale gray eyes, the essence of pearls, stole his equilibrium. Her pupils expanded as she studied him, and while her stance didn't suggest she'd forgiven all his blunders, a hint of affection lifted the edges of her lips.

"Coffee's ready." Muriel extended a cup to Leland, but

withdrew her hand as he reached for it. She sniggered. "You might want to get dressed first."

Leland couldn't decide whether this was some kind of game, or maybe Muriel's unorthodox wooing, but her unrelenting stare while he lost his towel and donned his clothes brought a wave of heat to his person that surpassed a third-degree burn.

When an indecipherable expression accompanied Muriel's second offering of coffee, he pushed her perplexing theatrics aside, pressed his greedy lips against the mug, and savored the first drops of caffeine as they tumbled down his throat.

Her eyes never left his face, and although she acted as if she were ready to delve into a deep conversation, none materialized. Muriel's customary dialect was a pantomime Leland generally failed to understand, and over the course of twenty years, the silence and innuendos had taken a toll. Could he—could they—learn to speak the language of their hearts?

"I hope you don't make a habit of driving alone in the middle of the night."

"I hope you don't make a habit of entertaining people of dubious character," Muriel replied as she topped off Leland's coffee.

"Touché." He raised his cup. "Thanks. But seriously, why not wait until morning?"

"I didn't want to see another sunrise until I'd seen you."

Her reply was poetic, music to Leland's ears, assuming the catalyst was reconciliation and not reckoning.

"After all these weeks, why the hurry?"

Muriel turned aside, breaking eye contact. "When you told me you didn't want to be around me, I thought I'd oblige. Give you plenty of time away from me."

"About that."

"Let me finish. I went to the football game last night, and

during half time Fern and I wandered away from the stands so we could talk. She had what you'd call right smart opinions and suggestions, but those didn't compel me drive to Charleston in the wee hours of the morning."

"What, then?"

"The short end of the story is that after the game, we lost June."

Leland choked. "You lost her?"

"While everyone streamed out of the bleachers and into their cars, she let go of her brother's hand. The crowd swept her up and carried her out to the parking area. It's hard to guess how long that little girl wandered around the cars, dodging people going to and fro and vehicles pulling out of parking spaces, but she found Fern's car, hopped inside, and while she waited to be found, she fell asleep."

"She's all right?"

"Yes, but two hours passed before we found her."

Leland wiped his palms across his cheeks and rubbed his forehead with his fingertips. He stammered when he said, "I can't imagine."

"I ached and I feared for that child, but all the while we searched, an unrelenting grief befell me, its presence so heavy I thought I might suffocate. During every second that ticked by, and every moment Percy and Fern feared their child was lost to them, I envisioned you, alone in Charleston. Lost to me."

"Come here." Leland wrapped his arms around Muriel and pressed a kiss to her neck. "I'm a pig-headed fool and I'm sorry I pushed you away."

"I'm sorry you took offense at my thinking we'd be better off living in Charleston than in Elizabeth. I know you call that place home."

"Do you call it home?" Leland asked as he took a step

backwards.

Tears brimmed, but Muriel didn't make an effort to acknowledge them. "If you have to ask, I reckon Fern's half-time analysis was right. All along, I've considered myself transparent, and my intentions and my opinions obvious. To hear Fern talk, I've frustrated every last one of you because you can't decipher my moods, my motives, or my thoughts."

Leland couldn't have said it more plainly than Fern had. Muriel acted as if everyone was a mind reader. The fact that it pained her when she recognized the hurt she'd inflicted, ripped him to the core. It's not as if he were any better in this communication business. While she guarded her vulnerable spirit in the only way she knew how, he spilled his high horse, know-it-all attitude with aplomb. The coffee, now consumed, churned in his stomach as his self-described *stupid, stupid, stupid* reappeared.

"Listen for a second," Muriel said. "I admit I like Charleston. And why not? It's at the top of the heap in terms of prosperity, industry, transportation, community, recreation, and the arts, not to mention its fine shopping venues like the Diamond department store. But Elizabeth is my home, Leland. *Home.* I only suggested we move here because this is where the jobs are."

"Why not Parkersburg? It's a mite closer to Elizabeth than Charleston." A train's shrill whistle pierced the air, as if to punctuate Leland's remark. After all, it was Muriel who insisted Charleston was *the* place for him to work.

"Why not Parkersburg? Leland, your niece is here. She's young. She's homesick. Don't you think it's more fitting for her family to join her in this direction than to take off in the other?"

Understanding smacked Leland with the force of a freight train just before it derailed. First, the caboose, his lofty opinion that safeguarded the rest of the cars, teetered. Next, the Pullman, the place where he could ignore the outside world and imbibe his selfish desires, toppled. One egocentric car after another fell off the tracks until, finally, the engine, the leader and the crux of it all, plummeted into a bottomless gorge.

"That's why you picked Charleston? Why you offered to find a job and come here too?"

"If you have to work here, this is where I want to be. You big lug, it's not the city lights or the prospect of living in an apartment on a main thoroughfare that calls me here." She waved her hand around the cramped, smelly room. "I want to be with *you*."

The apologies, the sorrow, and the reconciliation came in the form of a welcome, soft whisper. What followed was more akin to thunder—the awe-inspiring kind.

Chapter 15

Leland parked the car at the curb, rounded the vehicle, and opened Muriel's door. She smoothed her skirt and ran her fingers along the edge of her collar.

"Do I look all right?"

"More'n right. You have a special glow about you this morning."

Muriel swatted Leland's arm, hefted her shoulders, and took on an air of determination. "Will you wait here for me?"

"You don't want me to come inside?"

"Well, I don't want anyone to think I need to bring my husband along."

"I'll stay out of the way and pretend I don't know you. Maybe I'll find the non-fiction section and do some Dewey Decimal reshuffling while you make your case."

"Don't you dare."

"Which? Come in with you or shuffle books?"

"Just mind yourself. Your reputation precedes you, Mr. Dugan."

Leland slapped his hand against his thigh, but he swallowed his guffaw when Muriel gave him her I-mean-it glare. The last time Muriel encountered Leland in a library setting, he had just decked Percy for trying to steal his girl. That was more than twenty years ago, but the memory was so vivid it could have been yesterday. Muriel's recollection of the incident hadn't faded either.

Leland walked ahead of Muriel, took the dozen or so steps toward the old stone building, and gawked at the ivy. The dark green creeper swamped the building with the same zeal as kudzu encapsulated unwary vegetation and devoured the South. Ivy clung to the eaves of the third floor, and as it trailed downward, it smothered the paired columns on either side of the entryway, continued down the façade, and finally tangled with the bushes edging the ground floor. Only the low metal dome that rose into the Charleston skyline was immune to the persistent vines.

As soon as Muriel joined him at the entrance, he opened the door, gave her a wink, and ushered her inside. She ignored him as she walked to the librarian's desk, which sat right inside the door. Leland took inventory of the lobby, deciding where he might linger while Muriel conducted her business.

Off to the side of the doorway were reading rooms. A plaque indicated the building was erected in 1902 as an annex to the former Capitol building. Former, as in the Capitol burned to the ground in 1921. The Charleston Library Committee turned the annex into a library in 1909, and the County Board of Education turned it into Kanawha County Public Library in 1933.

Apparently, the county didn't own enough books to fill the massive structure, because the building directory listed Morris Harvey College as occupant of the second and third floors, and the West Virginia Medical Library as the basement tenant.

Leland set his sights on an aisle of bookshelves. When he found the non-fiction section, he clasped his hands behind his back just in case Muriel peeked over her shoulder to see if he was behaving. Leland hadn't attended college like Muriel had, but he was right proud of the diploma he earned while he was in the Civilian Conservation Corps. That piece of paper seemed to have played a part in landing the quality control job at the Libbey plant instead of one requiring manual labor.

The library was a perfect fit for Muriel, what with her degree in Library Science. Leland moved beyond Muriel's eyesight, examined another rack of books, and deemed them shelved in the proper Dewey Decimal order. For a brief moment, he felt he was performing a quality control assignment for the county.

When he heard high heels clicking on the floor, Leland peered around a shelf, confirmed the clicker was his wife, and walked to the foyer. The tight-lipped librarian, whose haughty manner was more suitable for a throne than a desk, eyed him suspiciously as he headed toward the exit. She turned away when he dipped his head and offered a nonchalant, "How do?" If Muriel landed a job here, Leland would have to stay far away.

Muriel stood next to the car, her arms folded across her bosom and deep lines framing her downturned mouth. "They're not hiring."

"You knew that was likely."

"I was hoping."

"I reckon they don't have openings often. That snooty librarian's probably worked here since Dewey invented his decimals."

"Since 1876?"

"If you ask me, she's been practicing her scowl at least as long."

Muriel's shoulders slumped. "What did you do?"

"Me? Nothing. I behaved. Honest."

Muriel glanced down Lee Street. "I guess I'll try my second choice." When she started to step off the sidewalk, she turned around and asked, "You coming?"

"Yes'm." Leland wove his hand around Muriel's arm, but when they'd gone about half way across the street, she stopped.

"I didn't know that was there."

Leland tugged her along until they reached the opposite side of the street. "What?"

"The *Charleston Gazette*," she said as she pointed down Hale Street.

"I guess I never paid any mind to it either. You want to stop in and introduce yourself to Percy's newspaper boss?"

"No. It's just odd that after all this time we see where Percy sends his editorials. Can you imagine how different things would have turned out of he'd taken a full time job with them?"

"I reckon he might not have married my sister, and we wouldn't be having lunch today at Three Squares Diner because Ellie wouldn't have been born and wouldn't be there to take our order."

"Among other things. Choices have repercussions."

"Are you having second thoughts about finding work here?"

"No," Muriel replied as she walked toward Capitol Street.

Leland stretched his neck as they neared the corner occupied by Kanawha Valley Bank. The skyscraper, with its twenty stories soaring into the blue expanse, was Charleston's tallest building. More amazing was the bank's survival, as the institution moved into its new quarters just one month before the 1929 stock market crash.

Muriel's pace quickened as she passed the bank and the Diamond came into view. Narrow striped awnings extended over the windows, keeping the sun from glaring into the eyes of passersby who admired the merchandise on display. A handful of people loitered near the curb, waiting for the next city bus to come along, while pairs or trios of shoppers contemplated the tempting offerings behind the glass. If not for Muriel's hope for gainful employment herein, Leland would have swept her off her feet and hauled her back to the car. Everything about the Diamond made Leland's wallet feel lighter, and it was pert 'near empty already. As they entered the department store, he slid the button on his back pocket into the buttonhole, just in case the contents tried to float away like a helium balloon.

"How do I look?" Muriel asked again.

"Same as you did when you went to the library. Fine. Professional."

"I wish I had one of those outfits in the window. I'd feel more confident."

"Just show them what you know. Why, you could run this whole store."

"I don't know about that." It wasn't like Muriel to need reassurance. The woman was smart, decisive, and capable. The Diamond, though, intimidated her. Leland glanced at the clothing the clerks wore, and he examined the attire of the shoppers who sniffed perfume and tried on hats. The high-class retailers got it right when they claimed Charleston had become the place to shop, drawing fashionable, well-heeled folks from all around the region. But, clothes were just covering. Why would Muriel care?

"Just tell them you run the whole operation at Bigler's General Store."

"I don't know how long I'll be." She checked her watch. "Let's meet right here in, say, thirty minutes. If I'm not here, come back every fifteen minutes. That way, you can rummage through all the different merchandise and not be bored to death."

Leland was not what the women called a window shopper. Maybe he'd ride one of the elevators. That might be entertainment enough.

"Sounds like a right smart plan. You go on to their office and don't worry about me. After you impress them, I'd like to take my gal to lunch. You hungry yet?"

"Starved." Muriel gave Leland a peck on the cheek and disappeared down one of the aisles.

Leland took his maiden voyage in an elevator and his first ride on an escalator. One floor housed a studio for portraits or an artist's rendering of the subject, another announced the upcoming visit of a famous author who promised to sign copies of his latest book. Elsewhere, tucked into a corner behind the hair salon, where management had yet to discover how to mask the scent of ammonia, he saw a sign for customers who needed help buying the perfect wig.

During his floor-to-floor exploration, Leland preferred the three fast elevators to the escalators, mostly because he could chat with the operators while they hoisted shoppers to their destinations. When he finally remembered to check his watch, he took brisk strides until he found his frazzled wife waiting beside the front doors. Her expression suggested she was no longer starved, but famished. Unfortunately, she looked ready to take a bite out of him.

❧

A parade of cirrus clouds cavorted beneath the midday sun, their wisps pressing dainty shadows against the sidewalks and streets. Except for the swirls of wind that encircled the high-rise buildings, a gentle breeze accompanied pedestrians as they walked through the business district. The cool air, a precursor to autumn's chill, toyed with Muriel's hair and ruffled the edge of her skirt.

Muriel had walked out of the Diamond before Leland could ask about her interview. She led the way as they retraced their steps, crossed Lee Street, and continued toward Quarrier Street. Her indifferent expression was typical of the old Muriel, the woman who just hours earlier had promised to share her thoughts to avoid more misunderstandings.

"Well? How'd you do?"

"I start on Monday."

"Whoo-ee! I knew they'd want to hire you when they saw how smart you are."

"I didn't get a job in their offices."

"Did they make you a supervisor over of one of their departments? There's enough of them, for sure."

"The store managers like to encourage their employees to work their way up the ladder."

"Nothing wrong with that."

"Except I start on the very bottom, below the ladder's first rung. Literally. They offered me a clerk's position in the basement."

Leland squinted as he recalled the sights he encountered each time the elevator operator opened the doors to a different floor. If he got a peek at the basement level, nothing special came to mind.

"What's down there?"

"A little bit of everything. It's the budget store." Disappointment filled every tiny fold that stretched across Muriel's forehead. She expelled a puff of air when she said, "Probably where most of the locals shop."

"Nothing wrong with us locals."

"I know. You're right, and since the hoity-toity types who shop above ground won't need my help, I won't have to fancy up my wardrobe. Maybe, after the sun fades them and the managers consign them to the basement bargain bins, I can buy a few of the outfits they put on the mannequins."

Where her face was expressionless, Muriel managed to convey her displeasure by her tone, which was part resignation, part sarcasm, and part bitter.

"You don't have to take the job."

"If I want to live in Charleston with you, I have to work. You can't afford a bigger apartment on your salary, and it's too small for the two of us."

"True, but if you take the job at the Diamond, you can keep hunting for one more to your liking. Maybe the library will call you back."

"I doubt it. Mrs. Methuselah isn't about to retire anytime soon."

Leland and Muriel turned left onto Quarrier Street where they had to sidestep two crows squabbling over food scraps. After walking another block, Muriel paused in front of the ballet studio. "Whether I land a job at the library eventually or work my way to the top floor of the Diamond, at least we'll be near Ellie. Won't she be pleased?"

"Sure she will. I remember how hard it was to leave home, and I took comfort in sharing my CCC adventure with Percy. Ellie has nice roommates, but that's not the same as being around your own."

"You were a mite out of your realm in Nevada," Muriel said as a hint of levity erased a measure of her discouragement.

"Ain't that the truth?" Leland turned in the direction of Three Squares Diner, but before he stepped forward, he took in the sight of his wife. "Your smile still leaves me speechless, Mrs. Dugan. I don't think you know how beautiful you are, inside and out. Let's mosey on down the way and see if we can get Ellie to order a couple of burgers for us."

When they reached Dickinson Street, Leland escorted Muriel into the bustling restaurant. Ellie stood with her back to the door, her blond ponytail bobbing as she took her customers' orders. She spun around and handed her scribbled list to the short order cook, and when she caught sight of her kin, her face beamed. If not for being in her workplace, she might have hopped across the room and jumped into their arms.

"What are you two doing here?" Ellie asked as she led them to a booth, wiped down the empty table, and ran her cloth over the tops of the vinyl cushions. She gave them a hug as they took seats on opposite sides of the table.

The interior of the diner, with its black and white tiled floor, bright white walls, and gleaming chrome trim everywhere, was similar to Elizabeth's Theatre Restaurant. Instead of cherry red seats and tabletops, Three Squares' owners opted for royal blue. The place was humming with lunchtime customers, their conversations occasionally interrupted by the spit and sizzle of the grill. Hot grease infused the air with the pungent aroma of beef and onion and drew a noisy gurgle out of Leland's belly.

Ellie laughed. "You hungry, Uncle?" She didn't wait for a reply, but pulled a pencil from behind her ear and hovered her hand over her tablet. Instead of taking their order she asked, "Why didn't you tell me you were coming?"

"My plans were last minute," Muriel replied.

"Well, it's good to see you. I get off in half an hour, so can you take your time eating? I'll save three slices of carrot cake if you'll let me join you for dessert."

"Don't you have to work until the lunch crowd disappears?" Muriel asked.

"Trust me. After one o'clock, this place will empty out faster than church pews on a potluck dinner Sunday."

While Leland and Muriel dined, Ellie and the other waitresses managed to wend their way around customers and tables as they delivered food, collected empty plates, and refilled coffee cups.

Muriel dabbed her lips after she ate the last of her chicken salad sandwich. Her expression was a heap more content than when she'd left the department store, satiated. Filling hunger with the right kind of sustenance does that to a person. It appeared that she had taken time to count her blessings, every one of which trickled down to Leland. The soft whisper that drew them back together tugged at him, a testament to unmerited grace.

True to her promise, Ellie carried three servings of carrot cake to the table. After pouring two cups of coffee and a glass of water for herself, she untied her apron and slid into the space next to Muriel.

Ellie's powder blue uniform brought out the sapphire hue of her eyes, but the outfit's white collar drew the warmth out of her fair skin and stole the gloss from her silky hair.

"Are you feeling all right?" Leland asked.

"I'm tired. Why?"

"You're a mite pale."

"I'm fine. Except for my feet. They always hurt, but I can't complain. It's just part of dancing."

"Something's bothering you," Muriel said. "Would you rather tell your aunt and uncle all about it, or do you want me to sic your parents on you?"

"Oh, no. Anything but that."

While Ellie toyed with her cake, Leland let his cream cheese frosting tantalize his taste buds. He was paying heed to the conversation, for sure, but when Muriel gave him the eye, he lowered his fork to his plate.

"I'm trying to find another place to live," Ellie said.

"What did those girls do?" Leland asked. "Did they steal from you?"

Muriel turned sideways, and in a low voice she asked, "Do they entertain people of dubious character?" She stared at Leland while she asked the question, which was downright rude, but her arched eyebrows said she was poking fun.

"It doesn't have anything to do with Kay or Norma. It's the landlord. The lease they signed only allows two tenants. I need to find another place to live, but so far I haven't found anyone to share the rent."

"What about one of the other dancers?" Leland asked.

"The only one who needs a roommate is Jerry, but he doesn't fit my criteria."

"Jerry? You're taking ballet classes with men?" Leland asked.

"Why does that surprise you? Mr. Van Damme is a man."

"I know, but I never gave it much thought. What do you call a male ballerina anyway?"

"Just so you know," Ellie said, "the only one who earns the title of *ballerina* is the principal female dancer of a company. So, you'd best not call me a ballerina when you're among my dancing friends."

"What should we call you?" Muriel asked.

"I'm a *danseuse*. My male counterpart is a *danseur*. Given his artistry, technique, and talent, Mr. Van Damme is a *danseur noble*, but in Belgium he held the title of *danseur étoile*. I like *étoile* much better. It means *star*."

Before Ellie could introduce more of her French vocabulary, and since the mention of Jerry was irrelevant, Leland said, "Let's get back to the apartment dilemma. How much notice did the landlord give you?"

"I have to be out by the end of the month."

"This month?" Leland asked. What was today? The twenty-fourth. "He gave you less than a week?"

"No. I've known about it since the fifteenth, so technically he gave me two weeks' notice." Ellie scrunched her face, much as a toddler who had her eye on a plate of cookies. "Um, Uncle

Leland, if I can't find anything, can I stay with you for a while? I promise I'll find my own place soon."

Leland watched Muriel out of the corner of his eye and prayed she would not utter the simple answer to Ellie's complex question. It's not as if his apartment could accommodate three people. Once Ellie understood their predicament, she would understand, although understanding was hardly a fix.

Leland cleared his throat. "I don't know how—"

Muriel interrupted. "We'll make room."

"We?" Ellie asked.

"As of Monday, I'll be the newest sales clerk in the Diamond's bargain basement."

Puzzlement washed over Ellie as she studied Muriel's face and digested her comment, but the barefaced emotion it induced was potent enough to knock Leland out of his seat.

"You're coming to Charleston?"

"I am for now."

"For how long?"

"I guess we'll have to see." Muriel's iridescent gray eyes caught Leland's attention and set his heart aflutter, as if he were an adolescent schoolboy. She pointed across the table and bumped her arm into Ellie's shoulder. "I missed him, if you can imagine that."

"Oh, wow," Ellie said as her mouth fell open. "Maybe I have the perfect solution for all of us."

Chapter 16

The two-story brick house on Truslow Street was just a stone's throw from the center of the city. Some might call it a continuation. The residence sat on the side of the one-way street where folks could park their cars, and like the other homes lining the boulevard, it had a miniscule front yard barely wide enough to accommodate a well-trimmed bush and a few square feet of grass. Edging the lawn was an equally narrow sidewalk. Despite those tight boundaries, a short brick wall defined a covered porch that stretched across the front of the abode. It offered a pleasant respite at the end of the workday, or dance day, depending on who was doing the resting.

Leland propped his feet on the edge of the railing, stretched his arms, and clasped his hands behind his head. It was chilly, but after all the unpacking and organizing they'd done the night before, the moment invoked a sense of contentment.

Fern, the only other person to venture outdoors this morning, pulled on the neck of her sweater until it reached her chin. When a bus rattled past, she pressed her nose into the yarn and waited for the plumes of exhaust to dissipate. "This is a nice house, but I don't think I could get used to the noise. Does this town ever shut down?"

"Don't think so."

Just beyond the sleepy residential section, Truslow Street yawned into a commercial district that ended at the junction of Kanawha Boulevard. The city buses were plentiful and their routes accommodated Ellie and Muriel's inconsistent schedules pretty well. In the vicinity of the Diamond and the dance studio, the Elk River met the Kanawha River, and just beyond the opposite bank, the C&O Railway carried goods toward Huntington or Logan. Each morning, Leland drove to Kanawha Boulevard, crossed the Kanawha River at Dickinson, and then took MacCorkle Avenue to the glass plant.

"How are the Tigers doing?" Leland asked.

"Six wins. Except for the first game with Sistersville, their opponents haven't scored a point."

"No fooling?"

"They scored twenty-six against Spencer, twelve against Ripley, and last week they put thirty-nine on the scoreboard against Harrisville."

"Thirty-nine? Wish I'd seen that one. No wonder Roy and Wayne decided to stay home this weekend. Maybe next time they'll come visit with you."

"Maybe, but only if our next trip comes after football season ends."

Leland tipped his chin. "How do you like being in charge of the general store?"

"I just do the same as I always did. Becca is working most of Muriel's old hours, and Nettie comes into the store when one of us needs a break, but otherwise, things haven't changed. I appreciate that Muriel still handles the books."

"You don't need to worry about that part. Since she still owns the store, it's her responsibility."

"I know, but with Becca learning how to keep track of the ledgers, I hope Muriel doesn't feel as if we're trying to take her store away from her."

"She doesn't think any such thing. She's the one who offered to teach Becca, more'n likely because we don't know when, or if, we can move back home."

"That makes me so sad."

"Seeing how we're in this house, I can't complain about the way things worked out. Ellie was right, you know. Moving here was perfect, just like Muriel's timing. Ellie couldn't afford this place on her own, and Muriel and I wouldn't have known about it if we hadn't stopped at Three Squares Diner after Muriel accepted the job at the Diamond."

It was Norma, one of Ellie's roommates and a fellow dance student, who mentioned that the home her aunt had inherited might be an answer to Ellie's plight, but the logistics were insurmountable until Muriel and Leland became part of the equation. After the owner confirmed the source of the rent payment, everything fell into place. The owner's offer to leave the furnishings eliminated her need to dispose of the goods, and gave Leland and Muriel the option to leave their belongings in Elizabeth for the duration. Ellie described the transition as finely tuned choreography.

"Ain't it funny how life works out?" Leland asked.

"What do you mean?"

"Well, I don't think any of this move was coincidental. No, ma'am."

"Ma'am? You're the old one here."

"I'm just being respectful. Once a person reaches forty, I think they've earned the right to be called *sir* or *ma'am*."

"I'm only thirty-eight."

Leland hesitated too long before he replied, "I'm just joking.

I knew that."

"No, you didn't. Now, you're just fudging your backpedal." Fern was a pretty sharp gal, but rather than admit her statement held more truth than his did, Leland elected to finish sharing his opinion.

"Where was I? Oh, talking about coincidences. Some might slough off the timing of events, but wise folks who admit they lack control in most things know they ought to thank the Orchestrator of every good thing for His loving kindness."

"I think Percy and I are as grateful as you and Muriel are. We're relieved Ellie's living with you."

"We're happy to oblige, and we're proud of her, the way she's working hard and turning herself into a mighty fine dancer."

Ellie poked her head out of the front door. "Pancakes are done."

"You don't have to tell me twice," Leland said as he helped Fern to her feet.

After breakfast, June stood on a chair while she took soapy plates from Fern and held them under the running water. Muriel was quick enough with her drying chore to place her hand under June's slippery fingers while the child "helped" the grown-ups.

Ellie sat at the table with Leland and her father, chatting nonstop about her ballet lessons.

"I am so excited to be on my toes, although my feet and every muscle in my body ache from sunrise to sunset. Those *pointe* shoes are murderous."

"Why doesn't he go easier on you?" Percy asked. "Let you get used to them."

Ellie's hand flew to her mouth, as if Percy's question was the joke of the century. "Go easy on us? Never. Mr. Van Damme is like a racehorse that isn't happy unless he's galloping at full speed. If he's not teaching, he's dancing. He expects every one of his students to be on their toes—literally—from the moment they enter the studio until he's convinced that his lessons have heightened his students' passion for the art."

"I reckon you were zealous about dancing before you enrolled," Percy said. "Are you passionate now?"

"You bet I am. Mr. Van Damme doesn't just teach, you know. He performs with the pianists who share the studio space with him. The Hiersouxs, who came from Belgium like the Van Dammes, are famous in their own right. Mr. Hiersoux came to Charleston as a glassblower. You do know Charleston has a pretty impressive glassblowing community, don't you?"

"Can't say as I do," Percy replied.

Muriel craned her neck and spoke over her shoulder. "I knew about it."

Leland shared a knowing glance with Percy while Ellie was quick to continue her discourse.

"Besides glass work, Mr. Hiersoux is an accomplished pianist and conductor. In fact, he founded the Charleston Chamber Music Society. If Mr. Van Damme hadn't met the Hiersouxs, he wouldn't have moved to Charleston. He came at their invitation, and when they offered to play piano for his dance school, and share their studio to boot, everything fell into place."

"How does Mr. Hiersoux fit into the story of your sore feet?" Leland asked.

"You wanted to know why Mr. Van Damme was so demanding, so I thought I'd tell you what things are important to him. In order to make people more aware of ballet, he tours college campuses with his accomplished students. Once in a while, he returns to Europe and dances there."

"Do you think he'll take you on tour?" Percy asked.

Ellie's face flamed scarlet. "Not anytime soon, if ever. If he needs a dance partner, he takes Julianne Kemp with him."

"I've heard her name," Muriel said. "She's probably his best known student."

"That's true," Ellie said, "and she's a sight to behold. Well, they both are. The gist of all this is, if *I* want to be good—and you know I do—I have to give it my all, sore feet notwithstanding."

"Is that the door?" Fern asked as she pulled the drain plug and let the water gurgle down the pipes. She untied June's apron and helped her down from the chair.

"I'll get it." Percy started toward the front door, June fast on his heels.

June's squeal echoed down the hallway, and a round of near-hysterical giggles followed.

Percy hollered, "Can one of you bring out June's sweater?" He didn't wait for a response, but when the front door latched shut, it muffled the sound of June's unbridled laughter.

No one bothered to grab a jacket or sweater, but dashed outside instead. Leland recognized Danny, the little boy who lived nearby, but the puppy nipping June's fingers and licking her face was an unfamiliar companion.

The wriggly canine, which bore a strong resemblance to the Boston terrier owned by the people who lived behind them, also carried an uncanny likeness of the longhaired dachshund owned by the neighbor two houses down the street. It was hard telling how the mixed features might turn out as the pooch grew into an adult, but her current appearance brought about the same delight as any full-blooded, well-bred champion. June was beside herself with glee.

After Princess made everyone's acquaintance, Fern slipped into the house and came back with June's sweater.

"Don't you have a collar and leash for her?" Muriel asked Danny.

"No, ma'am. Not yet. We just brought her home."

"I think it might be a good idea for you to go out back and play with the puppy there," Fern said.

When the adults returned to the house, Percy and Leland went upstairs where the women had entrusted them to unpack boxes of towels and linens. Their assignment also included hanging curtain rods and patching gaps along the windowsills.

Fern called after them. "We'll be in the kitchen where we can keep an eye on the children."

Stuffing the linen closet took all of ten minutes, but the first window Leland and Percy attempted to repair was stuck fast to the frame, as were the next six.

Once they pried the first frame loose, Percy wrestled to hold the window open. Sure enough, the sash was shot.

"You might as well ease that back down," Leland said.

"Didn't the previous owner ever need fresh air?" Percy asked. "These windows are jammed so tight, it's as if someone glued them shut."

"Ain't that the truth? We'll worry about keeping them open come springtime."

Leland flinched when a spine-chilling *pop, pop, pop* interrupted the sound of children playing. The clatter ricocheted throughout the neighborhood, concealing its source, but the origin of a child shrieking at the top of her lungs was unmistakable.

June screeched while Danny screamed, "Princess!"

Fern flew through the front door while Percy and Leland raced down the stairs. Hot pain seared Leland's chest when he heard June wail, "S-s-she shot the puppy!"

Chapter 17

Leland cleared the threshold at the same time Fern sprinted to the sidewalk where June stood, shaking and bawling. Fern dropped to her knees and wrapped her daughter in her arms, soothing her child at the same time she ran her hands over her body, no doubt searching for wounds. Percy lassoed a kicking and screaming Danny, whose puppy had darted into the street.

Princess managed to run all the way across the roadway and climb the curb, but the thick hedge she encountered prevented her from disappearing into the yard. The confused animal tried to burrow under the shrubbery, but the tangle of roots didn't offer sanctuary. Danny kept calling for the dog, and when he captured her attention, she inched toward the pavement.

Leland dashed in front of an oncoming car, whose blaring horn stalled his heart almost as surely as an impact might have done. Having escaped the first of two imminent threats, he waved at the approaching bus. The driver hit the brakes before the front bumper sent Leland sprawling.

While the bus ambled on down the road, Princess eyed Leland with suspicion, and instead of seeking the safety of his outstretched hands, the panicked dog outmaneuvered her rescuer. The next driver to encounter the chaos braked so hard that his truck fishtailed.

Princess surrendered when she reached the middle of the street. She dropped to the pavement and rolled, belly up, her chest heaving as fast and furious as the coupling rods that turned a locomotive's wheels. Leland retrieved the terrorized pup and waved a thank you to the driver. The man glared at Leland, his curses joining the growl of his truck's engine as he sped down the street.

It didn't come as a surprise to see a handful of spectators gathered on the sidewalk, but the sight of his prim and proper wife taking on the role of a she-bear caught Leland off guard. Muriel wagged her finger in the face of their next-door neighbor, a pinch-faced, middle-aged woman named Betty Hastings, who stood with her feet apart, her hands planted on her hips, and her mouth flapping. Given Muriel's aggressive posture, Leland's anxiety lessened when the only weapon Betty brandished was her mouth.

"I told them to hush up. I warned them. That dog yipping and those wild things carrying on? They're breaking the law. Disturbing the peace."

Leland glanced at Betty's house, where the windows were closed against the chilly weather. She might have witnessed the children's playful antics from behind the glass, but her accusations didn't hold an ounce of truth.

"I know Danny. His folks let him run around the neighborhood like an animal." Strands of variegated black and gray hair hung limply from her crown to her shoulders, framing her fleshy jowls and accentuating her dark, beady eyes. Considering her physical attributes and her charming personality, she could audition for a Disney movie that needed to cast a wicked stepmother.

Danny clenched his hands, bared his teeth, and tried to squirm out of Percy's arms. When Percy held tight and whispered into the boy's ear, Danny quit wiggling, but his anger smoldered.

"Whoever this child belongs to," Betty said as she stared down her nose at June, "ought to teach her to mind her manners."

Muriel, who was already close enough to strangle the maniac, took a step forward. Betty, in turn, reached into her apron pocket and withdrew a long-barreled six-shooter, a veritable beast of a weapon. Before anyone could move, Betty pointed her gun into the air and pulled the trigger. *Pop. Pop. Pop.*

Princess wriggled and tried to leap out of Leland's grasp. Danny broke loose from a startled Percy, and June wailed.

"Y'all get in the house," Leland said as he shoved Princess into Percy's arms and bolted toward Betty. He pushed Muriel aside, grabbed the gun out of Betty's hand, and flung an arm around Danny, who was trying to kick Betty's shins.

"How dare you," Betty hollered. She scanned the faces of her neighbors and yelled, "Somebody call the police."

"They're already on the way, you old bat," a young man replied.

The police pulled in front of the house while Leland held the gun. He lifted his hands high while two officers approached him, weapons drawn.

"Nice and slow. Put it on the ground."

"Yes, sir." Leland said. He kept his eyes glued to the blond, who appeared to be the older of the two, although neither of them was old enough to have much experience upholding the law. "It's a cap gun."

"He's right," the redhead said as he retrieved Betty's firearm. "This belong to you?" he asked Leland.

"No, sir. I just relieved Mrs. Hastings of her lethal-looking peashooter. She's done a great job of terrorizing two children and a puppy, not to mention scaring the daylights out of the rest of us."

The blond took the gun from his partner and turned it over. "Nice piece, Betty."

Leland and Muriel traded glances. The cop knew the neighbor on a first-name basis.

"A Roy Rogers edition," the blond added. "Probably be worth big bucks if you hold onto it long enough. Be a shame to have to take it from you."

Leland peered at the cap gun. It *was* a handsome toy, with the cowboy's name imprinted on the metal and detailed etchings of flowers and vines on the grip.

"Ain't no law against shooting a cap gun," Betty said.

"Maybe not, but it's obvious you're creating an uproar. What's worse, you know this toy is the spitting image of a real-deal six-shooter. What if one of these folks thought you were about to shoot one of these children and they decided to come to their defense? You'd likely end up dead."

Betty wrinkled her nose while she worked her jaw back and forth. As far as Leland could make out, Mrs. Hastings lived alone in the house next door. She'd acknowledged her new neighbors with cold stares, but until now, had kept to herself. More'n likely she held a job, because she got on the bus each morning about the same time Leland drove to the Libbey plant.

The woman didn't seem to care about her tired wardrobe or unkempt hair, and more than once Leland had spied her sitting on her porch in the evening, wearing a faded robe, hefting a glass filled with amber-colored liquid, and staring into nowhere while traffic passed. She took the same care of her house and shrubs as she did her person.

The blond handed the gun to his partner, who returned it to

Betty. "Why don't you go on home and put that thing away? Set it on a high shelf where you won't think about it. You hear?"

"I hear you, Martin. But afore you go, you tell these people to mind the noise. I won't stand for it."

Martin dipped his chin and tapped the brim of his hat. "Never mind the neighbors. You just worry about yourself. Go on now."

As the hateful sharpshooter climbed the steps to her porch, Martin took note of Leland. "Y'all live here?" he asked as he gestured to the house.

"My wife and I just rented the place. And our niece."

Martin's eyes widened when they landed on Ellie. "Best I can do is advise you to steer clear of Mrs. Hastings. She invents excuses to rile up the neighborhood." Martin eyed Danny, who held Princess against his chest while he stroked the space between her ears. "If I was you, I'd keep the pup in my own yard. Be careful she doesn't get loose. Understand?"

"Yes, sir."

Ellie walked forward and put her hand on Danny's shoulder. "Why don't I walk you home? Maybe talk to your mom so she knows what happened. Okay?"

As Danny and Ellie started down the sidewalk, Martin called after his partner, "I need you to take down names and such, while I help explain this incident to the boy's mother."

The redhead looked ready to protest until Martin flashed a grin and waggled his eyebrows in Ellie's direction.

Leland gawped while he watched the lawman and the *danseuse* escort the traumatized victim to the safety of his home. If he wasn't mistaken, a lilt of laughter accompanied them.

Later, after Ellie deflected every question or comment regarding Danny's police escort and June's frayed nerves subsided, Fern and Percy packed their overnight bags. The whole clan gathered on the porch to say their farewells, taking care to keep their laughter and their voices low. Leland watched as the truck disappeared down Truslow Street, troubled that his sister left a day earlier than she'd planned, but understanding. June needed to sleep in her own bed tonight.

As Leland, Muriel, and Ellie ascended the steps, the young man who had called Betty an old bat walked toward the Dugan's house. Beside him was a woman who carried a plate of frosted brownies.

"Evening, neighbor," the man said. "I'm Cliff and this is my wife Naomi. We live three doors down, and we've been meaning to introduce ourselves."

Muriel accepted the plate from Naomi while Cliff turned toward Leland and said, "After the incident with Betty, well, if I were a drinking man, I would have brought you a bottle of booze."

"Cliff told me what happened," Naomi said in a hushed voice. "I'm not one to gossip, but Betty wasn't particularly friendly before her husband left her. Now? Well, you can see she's a pretty miserable person. As for the rest of us? We're just like Ivory Soap."

Leland drew his brows together. "Soap?"

"Haven't you heard Ivory's old slogan, the one that says their soap is ninety-nine and forty-four one-hundredths percent pure?"

"Why, sure we have, but I don't understand."

Naomi giggled. "This neighborhood is the same percentage friendly. We'll try our best to snuff out the antics of the exception."

Cliff winked at Muriel. "Welcome to Truslow Street."

Chapter 18

"Hurry up," Wayne said as he focused on the wall clock, its minute hand nearing the hour. "Once you open the door, they'll be gone." The boy was right. At least a dozen customers stood in a line in front of the general store.

Fern wrestled with the bundle, which was considerably larger than usual. Without consulting the storeowner, she'd taken the initiative to purchase fifty extra copies of *The Parkersburg News*, but judging from the fans waiting to purchase a souvenir, perhaps she ought to have ordered more. Would Muriel praise her for her foresight or reprimand her for being too conservative? "Will you give me just a minute?"

"What about me? I want one too." Roy hovered over the stack, his fidgety fingers preparing to snatch what was sure to become a piece of Elizabeth's finest memorabilia.

Fern eyed the growing queue. She should have ordered more. If every customer had children waiting at home, each with the same expectations as her boys, the newspapers would sell out in five minutes. It wouldn't do to rile the folks who lagged at the end of the line. Better to annoy a few than incense the rest.

"Grab a piece of paper and a marking pen," Fern said to

Wayne. "I need you to make a sign that says Limit Three to a Customer."

"That'll make 'em mad," Roy said as he lifted four copies off the stack.

"What do you think you're doing, mister?"

"What? One for me. One for Wayne. One for Uncle Leland, and one for you and Dad."

"Rules apply to us too. Put one back."

"Who's not gonna get one?"

"We'll worry about it later."

"But—"

"If we have any left after two o'clock, you can buy another one then. You'll have to wait and see, just like everyone else. Now, go on and get your copies out of here so they don't end up in the For Sale pile."

Roy acted as if his pants had caught fire when he clutched his booty and sped out the back door.

The folks in Wirt County earned bragging rights after the last of the high school's regular season games. Fern snuck a peek at the sports page where the headline read, *Wirt Tigers Capture Playoff Berth*. The subheading called St. Marys the *Final Victim*. As she skimmed the article, Fern beamed at the writer's choice of words: *Tiger lair, vengeance, aroma of the Class B championship floating on the air*. If Percy had decided to work for the *Charleston Gazette* fulltime, he would have penned something similar. Newspaper career aside, the entire Bigler clan, Ellie excepted, enjoyed the raucous event when it played out the previous day.

Before walking to the door and turning the lock, Fern glanced at the cover photo, in which four jubilant football players carried Coach Ray Walton across the field. At the click of the latch, Wayne's eyes grew to the size of a wide receiver's open arms. When the stampede bustled into Bigler's General Store, the only thing lacking was the sound of the high school marching band performing their victory march.

"Just three?" Andy Holly opened his wallet and picked out a twenty. "I'll give you this for five more copies."

"I can't do that," Fern said. "Come back after two o'clock. If we have any left, we'll sell them on a first-come, first-served basis. No limits."

"Well, I guess these will have to do," Andy said as he collected his allotted trio and plunked down his coins.

Fern counted out his change and said, "That was quite a game, wasn't it? Thirty-six points to the Blue Devils' six. Nice way to end a perfect season."

It *was* quite a game. She'd gaped at the crowd of two thousand, maybe more. It's not as if every business had the luxury to close on Veterans' Day, but given the mid-afternoon kick-off time, one would think that every soul in Wirt County had taken the day off work.

The Tigers and the Blue Devils faced off on a spectacular, autumn day. The afternoon temperature hovered around sixty degrees, and the only people who may have minded the breeze that skimmed across the grounds were the teams' kickers.

Stanley Palmer took two copies of the paper and while he paid, his son turned toward the customers waiting to purchase their own copies and tapped on the counter to get everyone's attention.

"Hey, y'all. I went home last night and tallied the scores. During Wirt's undefeated, ten-game season, they racked up a total of three hundred thirty-two points. Their opponents' combined scores totaled forty-one. Ain't that a hoot?"

The proclamation set off a round of foot stomping and Tiger cheers. Fern applauded with the rest, but when poor Mable Shoemaker from down the road poked her head into the store and yanked the door shut without stepping inside, Fern had to wonder at her decision to supply the town with newspapers at a few pennies a copy when she had customers too intimidated to come in to do real shopping. Regardless, this *Parkersburg News* edition had almost sold out, and the store hadn't been open half an hour yet.

When Roy climbed atop the counter and started yowling and flicking his bent hands as if he were a clawed animal swiping his opponents, he displayed a decent rendition of a valiant Wirt Tiger coming out of his lair. His antics earned whoops and another round of *Tigers, Tigers, Tigers.*

Fern scrambled on top of the counter and joined her son in a caterwaul duet, but when the front door popped open and everyone in the store grew silent, she and Roy stopped their mischief mid step. She relaxed after the sheriff came in, digested the scene, and dipped the brim of his hat.

"Morning, Mrs. Bigler. Save me a paper?"

The question set the customers a-laughin' and a-hootin' all over again.

Before Fern could tell the lawman to get in line behind the others, the next person to stride into the store earned a similar, panicky reaction. The visitor's taunting sneer resembled that of the Wirt High School mascot. Unfortunately, it appeared she'd left her avid fan persona in Charleston.

Muriel took in the scene, her features none too pleased, but when someone thumped on the door, she reached behind her and pulled it open. On the other side of the threshold was Leland, and in his arms was a sky-high bundle of newspapers.

"Hey, Fern, can you come down from there long enough to make space for these things?" He made it sound as if her standing on the counter was the most normal thing in the world.

She slid back to the floor and made room for another

shipment of *The Parkersburg News*.

"We thought y'all might need a pile of boasting copies, so we bought these from the distributor in Charleston." Leland cut the twine with his pocketknife, lifted the top copy, and asked, "Have we got any braggarts in this crowd?"

"Sure enough," Roy hollered. "Get on up here."

Roy started his King of the Cats strut again while Leland considered the invitation. The crowd thought they'd help the boy, chanting, "Leland, Leland, Leland."

Muriel covered her face with both hands when Leland leapt onto the counter. "I can't watch," she said when Fern stood beside her. "His foot isn't ready for this sort of lunacy."

Fern gave Muriel's shoulder a squeeze and said, "I need you to man the cash register until folks settle down."

"Why?"

"So I can protect your high-stepping dance partner."

Fern scrambled atop the counter, putting Leland between her and Roy. "Hang on to your uncle's arm," she hollered.

Muriel handed five copies of the newspaper to the sheriff—who'd assumed the front of the line was where he belonged—and counted out his change. He caught Fern's eye and gave her a wink. "Dang, this was fun."

"So you're not serving us a citation for disturbing the peace?" Muriel's face warmed at her obvious merriment.

The sheriff tipped his hat. "No, ma'am."

Fern regarded her sister-in-law, who'd cared enough for the folks in Elizabeth to get out of bed before sunrise to buy and deliver newspapers to them. Just as touching was watching her join the fun. She'd chiseled off a chunk of her mask. No, she wasn't dancing on the counter, but for Muriel, it was pretty much the same thing.

Leland squeezed the handles on the hedge trimmer, lopping straggly runners and squaring off the sides of the bushes. Movement caught his eye, leading him to take a gander at Betty Hasting's house, where a curtain rustled and a shadow fell across the window. She was doing it again. Spying. It was as if she had a sixth sense that drew her to the window or the front porch every time he, Muriel, or Ellie stepped out of the house. Betty's unremitting materialization was enough to give anyone the heebie-jeebies.

It amazed him that a mere fifty-six one-hundredths percent of the neighborhood could spoil the pure and pleasant hospitality of the remainder. The toy gun menace had kept to herself since she'd played the part of a peeved cowpoke who'd grown tired of life on the trail and weary of her fellow herdsmen. Leland oft envisioned her seated at her kitchen table, spooning cold baked beans out of a can and regretting the incidents that led her to hang up her spurs and live in solitude.

It's not as if he hadn't tussled with ugly realities now and again. Enrolling in the CCC wasn't on his list of wishes, nor was a stint in World War II. Both incidents were costly, but both taught mighty lessons that made him a better person, more grateful, more caring, more empathetic.

Most likely, the difference between his response to his circumstances and the way Betty let hers steal her present and jeopardize her tomorrows came down to faith. When Leland fell to the bottom of the heap, when his soul was parched, he heeded the psalmist who described his plight using words that revived Leland's downtrodden condition. It is He "who covers the heavens with clouds, who prepares rain for the earth." On more than one occasion, Leland had needed a good drenching. Betty might need something akin to a baptism of the spiritual kind, but that wasn't his assignment.

He stood back, inspected his work, and deemed the yard prepped for winter. He'd borrowed an extension ladder, pulled a mess of slimy leaves out of the gutters, drained the water hoses, and pulled the dead annuals out of the flowerpots Muriel kept on the back stoop.

As he took his bush-trimming clippings to the back of the house, his shoulders drooped at the sight that was Betty Hasting's yard. She'd used a dull-edged push mower on the grass a few times, but since the yard was mostly dirt, her efforts went unnoticed. Before he pulled off his work gloves, Leland walked next door and started lopping overgrown bushes. After he heaped piles of weeds next to the hedge clippings, he raked the mess and stuffed it into their spare garbage can.

"What do you think you're doing?"

Leland flinched at Betty's appearance, but more so at her nasty tone.

"Just straightening up."

"Who said you could come over to my property and take your bloody hatchet to whatever you please?"

"I took care not to trim anything but the bushes, and I pulled a few weeds while I was at it." An understatement, if ever there was one. "Would you like me to empty out your gutters?"

"How dare you? I told you before. I know my rights, and *your* rights don't include trespassing. How you'll explain yourself to the police is your problem. I'm going to call them now."

"Mrs. Hastings," Leland said as he splayed his hands, "I don't mean to be a thorn in your side, nor do I mean to be a poor neighbor. Honestly, I thought you might want me to give you a hand, but I apologize for offending you. It won't happen again."

"It better not." She curled her nose, as if all the work Leland had done was distasteful. He knew better. She waited until he finished before interrupting him. She just didn't know how to say thank you. Well, that wasn't the case. Betty Hastings didn't *want* to say thank you.

"I'd like to call a truce, ma'am." Leland used his best, soft-spoken country boy voice. She met it with another snarl.

"I don't think so. You stay on your property. I'll stay on mine."

"Yes, ma'am." Leland watched her stomp up her back steps. He winced as she slammed the back door hard enough to make the glass rattle, and tried to hide his satisfaction as he admired the transformation of his not-too-neighborly neighbor's yard.

Muriel was halfway to the house when Leland rounded the corner, tugging off his gloves. Where had the time gone?

"Are you early?" He gave her a quick peck on the cheek, careful not to touch his grimy clothes against her work outfit.

"No." She examined the yard. "You've been busy."

"I have." Leland bunched his gloves and lowered his eyes. He should have watched the clock. "Um, I reckon it's a tad late to put the pot roast in the oven."

"I get off work at three tomorrow. I'll fix it then. We can have grilled cheese tonight."

"I'll help."

Muriel plucked a sprig of greenery out of Leland's hair. "No need. Besides," she added as she sniffed, "I think you could use a shower." She surveyed Betty's house. "Did she ask you to work in her yard?"

"Um."

Muriel's eyes narrowed. "Did she pay you to do all of that?"

"Why don't we go in the house?" Leland pressed his hand to Muriel's back and steered her toward the front door. Once inside, he said, "It's not about money. I'm heaping kindness."

"What? Did you offer to do all of that work for nothing?"

"No, not exactly. I finished with our yard and thought I'd just meander over and keep working. Instead of letting antagonism simmer—I'm weary of it—I'm heaping kindness on her."

"I'd rather you returned fire with fire."

"Same thing."

"How so?"

"Scripture says when you give your enemy what he lacks, it's like heaping coals of fire on his head, overcoming evil with good."

"I don't think I'd have bothered." Muriel studied Betty's property. "Has she seen your kind work?"

"She sure has."

"And did your good overcome her evil?"

"It didn't quite work out that way."

"Did she at least thank you?"

"She dropped her threat to call the police on me for trespassing and destruction of property."

"She what!"

"That's right, darlin'. She returned my generosity by heaping scalding venom and warning me off her property with promises of retribution, the likes of which I'd never imagined."

Muriel's response was a deep growl.

"I reckon I'll have to dispense more hospitality. In the meantime, I'm so wounded by her reprimand that I need you to extend genuine, unconditional, compassion my way." Leland waggled his eyebrows.

"Tell me again after you've had a shower."

Chapter 19

"I feel like a princess in a fairy tale," Fern said as the bus pulled to the curb in front of the Diamond.

"According to Dad, you've always been one," Becca said as she gripped her pocketbook and stood.

Fern sidled next to Becca, but left enough room in the aisle for Ellie to merge into the throng of passengers waiting to disembark. Judging by the surge of pedestrian traffic, the Diamond was everyone's destination, and if one were to judge by the window displays and the festooned streetlights, the end of the line marked the entrance to an enchanted kingdom.

Fern's mind wandered while she fumbled to catch her glove and shove it into her coat pocket. "I've always been one what?"

"Dad's fairy tale princess," Becca said as she stepped onto the pavement, Ellie right behind her.

"He told you that?" Fern's cheeks warmed, not at the memory, but at Percy having shared their personal affairs with the children. Then again, what better way to teach them about a man treating a woman with respect and tenderness? His willingness to expose that part of himself to the girls drew a lump to her throat. "I'm not so sure it fits anymore."

"Why wouldn't it?" Ellie asked. "I think it's sweet."

"And romantic," Becca said.

"While we're wrapped in our imaginations," Fern said, "why don't we enter the grand castle, better known as the Diamond, and see if we can find buried treasure?"

Becca chuckled as she said, "I think you're confusing princesses with pirates."

Ellie swooped in front of both of them and donned a Cheshire cat grin. "I don't know about either of you, but I'm ready for a treasure hunt." She rubbed her hands together and eyed Fern's pocketbook. "You brought Dad's wallet, didn't you?"

It had been too long since Fern had an afternoon to spend with her grown-up girls. The city's downtown district wouldn't have been her first choice, but when Muriel said the Diamond made as much of a fuss over the holidays as New York City's Macy's department store, Fern couldn't escape Ellie and Becca's excitement. Muriel, who had started her workday earlier, promised the excursion would be a blast.

Aside from visits to Ellie's apartment and to Truslow Street, Fern's travels to Charleston had been few. *Dirt poor* was a kind term for her growing up years, and a visit to the city for the whim of it was unthinkable. She wasn't a stranger to the amenities that beckoned people to part with their money, but seeing them in person presented an awareness that left her both awed and apprehensive.

Becca, whose excursions to Charleston were equally infrequent, didn't act concerned about the frenetic pulse that radiated from the city's core. Instead, she looked as eager as she had on her first day of school, ready to unwrap and sample each course of the banquet spread before her. If the day ended without the treasure hunt giving Fern a case of indigestion or emptying her billfold, she would deem it a success.

Becca and Ellie stood side by side, gazing at the scene depicted in one of the windows. It took after a theater setting, a room bedecked not just for a get together, but for an opulent evening. Floor length gowns of silk, satin, and chiffon graced the doe-eyed mannequins, every piece and accessory befitting the fashion and styles favored by Hollywood's stars. Equally fine was the attire for the male partygoer, from dapper silk suits and ties to sophisticated wing-tip shoes.

When a shoulder jostled Fern, she turned to the stranger and offered an automatic, "Excuse me." Instead of accepting that she was the offender, the fur-draped matron used her elbow to sidestep Fern, stealing the view.

In the distance, a freight train chuffed, a reminder that for every shopper who exchanged money for goods, someone had to earn it first. It called to mind the coal miner, the engineer, and the pharmacist who dispensed healing balms, the sales clerk and the waitress, the construction worker who welded steel to erect a new skyscraper, and the laborers who manufactured glassware or pottery.

Fern didn't have a quarrel with the well-to-do families who had generous supplies of money to exchange for merchandise, but the better part of the people who lived in the region worked hard to make ends meet. The Great Depression ended two decades earlier, but the lessons learned while it dominated and crippled the country were hard to put aside. She was Percy's princess, all right, albeit a practical one.

The three women followed Leland's advice to make a quick survey of each floor instead of losing time in one department. They trooped through the offerings on the street level, and when they passed the lingerie department, Ellie stopped in front of a Burlington Hosiery display. "Well, I didn't expect to see this. I think Americans are finally becoming aware of the ballet. Should

I buy a pair?" She held a package that had a simple sketch of a ballerina next to the label, Ballet Brand S-t-r-e-t-c-h.

"Do you need a pair of stockings?" Fern asked.

"No. I'm just excited to belong to the generation that's introducing the country to a treasured art form." Her face was pure mischief when she performed a pirouette in the narrow aisle.

Becca blushed when a young man stopped to watch Ellie's impromptu demonstration. She tugged Ellie by the elbow. "You're drawing too much attention. Can we please go now?"

Up the escalator they went, inspecting an entire floor filled with clothing and another floor overflowing with everything one might need to furnish a house. If June hadn't stayed home with Percy, they would have spent the rest of their outing on the floor offering children's wear, for beyond the clothing racks was the toy department. Bedlam reigned as children ran from aisle to aisle, yanking on their parent's sleeve or calling for them to "Come see!" When the upward-bound escalator delivered the threesome to the level displaying housewares, a welcome calm accompanied them.

Fern stood in front of an array of Sunbeam appliances and gadgets, trying to grasp the inventors' cleverness. "What would we do without electricity? Who, do you suppose, decided we needed electric everything?" She waved her hand in front of the wares. "Electric fry pans, blankets, shavers for men, shavers for women, drills, saws, and sanders. What's next? Electric toothbrushes?"

They plodded onward, gawking at all the things meant to simplify life.

"Do you need any of these?" Becca asked as they walked past vacuums, silver, and china.

"No, but . . ." Fern veered toward the bookshop.

"I'll bet we could find something for Dad in here," Ellie said.

"Can we see what they've got?"

Reading titles and thumbing through pages were free. "Sure," Fern replied. "Why not?"

Why not? Because she had a weakness for books, not because she was an avid reader, although she did like to read, but because it would be easy to buy enough volumes for Percy to amass a library. Fern dropped her change into her pocketbook, accepted the striped Diamond bag from the clerk, and tucked her single book purchase into the crook of her arm.

They rode the elevator to the lower level, timing their arrival to coincide with the end of Muriel's work schedule. The clamor in the bargain basement was as intimidating as the ruckus in the toy department, except here, children weren't vying for their parents' attention. Shoppers parried for the one-of-a-kind, last-of-a-kind deals before they disappeared into another customer's bag.

The expression on Muriel's face suggested she'd engaged in hand-to-hand combat. Fern picked an orphaned strand of aqua thread off her sister-in-law's sleeve. "You look as worn out as the knees on Roy's dungarees."

"No doubt. I'm a tar'd sales clerk with frayed nerves and threadbare momentum. Y'all might need to carry me upstairs."

Muriel didn't often fill her conversation with West Virginia speak, a testament to her fatigue. Sure, she'd throw in an *I reckon* and a *y'all* now and again. But *tar'd* instead of tired?

"I thought this day wouldn't end," Muriel said. "It's going to get much worse as Christmas nears."

Ellie and Becca jabbered incessantly while they waited at the curb for a bus to take them to Truslow Street. Dusk had settled by the time they emerged from the opulent palace. Glowing white lights framed the red sign that stretched above the Diamond's entryway, but the light emitted by the window displays drew

Fern's eye. Their luminous golden hue spilled onto the sidewalk and competed with the colorful lights strung from one side of the street to the other. If not for her appreciation of the simple life she had in Elizabeth, the glamour of it all might be a credible tempter. She studied Becca's enrapt expression with apprehension while Ellie's enthusiasm, the city lights, and all things new spun around Becca like a weightless, imperceptible spider's web.

A light rain, on the cusp of sleet, began to fall while the driver rambled from one bus stop to the next, and when they reached their destination, a glassy film covered the sidewalk.

Becca checked her footing before reaching for Fern's arm. "Be careful."

Fern held onto Becca and reached for Muriel, and Muriel did the same for Ellie, until their line resembled the beginning of a firemen's bucket brigade. As the bus pulled away from the curb, however, the space between the bus stop and the house lacked the dozen or so swarthy firefighters who might have passed each gal along until they'd transported them to the safety of the front porch.

Instead, the foursome hung onto each other, testing the pavement and holding one another up when one of them lost their footing. Muriel's "whoops" rang into the air as one of her feet went left while the other veered to the right. How she didn't pull all of them to their keisters was an achievement in itself.

"Would you quit laughing?" Muriel said to Fern. "Your shoulders are shaking so hard you're going to steal what's left of our balance."

"As long as this is a group effort, we're okay," Becca said as she braced her shoulder against Fern.

"She's right," Ellie said. "Listen up, y'all. Pretend you're a *danseuse*. On the count of four, we'll all step forward on our right foot. Are you ready?"

"Ready," Fern said. She lifted the heel of her foot while Ellie counted.

"One, two, th—"

"You lousy, loudmouthed drunks. What's wrong with you people?" Betty Hastings stood on her porch, wagging her finger. Fern squinted at the eerie shadow cast by the woman's ceiling fixture, one that made it appear as if Betty had grown a pair of devil's horns. When Fern inspected the anomaly, the humps turned out to be eyeglasses resting on top of the woman's head.

First, Fern worried she'd choke, but things spiraled downhill from there. When she pulled her hand out of Becca's grasp, the action sent a wobble down the line that threatened to be the group's undoing. Instead of covering her gaping mouth as she'd intended, the snigger she tried to bury grew into an uncontrollable horselaugh. Once it escaped her lips, it resonated throughout the neighborhood.

"You ought to be ashamed, the lot of you," Betty hollered.

"I'm so sorry," Fern whispered to Muriel. When a snort escaped Fern's lips, it roused peals of laughter from all three of her companions.

Leland opened the front door, examined the scene, and started down the stairs.

"Stop," Muriel yelled. "It's a sheet of ice out here."

Good thing the man was fast on his feet, leastways while they still had traction. He minded his steps while he gathered the women, one at a time, and ushered them into the house, all the while Betty shouted insults.

Fern stood in the entryway with the others, brushing off her coat and trying to quit acting like a silly schoolgirl. "I think I ought to apologize all around. Girls, I don't want you to think my reaction was appropriate."

When an unchecked round of belly laughs drowned out every syllable, Fern gave up her scolding and followed them into the parlor.

"Oh, no," Becca said as she watched the scene beyond the window. "Did she call the police?"

Ellie leaned over Becca's shoulder and pulled the curtains apart so she could see the car that idled at the curb. The patrolman in the passenger seat rolled down the window and waved. Ellie's face turned a bright shade of pink when she waved back.

As the patrol car pulled away, Becca asked, "Who was that?"

"You know about the incident with Mrs. Hastings and the neighbor boy's dog," Leland said. He winked at Ellie before he added, "I reckon the officers' frequent appearances discourage Mrs. Hastings from making more trouble."

"Don't you believe a word he says," Muriel said. "I think Ellie can give you the honest answer."

Ellie's explanation during dinner was evasive, but it was plain to see she didn't mind if Betty's complaints had drawn the policemen to the front door. She put down her fork and dabbed her napkin to her lips. "Can I change the subject now? I've waited all day long to tell y'all my news."

Becca didn't waste a second. "Spill it."

"Mr. Van Damme is tough as nails, and he expects us to work hard and do our best, but he really, really, really cares about his dancers. He said I've come along quickly with my lessons and he invited me to go to the next college visit. I get to perform. For real. I am so excited."

Once Ellie got started, no one dared interrupt. She carried on as fast and non-stop as a seventy-eight rpm record. "See here," she said as she placed a program on the table. "This is from a college visit the academy made several years ago."

Fern inspected the dog-eared cover.

TWENTY-THIRD SERIES OHIO STATE UNIVERSITY CONCERTS

THE OHIO STATE UNIVERSITY
SCHOOL OF MUSIC

presents

ANDRE VAN DAMME
AND COMPANY

WEDNESDAY, FEBRUARY 20, 1952
8:15 P.M.
UNIVERSITY HALL

Ellie opened the folded paper and ran her finger down the first page. "The program started with *Le Spectre de la Rose*. Mr. Van Damme danced the part of The Spirit. Underneath is an explanation of the story, which is about a secret lover's gift of a rose. Next was one of Ravel's pieces, *Pavane pour une Infante Defunte*."

Fern read the fine print while Ellie glossed over the details and moved on to the next selection. Not so romantic, this particular piece by Maurice Ravel, as it spoke of death.

"After that," Ellie said, "they performed Brahms' *Guerriere*, a war dance, and Ravel's *Bolero*." Ellie almost popped out of her chair when her finger slid to the title of the last production. "Following a second intermission, they performed Act One of *An American in Paris*."

"George Gershwin's *American in Paris?*" Muriel asked. "But that's modern, jazzy."

"That's true," Ellie replied, "but Mr. Van Damme doesn't limit dance to traditional operatic ballets. His repertoire includes classic and modern as well." Her finger slid down a few lines. "And, see this note? 'Choreography by Andre Van Damme. Choreographed by special permission.' He's so well known and respected that composers give him freedom to create his own interpretations. Isn't that crazy?"

Fern tried not to gawp, not just at the academy's diverse offerings, but at Ellie's use of the foreign terms and the ease with which she pronounced the names of the musical pieces. They rolled off her tongue with the confidence of a college-educated linguist. Fern tried to keep up. Leland's face, on the other hand, had glazed over completely.

While Ellie prattled on about Mr. Van Damme's accomplishments, Fern read the last page of the program, which described the story behind Gershwin's composition. If the concert as a whole wasn't enough to impress Fern, the final statement floored her.

> The Andre Van Damme Ballet Concert was brought to Ohio State University through the courtesy and under the auspices of Baron Silvercruys, Belgian Ambassador to the United States of America.

What was next? Would Ellie perform for presidents? For royalty? Fern saw no limit to the possibilities. She eyed her daughter, whose fervor exploded around her like soundwaves—soundwaves that multiplied as they emanated from their source. Like an echo, Ellie swept others into her passion long after she'd shared her original report.

"I can't believe I get to participate in something like this," Ellie said.

In the midst of the ensuing congratulations, Ellie beamed, as she should, but she failed to miss the pain that edged Becca's eyes and mouth. Fern swallowed hard. Becca, her unassuming, contented, and quiet firstborn, hungered for more. This unexpected awakening could bring delight, or it could wound her. The path was fraught with perils, none of which Fern could control.

Chapter 20

"Mom?"

"Hmm?"

"What if Dad hadn't returned to Elizabeth after he finished working with the Civilian Conservation Corps?"

Fern didn't dare take her eyes off the road, not when the tires might encounter a patch of slick pavement where the steep mountainside had obscured the melting properties of the sun. Becca's sunglasses, like the terrain, prevented her mother from seeing the source of her daughter's uncharacteristic detachment. Becca's tenor, like the question, unsettled Fern.

"I don't know what you're asking me."

"Did you ever have your eye on another boy?"

"Are you asking if I had a second choice?"

"I don't like the way that sounds," Becca replied, "but I reckon that's close enough."

"When my father decided to marry me off to a widower who was as ancient as an Egyptian pyramid, I decided right then I didn't mind living alone."

"You never had another boyfriend?"

"I had a mighty big crush on a boy when I was six, but by the time I turned seven, I changed my mind."

"So, if you hadn't married Dad, you'd have turned into a spinster."

"Well, I hope not, but I'm happy I'll never know." Fern ventured a quick glance at Becca. "Why are you asking me these things?" As Fern asked, she knew the answer. Becca's sigh weighed heavier than a thousand *what ifs.*

"Going to Charleston triggered possibilities that I hadn't considered before. Ellie and I spent half the night talking, although it was mostly Ellie carrying on about the ballet and getting to know Martin."

"The policeman?"

"Does she know another Martin?"

"I don't think so, but I wasn't aware she'd spent any time with him."

Becca turned her face toward the passenger window. "Maybe I wasn't supposed to share that."

"Maybe you ought to."

"It's nothing major. He dropped by Three Squares Diner a few times while Ellie was working. That's all."

That's all? Fern's imagination whirled. Maybe Leland could devise a means to interrogate the young man.

When Becca faced forward again, Fern asked, "Does Ellie's happiness take away from your own?"

"That's not what I'm saying. No. But, when she goes on about her dancing, she has a spark in her. You saw her in the Diamond when she spun around in the lingerie aisle." Becca paused for a moment. "She reminds me of a butterfly."

"How so?"

"I don't know anyone who doesn't stop whatever they're doing when a butterfly flutters by. The insect's delicacy, its grace and beauty, demand attention. Ellie's like that. I mean, didn't you see the boy who stared at her? He was entranced."

"You sound a mite jealous."

"Oh, no, no, no. I'm not. Honest. I don't want to be Ellie. I'm happy for her. We're different in most ways, but after yesterday, I realized I'd like something to light a spark in me too. I don't have any idea what might make me feel that way, but the prospect excites me. Are people passionate about one thing or another when they're born, or does it come along later?"

"Both, I reckon. Ellie's been dancing since she could walk, but your dad didn't have a notion to write until he was in his twenties. Don't fret over it, Becca. In time you'll find your niche."

"Will I? In Elizabeth?"

Was this conversation about living in a tiny, isolated town? "Are you worried you won't find a proper husband in Elizabeth?"

"It's slim pickings."

"If you'd venture from behind the store's cash register once in a while and attend a few community events, you'd have a better chance of meeting someone new."

"Maybe. I don't know. But you have to admit that country life spawns far more redneck mountain men than it does cerebral types like Dad."

"Cerebral types?" Fern laughed. "That's an appropriate term for your father. I'll have you know, that trait intimidated me more than any other. I am not your dad's intellectual equal, but I'm still his fairy tale princess, so I think we're not in danger of unraveling anytime soon." Fern snuck a peek at Becca when she said, "I'm also rather taken by your dad's he-man attributes. You don't necessarily have to forego one for the other."

When Becca blushed, her innocent reaction and its familiarity touched Fern. She'd walk a desert from end to end if it would bring as fine a man to Becca as Fern had found in Percy.

Fern's smile broadened when she said, "In case you didn't

know, he's also part hillbilly, so he and I do have at least one thing in common."

Becca slunk down in her seat. "Maybe we ought to talk about football."

"That's a touchy subject these days. After the Tigers lost to the Monongah Lions in the playoffs, people's celebrations turned to grumbling. Regardless, you should have gone to the game with us."

"Why? I heard the fourteen to thirteen score less than an hour after the game ended, and I didn't have to suffer through the cold."

"You never know. You might have run into a handsome, cerebral, football fan."

"Mother..."

"I'm simply suggesting you shouldn't wait for him to find you in Bigler's General Store."

"I'll keep that in mind."

"On a serious note, Becca, sharing a life is more about immersing the other person in immeasurable, never-ending offerings of love than expecting the other one to make you whole. Whether a suitor sweeps you off your feet or not, you determine whether you lay hold of joy."

From the corner of her eye, Fern saw Becca purse her lips and blink her eyes. The air weighed heavy again.

"I'm glad you see it that way," Becca said, "because I'm pretty sure I want to move in with Uncle Leland and Aunt Muriel for a spell, or as long as it takes for me to discover what will ignite a fire in me."

What! No, no, no. First Ellie, then Leland and Muriel, and now Becca. No!

"How did it go?" Fern held the receiver to her ear while she stretched the cord far enough to grab the dishtowel. She wiped her hands while Ellie's animated voice carried through the telephone line.

"It was fantastic."

"Hold on while I turn off the burner." Fern pulled the pot of near-boiling tomato sauce off the heat and stirred it one more time. Dinner would be late, but this was news. Important news. She picked up the telephone and took a seat at the table. "All right. Tell me everything."

"Well, first off, this college visit wasn't anything like the one the academy attended at Ohio State. I mean, not only is Glenville State College tiny in comparison, it's . . . well . . . Glenville's just a dot on the map, not that Charleston is huge. Am I making any sense?"

Fern wiped her hand across her mouth, as if she needed to hide her response from Ellie's view. If Fern compared Becca's slow and deliberate conversation to a predictable, steady drip, Ellie's banter was a leaky pipe with the force of a gusher behind it.

"About Glenville? I reckon the size of the town and the school didn't come as a surprise." Glenville State had a long history, but it was a small college tucked among the hills and hollows of Gilmer County, a hundred miles or so from Charleston.

"It didn't, but after I bragged over that old OSU program, I thought I ought to lower your expectations."

"I didn't have any expectations, honey, just hopes. I hope you performed well and you enjoyed yourself."

"Oh, I did. At least I think I performed well. I know for sure I enjoyed myself. It took longer to get there and back than it did to perform, but the auditorium was full and the audience was enthusiastic."

"Well, that's good to hear. What did you dance?"

"I was part of the dancers who performed *Pavane of the Sleeping Beauty*. It's from Ravel's *Mother Goose Suite*, which is a collection of fairy tale pieces. The one about Sleeping Beauty is a little sad and haunting, and the music is rather simple, but it's also delicate and moving."

"I wish I could have seen it."

"Me too." Ellie's voice perked up seconds later when she said, "Afterwards, a few of the students waited to talk to us. They were mostly girls, but a couple of boys expressed their interest, although Kay and Norma both swore they only wanted to flirt. Which is too bad, really, because Mr. Van Damme still needs to recruit male dancers so the girls don't have to fill those parts. I'd dance a male role if Mr. Van Damme asked me to, but I'd rather wear mascara on my eyelashes than to use it to draw a mustache on my upper lip."

"He'd have you do that?"

"I'm kidding about drawing a mustache, although I suppose it could happen. More than likely I'd have to wear a bulky costume, or maybe a mask, to hide my being female."

Before Fern could reply, Ellie said, "Oh, yikes. If I don't leave here in five minutes, I'll be late to work. Give Dad a hug. Love you. Bye."

After a click on Ellie's end, the phone went silent. Fern placed the receiver back on the cradle, put the pot back on the burner, stirred the sauce, and turned on the heat, reversing her earlier steps. Now, if only she could do the same with her fleeing kin. Refrain Becca, call back Ellie, lasso Leland, and hog-tie Muriel. Bring 'em all back to Elizabeth. Although the thought was futile, and not particularly funny, Fern enjoyed the vision of her hogtied sister-in-law.

※

"Happy New Year, Mrs. Bigler." Paul Anders, Percy's employer and owner of Anders Oil, scuffed the soles of his boots against the mat that lay just inside the general store's front door. He removed his hat, tugged off his gloves, and loosened his wool scarf.

"Good morning," Fern replied. "Did Percy send you over to keep me company? Business is slower than a fly doing the backstroke in a pitcher of molasses."

"I don't have much time to chat these days. 'Tis our season for completing our clients' quarterly reports and preparing annual summaries. We're as rushed as an accountant's office."

Indeed. Percy would miss more than an occasional family dinner for the duration. Getting food to the Bigler table required more familial cooperation than it had before Becca joined her sister in Charleston. She'd only been gone a week, but her absence left more than a tender wound and an empty seat at suppertime. Becca's departure dismantled the flexible schedule that allowed the women to fulfill obligations at the store as well as at home.

"What can I get for you?" Fern asked.

"I have a list," Mr. Anders replied as he pulled a scrap of paper out of his coat pocket. "Our son and his family are still visiting, and the youngest grandchild asked her granny to bake a yellow cake with chocolate icing. The whippersnapper doesn't ask for much, and their visits are rare, so Barbara is more than happy to oblige. Except her pantry doesn't have these things," he said as he handed the paper to Fern.

After Fern gathered a can of cocoa, a bag of Hudson Cream flour, and a bottle of vanilla, Mr. Anders handed over his cash, and she fished his change out of the register.

"I might have found the correct ingredients without your help, but I appreciate your saving me a good thirty minutes of guessing. Barbara and I are bouncing between the office and home, so I need to get back before one place or the other catches fire."

"Glad to be of help. Y'all take care."

The bell jangled as Mr. Anders pulled the door shut. Fern walked to the side window where she could see the corner of her house. It wasn't in flames, and neither was the general store, but she could appreciate Mr. Anders' comment about bouncing back and forth between the two.

Nettie planned to give Fern a break for lunch, but it would be hard to enjoy a meal while she tended to June, the last of her children to suffer through a bout with mumps. Ellie and Becca had come down with the disease at the same time, as had Roy and Wayne, but this third round with June wasn't any easier than the others had been. The child was miserable.

Fern walked to the register and scrounged for a piece of paper and a marker pen. She wrote HELP WANTED in bold letters. She should have posted the job opening as soon as Becca made her wishes known, but the mother in Fern hoped Becca would fret over the unknown, have second thoughts, and change her mind. As is turned out, it was Fern who did most of the wishing.

For the second time in the general store's history, a member of the Bigler family, extended or otherwise, couldn't fill all the hours needed to manage the shop. For the second time, Fern being the first exception when she fled her parents' home so as to avoid a wedding with the elderly widower, an outsider would be on the payroll.

Nettie came in through the shop's back door as Fern taped the notice to the front window.

"How's June?"

"Still not eating." Nettie hung her coat on the hook near the rear entrance and donned a navy blue apron, a throwback from the store's early days. "She tried to swallow broth, but she's so swollen that most of a slurp dribbles down her chin."

"Her fever and achy muscles worry me, but her inability to eat scares me. This could go on for another ten days, maybe longer."

"The swelling has finally leveled off, so maybe she's on her way to recovery." Nettie's reassurance didn't hide the shadows beneath her hazel eyes. She'd lost as much sleep over June's illness as Fern had.

As she walked to the counter, Nettie gestured to Fern's sign. "Did you finally concede?"

"I don't think we have a choice. We're in a fix because I didn't advertise sooner. I can't apologize enough. You're plumb wore out, and it's my fault."

"We can't see the future, Fern. I know why you've put it off. If I were in your shoes, I'd have done the same thing."

"How would you describe the job to an applicant?"

"What do you mean?"

"If I hire a clerk for a permanent job, and Becca runs home because she realizes she made a mistake, it wouldn't be fair to the employee. On the other hand, someone seeking a permanent job might be more reliable than a willing worker who plans to dive in and swoop right back out again."

"An employee with a long view is apt to be more loyal, and that generates a different type of accountability. I reckon they would make more of an effort to be courteous and dependable."

"That's what I was thinking. I just don't know how to be honest with the person who wants the job."

Nettie looked over her shoulder. "I know you need to get

over to the house, but let me give you another thought to ponder."

"I need wise counsel. Please give me some."

"Supposing you hire a clerk who expects to stay indefinitely. If Becca decides to come home, and if she wants to work at the store again, she can take over my hours. I'll retire. Work the garden. Knit mittens. Bake bread. Read more books. Turn on the television and watch *Father Knows Best, I Love Lucy*, and *I've Got a Secret*. I've plenty of choices. You go ahead and hire the best you can find and treat them as if they'll work alongside you forever."

"But—"

"Just take care of business today. Do what you need to do. We'll iron out the wrinkles if they come. Now, get going. Your baby needs you."

Fern planted a kiss on her mother-in-law's cheek. "Thank you."

She stole into the bedroom where her daughter lay in her bed, her head supported by two pillows, her puffy cheeks pink with fever. When June opened her dark brown eyes, they bore pain and misery, and a desperate plea for relief. The teardrops sliding down the sides of her face shattered Fern's stoic veneer into a thousand pieces.

As she cast her silent plea, words of the psalmist washed over her, wave after wave. She ran her fingertips over June's hand as she whispered, "He established the mountains, calms the roaring seas, and waters the crops. He established light and sun, set the borders of the earth, and made summer and winter. He gives favor. Favor." Fern squeezed her eyes shut. *Mercy. Please have mercy.*

Chapter 21

Leland lowered the serrated blade and pulled it back and forth. After the first few swipes, he lifted his hand and examined the meaty mass. The pot roast was so tender that the pieces fell away. Instead of messing with perfection, he placed the serving fork on the plate and handed it to Ellie, who sat to his right.

"Just stick your fork into however much you want and slide it onto your plate." He directed his next comment to Muriel, who sat at the opposite end of the table. "This is right nice."

"It sure is." Martin took the plate from Ellie, helped himself to a generous serving of beef, and passed it on to Muriel. "I'm not much of a cook, and my folks don't worry about family meals anymore, so this is a rare treat. Thanks for having me."

When Ellie asked if she might invite her policeman to dinner, Leland hadn't intended to interrogate the young man, but he couldn't help but examine every move, every blink, and every word. Like that last mouthful of information.

"You still live at home?" Leland asked.

"No. After I moved out, we still gathered for Sunday supper, but when my brother left, Ma quit bothering with it. Said it was too much effort." Martin turned to Muriel and said, "If this tastes half as good as it smells, I might have to move in with y'all." Sure enough, Martin was jesting, but even Ellie swallowed hard.

Becca helped herself to the pot roast before sending the plate on down the line. Right behind was a bowl with steaming potatoes, carrots, and onions, all infused with the savory flavor of beef.

Leland tipped the pitcher holding dark brown gravy and smothered the mouthwatering heap he'd piled onto his plate. After he offered a prayer of thanks, he tapped his fork against his glass. "This is mighty fine, indeed. Now, before y'all begin to eat, I want to declare this a monumental occasion."

Muriel lifted her face and settled her gray eyes on Leland. Her skin was as pale as could be, what with it being the middle of winter, but her dark lashes and rich brown hair set off her rosy cheeks and lips all the more. The sight of his wife still captivated him.

"We're waiting," Becca said.

"Where was I?"

"You were about to make a declaration," Ellie replied.

"Right." Leland cleared his throat. "This here marks the first time all of the Elizabeth transplants have gathered at their Charleston table, all at the same time, to break bread with one another. I, for one, want to express my thanks, not just for the food, but for all the good we've enjoyed. Should we make a list?"

"Becca's new job," Muriel said.

Leland turned toward Martin and said, "Having a seat at the table for guests."

"Generous kin who opened their home to me." Becca blushed when she saw Martin watching her.

Ellie almost burst out of her seat. "Dreams that come true."

"What dreams?" Becca asked.

"I'll tell y'all while we eat dessert. I don't want to take over the dinner conversation."

"I think you already have," Becca replied.

Ellie pressed her shoulders back at the remark, but Becca didn't sound or appear as if she meant to offend. Leland riveted his wide eyes on Muriel, but her perplexed expression implied that she was as ill equipped to decipher the exchange as anyone who lacked first-hand experience raising daughters.

"Okay, then," Leland said after he swallowed a bite of carrot. "Martin, why don't you tell us why you decided to join the police force."

"Well, I was an MP in the army, and when I returned stateside, I figured it couldn't be any harder to uphold the law here than in Korea."

"You served in Korea?" Leland asked. He ran his eyes over the young man's form, from his white-blond hair and youthful face, to his squared shoulders and his sturdy build. "How old are you, anyway?"

Muriel sent Leland a visual warning and cleared her throat at the same time Ellie clutched her own.

"I'm twenty-four."

Leland, mathematics wizard that he was, deduced that Martin was six years older than Ellie. That would be Strike One.

"I never met anyone who served in Korea," Muriel said. "No one talks about that war."

"You're right," Martin said. "While we were in Korea, most of the world was still trying to put life back together after the Second World War tore it apart. It's just as well, if you ask me. Most soldiers don't care to share stories involving combat."

"I agree," Leland said.

"Was it awful?" Ellie's solemn blue eyes searched Martin's face. Leland detected a tad of awe in his niece's expression, which did little to settle his unease.

"It was." Martin took a sip of water but directed his gaze at Leland when he added to his reply. "I know you served, so you know what it's like, seeing things no one should have to imagine, let alone witness. Serving in the war, though, woke me up. Turned me around."

"In what way?" Muriel asked. She gave Martin a kindly nod, but the pinched lines around her mouth alerted Leland to her misgivings over Ellie's choice of dinner guests.

"To be honest, I used to be a violent man."

Martin's confession forced four spines straight as ramrods and erased every manufactured smile. Ellie looked ready to cry.

"I ought to explain before y'all get het up about it. Before I enlisted, my best friend was alcohol. Like my father, I'm an alcoholic, and like my father, I'm a mean drunk."

Strike Two.

Martin gulped water this time. "In Korea, at times we'd have booze on post, and other times we'd be dry for weeks on end, but when a new shipment came in, most of the men got soused, including me. After an incident that I won't put to words, I quit drinking. Haven't touched a drop since."

"Well, that's commendable," Ellie said.

Whether she meant to convince the others or herself, Leland couldn't tell, not that it made a difference one way or another. It was still Strike Two.

"How do you keep from falling back on the bottle?" Muriel asked while she toyed with a potato.

"After that incident, I had a forthright visit with the chaplain. If I hadn't, I doubt I'd have made it home. I got saved, and now I'm a different man."

Leland would have sworn that Becca mouthed *do tell* before she lowered her face and jabbed a carrot with her fork.

"Enough about me," Martin said. He fixed his eyes on Becca,

who sat across from him. "Ellie says you're working in a camera store."

The transition to polite conversation startled Becca. She wiped her mouth with her napkin and said, "Um. I am."

"Which one?"

"Hawk's Photo Supply Company. It's near the corner of Summers and Lee."

"Are you taking photographs?"

Becca's cheeks flamed. "Right now I help with the orders and the inventory. As soon as I learn about the cameras, they'll let me work with the customers."

"Do you like it?"

Leland wanted to interrupt, seeing how their guest was working too hard to keep the discussion anywhere but on himself. This particular line of questioning, however, wasn't giving Leland the same level of indigestion as the previous subject, so he'd let Martin continue until Becca cried the proverbial *Uncle!* Which, given the present circumstances, was more real than cliché.

"I do like it," Becca replied. "Really. Once I settle into the work, I hope the owner will teach me how to take pictures. I mean, I always liked my Brownie camera, but compared to the ones they offer at Hawk's, a Brownie is child's play."

The banter fell into the mundane, and after Becca and Ellie filled every coffee cup and dessert plate, Ellie took her seat. It wasn't so long ago that her Uncle Leland had placed a tickly firefly in the palm of her hand. When that little creature lit up, Ellie's face had done likewise. She had that same air about her just then.

Ellie rested both elbows on the edge of the table. "Can I tell you now?"

"You'd better," Becca replied.

"Mr. Van Damme is forming a ballet company." Maybe it was

the excitement in Ellie's voice, or simply an opportunity for Martin to squeeze his gal, but when he reached over and pulled her into a hug, Leland had to retract his claws.

"He already runs the American Academy Ballet. I don't understand," Becca said.

"The academy is a school. A ballet company puts on professional performances. The company sells tickets to an event and pays the dancers. He'll let each of his students audition, but he'll only select the best for the ballet company. I am so excited. And, here's the wild part. He's already made a commitment to perform *Capriccio Espagnol* in April. April!"

Muriel was the first of the hearers to pull herself together, not that Ellie had a knack for pushing her enthusiasm beyond her audience's ability to keep up.

"You haven't auditioned yet?"

Ellie's blue eyes glimmered as bright as sunlight glinting on a faceted sapphire. "Next week. Oh, and guess where he scheduled the debut."

"One of the colleges?" Becca asked.

"Better. We'll perform at the Municipal Auditorium. I am thrilled."

While Ellie's excitement bounced from one wall to another, from one startled face to another, Martin wore a grin that couldn't get any wider without ripping his jowls. Leland, for his part, reclined in his chair, contemplating. Fern was joking when she told Leland to investigate the blond police officer who caught Ellie's notice, but if Leland were reading things right, Martin had the same ability to disappoint Ellie as a *no thank you* to her ballet company audition.

"Do we need to reserve seats?" Leland asked.

"Oh." Ellie obviously hadn't thought of that. "I reckon you can either purchase a ticket when you get to the auditorium, or maybe you can call ahead and reserve seats. I'll have to ask."

"Martin, will you be at the performance, assuming Ellie is among the performers?" Leland asked.

"You bet."

"If I find out I can reserve tickets, I'd better get your last name."

Ellie's posture stiffened and Martin's jovial expression fell faster than a duck hunter's prey did a nosedive.

"I was going to tell you," Ellie began.

Martin put his hand on her arm. "Let me. Mr. Dugan . . . uh, my last name is Hastings."

Leland clenched his jaw tight enough to pulverize the enamel clean off his teeth.

Martin's voice took on a sheepish tone when he said, "You see, um, Betty Hastings is my uncle's ex-wife."

Strike Three. *Somebody—anybody—escort this man out of the ballpark!*

Chapter 22

"Ellie," June squealed, "twirl me again."

"No more. I'm as a dizzy as your goofy dog." Ellie pointed to the collie pup that spun in a circle while she tried to grab her tail.

"She's got fleas," June said. "She's trying to itch 'em."

Ellie reached down and tickled June's ribs. "Is that why you need to twirl? Are you trying to shake off a swarm of fleas?"

June's giggles filled the air, a melody as pleasant as a warbling lark. When Ellie grabbed her little sister's wrists and whirled in circles again, June could hardly sputter out her reply, "I—don't—have—fleas."

Fern stood in the doorway, with Muriel peeking over her shoulder. "I think Ellie forgot that June has twice as much energy as she does."

Muriel let out an unexpected, long sigh. "I've missed the little darling. Roy, Wayne, you, Percy, Nettie. All of you."

"It's been a hard transition. Nettie acts lost sometimes, staring out the window, just like we're doing now, but instead of entertainment, most of the time she sees a yard where the sounds of family are just a shade of what they used to be."

"Leland and I talk about coming home one day, but neither of us sees an end to the circumstances that sent us away. If you were to ask my opinion, I couldn't tell you whether I thought Becca might decide to stay in Charleston or not, but I can't imagine Ellie surrendering what she's found there, especially since Mr. Van Damme selected her as a member of the ballet company."

Fern bit her lip. It wasn't just the ballet that might keep Ellie in the city. Visions of her with that boy, the one Leland was so het up about, stole more sleep from Fern than anything else did.

"Roy and Wayne haven't suffered much," Muriel said.

"Don't let those two fool you. They still fight with each other, but their quarrels are sharper than they used to be. When Wayne and Roy exclude June, and she whines about it, the boys seem to forget that she went from being part of a trio to taking a solo part."

Muriel checked her watch. "I need to collect my paperwork." Her focus wandered to Bigler's General Store. "How is Ron working out?"

"He's doing well. It's been a long time since a fellow worked in the shop, and I'll admit it's nice to have someone tall enough to reach the cobwebs or change a lightbulb without having to drag out a ladder. It was good timing all around when he moved in with his grandparents, although I'm sorry for the circumstances that landed him here."

"What happened?" Muriel asked.

"It was in the Parkersburg paper. Their neighbor got drunk, roughed up his wife, and went to a bar. When she locked him out of the house, he set a fire, front door and back. It didn't do much damage to their brick house, but the wind took the embers next door."

"To Ron's house."

Fern hesitated while the weight of the telling yielded another round of pity. "You know those old, stick-built homes are tinderboxes. By the time the fire department responded, it was too late. Ron wasn't home at the time. Otherwise, he'd be gone too."

Muriel pulled her bottom lip between her teeth, dismay clouding her features. "I wish he could warn Ellie. Martin was honest about his being an alcoholic. Said he's not had a drop in years, but—"

"But what happens when his appetite outweighs his will? Is that what you meant to say? What then? The people who surround him will pay the price. And what about the comment he made to y'all about having been a violent man? Good heavens, Muriel, it scares me half to death."

June ran past Muriel and Fern and scrambled into the house. "Is it time for lunch yet? I'm starving."

Nettie called to June from the kitchen. "Lunch will be ready in five minutes."

June tugged Fern's hand. "Come on."

"Go ahead. We'll be right there."

Ellie walked to the porch but hesitated at the sudden silence. The blush that colored her cheeks suggested she knew she'd been the subject of the hushed conversation. She straightened her posture and crinkled her nose, as if she were sniffing out a threat. "Something wrong?"

"Why don't you two go on in?" Muriel asked. "I left my papers at the store."

"I'll get them." Ellie pivoted and walked away.

"Oh boy," Fern mumbled.

"You have to talk to her."

"In due time. Let's enjoy lunch."

As they sat around the kitchen table, Ellie wagged a stalk of celery. "So, here's the story. My Belgian ballet instructor, who is now the Director of the Charleston Ballet, has chosen to choreograph and perform *Capriccio Espagnol*, a collection of Spanish-themed orchestral pieces composed by a Russian. It sounds crazy, doesn't it?"

"It makes the world seem right small," Fern said.

"Who's the composer?" Muriel asked.

"Nikolai Rimsky-Korsakov." Once again, Ellie's ability to roll French, Spanish, and Russian words and intonations off her tongue astonished Fern. Her daughter's adventure was creating a new woman out of her innocent girl, and Fern wasn't quite sure how she felt about it. On the other hand, she knew exactly where she stood on the subject of Martin Hastings.

"I've heard of him," Muriel said. "I'm not familiar with that particular music, though."

"He composed the *Capriccio* in 1887," Ellie replied, her defenses at rest and her excitement brimming. "Back then, critics warned that it was too bold, too *avant-garde*, but it turned out to be a smashing success. If you ask me, it's daring, even for today."

"Bold? Daring?" Fern asked. Never mind the *avant-garde*.

"The folk music, the dance, the costumes. Everything. It's festive, intense, and colorful. When the costume designer watched a recent rehearsal, she described one of the dances as sultry."

"You have a costume designer?" Nettie asked.

"We do. Set designers too. And, don't forget the orchestra. The production will be as top-notch as an event in New York City or San Francisco."

"Do you get to wear a costume?" June asked Ellie.

"I sure do."

"Can I see it?"

Ellie turned to Fern. "I don't know. Will you be there? Will

Dad come? Grandma?"

"We'll have to see," Fern replied. She hadn't considered that everyone would want to go, but, what if they did, including Roy and Wayne? They'd have to set aside money for gasoline and food, for seven tickets—nine if they paid for Leland and Muriel, ten if they bought one for Martin, heaven forbid. If they could afford all of those things, what would they wear? "What's the date?"

"Friday, April thirteenth, at a quarter after eight."

"I reckon your father and I need to see how to work things out. You can be sure we want to attend."

Ellie gathered the dishes and took them to the sink. After she sat back down, she said, "Tell me about Ron. He's pleasant and polite, and those blue eyes of his, why, they're as pale as ice."

"I hear a 'but' coming," Fern said.

"It's as if his friendliness doesn't quite come into focus. I mean, it's there all right, but . . . well, I don't know how to describe it."

"His parents both died in a fire a couple of months ago," Fern said.

"Oh. I'm sorry to hear that."

"They died because a drunk neighbor set a fire," Muriel said.

Ellie stared at Muriel. Fern closed her eyes. Muriel's personality traits did not include tact.

"Why did I need to know that part?" Ellie asked, directing her question to her mother, not to Muriel. "Is this a warning? Another hint about Martin? Instead of dancing around his little problem, which hasn't been a problem for years, why don't you just lay it out there so we can waddle through the manure?"

"I need to tend to the chickens." Nettie pushed back her chair and extended her hand to June. "Will you come help me?"

June followed, but she craned her neck to get one more view

of the muck that engulfed the kitchen.

Ellie turned on Muriel. "Has he done anything to give you cause for this confrontation?"

"I haven't witnessed anything untoward. The problem lies with what he claims to have done before."

Ellie crossed her arms in front of her chest. "That's right. Before. You heard him. He's not drinking. People change."

"That's true," Fern said, "but all it takes is one time to undo his best intentions. For an alcoholic, booze is as addictive as a narcotic."

"I know. But, he's not a drinker. Not any more." Ellie's voice grew strident and the muscles in her neck tightened as she came to her beau's defense.

"He said he drank hard when he was in Korea," Muriel said. "Things he experienced there disturbed him."

"He's not in Korea any more. Obviously." Ellie threw up both hands. "Why do I even have to tell you this?"

"We're worried for you," Muriel said. "Of what could happen." When she reached over and tried to put her hand on Ellie's shoulder, the girl twisted sideways, deflecting the action.

"Nothing's going to happen."

"You don't know that," Fern said.

"And you didn't know when you married Dad how things might turn out. You were lucky."

"I wouldn't call it luck. I knew your father pretty well. Knew his family, knew what mattered to him. I knew his heart."

"Martin has a hard job," Muriel said. "He sees things that can shake him up, just like combat. What if, Ellie? What if he takes a drink? You heard him when he said that violence accompanied his drinking."

This next part needed to come from Ellie's mother, not her aunt. Fern cut off Muriel's objections and stated them in the only way she knew how. "Your father and I could not bear any harm coming to you, especially at the hand of a man who had a history of brutality. Knowing what we do, how can you expect anything else from us? We want you to be happy, Ellie. Safe. Loved. Cherished."

"You heard him, Muriel. He said he found salvation. He didn't just quit drinking. He turned his life around."

"That doesn't erase his body's bent toward alcoholism," Fern said.

"Are you forgetting that all mankind has a bent toward sin?" Ellie's eyes flashed, anger and pain coming together in a flood of tears.

"We're not saying that alcoholism is an unforgiveable sin," Fern said.

"What you're *saying* is you don't believe the scripture that says when a man comes to faith, the old things pass away and he becomes a new creation."

"I do believe that," Fern said.

"Really? It's true, but it doesn't apply to Martin."

"Ellie . . ."

"No, Mom, you either believe it or you don't. Once you figure it out, let me know. I'm finished talking about it. Muriel, can we please go now?"

Chapter 23

Leland and Muriel sat on a bench along the waterfront, just west of the South Side Bridge, where the Great Kanawha River called to the winter-weary West Virginians who couldn't wait for the warmth of summer. A smattering of bold residents skimmed the water in colorful rowboats and sleek canoes, their crafts leaving slender trails as they floated across the watery expanse. Families dotted the grassy areas while bicyclists and an occasional roller skater circumnavigated couples walking hand in hand down the walkways.

"One could almost forget a busy city looms behind us," Muriel said as a soft breeze toyed with her hair.

Leland wrenched his neck and eyed the church spires, the skyscrapers, and the Capitol building's gleaming gold dome. Muriel had lived in a big city before, so maybe that slanted her perspective.

"You can tune out the noise?" he asked.

"The children laughing?"

Leland pinched his brow and looked sideways at his inattentive wife. "You don't hear that?"

"What?"

"Buses, horns, revving engines."

Muriel shrugged.

It wasn't just audible noise that poked at Leland's hills-and-hollow-bred nature. The disturbance came in the manner of a feverish pace of life and a nonstop wakefulness that was at odds with a man's peace and quiet. The clamor originating just beyond the opposite bank of the river drove Leland's opinion home. "What about that?"

"What?"

"The trains."

"I guess I don't notice them."

"Don't you know half of the folks who live in Charleston set their watches by the train schedule? They know the difference between the sound of the *George Washington* when it pulls its fancy Pullman cars into the depot and the chug of an engine pulling ordinary freight cars. Why, just the other day when I was outside eating lunch, one of the glass trimmers stopped chewing his sandwich and said, 'Number Three's a mite early today.' "

"You're joking."

"I'm not."

"Noise aside," Muriel said, "today is nothing short of sublime."

"True enough. You know, I've been thinking about what happened with Ellie and Fern when y'all went to Elizabeth. Maybe we ought to cool it where Martin is concerned."

"Her parents aren't here. We need to protect her."

"By driving her into his arms? Prohibition breeds temptation, don't you know?"

"You're right, but she's young and naïve."

"Maybe so, but she spoke the truth when she defended Martin. If he's truly reformed, saved or otherwise, it's wrong to punish him for what he used to be."

"It's not punishment, Leland. It's being cautious."

"Let me ask you this. What was your first impression of my brother Calvin? Describe his personality."

"Calvin? He was a little rough around the edges, but he doted on his wife and daughter, so I assumed the burly fella had a soft side. I liked him well enough."

"He wasn't sweetness growing up," Leland said. "Calvin was never much of a talker, and he didn't take to schooling very well, but no one made fun of him more than once, and that's the truth. He used his fists to communicate." Leland lowered his voice when he said, "I did my best to emulate my big brother, which had a lot to do with the trouble I caused when I was with the CCC."

"Fern said as much."

"She told on me?"

Muriel answered with a tiny wag of her head.

"You see what good can happen when a man reforms." Leland stuck his thumbs under his armpits and splayed his hands, his best rendition of a local yokel and as ridiculous a pose as he could construe.

Muriel pretended to ignore him and said, "Let's start by inviting Martin over to the house more often."

"You're a right smart woman. We'll welcome him, feed him, and watch him like a hawk."

"Count on it."

"I have one more serious piece to talk about."

"You know, Leland, I wouldn't mind a day without drama."

"Well, this is pretty high on the list of marital disputes."

Muriel narrowed her eyes, but her expression was humdrum. "Did you decide to heap more kindness on Betty Hastings?"

"No, although I ought to spruce up her side yard. It's getting unruly already."

"She'll turn you in to the police."

"And I'll finagle a get-out-of-jail-free card from Ellie's beau. No sweat."

"So, what's on your mind, my fearless one?"

"I need to empty our bank account." Leland thought to let that sit for a moment, but money could elicit as negative a response as a confession of infidelity, not that Leland knew anything about the latter.

When Muriel's wide eyes returned to their normal size, the edges crinkled. Her outlandish response drew the notice of everyone within thirty yards. Muriel was not a laugh aloud kind of person. Hers was more of a titter or a chuckle-huff, which was a cut short snort hidden behind the guise of a chuckle. When she quit making a spectacle of herself, she wrapped her hands around her ribs.

"You had me there." Muriel pulled in a long breath and almost went into hysterics again. "Which account? The one with a dollar, or the one with five?"

Now, that wasn't funny. "After all these months we've only set aside six dollars?" Leland asked.

"Thereabouts."

"I guess I might have misspoke."

"About emptying our bank accounts?"

"About telling Fern we'd buy everyone's ticket to the ballet performance."

This rendition of Muriel's wide-eyed response wasn't humorous. Not at all.

"You offered to buy?" Muriel asked.

"I did."

"How many?" she asked.

"A heap of them."

"Who's coming?"

"First off, Ellie's grandma. So Nettie, one. Fern and Percy make three. With the boys and June, that's six. Plus Becca, you and me, and Martin. So, that makes ten. Or thereabouts. Just so you know, this list came from Fern, except she didn't include Martin."

"Well, maybe you ought to invite Betty Hastings and Martin's partner. We'll just buy an even dozen." Muriel's tone was more flabbergasted than sarcastic.

A smart man would proceed with caution. A measure of wisdom would be welcome, as well. "Ten's plenty," he replied.

"How much are they?"

"I guess it depends on where you sit. Cheap seats are a dollar, so-so seats are a dollar and a half, and the best in the house are two bucks."

"The best seats would cost more than a day's wages," Muriel said. "How can we do that?"

"I reckon we'll have to go with the dollar seats after I collect my next paycheck, and then we'll find a way to make do with what's left."

"We'll manage," Muriel said.

"Maybe it's time to ask Becca and Ellie to help with the household expenses. Fern thinks they're already paying a fair share. I know we talked about it before, but it wouldn't hurt for them to take on a bit of financial responsibility."

"But they make so little."

"And you make a lot?" Leland hadn't meant to make Muriel wince. She went to her clerking job at the Diamond, and she didn't complain, but it was as clear as the cloudless blue sky overhead that she'd set her hopes on working in the library. Once in a while, she stopped in and borrowed a few books, but the librarian, the one she dubbed Mrs. Methuselah, still sat on her throne by the front door.

Muriel cleared her throat and turned sideways so she could look Leland square in the face. "Let's buy the dollar and a half tickets."

"You just said we didn't have that much."

"We don't have that much in the bank." The way she acted—wise, shrewd, and clever—reminded Leland why she'd been the one to sweep him off his feet.

"Then where?" he asked.

"Every smart woman has a cash stash, Leland. Surely, you knew that."

ஐ

If Fern's first impressions of the Diamond left her in awe, the Municipal Auditorium rendered her thunderstruck. Her pulse quickened as they parked the car and walked to the corner of Truslow and Virginia Streets. The structure was dissimilar to the classic, post-Colonial, and Italian Renaissance styles that dominated Charleston's landmarks. The fan-shaped building faced the intersection, and the placement drew one's view to the tower block positioned front and center. Above the entrance, bold red letters identified the building by its name.

"Wow." Fern gaped at the monolithic steel and concrete façade. The building was as imposing as it was stark. "It's a lot different up close."

Nettie squeezed June's hand. "It makes me feel small. Does it make you feel small too?"

"I am small, Grandma."

"So you are, but you're growing fast."

"That's because I go to school now."

"I love the art deco design," Muriel said. "It's simple but stunning." She pointed to the large windows on the tower block.

"That's the landing between the street level and the mezzanine. We can't see from here, but it's where we'll find the grand central staircase, or so I hear. One of the clerks at work said the smaller block towers have staircases, too, but I intend to climb to the mezzanine in style."

"I thought our seats were on the first floor," Fern said.

"They are, but we have to walk up the grand staircase."

"Why?" Nettie asked.

"Because we can." Muriel winked at June. "You'll come with me, won't you?"

"Can we, Mommy?" June's rosy cheeks matched the embroidered flowers on the dress Muriel found among the Diamond's bargain basement offerings. In fact, Muriel used her eagle eye and employee discount to outfit the bigger part of the gals' ensembles. She could say what she wanted about the benefits of taking a job at the library, but when it came time for Muriel to relinquish her job at the department store, Fern would miss the occasional purchase of quality wear at a steep discount. Turned out, she rather liked fashion.

"If we have time." What a silly reply. Of course, they had time. They'd arrived thirty minutes before the performance was to begin. Leland, Percy, and the boys promised to join the womenfolk in twenty minutes or less. In the meantime, the men of the family planned to find an activity that would ward off captive audience fidgeting. Or so Percy had surmised.

"I wish I'd brought my camera," Becca said.

"I don't think they'd let you to take one inside," Muriel replied. "One flash from a sneaky photographer's bulb and the conductor might stop the orchestra until the usher escorted the offender outside."

"Guess I'll have to wait until I earn a spot with a newspaper. They'd let me take a few shots if I had the right credentials."

"Did your father suggest that?" Fern asked.

"No. I just thought of it." When Becca lowered her face and peeked through her dark eyelashes, she reminded Fern of a shy schoolgirl. "If I'm ever good enough to be a professional photographer, do you think Dad could help me land a job at the *Gazette*?"

Muriel's, "I don't see why not," silenced Fern's cautious, "We'll have to wait and see."

Given her druthers, June might have ascended and descended the so-called grand staircase until her legs gave out. Fern expected ornate architecture that rivaled the photographs she'd seen of Radio City Music Hall, or the staircases depicted in *Gone with the Wind*. The Municipal Auditorium's central staircase was prominent, but otherwise, it was just a flight of steps. The simplicity of the structure didn't deter June. After her first round trip, she talked Muriel into climbing to the mezzanine a second time.

Fern, Becca, and Nettie stood below, watching.

"I wish you had your camera," Fern said to Becca. "What I wouldn't give to capture that sight."

When June waved to the group, Nettie blew her a kiss. "Look at her. She's thrilled."

"If I had brought my camera, I'd entitle the picture, *Pure Glee*."

"That says it all," Fern replied. At this moment, in this tiny fragment of her lifetime, June was a storybook princess whose joy brought a lump to her mother's throat. When Fern considered the rest of her tribe, she had to dab moisture from the corners of her eyes. Wherever they landed in life, they were hers forever.

Becca found their row in the auditorium, slid toward the center until she found her designated spot, and lowered herself to the upholstered seat. She crooked her finger at June and patted the cushion beside her. Since June still held her granny's hand, Nettie followed. Before Fern could scoot in next, Percy and the boys joined them in the aisle.

"My turn," Percy said as he squeezed in front of Fern. As he passed, he whispered, "It wouldn't hurt to separate the boys." He chuckled, but he spoke wisely.

"After you," Fern said to Roy.

Fern squeezed in next, followed by Wayne, Muriel, and Leland. That left one seat on the aisle. Martin was cutting it close, but Fern couldn't blame him for dallying. None of the nine people from Elizabeth was particularly imposing, but as a whole, they had the potential to send fear into any man who might come courting one of the clan's females. Fern's short brush with humor fell away. Try as she might, she couldn't come to terms with her objections to Martin Hastings.

The lights began to fade, sending a hush throughout the auditorium, and drawing goosebumps. Fern pressed her palms together and brought her fingertips to her lips. This was it. Ellie's debut. If the conductor didn't tap his baton on his music stand and get the musicians playing a tune, the whole auditorium might hear Fern's sniffling and carrying on. She was worse than her six-year-old daughter, overwhelmed with pure glee and barely able to contain herself.

As darkness fell across the room and the first notes of the instruments lilted into the air, Fern mustered a hint of self-control. A spotlight set the stage ablaze, and when the curtain rose, she bent forward so that she could see the aisle.

Where was Martin?

Chapter 24

Although six seats separated June from Leland, he heard the child gasp when the first dancer appeared on stage. Her reaction was contrary to Muriel's, who regarded the empty aisle seat with a judgmental huff. Martin's absence cast a light on his priorities, and if his lack of support caught Leland off guard, how might it disturb Ellie? If Martin had an excuse, it had better border along the lines of life and death.

Muriel slid her hand around Leland's arm, stealing about two square inches of their shared armrest. He curled his fingers around her slender hand, savored her sweet affection, and turned his attention back to the performance.

He regarded the costumed dancer who cavorted across the stage, Belgium's *danseur étoile*, Ellie's idol. If Leland had met the dancer on the street, he might have labeled him a longhaired pipsqueak. However . . . muscular thighs and calves defined his otherwise slight physique, and if the famous Andre Van Damme wanted to retain his decidedly European hairstyle, who was Leland to criticize?

The program identified Julianne Kemp as the dancer who played the role of The Girl. Although the title sounded ordinary, the dancer was exceptional. Leland might not know what to call her, but she was the principal female dancer throughout the production, and although he wasn't familiar enough with ballet to define the artistry that made the woman stand out from the rest, she carried herself with a heightened level of grace and elegance. Her movements were as fluid and effortless as a ripple in calm waters.

He'd enjoyed the Kanawha Players' rendition of *Girl Crazy*, to be sure, but this ballet was entertainment of a different magnitude. It wasn't just the scale of the building and the stage, or the size of the audience that impressed him. The professional sets, the costumes, and the orchestral effects were grand, grandiose, super, superb. But, the most noteworthy asset came in the form of a lithe blond *danseuse* who was but one of the Spanish villagers who frolicked to the lively folk melodies.

Ellie's movements, perfectly synchronized with those of her peers, were deliberate and precise. It was hard to imagine that his niece had transformed from a barefoot, dancing-in-the-grass teenager to a professional performer, especially when he considered the short duration of her training. Unlike a couple of the other dancers who wore tentative, nervous expressions, Ellie personified a genuine Spanish gypsy who was having the time of her life.

The final movement, a selection entitled *Fandango Asturiano*—whatever that meant—touched Leland's core, in that the percussion instruments set his chest a-thrummin'. It was as if the audience was part of the dance, whether they wanted to participate or not, for no one could escape the rush, the pounding, and the formidable tremors that engulfed the auditorium. In a word, it was magnificent, or as Ellie might say, *magnifique*.

The performance earned a standing ovation, a second curtain

call, a few whistles, and shouts of "Bravo." If Percy's puffed-with-pride chest were an indicator, he'd pushed aside all manner of misgivings that attended Ellie's departure from Elizabeth. And Fern? Well, few things rendered her silent. As the crowd exited the auditorium, Fern stood in front of her seat, staring at the empty stage. Before Percy grabbed her elbow and steered her toward the aisle, she had to press her handkerchief to her eyes and her fingertips to her lips.

A twinge of jealousy engulfed Leland's neck in prickly heat. He thought he'd put envy behind him a long time ago. What would it be like to rear a child, to guide her toward honorable and praiseworthy goals, and to partake in an event like this, where the child's deportment, values, and skills were laid bare? Ellie's accomplishment, her passion, and her joy were apparent, and although he was merely the uncle, he was genuinely thankful. Thankful for kin, for a decent job, for a remarkable wife, and for all the good that came along when they pulled up stakes and moved away from home. Jealousy was an unwelcome burden.

"What are you doing?" Muriel asked as she watched Leland grind the toe of his shoe against the lobby's floor.

"Putting out a bad habit."

Before she could demand an explanation, June skipped over and tugged Muriel's hand. "Can we go upstairs again?"

"Again?"

"While we wait for Ellie."

"Aren't you tired?"

"Nope. I want to pretend I'm a movie star. Can we?"

Leland had to chuckle. The grand invention of television brought all sorts of ideas into the living room. If Fern thought it was hard to let Ellie join the ballet, the notion of putting June on a train traveling to Hollywood would set Fern spinning down the hill, straight to the bottom of the hollow.

Ellie, accompanied by her former roommates, Kay and Norma, came into view. They had changed into street clothes, but their cheeks were as flushed as if they still wore stage makeup. Their dazzling smiles and glimmering eyes didn't need a spotlight to reveal their jubilation. The roommates had to have been among the villagers who danced alongside Ellie, but Leland had been so fixated on his niece that he hadn't noticed the other two. The friends exchanged hugs before they ventured to their waiting families.

"Bravo," Nettie said as she planted a kiss on Ellie's cheek. She stepped back and stared at her granddaughter, pressed her hands together, and clapped. "You were beautiful."

"Stunning," Fern said as she swatted at tears . . . again.

"I'm speechless," Percy said.

"You? The word master?" Ellie was the spitting image of her mother in that instant, her eyes brimming and her blush heightening. She displayed, all at once, pleasure, confidence, innocence, and humility.

Percy pulled her into a hug. "You must be overwhelmed. When I think about you taking dance classes, working at the diner, rehearsing, and finally performing . . . well . . . right now I'm just plain awestruck."

"We all are," Muriel said. "You were incredible."

June peered at Ellie, waiting.

"What about you? What was your favorite part?" Ellie asked.

June pivoted toward the front of the building. "The movie star stairs."

"Movie star stairs?" Ellie turned to Fern for an explanation, but it was Muriel who enlightened her.

"June fancied herself a celebrity when she walked up and down the central staircase."

"Ah, I see." Ellie pulled in her bottom lip with her teeth as she made a show of examining her baby sister. "Before we leave, will you show me how elegant you are when you walk down those steps?"

"Can I?" June asked her father.

Percy extended his hand to June. "You know, darlin', a wise father knows when he shouldn't interfere with his daughter's dreams." He gave Ellie a wink. "I reckon you can climb to the top and then tell us what the world looks like from that lofty view."

While June played the part of the starlet, Ellie tugged Leland's arm. "Where's Martin? Did he have to leave?"

Why ask him? Percy and the others stood at the bottom of the staircase, forming a June Bigler fan club. While June giggled—with a heap of encouragement from her kin—Ellie's question conjured a storm cloud that could turn the joyous occasion into a washout.

※

Ellie rode with her parents to the house on Truslow Street, but said nothing of the unanswered question about Martin. After her family left for Elizabeth, she went to bed. When morning came, Leland steeled himself for an emotional quagmire. Once again, he and Muriel were inexperienced and unprepared.

As Leland walked into the kitchen, Muriel filled a coffee mug and handed him the steaming brew. He liked his coffee strong, black, and hot. Muriel poured herself a cup, added a generous splash of cream, and waited for hers to cool.

"Are the girls up?" Leland asked.

"Becca's still in bed, but Ellie took her coffee to the front porch."

"She say anything to you?"

"Besides 'good morning'? No."

"I can't believe that boy didn't so much as come by and offer an explanation or leave a note. Something."

"I know."

"We can't let her get all het up about him. She has every right to celebrate, and I'm not going to let Martin Hastings take that away from her."

"What to you propose to do?"

"Do?" Leland replied. "Nothing. I'll just lend an ear and see if it overhears anything."

"She doesn't need both of us pestering her. I'll stay here."

Leland took a slug of coffee before he walked down the hallway. The front door hung open, inviting the chilly morning air to sneak into the entryway. Muted noise from the street, the town center, and the distant factories and railroad filtered into the house. The sound of a vehicle pulling to the curb drew Leland to the front window.

When a patrol car came into view, he backed away from the glass, out of sight but not out of hearing. He'd let Ellie's worthless skirt chaser voice his excuse, but he wasn't leaving the immediate area. If Martin needed to be ushered off the premises, Leland would oblige.

"Good morning." Martin sounded cheerful, not penitent. When Ellie didn't reply, he said, "Coffee smells good."

"It is." Ellie could have acquiesced and offered him a cup, but she didn't. Good for her.

"Hey, about last night."

"Where were you?"

"I was there."

Leland's nose twitched while he held back a snarl and more than a few biting words.

"You never took your seat."

"No, I didn't. That's why I'm here. I want to explain."

The metal legs of a chair scraped the floor. Martin's sigh was heavy and loud. From his perch inside the doorway, Leland kept his eye on the car, where Martin's partner sat in the passenger seat with the window down, his fingers tapping the doorframe.

"I was a few minutes late, but the second I walked into the auditorium, I saw you. My shift ran long at the station yesterday, so I was still in uniform. I guess that's why the usher didn't make me take my seat. He let me stand by the door for a while. He must have thought I was hunting for a criminal." When Martin sniggered, Leland wanted to cuff the copper's mouth. Not that he would have, but nothing about this was funny.

"Was I so awful that you didn't want to watch the rest?"

"You were incredible."

"Then why didn't you stay?"

"Because the longer I watched you romping on that stage, with all those men leering after you, the more it burned me up."

Leland's spine stiffened. He lowered his cup to the side table, clenched his jaw, and tried counting to ten.

"Romping? Leering?" Ellie asked. Her voice pitched higher. Good girl. "Romping? Like a two bit hussy in a burlesque show?"

"Who cares whether you call it ballet or burlesque? Either way, it riles men into a lather."

"That's just plain sick."

"You don't have to get all cranked about it," Martin said. "You wanted to know why I missed your show. I'm telling you straight. The longer I watched you parade around, the angrier it made me. I know when to walk away, which is exactly what I did. That's why I wasn't there."

"I think you and your buddy need to hit the road." Ellie had perfect control of her voice, and her directive didn't leave room for misunderstanding, but Leland didn't relax his fisted hands.

"Aw, don't be like that. Now that you're done with the show, we can go back to where we left off."

"You are so full of yourself. You insult me. You couldn't care less about what matters to me."

"I thought I mattered to you."

"Well, we were both mistaken. Go away."

Martin's partner waved at him from the patrol car. "Hastings, we have to roll."

"We'll talk about this later." Martin's footfalls sounded on the steps. "I'll be back."

"Don't bother."

"Aw, you'll come around." Martin's laugh rose into the air. "I'm worth it and you know it."

Chapter 25

"I don't know about you," Fern said as she, Nettie, and Muriel walked into the Charleston High School Auditorium, "but I'm as excited to see the American Academy Ballet recital as I was to see the Charleston Ballet's debut."

Just six weeks had passed since Ellie performed in *Capriccio Espagnol*, and tonight she would participate in two of the academy's recital numbers.

"This is an interesting venue," Muriel said as she inspected the interior of the building. Images of the high school's Mountain Lion mascot eyed every passing visitor, while vibrant shades of gold and blue blazed down the hallways, distinct contrasts from the interior trappings of the Municipal Auditorium.

"Compared to the Wirt Tiger's territory, this place is huge," Fern replied. "I'd wager that the students enrolled here outnumber the people who live in Wirt County."

High school setting aside, once they settled into their seats, Fern detected the same air of expectation that she witnessed at the ballet company's first performance. With the recital set to begin in fifteen minutes, it appeared that this was a sold out event. After the newspaper reports praised the ballet's debut, it was no wonder that people rushed to fill the few remaining empty seats.

Unlike the *Capriccio Espagnol* ballet, which had been a family affair, the Bigler and Dugan attendance for the recital was sparse. Becca had to work at the photo shop and Percy stayed in Elizabeth to attend a school function with the boys. When Percy offered to keep June during the recital, and Leland discovered he'd be the only male in attendance, he bowed out.

Fern studied the auditorium, where another daunting pose of the school's mountain lion served an unsettling reminder. As soon as Wayne started summer practices for Wirt Tiger football team hopefuls, school functions would multiply. Excited as Fern and Percy were about Wayne's gumption, his schedule would make excursions to Charleston more of a challenge than they were already. If he made the team? Well, they'd deal with the crazy schedule one game at a time.

When the spokesman stepped to a microphone and welcomed the audience to the recital, Fern skimmed through the program. This was Ellie's moment, not the time nor place to worry about timetables. Fern shoved aside the image of an overfilled calendar and searched for her daughter's name among the performers.

At the beginning of the program, Ellie was one of about twenty dancers who performed Ravel's *Pavane of the Sleeping Beauty*, the same piece she danced at Glenville College. The sight of her daughter on stage squeezed Fern's chest, the ache a muddle of pride, exhilaration, and yearning. Fern's inability to fathom what Ellie experienced as she performed left Fern stymied, if not in awe. Nettie reached over and clasped Fern's hand, as if she, too, were disoriented.

Next was a rendition of *Hungarian Dance no. 6* by Brahms, followed by *Variation* by Tchaikovsky. Ellie had mentioned earlier that Marie-Claude Van Damme, the soloist who danced to

Tchaikovsky's piece, was the elder of the Van Damme's two daughters. Following her lovely performance was the pianist, John Jud, whose fingers leapt across the black and white keys as he played works by Chopin and Debussy.

So many dancers took the stage during the performance of *The Seasons*, by Glazunov, that Fern struggled to locate Ellie. More than likely, every single academy student participated in the presentation. During the infrequent moments Ellie came into view, she was the picture of elegance, her expression one of joy.

The final selection, another of Ravel's compositions, was *Empress of the Pagoda*. A dozen dancers executed the work with poise and grace. Given the ages and expertise of the students, Mr. Van Damme had every right to boast of their accomplishments, yet the humility he wore at the close of the recital touched Fern.

❧

"You haven't said a word." Muriel glanced sideways at Fern before she lifted her teacup and took a sip.

The location of their booth at the rear of the restaurant muted the conversations of the other customers. It was near closing time, but this little outing was a rarity, a moment to savor. The journey back to Elizabeth could wait for a while.

Fern considered Ellie, who sat across the table, next to her grandmother. The girl's transformation into a professional artist and the resolve and talent needed to fulfill that goal stunned Fern. Ellie raised an eyebrow, as did Nettie.

"I think I'm overwhelmed," Fern said.

"In what way?" Ellie asked.

"I think I should know what to expect, in a small way, when I sit down in an auditorium and watch you dance. Both times, though, I've been astounded."

"That's not a bad thing. I'd worry if you were bored, or disappointed, or a dozen other things. I take *astounded* as a compliment."

"You should," Nettie said. "You, and all of the students, performed magnificently."

"Thanks, Grandma."

"Tell me," Fern said as she stirred her tea, although she'd not added anything that required mixing. "When you're waiting just out of sight, moments before you enter the stage, how does it feel? What goes through your mind?"

Ellie paused for a long while. Finally, she asked, "How much time do we have?"

"As long as it takes," Muriel replied. "If it gets too late, your mother and grandmother can spend the night."

"Well, we can't," Fern said, "but I'll sit here long enough for Ellie to tell me."

"I can only guess," Ellie said, "but I reckon that dancing, in some respects, is similar to childbearing."

Fern studied Ellie's expression to see if she was making a joke, which she wasn't. Nettie nodded, as if in agreement. And Muriel? Well, Muriel just stared at Ellie.

"Tell me how you felt when you first found out you were expecting Becca."

An easy question. How could Fern forget the moment the doctor confirmed her suspicion? "I was thrilled, excited, grateful."

"When I found out I could take dance lessons, my excitement probably rivaled yours." Ellie watched her mother. "I was almost a teenager when June came along, and I remember you didn't feel too well, at least at first."

"Well, I may have been skipping with joy and anticipation, but I was tired all the time. Regardless, when it comes to carrying babies, mothers learn to live with the transformation."

Ellie acted as if she could identify with the circumstances. Goodness, she didn't know the first of it. How could an expectant mother describe that first whisper of life, the mysterious, delicate movement inside her?

"Since my first lesson, I've suffered sore feet, achy muscles, tender toes, leg cramps, stretched ligaments, and more. We rehearse so many times, I'm surprised my legs don't run through the steps while I'm asleep." Ellie knitted her brow and regarded Muriel. "Y'all don't hear me hoofing across the floor in the middle of the night, do you?"

"I wouldn't tell, even if you did," Muriel replied.

"When the concert starts, my heart races so fast it's a wonder I don't pass out, but just before my entrance, a peacefulness falls over me. Every tiny detail comes together, and I know what I'm to do. I step onto the stage and I dance."

The similarities between childbirth and a ballet performance may have sounded like sheer nonsense to anyone sitting in the proximity of the booth. Had Leland joined them this evening, he'd have keeled over at the first mention of pregnancy. The thought drew a wry smile to Fern's lips.

"No question, the outcome is worth the sacrifice. When I held each of my babies in my arms, I counted every toe and finger and brushed my fingertip across tiny pink lips. I couldn't wait for two big eyes to open and focus on mine."

"When you have your first child," Nettie said to Ellie, "I want you to recall this conversation. I think you'll be surprised at your insights."

"Yours is a good analogy," Fern said. "I feel as if I'm wearing your *pointe* shoes right now."

When the waitress came to the table to see if anyone needed anything else, Fern caught Muriel's expression. It was the same one Becca wore when she realized the world beyond Elizabeth had much to offer and she recognized she might be missing life-changing opportunities. Muriel, though, didn't have a remedy for the missing pieces in her life.

"Mom?"

"Hmm?"

"I have one more question."

"What's that?"

"If you're wearing my *pointe* shoes, do your feet hurt?"

If only Fern could bury the ache that accompanied her laughter.

Chapter 26

It wasn't often that Leland had to work late, but after a piece of machinery broke down and slowed the manufacturing process, he had to take special care to inspect the glass that came through the line after the maintenance crew completed the repairs. The customer's contract didn't leave room to renegotiate the shipment date, so it was hitting near sunset when he pulled his car in front of the house. The official Charleston Police Department cruiser parked at the curb set his empty stomach churning.

Martin's redheaded partner slouched against the front fender, a cigarette dangling from his mouth. He turned toward Leland, and when their eyes met, he offered an apathetic shrug.

Leland took the steps to the porch two at a time. Ellie sat in a chair with her arms wrapped around her middle. Martin sat a few feet away, stretched forward with his elbows resting on his knees.

"You all right?" Leland asked.

"For now."

"Where's Muriel?"

"She's pulling laundry off the line."

Leland gave Martin a warning glare before he strode into the house. He walked down the hallway, through the kitchen, and out the back door.

"Sorry I'm late." After Leland shared a quick kiss with his wife, he pulled a sheet from under the clothespins and started folding. "How long has he been here?"

"About ten minutes. I've kept an ear out for any sign of a confrontation, but Ellie's determined to make him understand he has no reason to be here."

"It riles me, him pestering her. Something's wrong with that boy, and I don't just mean his brushes with alcohol and violence." Leland dropped the haphazardly folded sheet into the basket and planted his hands at his waist. "Sounds stupid of me to have said that. Knowing what I do, how can I leave Ellie alone with him?"

"Leland," Muriel said as she grabbed his arm, "I don't disagree, but watch how you handle him."

"I don't aim to make things worse, but he needs to leave."

Leland walked alongside the house and recognized the sound of an argument along the way, but he was unable to decipher the words. When he reached the steps and Ellie's red-rimmed eyes fell on him, Muriel's warning vanished faster than a busted ax-head could fly off the handle.

"Martin, it's time for you to get back to work."

"We're not finished."

"Yes, you are." Leland pushed out his chest, stood taller.

"This is none of your business."

"She's my kin, so it's all my business." Leland clenched his teeth. What an arrogant runt.

Martin pulled himself out of his seat, ran his tongue along the inside of his mouth, and made a show of resting his hand above his firearm.

Leland narrowed his eyes. "You fixing to use that thing or are you just inflating your swagger?"

"Are you threatening me?"

"Am *I* threatening *you*?" Leland's dry laugh brushed color onto Martin's cheeks and neck.

Ellie's blue eyes widened when Martin's fingers twitched.

"Go on inside," Leland said. Once the door closed behind Ellie, he glared hard enough to burn holes in Martin's eyes. "Get out of here."

"Or what? You gonna call the cops?" Martin raised his voice as he jutted out his chin.

"You need help there, partner?" the redhead asked as he pushed off from the fender.

"We're just fine," Martin called back, loud enough for everyone in the vicinity to hear.

"If you think you can hide behind your badge, you're mistaken," Leland said. "I have no qualms about going to the police station to have a chat with your superiors."

Martin crossed his arms. "Wouldn't be hard to find a reason to take you in, save you some gasoline."

"So you say. Now let me have my say, Officer Hastings. Ellie has made it clear. She doesn't want your company. You've bothered her at the diner more than once, and you keep showing your face here at the house. When you don't come to the door, you drive around the block, over and over again. All of those things, when you put them together, describe harassment and intimidation. If you don't want me to file a complaint, you need to leave right this minute."

"Dwight," Martin hollered. "I need you to come here."

Martin's partner acted none too pleased to have Martin order him to the porch.

Betty Hastings slammed open her front door, stumbled down the steps, and staggered toward the side of her yard. "How many times do I have to tell y'all to shut up?" She slurred her words while she tried to fix her glassy eyes on the altercation that interrupted her date with the drink. She aimed her Roy Rogers collector's item at the noisemakers, her hand wavering all over the place. "I demand silence," she shrieked. *Pop, pop, pop.*

Dwight stood in the space between the gun-toting drunk and the arguing men. "What's it gonna be, partner? If I was you, I'd escort the auntie back into her house, make my peace with letting the ballerina go, and get back to work." He stood tall despite the hateful stare Martin leveled at him. Good to know that one of the two was interested in keeping his job.

Martin crossed the yard, clamped his hand around Betty's upper arm, and spit out his words. "Get back inside." He escorted his insufferable kin to her house, and when he opened the door to help her in, he grabbed her cap gun. "Give me that thing."

When Dwight's gaze landed on Leland, he shook his head and frowned. If Leland heard him right, he mumbled, "Enough of this."

Martin spun the Roy Rogers toy with the confidence of a hired gunslinger and slipped it into his waistband. He crossed the yard and walked toward the car. Before ducking inside, he yelled, "Tell Ellie I'll keep an eye on the neighborhood. See you soon."

※

Fern held the telephone receiver to her ear, listening to Leland's latest update on Martin Hastings. She twirled the coiled wire around her finger as she paced.

"No," Leland said, "he hasn't gone to the diner, and Ellie hasn't seen him anywhere near the ballet school."

"But..."

"Well, she's pretty sure he's still watching her. Following

her."

"You ought to go to the police."

"And tell them what? I can't just walk into the precinct and accuse one of their own of menacing Ellie. Since I warned him away, none of us has seen him."

"But Ellie senses he's still around."

"She has good reason."

Fern jerked to a halt. This was too much and it had gone on too long. "What reasons?"

"Things left on the front porch."

"What kind of things?"

"One time it was a rose."

"And the other times?"

"Once it was a joker from a deck of playing cards. He'd colored the hair red and the eyes green, so I reckon he left that for me. The last time it was a cutout heart, like a Valentine, but instead of saying *Be Mine*, it said *You're Mine*."

"Do you still have those?"

"I sure do."

"You either promise to take those to the police today, or I'll be there first thing in the morning to do it myself. Do you hear me?"

A prolonged silence sat between them. "I worry that he'll up his game if we provoke him."

"And I worry that we're giving him the opportunity to do harm." Didn't Leland understand? While he blathered on, Fern let her anxiety run its course. Which of the two of them was right?

"Talk to Percy. Whatever the two of you decide, I'll do. Just realize that when you call a man's character into question to those who have authority over him, you jeopardize his livelihood. If he's out of a job, he'll have more time to make the situation worse."

"Take care of her, Leland."

"I'm doing my best, Sis."

"I know. I'm just scared."

"I didn't mean to upset you. It was Becca who asked me to call you in the first place. Hold on while I put her on the line."

"Mom?"

"Hey, girl. How are you?"

"I'm great."

"No troubling news?"

"No. Just the opposite. You must have told Dad my idea about becoming a photographer for the newspaper."

"I mentioned it to him. Why?"

"Because a customer came into Hawk's Photo Supply today and asked for me by name."

"Who?"

"His name is Larry Tanner. He's a photographer for the *Charleston Gazette*. Do you know him?"

"I don't recall the name."

"He told me that when Dad first wrote his editorials about the Civilian Conservation Corps, he went to a few of the nearby camps and took photos to go along with Dad's commentaries. He said he got to know Dad pretty well, although they mostly talked to each other by phone."

"What did he want?"

"He offered to let me tag along while he worked."

"What about your own job?"

"I'd just go on one of my days off." Anticipation tinged Becca's voice. "He said he'd treat me like an apprentice, although he couldn't pay me, but he said he'd bring an extra camera and film so I could take pictures right along with him."

"That's awfully generous."

"I know. And, there's more. He said if I wanted to learn, he'd teach me how to develop the film. They have a dark room at the newspaper office."

"It sounds like going to school, without the tuition."

"I know. I am so excited."

"What kind of things does he photograph?"

"Everything, I guess. The news."

"Does that mean you'll take pictures of crime scenes or accidents?" More than anything, Fern wanted to hop into her car, fetch both girls, and bring them home to the uncomplicated existence she'd savored her entire life. Couldn't they find their callings here? Fern stared at the Kit Cat clock that hung on the wall, its black and white tail swishing back and forth. The answer was simple. Times change. That, and the girls craved for more than what they could find down home.

"Crime scenes? Oh, I hope not."

"Maybe you'd better ask for particulars before you accept his offer."

"Can't you just ask Dad if he thinks it will be all right? I mean, it has to be. Otherwise, he wouldn't have asked Mr. Tanner to visit me at work."

"I reckon that's true."

"I have the day off tomorrow, and I really, really want to go along. What do you think?"

"You won't know if this is what you want to do unless you see what it's all about. Promise me you won't put yourself in any danger."

"I'll watch my step."

"If you run into any trouble, you call home."

"I will."

"Oh, and one more thing."

"What?"

"If you work with Mr. Tanner past dark, you either have him

drive you home or call your uncle to pick you up. I don't want either you or Ellie out by yourself, and you know why."

"Yeah, I do. We're watching out for her, so don't worry."

Don't worry? The child was telling the mother to set aside the instinct that helped the child reach adulthood. If not for Fern's nerves being as taut as a piano wire, she might have laughed. Instead, after they ended their call, she sat at the table, stretched her arms across the surface, and buried her face in the crook of her elbow.

When the back door slammed open and shut, and footfalls belonging to adolescent boys jostled the floorboards, Fern furrowed her brow. June's lighter gait sounded out behind them. Now what?

"Mom?" The quavering voice belonged to Roy.

"What?" Her garbled reply sounded puny, lackluster, and downright tired.

"Uh, I think Wayne needs stitches."

Fern wrestled her eyes open, took in the splotches of blood on Wayne's boot, and examined the slashed skin above his knee. It wasn't an emergency, but neither was it pretty. A butterfly bandage would probably work just fine.

"Roy, go get the first aid kit out of the bathroom."

"June, fetch a washcloth, but not one of my good ones."

"Wayne, you need to keep your mind off your injury, so start counting the reasons I'm the best mother in all of Wirt County."

"Huh?"

"I'll help you get started. Number one. She doesn't pass out at the sight of blood." Fern went to the sink, washed her hands, and filled a pan with warm water. "Your turn. What's the number two reason?"

"Huh?"

Chapter 27

Muriel placed her home-baked pie on the table and turned it around so everyone could see her pie crust artwork. She pressed her palms together. "Well?"

Leland took a sip of coffee, a cowardly delay. Maybe Becca or Ellie would ask the obvious.

Muriel's cheeks, flush with pleasure, radiated the same hot pink hue as the cherry juice that stained her fingertips.

"Um, what's the cutout supposed to be? Angel wings?" Ellie squinted at the peculiar design. Normally, Muriel finished her cherry pies by weaving a lattice top. When she baked apple pies, she carved an apple shape, complete with two leaves adorning the top of the fruit. But this?

"Angel wings? No. Look again." Muriel turned the bakeware so Ellie could get a straight-on view.

Ellie's second guess was a brilliant, "Um."

"Becca?"

Leland crossed his fingers. If Becca didn't figure it out, he was next in line.

"A butterfly?"

Muriel snorted. "Am I that bad an artist?"

Surely, she didn't expect Leland to answer. He'd toss out a few random words, see if she'd reward him with a hint or two. No, she'd already hinted when she announced that this was a celebratory pie. A wide grin stretched across his face.

"I know. Mrs. Methuselah retired. That there mystery shape? Why, it's an open book, and it means you got a job at the library. Whoo-ee! Am I right?"

"Yes, it's a book. No, Mrs. M didn't retire, as far as I know, so the county didn't offer me a job."

"Then what?"

"You're sharing dessert with the new State Law Library librarian. I start a week from this coming Monday."

"Well, whoo-ee anyway. I knew it would happen sooner or later." Leland jostled the table when he got up to give Muriel a hug, sloshing coffee all over the place.

The girls offered their congratulations while Ellie pushed linens out of the way and Becca scrambled to grab a rag.

"Leave it be," Muriel said. "I'll just buy a new tablecloth when I enjoy my last spending spree at the Diamond."

"Oh," Ellie said, her jubilation falling down a department store level or two. "No more employee discounts."

"No more shopping sprees?" Leland didn't have a quarrel with that.

"Oh, we'll still splurge," Muriel replied. "It'll just cost more."

Leland reached for his wallet, a spontaneous, defensive movement.

Muriel caught him, gave him a silent scolding, and sighed. "Mr. Dugan, let go of your hard-earned cash long enough to eat your pie."

"I may have lost my appetite."

Muriel clicked her tongue against her cheek and said, "I'll tell you about my salary later. It'll more than replace my Diamond discount." She cut a huge slice of pie and pushed it toward Leland. "Eat up."

"How'd you hear about the job at the law library?" Ellie asked.

"You'll laugh. I took a walk on my lunch break last week and was making a lap around the Capitol Building. When a young woman almost knocked me down, she apologized, said she was new to Charleston, and asked if I could give her directions to the law library. When she showed me the address she had scribbled on a piece of paper, all I had to do was turn around and direct her to the Capitol Building."

"It's right there?" Becca asked.

"It's been right under my nose all this time. I took the opportunity to escort the lost legal secretary into the building, and I followed her all the way to the east wing. While I was there, I had a little chat with the woman at the front desk. I'm embarrassed to tell you that the State Department of Archives and History has a library there too. I wish I'd known about these earlier."

"A law library, though. Won't you be bored? I mean, how much work could they have for you to do?" Leland asked.

"Oh, I think I'll be plenty busy. They have near a hundred thousand works on file. Their holdings include textbooks on every legal topic imaginable, and a host of State reports and court decisions made, not just in West Virginia, but in the US, Canada, and England. I'm trying not to let it intimidate me."

"I can't believe they just happened to have an opening," Ellie said.

"I'd call it perfect timing," Becca said.

"I'd rather call it providential." Muriel asked at Leland, "What would you call it?"

"A gift."

"Like Mr. Tanner becoming my photography. mentor?" Becca asked.

"Just like that," Leland replied. "Speaking of which, where did the paper send you today?"

"The *Gazette* sent Mr. Tanner to take pictures for a story about the modernization of the automobile."

"Ooh, I'd like to have tagged along. Where'd you go?"

"Well, let's see. First stop was a General Motors dealership where we took pictures of the family work wagon. I think that's what Mom and Dad need to buy. It's one of the few cars with enough room for the whole family without having to tie one of us to the roof."

"I'll bet they're pricey," Leland said.

"Everything in the showroom was pricey. Fancy. Wide whitewall tires. Two-toned paint. Lots of chrome. Fancy schmancy."

"Where else did you go?"

"Ford was next. I think you would have liked their newest line of trucks."

"I could see myself in one of those. What do you think, Muriel? It's just the two of us, you know."

"What do I think? Just the two of us? Leland, how many people are sitting around this table right now?"

"Well, you know what I mean. No offense taken, right girls?"

Becca and Ellie both rolled their eyes, which was pretty cute.

"So, no truck for this hardworking laborer. What else?"

"I thought I'd found the lap of luxury when I sat in one of the new Buicks."

"You got to sit in them?"

"Well, how else could I take a picture of the interior?"

"Did you get to drive one?"

"No."

"Peek under the hood?"

"No. I thought their hardtops were handsome. My favorite was a yellow one with a black top and red trim."

Muriel wrinkled her nose. "Sounds gaudy."

"It was classy."

Leland lounged in his chair, posing like a proud-as-a-peacock uncle while he listened to his niece carry on about automobiles. Percy would have gotten a kick out of this conversation, for sure.

"The last place we stopped was an Oldsmobile showroom. Uncle Leland, I could hear your, 'Whoo-ee,' soon as I stepped inside. If I thought the Buick was plush, the *Ninety-Eight* flabbergasted me. They called the design *Starfire Styling*, which was pretty accurate. That vehicle was out of this world."

"Go anywhere else?"

"We did, but it wasn't related to cars. I don't think you want to hear about it."

"Why not?" Muriel asked.

"It was pretty awful."

"Your mother worried about Mr. Tanner's work exposing you to ugly news," Leland said.

"I know. He wouldn't have taken me with him if he'd had time to drop me off, but when he checked in with his office after lunch, and his boss found out we weren't far from an accident scene, he told Mr. Tanner to get right over there."

"What happened?" Ellie asked.

"A little girl got hit by a truck."

"Where?" Muriel asked.

"On Morris Street, less than a block from the railroad tracks."

Leland winced. "The New York Central tracks?"

"Yes."

"Rough part of town," Leland replied.

"It's not far from here, but it might as well be a different universe. I didn't venture far from Mr. Tanner."

"Did . . . did the little girl survive?" Ellie asked.

Becca shook her head. "It sounds as if its commonplace over there. Parked cars line both sides of the street, making it impossible for a driver to see a child who's trying to cross the road. Traffic is heavy with trucks moving goods to and from the railroad terminal. According to the people Mr. Tanner talked to, the neighborhood children know better than to step into the street."

"Except for the one who was hit."

"She was different."

"Different?" Muriel asked.

"Deaf. She misunderstood her playmate's signal. Instead of waiting, she thought it was time to run. And, so she did."

"That's awful." Ellie pressed her shoulders back and slumped in her seat. "The paper didn't want a photo of the body, did they?"

"No," Becca replied. "Mr. Tanner went to take pictures of the witnesses and the victim's family. Not that another story about one more accident will prevent the next one."

"Did you take pictures?" Leland asked.

"I stayed back a ways, taking a few shots of the crowds milling around, but the strangest thing happened. Whatever they do at the rail yard, whether they're switching trains from one track to another or joining freight cars together, I couldn't tell you. But with all that metal slamming against metal, I must have flinched a dozen times. Probably looked like a dame with a bad case of hiccups. After one particularly loud crash, someone behind me giggled. When I turned around, three little children were staring at me. The girls were twins, plain as day. A boy, probably their little brother, held tight to his sister's sleeve, scared half to death."

"Because of the accident?"

"He seemed nervous about being so close to a white woman. Let me tell you, those children were beautiful. The girls had eyes as dark as midnight, and their lashes were darker still. And their skin? It was the color of Uncle Leland's strongest cup of coffee. They were barefoot and their clothes worn thin, like most of the children in the area, but their innocent curiosity captivated me. I'll have to show you the pictures after they're developed."

"You took their pictures while you were supposed to be taking news photographs?" Leland asked.

"Mr. Tanner didn't set any rules. He said I should experiment. Today's experiment was in portraiture." When Leland scowled at her, Becca asked, "Would you rather I had taken photographs of a corpse?"

"Of course not."

"Then why are you upset?"

"I'm just wondering how you'll explain the particulars surrounding your apprenticeship to your folks."

"Well, Uncle, I don't aim to tell them everything."

Chapter 28

Fern shoved another box onto the shelf in the back room and dusted off her knees. Think. It had only been three months since she moved the general store's school supply inventory to make room for seasonal goods. During the summer, men expected a larger inventory of fishing line, nets, and lures, and the women had more need for canning jars than Big Chief writing tablets, pencils, rulers, and ink pens, so she'd put the school supplies in a box. Somewhere in the storeroom.

"Hello?"

Had she been so engrossed in her search that she hadn't heard the bell jingle?

"Be right with you," she called out.

"Mom?" Becca stood in the doorway, clutching her pocketbook in one hand and hugging a large envelope to her bosom.

"You're early," Fern said as she gave Becca a hug.

"No, I'm not." Becca peered at Fern's face, lifted a finger, and daubed at Fern's cheek. "What are you doing?"

"Searching for the school supplies. I swear I put them right over there, but I can't find them."

"You look frazzled. Are you all right?"

"That's a fair question. Nettie and I got it into our heads that we could keep the same size garden this year, but we've worked ourselves silly all summer, and the canning season's barreling down on us."

Fern wouldn't blame her fatigue on age, although it had a bearing on both of them. Nettie was a workhorse, for sure, but she wasn't twenty any longer. Neither was Fern.

"Can't you get the boys to help?"

"Oh, we could, but Roy and Wayne lack the determination and efficiency we womenfolk have mastered. Besides, Wayne's preoccupied with football practice."

"Let me put these on the counter and I'll give you a hand."

"Need something?" Ron appeared behind Becca, his lanky form bowing forward so far that his face stretched over top of Becca.

"I can't find the school supplies," Fern replied.

"I set them out this morning, at the end of the center aisle. Isn't that where you wanted them?"

"Yes, but I didn't expect you to do that. I was just talking to myself. More or less."

"You tell me what you need, and I get it done."

"So, I see. Thank you."

Becca's hazel eyes honed in on Fern's face again. Becca angled her head toward Ron, who still towered over her.

"Oh. Ron, I don't think you've met Becca. Becca, this is Ron O'Dell."

"I'm the person who took your job." Ron took a step backwards and arched his eyebrows as Becca turned around, but a dimple betrayed his levity. "You're not here to kick me out the front door are you?"

"Nope. I'm just visiting."

"Are you the photographer?"

Becca's blush was uncharacteristic, but maybe those baby blue eyes unsettled her as much as they had Ellie the first time she met the new clerk. Or, perhaps the photographer title embarrassed her.

"I'd like to be. Maybe one day."

Ron gestured to the envelope. "Are those your pictures?"

"They are." Becca turned back to Fern. "This is the first batch I developed myself." Her face colored again when she said, "Well, with Mr. Tanner's help, anyway."

"Will you show them to me?" Ron's eyes darted from one female to the other. "I mean, if you have time and you don't mind, I'd like to see some pictures of Charleston. I haven't been there in a long while."

Fern spun her finger in a circle and pointed toward the shop. "Let's go spread them on the counter."

Becca placed about two dozen photographs across the surface, their glossy finish catching the overhead lights. Fern and Ron started at either end of the array, gawking at the scenes and portraits, and sidestepping each other when they met in the middle. Becca stood behind the counter, hands clasped at her waist. Furrows marked her brow while she waited.

"These are really good," Ron said. "You have a way of catching light and angles. See, the way you captured this building and this street?"

"Um."

"Well, it makes my eyes wander from one corner of the photograph to the opposite side. That's what makes this a fine piece of art."

"How do you know that?" Becca asked.

"Friend of mine, his father was a pretty good artist. He'd lug his easel outside and paint a landscape while his son and I would catch tadpoles or terrorize frogs. When we'd get worn out, I'd watch him paint. He liked to talk—his wife didn't give him space for two words back at their house—and he had a smooth, deep voice that always drew me to him. When he gabbed about color and perspective and such, I listened."

"Do you paint?" Becca asked.

"I'm too fidgety for that sort of thing. I'd rather be outdoors chasing after varmints or stomping my foot while I slide my bow across my fiddle."

"You like music?"

Becca and Ron were so engrossed with one another that Fern may as well have fallen through the cracks in the floor.

"I sure do."

Fern lifted a photograph of three young children. Ron could say what he liked about the street scene, but . . . "Tell me about this one."

"Aren't they beautiful?" Becca asked.

"The way they're watching the camera? I don't know how to describe their eyes. This is captivating," Fern said. "Did they print this in the paper?"

"Oh, no. No, no, no. The *Gazette* hasn't printed any of my photos. I'm an unofficial apprentice."

"Well, if I opened the paper and saw this, I'd read the article for sure, especially after all the news about the unrest down South. It disturbs me when I hear about senseless murders and bus boycotts. This picture, well, it's a reminder that we're all precious, no matter our roots."

"Thanks, Mom."

When Fern picked up another photo, she choked. She had to cough a few times to clear her windpipe. "Is that who I think it is?"

"I meant to take that out."

Ron leaned over so he could see. "Who is he?"

"Martin Hastings," Fern replied. "Where were you when you ran into him? He wasn't at the house, was he?"

"No, this was near a rockslide. When Mr. Tanner and I arrived to take photos, Martin and his partner were directing traffic."

"Did Martin see you?"

"Oh, he sure did."

"What does that mean?"

"He tried to wave me over to him, but when I wouldn't oblige, he left Dwight—that's his partner's name—to come talk to me."

"What did he want?"

"To make sure I knew he was still keeping an eye on Ellie."

"What!"

"I know. He's been out of sight for several months, but Ellie's right to be vigilant."

"Tell me what he said."

"First, he asked if Ellie enjoyed visiting Marshall University."

"He knew she performed in Huntington last week?"

Becca bit her bottom lip. "Somehow he knew the dance academy was performing there."

"How?"

"Maybe he knows one of the other dancers. Maybe he sends Dwight or another policeman to the studio to poke around and ask questions. It's not as if their campus touring schedule is a secret."

"For Ellie's sake, it ought to be." Fern walked behind the counter and sat on a stool. "I thought Martin Hastings was history. Gone."

"Are you going to tell Dad? He'll have a fit."

"He needs to know." Fern closed her eyes, but an image of

Martin prowling around, shadowing Ellie, nearly buried her.

"What did Ellie say when you showed this to her?"

"She hasn't seen it yet, but you have to trust her. She's careful not to walk home alone, to go to and from the diner alone. It's been a while since he's shown his face, but Ellie hasn't let down her guard. Uncle Leland hasn't either. I think we all know that Martin's not quite right."

"He's obsessed," Fern said.

Ron hadn't said a word, but his expression suggested that his mind was spinning. "Back when I was a boy, the neighbor brought a stray dog home, a dark red Irish setter. Seemed like an all right animal whose owner had taken good care of him. Dog behaved as long as the father was around, but it used to torment his daughter. Once, the daughter was playing on an old tire swing, and her daddy called her to come into the house. Every time the girl went to get off the swing, that dog bared his teeth and growled at her. Her daddy got pretty mad when she wouldn't come in, but he finally caught on to what the dog was doing."

"Sounds like Martin," Fern said. "Plays the part of a decent, law-upholding policeman, but he has a shady side."

"That neighbor told the dog to get into the barn, which he did, because he obeyed the man. He carried his daughter into the house, grabbed his shotgun, and did away with the dog."

Becca, sensitive girl that she was, recoiled. "Couldn't he have found another home for the dog?"

"I reckon that the previous owner didn't have the gumption to destroy the dog, so he let him loose, gave him another chance. What he did was give the dog another opportunity to maim a child, or worse."

"Well, we can't exactly order Martin to the barn," Fern said. "I'm hoping you're telling us this story because you have a suggestion."

"No, ma'am. I don't, but I'll give it more thought. I mentioned the incident with the setter because, when Martin finally accepts Ellie's rejection, it's not as if he'll lose his bark and his bite. He'll go after another woman he thinks he can manipulate. You ought to be able to put a stop to it, although his being a cop makes it harder."

"Sure does," Fern said.

"Say, iffen you don't mind me changing the subject," Ron said to Becca, "would you like to hear some genuine hillbilly music tonight?"

"Me?"

"You said you like music. Just happens that I'm playing my fiddle at the Summer Swing Festival. Wanna go?"

"Tonight?"

"We start playing at seven o'clock."

"Mom, do you mind if I stay over, assuming Uncle Leland doesn't care if I keep his car overnight?"

"You don't have to ask. We'll always have a place for you."

"Well then, excuse me while I make a phone call."

Chapter 29

Leland bolted upright, the thumping on the front door jarring him awake with the same force as a stick of TNT—not that he was back in Hawthorne, Nevada, laying dynamite for the canyon road—but the incessant pounding kindled hair-raising memories.

"What in the world?" Muriel asked.

"Stay here."

Leland climbed out of bed and hopped on one foot while he pulled on his trousers. He scrambled to the landing where he bumped into Ellie and Becca.

"What's going on?" Becca asked.

"Stay here."

Leland turned on the porch light and yanked the door open. Betty Hastings stood beneath the ceiling light, dripping wet. She looked like she'd waddled in a pigsty.

"Get over here. Hurry up." Betty turned around and tottered back toward her house.

Leland followed, barefoot, stumbling on loose gravel and stubbing his toe on the neighbor's uneven walkway.

She led him to the side of the house and stopped in front of the water spigot. "Turn that thing off," she hollered.

How many bottles of booze had she emptied tonight? The faucet wasn't running, wasn't dripping. Although . . . the ground beneath the spigot appeared to be the source of Betty's mud bath.

"It's already off," Leland said.

"No, it's not. I've turned the handle hard enough to break it, but the water's still pouring."

Leland scanned the side of the house. Aside from the dirt-caked neighbor, nothing appeared to be out of order. "Where?"

"The bathroom." Betty stared at Leland as he if were an imbecile. She ought to have looked in the mirror.

"You have water leaking in the bathroom?"

Betty gaped, tossed another you're-so-stupid glare at him, and said, "That's what I'm telling you."

"Why are you out here?"

"To turn off the water."

"The main?"

"Yes, the main. Can you help or do I need to call the water company?"

"Let's go inside and check the bathroom."

"Fine."

When Leland and Betty traipsed back to the front of the house, Muriel, Ellie, and Becca were standing on the front porch—the Dugan porch, not the crazy neighbor's porch—listening in to Betty's inane chatter.

"Y'all can get on back to bed. I might be a while."

Given the disorderly and unkempt exterior, Leland didn't have any preconceived notions of cleanliness or neatness, but he was ill prepared for the sight of Betty's domicile. The stale air was a suffocating blend of cigarette smoke, garbage, mildew, and alcohol. He choked down the protective layer of phlegm that rose in his throat, bypassed furniture draped in piles of clothing—none of which smelled laundry fresh—and sidestepped mounds of who-knew-what that littered the floor.

He heard the hiss of water spraying at the same time his bare feet encountered wet carpet. The hallway was soaked, but the floor in the bathroom was under water. Leland reached beneath the sink and turned the shutoff valve. Betty didn't have a broken pipe. A loose fitting caused the mess. All she needed was a dab of solder—although a bulldozer might be a better option if one considered the overall condition of her abode.

Betty stood in the doorway, her arms crossed and her bleary eyes weaving over Leland's apparent heroics.

"How long has this been running?" Leland asked.

"I heard an odd sound around dinnertime. Thought it was outside."

Leland's shoulders drooped. It was well after midnight. "I think we ought to check the basement after we mop this up."

"Why? The leak's right there."

"Yes, ma'am, but all this water's got to go somewhere, and most often, it takes after gravity."

She didn't understand, and Leland didn't care to explain. Armed with a bucket, a mop, and a couple of towels, he sopped up the water in the bathroom. After Betty put on dry clothes, she made a feeble attempt to towel-dry the hallway carpet.

"Don't turn that handle until you get a plumber to come out and put solder on the pipe. All right?"

"Can't you do that?"

Could he? Sure, if he bought flux, solder, and a propane torch, and if he had the motivation to do so. His own *heaping kindness* proclamation was about as welcome as Betty's midnight emergency, but there it was, staring him in the face. Or, rather, there *she* was, staring at him. "I'll buy what I need tomorrow."

Leland took the damp towels from Betty. He ought to pull the carpet up, get air under it, but that would make him responsible for putting it back down when it dried. If he had his druthers, he would never walk through Betty's front door again, except to apply a ring of solder around a leaky pipe.

"Let's go downstairs."

The trip to the cellar led Leland through the kitchen, and after he made a mental note to buy rattraps for the exterior of his own house, he went downstairs.

"Why don't you go press more water out of the carpet while I mop the floor?" Leland asked. After he watched Betty go upstairs, he assessed the basement. It was probably the cleanest place in the house. A clothesline ran from one side of the room to the other, and a short rack of laundered clothes hung from wire hangers. How did Betty Hastings manage to put herself in order every morning, walk herself out the door, and hold down a job? How did she function?

By the time Leland turned out the basement light, the clock on the kitchen wall read half-past two. He followed the sound of Betty's snoring to the living room. The liquor bottle hadn't been on the end table when he'd come inside, so most likely she hadn't fallen asleep, she'd passed out. Without a sensible reason to roust the woman, Leland crept out the front door and walked back to his little slice of paradise where a long, hot shower might erase his skin-crawling introduction to Betty's housekeeping.

※

The sweet scent of burning wood filled the living room. When a spot of sap popped and sent sparks up the chimney, Muriel peered over the rims of her reading glasses, studying Becca. "You've been awfully quiet the past couple of days."

Leland lowered the newspaper and watched Becca while she gathered an answer. She wasn't one for idle conversation or empty replies, and Muriel's simple question provoked a lengthy silence.

"Did Mr. Tanner take you on another tough photography assignment?"

"No. When we went out the other day, I enjoyed our first stop. Since the election is just around the corner, the paper sent Mr. Tanner to the Daniel Boone Hotel to take pictures. Did you know that West Virginia legislators used to hold their meetings at the hotel, making it an unofficial location for the state government?"

"No, I didn't," Leland replied.

"Over the years, a heap of politicians, high society folks, and celebrities have stayed there, including President Eisenhower. Since he's running for re-election, Mr. Tanner's boss thought we ought to remind folks that Charleston has hosted important dignitaries. It's a pretty impressive building, with a gorgeous lobby and mezzanine, and enormous banquet rooms. Every detail is as luxurious as the interior of the Capitol Building. You should have seen the dining area."

"Maybe we should have lunch there," Muriel said.

Better to steer this conversation elsewhere. "Who else has stayed there?" Leland asked.

"President Hoover, President Truman, Eleanor Roosevelt, and Gene Autry, for starters."

"Ooh, Gene Autry. Now, his television show is one I don't want to miss. If you'd like, I can sing a verse or two of "Back in the Saddle Again." Just wait a minute while I fetch my guitar."

"Leland?" Something in Muriel's expression put his rear end back into his chair.

"Yes'm?"

"We were talking about Becca and the *Gazette*."

"Right." Leland reigned in his rambling concentration and

guided it back to his niece, although now that the Autry tune was rolling around in his brain, it took a ton of effort to keep his humming to himself.

"What happened after the hotel visit?" Muriel asked.

"We went back to the newspaper and started to develop our film, but just as we got started his boss asked him to run out to one of the chemical plants in South Charleston. Someone called in a report of a chlorine leak."

"You didn't go, did you?" Leland didn't mean to sound alarmed, but the paper took a risk in sending any of their employees to an accident like that. Becca had no business putting herself in harm's way. She was an unpaid tag-along, a mentor's eager pupil.

"Of course not," Becca replied.

"I don't recall hearing anything about a chemical spill," Muriel said.

"One of the plant's employees overreacted. It wasn't serious enough to make the news."

"So, what's bothering you?" Muriel, who'd taken to reading legal decisions instead of fiction and nonfiction books, set aside her current material and took off her reading glasses.

"I developed photos while he was gone. My roll of film had mostly portraits." Becca's shoulder inched up, as if an apology were in order. "I see more than a face when I press the button that opens the shutter. The lines and wrinkles tell a lot about a person. Laugh lines don't leave the same marks as worry lines, and the crinkles around the eyes and mouth of someone who wears a perennial smile are far different from the deep crevices that frame a smoker's mouth. And, then there's the eyes themselves. They can light up with happiness or depict something dark and brooding."

"You sound, though, as if capturing those features is a bad

thing," Muriel said.

"It's not that. It bothers me when I compare my photographs to the ones Mr. Tanner takes. He does the news. His film has smoke billowing out of burning buildings, smashed cars, and storefronts with broken glass where robbers crept inside during the night. I love photography. Don't get me wrong. But it can depict the good and the bad. Ugly things make their way to the printed page far more often than anything positive or uplifting does. I'm just the apprentice, but I think people are more interested in bad news than good."

"Oh, I don't know if that's the case," Leland said as he considered the voluminous small print that filled the very pages he held in his hands. "Maybe, because we're more concerned about the bad, we feel the need to stay informed." Was that the truth? Is that what drew him to the newspaper?

"Is it normal for a city the size of Charleston to have so much bad news? Was I blind to the constant suffering before I moved here?"

"People have their share of hardships in Elizabeth," Muriel replied. "Here, though, with so many people, it's multiplied."

"Which makes it an everyday occurrence. It's just so demoralizing. Every time I help develop Mr. Tanner's film, the weight gets heavier and I can't shake it off."

"Do you think you need to take a break? Maybe you could spend more time learning how to use the different brands of equipment they sell at Hawk's." Muriel gathered her papers, a sure sign that she'd made her suggestion and it was up to Becca to come to her own conclusion. Not that her method had always worked so well with her husband, but at least Leland recognized the approach.

"Maybe," Becca replied.

Leland bit his tongue, uncertain whether his insight might

earn him an understanding nod or a silent reprimand. While he studied Becca's downcast spirit, the words broke loose.

"Nothing wrong with going back home, iffen that's where you belong."

A rush of air blew into the room when the front door flew open. It slammed shut with enough force to send a tremor across the floor. Leland leapt to his feet. Ellie stood with her back braced against the door, panting, her eyes wide with fright.

"What's wrong?"

She answered between gasps. "I heard someone behind me."

Leland grabbed Ellie by her elbows and led her into the parlor. "Sit tight. Don't come outside."

He grabbed the flashlight he kept near the door and clambered down the steps, swinging the beam along the sidewalk and the street, behind bushes, and around the sides of the house. Save for a startled cat, the area was quiet. A second sweep around the house and into the corners of the yard failed to expose anything amiss.

When he walked inside, Becca and Muriel were hovering over Ellie. Color had returned to her face, but she was still shivering. Leland willed his throbbing chest to relax, to no avail. Filling his lungs to their potential wasn't in the offing either, but he wanted to calm everyone, not stir 'em up.

"I didn't see anything, but I want you to explain why you didn't call me to give you a ride home from work." He didn't mean to lecture, but how could Ellie ignore Martin's behavior?

"Norma got on the bus with me, but I misunderstood her plans. She got off a few stops before I did." Ellie's shrug was more apologetic than defiant. "I'm sorry for the fuss."

"We're just happy you're safe," Muriel said. "I don't like this. The little hints, like a flower left on the porch, make my blood boil, but Martin having the audacity to follow you down a dark sidewalk is intolerable. I think we need to call the police."

Ellie threw up her hands. "Call the police? What good will it do? Nothing's changed. He's *still* the police."

Chapter 30

Fern lowered her coffee cup to the table and watched Nettie dribble a generous portion of honey into her hot tea. A slender swirl of steam rose into the air, adding to the condensation that fogged the kitchen windows. Muriel peeked into the oven before taking a seat.

Although they'd been up since dawn, their day started hours after the men had traipsed out of the house for the sake of the hunt. Thanksgiving dinner, as always, took a back seat to deer season. The men were adamant that it was their duty to answer the instinctive call despite the depletion of the herds at the turn of the century. If the state's white-tailed population, which was staging a healthy comeback, had to endure a season with hunters armed with bows, muzzleloaders, and firearms, Fern, Muriel, and Nettie could rearrange the dinner schedule to accommodate their menfolk.

"Close your eyes," Fern said. Nettie obeyed without so much as a pause, but Muriel waited for an explanation that might compel her to do likewise. Fern shut her eyes to Muriel's lack of response, and said, "What do you smell?"

"Nutmeg, cloves, and cinnamon," Nettie replied.

Fern inhaled a myriad of mouthwatering scents. Preparations of the magnitude demanded by a traditional Thanksgiving dinner were exhausting, but at the same time they induced a sense of contentment and... well... thankfulness. "Yeast."

"Onions and celery." Ah, Muriel decided to join the sightless survey.

"Baked apples." Nettie insisted on baking two apple pies, not that Roy could eat them by himself, but she believed that if he didn't like pumpkin, he still needed a sweet dessert to finish off his feast.

"Sage," Muriel said.

"Why are your eyes closed?" June crossed the room and pulled out a chair, but Fern grabbed her around the waist before she could sit.

"Come here, you." Fern lifted June to her lap. "We were testing our senses. Close your eyes, take a sniff, and tell me what you smell."

June squeezed her eyes tight, wrinkled her nose, and inhaled. "Turkey." She opened her dark brown eyes and drew them wide. "I *love* turkey."

"Me too, but it won't be ready for a while. Do you want an apple?"

"Nope. I want to wait for turkey."

"Where are your sisters?" Nettie asked.

"In the parlor."

"Are they watching the Macy's parade?"

"It's over. I want to play a game, but Ellie and Becca are whispering about boys."

"Which boys?" Fern asked.

"Becca wants to know about Martin, and Ellie wants Becca to talk about Ron."

"Ron?" Muriel asked.

"You know. The one who works in your store."

"Ah, that Ron. What are they saying?"

"Ellie wants to know if Becca likes his blue eyes. She called them *baby* blues."

"And what did Becca say?" Fern asked.

"She said his inky black hair makes his eyes light up." June studied Fern's face and pulled on her mother's earlobe. "Why do they talk like that?"

"They're just being silly girls. Tell me what Ellie said about Martin."

"She said he's not nice. But, he's a policeman. Aren't policemen supposed to be nice?"

"They are. Mostly. Once in a while, though, one of them might get confused about what's right and what's wrong."

"Like Martin? Is that why he bothers Ellie?"

"How did he bother her?" Fern asked. Last she heard, Martin hadn't made an appearance in weeks.

"He asked for her car giraffe, but I don't know what that is."

"Car giraffe. Car giraffe," Muriel repeated. "I can't decipher that one."

Neither could Fern. "Ellie, can you come here please?"

"I wasn't supposed to tell," June said as her face flushed.

"Did she ask you to keep a secret?" Fern asked.

"Uh huh."

"You need me?" Ellie stepped into the kitchen, studied the women's expressions, and let her gaze linger on June. She licked her lips and swallowed. "What?"

"What did Martin want?"

"June? What did I tell you?" Ellie sighed. "I planned to talk to y'all about it after supper."

"Tell me now."

"Mommy wants to know about the car giraffe."

"The what?"

"What you said to Becca."

Becca, who'd come to the doorway, chuckled. "Not a car giraffe. An *auto . . . graph*. Autograph."

"Ellie?" Fern didn't mean to sound anxious, but how could she not?

"Oh, boy." Ellie sat and motioned for Becca to do the same. "You know we toured several campuses in Ohio. While we were in the Columbus area, we went to Otterbein University. When we finished our performance, Martin was waiting outside the building. He had a copy of the program and asked me for my autograph."

"He followed you to Ohio?" Fern pressed her hand to her throat. "Ellie."

"One of the girls told Mr. Van Damme, and he made every one of us promise to keep an eye on each other. He couldn't do anything else, Mom. It's not as if Martin broke the law."

"Yes, he did."

"That's debatable. Can you picture us in a courtroom? She said this, he said that. It would be awful, and I don't think he'd get so much as his hand slapped."

"Why does your schedule have to be public information?"

"Because the purpose of the college visits is to promote dancing. Mr. Van Damme wants to grab as much publicity as he can." Ellie summoned a cheerful tone when she said, "He's still trying to recruit male dancers, and if he's successful, maybe one or two of them can become my official bodyguards." The *pfft* that followed was more convincing than her sentiments.

"Oh, Ellie." The emerging distaste was so off-putting that the once-savory aroma in the kitchen may as well have been soot and ashes. "This has to stop."

"May I make a suggestion?" Muriel asked.

"Please do," Fern said.

"Percy has a lot of contacts at the *Gazette*, and any number of them might have a colleague in the police department who would want to know about an officer's inappropriate behavior."

"But any complaint, or hint of a complaint, has the potential to make Martin retaliate."

"Fern, his going to Columbus was rash. How bad will you let things get before you ask for help?" Muriel turned to Ellie. "Don't you want to quit worrying over where he'll show up next?"

Ellie, in turn, bit her lip and passed the question on to her mother. Fern didn't have a solution. As much as she wanted to lock Ellie in her bedroom and forbid her to return to Charleston, it was Martin's behavior that had to change. Fern would not let him steal her daughter's dreams. But, what were they to do?

"What about his partner?" Becca asked. "Dwight."

"What about him?" Fern asked.

"That last time he and Martin had to calm down Betty Hastings, Dwight seemed pretty tired of Martin's shenanigans with Ellie. Maybe Dad, or maybe Uncle Leland, could ask Dwight to say something to their supervisor."

"That's a stretch," Fern replied. "What if Martin turns on Dwight?"

"I think Martin probably respects his partner," Muriel said. "On the other hand, he views Ellie as a piece of property."

Fern tapped her finger against June's chin. "We aren't going to talk about this again until after we've had dinner and eaten so much pie that our bellies can't hold one more bite. You hear?"

June put her finger to her lips. "Shh. It's a secret," she said as she angled toward Ellie.

"I'm not asking you to keep a secret," Fern said. "I'm asking you to talk about other things until we've had our dinner. This is a special day and a very special meal, and I want everyone to enjoy it. All right?"

"Okay."

June hopped off Fern's lap and ran back into the parlor where she entertained herself until the back door opened and the men trudged inside. She ran into the kitchen. "Did you get a deer, Daddy?"

"No, darlin', we did not. Someone must have told them we were coming. We didn't even see one."

"I didn't tell," June said. "And . . . guess what?"

"What?"

"I don't have a secret."

⁂

"You won't believe who came into Three Squares Diner this evening," Ellie said as she tugged off her gloves and hung up her coat. She stepped out of the way so Becca could add her outerwear to the tiny closet, and went into the living room where Leland was watching television.

"Who?"

"Martin Hastings."

Leland's pulse soared at the mention of the name, but before his mouth caught up with his temper, Becca stepped into the room and said, "With a date. I saw them. When I went to the diner to meet Ellie so we could ride the bus together, they walked right by me."

Leland turned off the television while Ellie and Becca sat next to each other on the sofa. They were dissimilar in appearance and personality, but they shared the same good roots. They both had good sense, admirable ideals, and tender hearts. Martin Hastings didn't merit the time of day from either of them.

"Tell him what you told me," Becca said to Ellie.

"They came in about an hour before closing, ordered a couple of burgers, played a few songs on the jukebox."

"Do you think it was all for show?" Leland asked.

"Not on her part. The girl was pretty and she hung on to his every word. His smooth talking left her mesmerized, which is just what he wanted. He ate it up."

"His timing is suspect," Leland said.

"I thought the same thing."

"I'd wager that he got a lecture. Your dad intended to call that reporter friend of his, the one at the *Gazette* who covers the police beat. Maybe someone delivered a message to Martin that he didn't dare ignore."

"I haven't talked to Dad, so I don't know."

"Did his date keep his interest the whole time?" Leland asked.

Ellie tipped her head from one side to the other, as if she were trying to determine which side of the scale should hold her answer. "He pretended to ignore me, but whenever I was nearby, he made sure I got an eyeful and an earful. 'Oh, let's catch a flick tomorrow night,' " Ellie mimicked. " 'Let's go cut a rug down at the dance hall.' My favorite was when he said, 'You're prettier than one of those fancy ballerinas on toe shoes.' It's a good thing I wasn't his waitress. I'd have served him a knuckle sandwich."

"Sounds as if he was putting on a show. If Martin received a warning to behave himself, he defied the order when he bothered you at work. If you ask me, Martin's playing people. Don't let down your guard."

"I won't."

"If he shows his mug again, you call me to come get you. Or Muriel. If you can't reach either of us, call a taxi."

"I will."

Leland turned to Becca. "That goes for you as well. If Martin shows his face, call for reinforcements."

"All right."

"Dinner's ready." Muriel stood in the doorway, listening. Leland didn't know how much she'd heard, but the two of them had talked about the situation enough times that he knew she would agree with his proclamation.

Muriel served homemade vegetable soup and fresh dinner rolls that she'd purchased at the bakery located just down the block from her bus stop. It was a tad late for supper, but sharing a meal was more important than eating at a prescribed hour. When a siren sounded in the distance, Ellie scowled.

"If I could talk Mr. Van Damme into taking me on a European dance tour, we might get rid of Martin."

"Would you want to do that?" Becca asked.

"I was joking. I don't think he'll extend that invitation to me anytime soon."

"But, would you? If he asked?"

"Sure, I would."

"Europe? I can't imagine."

Ellie wagged her spoon at Becca and asked, "Did you think the *Capriccio Espagnol* performance gave a fair representation of Spanish life?"

"As far as I could tell," Becca replied. "It looked real enough to me."

"Mr. Van Damme wanted it to be authentic. He knows how to recreate a scene because he has traveled to so many places. You should hear him talk about the people in France, or Belgium, or Italy. He knows their customs and their histories, and can describe street scenes in such detail that they become the source of the stage sets."

"He has a lot to brag about," Leland said.

"It's not about his pride. You should hear how excited he gets when he talks about his experiences. He's so passionate, it slides off him and wraps around his students like a second skin. It's as if we're part of the story. That's why he tells us. The most important thing, though, is that he *knows* how people dance in different parts of the world, and he wants us to duplicate the movements, to identify with the culture. If his dancers accomplish that, the audience can too."

This was the reason Ellie didn't let Martin Hastings derail her. Her excitement was intense, so much so that the level of enthusiasm in the kitchen bade Leland to turn on the radio, find a lively tune, and kick up his heels.

He pushed his chair away from the table and extended his hand to his wife. "Come on into the living room."

"Why?"

"Just come on. Grab Ellie's hand. Ellie, you grab Becca. Y'all follow me."

"What about the dishes?" Muriel said.

"What about 'em? They'll be here an hour from now."

He had to tug Muriel's hand pretty hard to convince her to get out of her chair, and he pert 'near had to drag all three of them down the hallway. They mumbled while he picked out one of his favorite records and set it a-spinnin' on the turntable.

As the high-spirited bluegrass tune filled the air, Leland rubbed his hands together. "Take your corners, ladies, it's time for an *allemande* here, a *do-si-do* there, a *swing your partner* or two, with a heap of *sashaying* in between. Let's get our blood a-pumpin' and our feet a-tappin'. Whoo-ee!"

Chapter 31

"You sure you don't want me to walk with you? I mean, I feel pretty silly sitting here while you're freezing your—"

Becca arched her brow. "My what?"

"Your film. That's what I was just about to say. Freezing your film."

Becca gazed out the side window, hiding her face from Leland. Her voice, though, was as cheerful as a woman who greeted the morning sun with a melody, which is what Becca usually did. Leastways, she wore a happy tune since she quit shadowing the *Gazette* photographer while he made his rounds for the newspaper.

"I love that about you," Becca said. "You don't worry about saying what's on your mind."

"It takes too much effort to contemplate how five different people might react to what I have to say."

"I know you want to be a gentleman and all, but I pay more heed to what I'm doing if I work alone." Becca's attention wandered down Morris Street, as if she were recalling every detail of the scene she encountered when the truck hit that little girl. "I'm hoping a few of the children will let me take their pictures, maybe the very ones I captured on film the last time I was here. They were hesitant to trust me, you know, so I'm pretty sure they'll run if they see you."

Leland ran his eyes over his form. "Truth be told, I'm pretty easygoing."

"I know. Just sit tight and drink your hot cocoa."

"I'll look suspicious lollygagging here all by myself."

"No one is watching you."

"Well, not right this minute, but if I sit here long enough, someone's bound to tell me to move on down the road."

"If they do, don't scare the daylights out of me by sneaking up behind me and blaring the horn."

"Right."

"I won't be long," Becca said as she slid out of the car and closed the door.

Leland took a sip of his cocoa and conducted a three hundred sixty-degree inspection of his surroundings, which required the use of the rearview mirror when his neck reached its turning ratio limit. The traffic on Morris Street, like other roads near the rail yard, had turned the snow into a mixture of slush, grit, gravel, and dirt. Every vehicle that passed sprayed another layer of grime onto Leland's car.

If Becca had asked him which of her newspaper apprentice excursions he preferred to recreate with her, he'd be in the Buick dealer's warm showroom, relaxing in the driver's seat of that yellow hardtop she'd liked so much, the one with a black top and red trim.

In front of the houses situated among the neighborhood businesses, patches of wet snow clung to the dead grass. The sun wrestled its way around a mass of cumulus clouds, their forms as dense and as stark white as the meringue Muriel whipped for her lemon pies. Leland licked his lips. Pie would go right nice with his hot cocoa.

Becca stopped in front of a barbershop, and when a man and young boy exited the building, she waved to them, shared a short conversation, and stepped back a couple of paces. After lifting her camera and taking a few photographs, she reached into her coat pocket, pulled out a couple of Tootsie Pops, and handed one to each of them. The youngster let his father lead him down the sidewalk while he kept his eyes glued on Becca. When they reached the corner, the boy raised his lollipop and waved.

The Tootsie Pops were Leland's idea, mostly on account of Gene Autry being a big Tootsie Roll fan. Becca had purchased a generous supply, and if she passed out every one of them, Leland would be fogging the car windows for more'n a few hours. Well, she couldn't give away *every* one of them. Leland dug into his pocket, pulled out one of the Tootsie Pops he'd snagged out of Becca's supply, and examined the wrapper's purple lettering. He liked grape all right.

When Becca approached people as they passed on the sidewalk, some declined her request and kept on a-goin', but others didn't mind posing for her. The children, although playing shy at first, bubbled with pleasure by the time she'd taken her shots, and that was before she surprised them with the sweet treat. No question, Becca loved photography, just not the type that filled the newspapers.

Leland jumped almost high enough to smack the ceiling when a man tapped on the driver's window, right next to his ear. Becca seemed fine, all the way down at the end of the block, but here he was, about to be robbed. And in broad daylight.

He eased his face toward the window, taking in the sight of a billy club while he slurped the purple saliva that threatened to run down his chin. The brass buttons stitched to the cuff that rested above the club-wielding hand belonged on a policeman's uniform, not a hoodlum's attire. When the patrolman bent down and stared into the window, the sight harbored more trepidation than relief. If the familiar man played his partner's game, Leland would most likely get a tour of the neighborhood precinct. He rolled down the window.

"Hey, I know you." Officer Dwight, last name unknown, opened the car door. "Step on out."

Leland couldn't see Becca without turning around. Maybe it was better that Dwight didn't know she was in the area.

"Morning. Something wrong?" The stick to Leland's Tootsie Pop wagged as he tried to talk around it.

"Aren't you the man who lives next to Betty Hastings?"

"I am."

"Ellie's father. Right?"

"Uncle."

"Right. I knew that. Martin has a tendency to talk from the start of our shift until it ends. I half-listen."

Leland didn't half-care what Dwight thought, or how much of an ear he gave to his partner, but he meant to give the young man more respect than his slurp suggested. If he could just get past the hard candy part and sink his teeth into the chewy chocolate center, he might act and sound a mite more civilized.

"Something wrong?" Leland asked a second time.

"Got a complaint about a stranger hanging around, looking for trouble. Is that you?"

"Well, I reckon you could say I'm hanging around, but I'm no troublemaker."

Leland turned toward the heavy footsteps coming his way and, sure enough, Martin Hastings stepped alongside Dwight.

"What are you doing here?" Martin asked.

"Passing time." Leland started to reach into his coat pocket.

"Whoa. Keep 'em where I can see 'em." Martin's fingers

twitched as his hand flew toward his service weapon.

"Leland raised both hands. "Sorry. I just meant to offer you a Tootsie Pop. Want one?"

"No," Martin said.

"What flavor you got?" Dwight asked.

"Whichever you want."

"Using two fingers," Dwight said, "could you pull out a cherry one for me?"

Leland flicked his eyes in Martin's direction. "Well?"

"Go ahead."

It took three tries before Leland managed to pull a cherry flavored lollipop out of his pocket, and when he offered the orange and the raspberry flavors to Martin, he selected the orange one. So, there they stood, all three of them licking Tootsie Pops, just as if they were old friends.

"Why are you hanging out here?" Martin asked.

"I'm helping my niece."

Martin swung around, searching for Ellie, no doubt. When he couldn't find her, he turned a circle and scoured the area a second time.

"I'm helping Becca. She's taking photographs, and I didn't want her to come here by herself."

"That her?" Dwight asked as he caught sight of Becca.

"Sure is."

"Don't let her wander too far," Martin said. "This is a mixed area, if you know what I mean."

"That's exactly why she came here. See for yourself."

Becca knelt on the sidewalk, talking to three children who posed for her while they sat on the stoop in front of a house. From Leland's distant perch, he could hear the children giggling. It would warm Becca right up if those were the same children whose portraits she'd taken before.

"Dwight," Martin said, "would you go in the hardware store and tell the owner that everything's all right out here?"

Dwight didn't look too pleased, but it was apparent that Martin had prepared a speech for Leland. Once Dwight went inside, Martin put on a real nice face. Congenial. Polite. Respectful. Whatever it was he wanted, the answer would forever be a resounding *no*.

"I'm glad we ran into you today, but sorry about treating you like a suspect."

"I'm obliged that you didn't haul me to the pokey."

Martin must have remembered the time he threatened to do just that. His face flushed. "I wanted to ask if I could stop by your house and apologize to Ellie, but I ought to start with you. I apologize for the way I treated you, your wife, Becca, and Ellie."

Martin's apology sounded genuine, and he gave the impression that he was uncomfortable, the way most people do when they have to admit they've made a blunder. Martin's offenses, though, were many, and they were hardly trivial. The man knew how to bluff. The apology was bait, and Leland wasn't biting.

"No." Leland clenched the chocolate center between his teeth and pulverized the mass until it was soft enough to swallow.

"I'd really like to explain."

"Ain't interested."

"I know I was wrong."

"Then you should know to stay away."

Dwight climbed into the patrol car, turned the ignition, and pulled alongside Leland and Martin.

"Let's go," Dwight said.

As Martin lowered himself into the passenger seat, he asked again. "May I just stop by?"

"No." After Leland watched the car disappear around a

corner, he climbed back into his driver's seat and pulled what was left of the Tootsie Pop stick out of his mouth. It resembled a tiny spitball.

Chapter 32

Percy switched off the television and returned to his favorite chair. It sat at an angle to the front window where it gathered the room's natural light. With the sunlight fading behind the hills, he turned on the floor lamp and picked up the latest issue of *The Saturday Evening Post*.

"His speech was a mite different from the last one. Shorter, too." Fern sat on the sofa, her fingers working nonstop on her newest knitting project.

"Eisenhower proved himself during his first term, so maybe he didn't feel the need to make a list of promises," Percy replied.

"Four years ago, he started his inaugural address with a personal prayer. That stuck with me." Fern stopped mid row, scowling at the dropped stitch. A year ago, she would have ignored the mistake, but she'd seen too many of her creations unravel to ignore the obvious need to backtrack. She held her breath with each slip of the yarn from one needle to the other. As long as her eyes didn't veer from the task, she could talk while she repaired. "The man won the highest office in the country, but instead of acting prideful, he prayed for discernment and guidance."

"He needed it then. Needs it now. He didn't pray this time, per se, but he said we—meaning the whole country—ought to seek the blessings of the Almighty."

"I reckon that's why I still like Ike." Fern was a late bloomer when it came to finding activities to fill her time. Empty hours were infrequent, but when Nettie suggested that knitting might be therapeutic, Fern gave it a go, and since winter set in, she'd put mileage on her needles. Each of her knit and purl stitches helped to close the distance that separated her from Ellie and Becca.

"You heard his warning, though." Percy, who hadn't opened his magazine, rolled it into a tube shape and tapped it on his thigh. "We're enjoying a season of prosperity and the world is holding a fragile thread of peace, but he was right in describing the earth as a perilous place."

"I didn't know that a third of the world lives in poverty. Fact is, Percy, until wars forced Americans to consider folks who live outside our borders, I never gave much thought to the ways of the rest of the world. We've both lived in poverty, but I reckon it's a lot worse in places where the land isn't fit to till or where dictators hold people low."

"Communism," Percy said, his voice muted and his eyes betraying his frustration. "Russia. Germany."

"I liked the way President Eisenhower described peace as the climate of freedom, but he had to go and put hard-to-reach conditions on it, saying that justice and laws that value freedom come before peace. It takes a lot of cooperation for those things to happen. So far, I'm not impressed with the level of support from leaders around the globe."

"Power mongers will always kindle war and oppression."

"They make the president's ideas sound like a wish list."

"We have to hold to hope."

"And a prayer," Fern added.

"Which takes us back to the beginning of both speeches," Percy said as he unrolled the *Post* and flipped a few pages. Before he could have scanned a headline, he plopped the magazine down again.

"What?" Fern held her yarn perfectly still while she glanced across the room. "You know that word you taught Roy the other day? Flum something or other."

"Flummoxed?"

"Yes. The way you explained it? Well, that's what your face looks like right now."

"Naw, I'm not confused. I'm restless."

"You?"

"Sure am. When's the last time we took a vacation?"

"Does the Tigers' playoff game count?"

"No."

"Well, by my count, it's been going on a lifetime."

"That's what I figured."

Fern leveled the tip of a knitting needle toward Percy's reading material. "Is that sophisticated magazine giving you wild ideas?"

"Maybe. I think we ought to climb into our car and take a road trip."

Fern slid her yarn down the needles and set her task aside. "First off, are you suggesting a vacation with the whole family? Because if you are, we need to buy one of those family work wagons Becca talked about. And we're not doing that."

"I was thinking of a private affair, Mrs. Bigler. A vacation with me and my missus." Percy's eyebrows leapt to his hairline, making room for the grin that took over the rest of his handsome face. Neither laugh lines, crinkles at the edges of his hazel eyes, nor gray strands intruding into blond had the power to diminish the effect the man had on Fern.

She pressed a shoulder forward and leveled a sly, now-you're-talking-mister reply. "If we stay close to home, maybe we could stay for an extra night or two."

"You want to rough it at one of the state parks?"

"Only if you'll wrap me in a warm quilt before we go outside and count the stars."

"Do we need to wait until spring?"

"I like winter just fine, Mr. B."

◆

"Sure was nice of Leland to haul Becca all the way to Elizabeth so we could take our trip." Fern fastened the lid on the thermos and set it on the floor, between her feet.

"I wish we could have waited for the weather to clear. This is making me weary." Percy had already endured three hours of rain splattering the windshield, the intermittent swipe of the wipers barely keeping the road in view.

"Me too, but it might be five more years before one or the other of the girls can help out at the general store for a couple of days. I'm grateful Becca's boss gave her time away from work." Fern studied Percy's profile, and although he had to mind the snaking roadway, he knew she was watching him. "I can't help but feel guilty about leaving the store and the care of three school-aged children to Becca and your mother."

"They offered. Sit back and enjoy it."

Fern trusted Becca and Nettie, and she could trust Percy to drive safely. He didn't need a copilot. She eased her shoulders back and ignored the predictable squeak of the wipers against the glass. "When will you tell me where we're going?"

"I reckon I can tell you now. We have reservations at

Cacapon State Park."

"Isn't that all the way over to Maryland?"

"About as close as we can get without crossing the border."

"I thought you wanted to stay near home."

"The park is in West Virginia, which makes it near home. It's still a piece down the road, but we'll get there soon enough."

The sound of tires on gravel nudged Fern from her unintended nap. Rain had turned to drizzle, and despite the bare branches on the deciduous trees, their lofty limbs provided an impressive foreground for the evergreens that soared upwards. As Percy navigated the roadway, Fern rolled the window down far enough to take in the scent of wet leaves, dank air, and wood smoke.

"I hope you don't mind," Percy said, "but instead of booking us a room in the new lodge or in one of the cabins, I reserved us a spot at the original lodge. Nowadays, it's called the Old Inn."

The new lodge sat on the rise of a hill, its long roof stretching across eleven dormers, each with two wide windows. "How many rooms does that thing have?"

"Forty-eight. Not private enough for me," Percy said.

It was too touristy for Fern as well, and a cabin would have been fine, but when the Old Inn came into view, her pulse quickened. The building wasn't as enormous as the new lodge, but it was massive in its own right. More than the new accommodations, it fit its surroundings. Fern recognized a sense of belonging. This wasn't just close to home. This was *West Virginia home* at its finest.

"It's beautiful."

"Most folks don't call a log-built structure beautiful," Percy replied, "but part of the reason I chose this is its history."

"It has Civilian Conversation Corps written all over it. I love those stone fireplaces. And, that porch? Why, I could sit there all day, rain or not, and watch people a-comin' or a-goin'. I can't wait to see the inside."

It was hard not to gawk at the interior. Fern inspected the sitting room, the dining room, and a common room. Hand-hewn log beams drew her eye to the ceiling, its wood darkened with age. Although she didn't have a view of the kitchen, the sound of employees making preparations for the next meal carried into the public areas, and the aroma that filtered through the air stimulated her appetite.

When they entered their room, Fern dropped her pocketbook onto the double bed and spun in a circle as she inspected every nook and cranny. Dark wood framed the windows and the doors while carefully fitted planks, blackened by age and wear, covered the floor. The walls were wormy chestnut and knotty pine, joined in tongue and groove fashion. She ran her hand over the small chest of drawers. "Did the CCC men build the furniture too?"

"I imagine they did. You can be sure that all of the hardware you see is hand-forged iron."

Fern looked out the window where a wispy layer of fog had settled. "Doesn't it make you proud, your having been a part of the Corps?"

"When I recall that time, I'm more apt to say I'm thankful than proud. President Roosevelt's program put me to work and helped me finish my education." Percy waved his hand from one side of the room to the other. "Seeing this place, well, it reminds me how blessed I am." He walked over to the window, pulled Fern into a hug, and pressed a kiss to her cheek. "I was full of gratitude when I returned to Elizabeth. Making a home there with you made it sweeter still."

Fern swiped at her eyes and batted Percy's arm away. "What are you doing, making me all weepy?"

"I'm just tugging at your heartstrings. Seems appropriate

since today is Valentine's Day."

It was all Fern could do to keep her mouth shut. She'd plumb forgot, and she wasn't likely to find a trinket at the Old Inn that she could pass off as a memento of the day. Maybe the answer to her dilemma lay just a few feet away.

"Is that the bathroom?"

"Sure is."

"Does it have a bathtub?"

Percy snuck a peek into the room. "It does."

This road trip was more than a good idea. It was brilliant. That little bottle of bubble bath Fern had stashed in her suitcase would instigate more romance than a greeting card. She couldn't hide her delight, especially when one of her brother's favorite exclamations came to mind. *Whoo-ee!*

Chapter 33

"If it weren't winter, and if we were avid hikers, we could test our middle-aged mettle with a trek to the very top of Cacapon Mountain." Percy's cheeks and the tip of his nose were red from the cold.

What may have been a leisurely gander around the park in pleasant weather was turning into a chore, and the woolen scarf wrapped around Fern's face wasn't dense enough to protect her skin from the wind's nippy bite. Percy acted as if he didn't mind the cold, or perhaps he'd worked up a sweat. He'd unfastened the top button of his coat and tugged the collar of his plaid flannel shirt away from his neck.

"Just describe the sight to me. I'll close my eyes and see it that way." Fern's scarf muffled her voice, but it wasn't as if she had to talk loudly for him to hear her. Aside from an occasional bird flitting around the trees and the persistent tapping of a nearby woodpecker, the area was quiet. All the rest of the guests who'd booked a Valentine's vacation with their sweethearts were lounging in the lodge, the Old Inn, or private cabins, savoring the warmth of flames licking wood in the fireplaces. Fern had been keen on walking trails, but as the morning wore on, the wind picked up, the sun fled, and the temperature plummeted. She was ready to join the others in front of the fire. Instead, she closed her eyes. "Paint one of your word pictures for me."

"If we hiked all the way to the top, we would have a panoramic view that included West Virginia, Virginia, Maryland, and Pennsylvania. We'd be able to distinguish the West Virginia terrain because the view of the other three states would pale in comparison. That, despite their borders running alongside those of our magnificent Mountain State."

"You're funny."

"I'd rather you call me charming."

"Oh, you're that too. Finish your picture."

"Stretched out before us would be forest, as far as we could see. A red-tailed hawk, or maybe a pair, would soar above the tree line, borrowing the air current so they didn't have to flap their wings. If we were bold enough to be at the summit after dusk—which we are not—whippoorwills would serenade us while we kept watch for black bears."

"I wouldn't mind seeing a bear off in the distance."

"That'd be something, wouldn't it?" Percy spread his hands out. "Just like what you see right here."

"What do you mean?"

"Twenty years ago this land was clear-cut, and until the men in the CCC replanted, it was worthless. Fact is, the bare hillsides contributed to flooding. Nowadays folks call the ridge along Cacapon Mountain the Emerald of the Eastern Panhandle."

"I'll bet it's pretty in summertime."

"The recreation areas might get a tad noisy when families arrive. I can envision the lake near the entrance, filled with rowboats and children wading along its banks."

"Noise or not, I'd like to come back. I'd like to go riding."

"Been a long time since we had a horse. I miss that too."

Percy wedged Fern's gloved hand into the crook of his arm and reversed direction, a wise decision overall.

"Do you miss the milk cow?" Fern asked.

"I miss the fresh milk, not the milking."

"Times change."

"They sure do. I think we should consider these past couple of days as practice runs."

"Practice for what?"

Percy pulled Fern's arm, drawing her body close to his. "For being alone, an old married couple with grown children."

"I hope you're not in a hurry. June won't finish high school until, um, 1968."

"Eleven years sounds like a long time, but the way I figure it, Mrs. B, we need to nudge our way into our no-longer-parenting years very slowly. I'd like to suggest we take a road trip every year. Maybe five or six years down the road, when Wayne's out of the house, and maybe Roy too, we ought to increase our adventures to two times a year."

"You're assuming that I won't mind when the rest of our youngsters leave home."

"*Au contraire*, I expect you to suffer serious bouts of melancholy. Preparing for the inevitable will ease the intensity of the suffering. If it doesn't, you and I will have spent memorable time together."

"We already have, Percy. We've enjoyed blessings galore. At those times when circumstances push my countenance low, I want you to remind me of another word picture."

"Something I said?"

"No. The psalmist. You close your eyes this time."

"Okay."

"Don't tell me what you see, but tell me how you feel when you hear, 'Let Him come down like rain upon the mown grass.

Like showers, watering the earth.'"

"Makes me think of cleanliness, a new start."

"Whenever I'm discouraged, remind me to appreciate the rain, to get up, and to start anew."

"I'll do that. Speaking of getting up, though, it's time we packed and started for the place where we enjoy those blessings."

The drive home felt half as long as the trip to the park, mostly because the skies were clear, and despite the unexpected flat tire.

"Hard to say where we picked up that nail," Percy said as he bit into his dinner roll.

"Can't complain, given the circumstances." Fern looked out the restaurant window. From her seat, she could see across the two-lane road. While the mechanic inserted a new inner tube, she and Percy enjoyed a hot meal. The gas station attendant noticed the low air pressure when he filled the fuel tank, another of those blessings that reminded Fern of rain upon the grass.

"Do you remember the first time we had a flat?" Percy asked.

The temperature inside climbed at least ten degrees. The story never failed to amuse Percy, and if Fern were lucky, he wouldn't share the tale with the waitress.

"I do."

"You were so cute. 'Tell me, Percy, why is it that tires only go flat on the bottom?' Remember that?" They'd been together long enough for Percy to perfect her vernacular, and he was pretty good mimicking her facial expressions to boot.

Fern's earlobes were tingling with heat. Her family didn't have a car when she was growing up, and until that incident, she hadn't considered the cause and effect. Her question tickled Percy so much that the science behind the situation must have been obvious to everyone but her.

"I knew as much about cars as you knew about a woman giving birth."

Percy's face turned crimson at her unexpected retort. Once he collected himself, he mumbled, "Touché."

Fern was pretty certain Percy wouldn't bother retelling the tire story anytime soon.

After their meal, and after parting with the last of their road trip money, they climbed back inside the car. Percy pulled onto the roadway, reached over, and patted Fern's hand. "Could have been a lot worse."

When they parked in front of Bigler's General Store, the sight of Leland's car caught Fern off guard.

Percy cut the motor and stared at Fern. "We were only gone a couple of days. What have they done?"

*

Leland stepped onto the walkway at the same time Fern and Percy exited their car. As Nettie helped Becca turn her dream into reality, Leland contemplated leaving a message at the Cacapon office, but doing so would have interfered with their road trip. No way was Leland going to steal any part of his sister's first genuine vacation. Now, though, he and a few others needed to tender an explanation.

Leland whisked the sawdust off his shirt and trousers as he walked to the car. "Welcome home. Y'all have a nice time?"

"Sure did." Fern shoved her hands into her coat pockets and gave him the same warning she used to wear when she wanted to tear the daylights out of him. Good thing they'd left that sort of behavior behind, right along with their childhood. "You want to tell us what's going on?"

Percy's expression suggested that he wasn't too excited about the transformation. Leland would start by reminding them of a truth.

"While you hear me out, you ought to remember that this building belongs to Nettie."

"And the store belongs to your wife." Fern took her hands out of her pockets and crossed her arms. "You don't need to remind me that I'm an employee."

"Don't get het up before you know what's happening here."

Percy, bless his fair-minded and not-easily-flustered heart, walked around the car and stood beside Fern. "Did my mother decide to take in boarders again?"

"No, but she did sign on a new tenant."

"What kind of tenant?" Fern asked.

"A brand new business."

"Is the business paying for whatever work you're doing?" Fern asked as she ran her eyes over Leland's work clothes.

"It's mostly cosmetic changes, using materials we found out in the barn."

Percy didn't take well to that response, but he didn't voice his objections. Yet.

"Let me show you," Leland said as he started walking toward the side of the building. "We stretched out the footpath so customers have plenty of room to walk to the entrance." When they reached the door that led to what had been one of two efficiency apartments, he pointed upwards. "Didn't take but a wee bit of wood to make an overhang. The proprietor wouldn't want people getting soaked coming and going."

When neither Fern nor Percy said a word, Leland held the door open and ushered them inside.

"Where'd you get the counter?" Fern asked.

"Ron and I made it from scraps. Looks right nice, doesn't it?"

"You put Ron to work on this? Who ran the store?" Judging by her clenched jaw, Fern was prepared to pounce.

"Nettie."

"Who took care of the children?"

"Most of the time they were in school. Other times, the boys helped out here. June helped her granny in the store."

One side of Percy's mouth twisted when he regarded the partition that separated the shop from a small storage area.

"Is that the door to Sassy's old stall?"

"Pretty smart use of things on hand, ain't it?"

Percy met Leland's thumb's-up with an air of disbelief. "You tore up part of the barn?"

"Sure did. It gives the shop a genuine country flavor."

Fern wasn't seething, but she was simmering. "Does the milk pail go in the empty corner?"

"No. That's where they'll put the old feed trough."

The glower Fern traded with Percy suggested that Leland ought to quit playing. Instead of having fun, he'd fanned a firestorm.

"Come on back here so you can see the rest."

"You cut a hole in the wall between the two apartments?" Percy's calm manner faded as they stepped from one unit to the next.

"This here is where the darkroom will go."

Fern stopped dead in her tracks. "The darkroom?"

"Yes'm. When the proprietor takes her customer's film, she has to have a place to process it."

"Nettie leased these rooms to a photographer?" Fern asked.

Leland nodded.

"A female photographer?" Percy eyed Fern as he asked the question.

"Sure enough. If y'all want to congratulate Elizabeth's first professional photographer, you can find her over in the general store, making a sign to hang right outside the door."

Fern's face flushed and she looked as if she were about to

start blubbering. "What's the name of this new business?"

"She was struggling with that. It's best you go on over and see for yourself."

Leland held the door open, which earned him a tap on the arm from Percy and a brutal slug on the same arm from Fern. Leland followed them into the general store, greeted Ron, whose deadpan expression contradicted his involvement in the affair, and stopped in the doorway to the back room.

Becca, who'd pulled her long hair into a ponytail, knelt in front of a large piece of metal, its background now a pale blue. Its oval shape and proportions bore distinct similarities to an old ESSO sign, the type that used to hang over a filling station's gas pumps. Ron wouldn't say where he'd acquired that piece of antiquity, but Becca had transformed it into a suitable and professional sign.

It had been a while since Becca wore absolute pleasure on her face, but at the sight of her parents, her eyes shimmered. Leland reckoned her joy had as much to do with moving back home as with opening her business. When she pushed a lock of hair out of her face, she left a streak of navy blue paint on her cheek.

Becca scrambled to her feet, held her paintbrush at arm's length, and tried to pull her mom and dad into a hug. Both of them backed up lickety-split.

"What?"

"Wet paint," Fern said as she kept her distance.

"Oh. So, what do you think?"

"Of what?" Percy asked. "Your starting a business, your returning to Elizabeth, or the name of your shop?"

"All of it."

"I couldn't be happier," Percy said.

"I'm thrilled." Fern lifted her hand to Becca's cheek, smeared the paint instead of wiping it off, and chuckled. She turned to

Percy and said, "See what happens when we take a vacation?"

"Didn't you say something earlier today about life changing?"

"Yep. And this change couldn't please me more."

"Thanks." Becca blushed. "Before you go to the house, would you tell me what you think of my sign?"

Leland caught Becca's eye while she waited for her parents' response. She'd worried over this detail since she let herself consider that her dream might become a reality. In lettering as fine as a calligrapher's steady hand could produce, were the words, Still Life Portrait Studio. Small print along the lower edge of the oval read, Developing Services and Camera Supplies.

"I love it," Fern said.

"I do too," Percy said. "I don't know what word to use to describe my reaction."

"You don't?" Leland asked. "Mr. Dictionary is at a loss for words?"

"Give me a second." Percy's mouth twitched side to side, as if he were chewing. Finally, he tapped his lips. "I've got it. I'm gobsmacked."

"You're what?" Becca asked.

"Gobsmacked. Astonished."

Fern put her hand around Percy's arm and rolled her eyes at Becca. "He's tired, dear. He had a long day on the road. Just ignore him."

"Hey, now," Percy said.

"Gobsmacked?" Fern repeated. She started for the door, but paused. "Welcome home, Rebecca Bigler."

Chapter 34

Leland stood in the aisle until Fern and Percy took their seats, but snuck into the row before Muriel could step past him. Just this once, Leland wanted to share an artistic moment with the individual responsible for introducing him to indoor entertainment. Muriel was a tad miffed at Leland's bad manners until June settled into the seat beside her. He kept an eye on Nettie and Becca while they took the seats next to the aisle.

He'd never imagined the folks who lived in Charleston, a thriving business and manufacturing center, were so keen about art, but the city hosted multiple events every month. The Third West Virginia Creative Arts Festival was a weeklong affair, and tonight smartly dressed patrons filled the Morris Harvey College Auditorium for what the program described as *An Evening of Ballet and Music*. In addition to a performance by the Charleston Ballet, the audience would enjoy works presented by a violinist and pianist, a lyric soprano and her accompanist, and a solo pianist.

Leland nudged Percy's elbow, and asked, "What's '*Les Sylphides*'?"

Percy snickered at Leland's pronunciation, *less seel-fie-dees*. "It's *seel-feed*."

"You're guessing."

"No, I'm not. I looked it up."

"Where? You own a French dictionary?"

Instead of replying, Percy arched his brows. He *did* own a French dictionary. What a wiseacre.

"So, what's it mean?"

"A *sylphide* is a female forest spirit, so *les sylphides*"—where he came up with *lay* instead of *less* was another mystery to Leland—"which is plural, means we'll watch a ballet about a bunch of ghosts who live in the forest."

"If you say so."

Muriel, who had a vocabulary that rivaled Percy's, bumped Leland's shoulder. "After Ellie told me what they were presenting this evening, I did a little research."

"At the law library? Why? Did the forest elves have to hire an attorney?"

Muriel might have laughed if not for the backwards glance Leland's comment earned from the woman who sat in front of him. The elderly music enthusiast was as pleased to be sitting near a hillbilly as Leland was to inhale her sickly sweet cologne.

Muriel replied with a haughty tone, probably for the sake of the perfumed spectator. "Chopin composed the music, and the choreography takes after Michel Fokine."

Well, Leland could read that much. It was right there on the program's second page.

"The cast includes the forest sprites and a male dancer who plays the part of a poet. It's an eerie setting, usually with a Gothic castle in the background, but the dancers turn it into a romantic scene. *Les Sylphides* is a classic rendition of the Golden Era of Ballet."

"Which was when?" An occasional question meant that Leland was listening.

"The mid-1800s."

Leland didn't mind the schooling, but Muriel's fascination with a host of subjects boggled his mind. She loved history, a good portion of which was good to know, but the Golden Era of Ballet didn't concern Leland. Nor did he mind Percy's vocabulary lessons. Percy favored words, but for Leland, words were haphazard minefields, subject to misinterpretation—one of Leland's specialties—and speculation. Depending on the context or the tone, spoken or written, the same word could take on a myriad of meanings.

Leland liked numbers, figures that fit together in logical, predetermined formulas. After the program, if anyone were to ask, he'd tell how many dancers took the stage for each segment of the ballet's performance. Numbers weren't popular conversation topics, so few people appreciated his brilliance in the field.

Muriel was talking again, and he had no way to tell what he'd missed while his mind wandered to the land of integers. Iffen a choreographer were to create a ballet where each dancer represented a digit, why that would be quite the entertainment. They'd prance around the stage, forming an equation over here or a sum over there. Maybe he ought to share his vision with Mr. Van Damme.

"What are you laughing about?" Muriel asked.

If not for the start of the program, Leland might have had to dance around the question.

After the performance, Leland drove Percy, June, and Nettie back to the house. Percy had to coax June into her pajamas, but after he tucked his little one into bed, exhaustion overwhelmed her. Nettie excused herself minutes later and slipped into Ellie's room where June might give her enough space in the bed so she could get her shuteye.

Leland lowered himself to one of the living room chairs. "Do you think the *Gazette* will print any of Becca's photos?"

Percy, who sat on the sofa, rubbed his eyes. "I doubt it. Larry Tanner got permission for her to take pictures after the performance, but he was there too."

"His won't be fine, eye-catching portraits like Becca takes."

"Maybe, but since he works for the *Gazette,* they'll publish his photos."

"I reckon that's true, but Becca will impress the dancers and they'll all want to buy their photographs from her. She's got a good eye."

"She sure does."

"How's her business?"

"She's had customers trickle in for portraits, but she's selling more film and processing services than she's making money doing what she loves. She's patient, though, so it'll work out."

"I hope so."

"I think she'll get busy when it's time for school photos. The high school camera club is fine for pictures of the band and the football team and such, but none of the students has the expertise to do decent portraits."

"What about her and Ron?"

Percy's heavy eyelids lifted. "What about them?"

"Seemed to me, when I helped with Becca's studio, they were sweet on each other."

"I thought Ron just wanted to learn how to process film."

"What about him taking her to concerts?"

"So? Becca likes guitar. She likes music."

"You know, my sister thinks you're a romantic. When you act like you don't know nothin' about anything that's goin' on around you, I have to wonder how you pull off that charade."

Percy wiped the side of his face with the palm of his hand,

stretching his grin higher on one side. "You have a remarkable way of expressing yourself."

"You complaining about my grammar?"

"Not at all. It's entertaining."

"I don't aim to be funny."

"I know. That's part of the amusement."

"Listen here, Percy."

If not for the gals coming in the front door, Leland might have unloaded some integers on his brother-in-law. Like . . . *One, you don't know nothin'. Two, you just think you know everything. Three, you ought to quit poking fun at Leland Dugan. He's a right smart man.*

∽

Fern followed the aroma of coffee. She snuck past the living room where Becca slept on the sofa and dropped into a seat at the kitchen table, next to June.

"Ellie's fixing oatmeal." June's big brown eyes gleamed in the way of a child who enjoyed a sweet, uninterrupted sleep. If not for the joys of parenting, Fern might have acknowledged a twinge of jealously.

As Ellie lowered a bowl of oatmeal with brown sugar to June's place, she regarded her mother. "Why are you smiling?"

"Just happy to be here. Happier to have seen you dance last night. You were marvelous."

"Was I, or do you think your sweet talk will earn a spoonful of brown sugar?"

"Oh, that sounds lovely. Thanks for offering."

"Your mother is silly, June."

"So is yours." Not only were June's eyes bright, so was her wit. She was rested, carefree, and content, enjoying a rosy era that tended to fade with time. People underrated childhood until it was long gone.

Ellie served Fern and filled a bowl for herself, but when Leland strode into the kitchen and Ellie moved to get back up, he waved his hand at her.

"You did the cooking. I can get my own bowl." His countenance, like June's, was cheerful. Fern hadn't taken surveys, but it seemed as if men had an easier time at slumber than women.

Leland aimed his spoon at Ellie. "So, Miss Danseuse, what do you call those tiny little steps y'all take when you're frolicking on your toes?"

"*Bourrées?*" It sounded like *boo-RAY* to Leland.

"Those impressed me. How do you keep count of 'em and stay in step with the other dancers?"

"Practice. Hours of practice. *Les Sylphides* may appear to be a simple dance, but it's really difficult to do well. As you say, the precision is hard to master. You might think all of those dainty movements are effortless, but they are not."

Muriel walked into the kitchen and poured herself a cup of coffee. With her hair and makeup done just so, her appearance was a sight better than Fern's, who hadn't bothered to do more than run a brush through her hair.

Muriel slid into the chair next to Leland. "I loved the costumes, Ellie. The layers of white tulle rippled in the moonlight."

Leland turned sideways so he could see Muriel's expression when he asked, "What did you think of the poet's garb?"

"What about it?"

"I hear Ellie talk about the ballet company needing to find male dancers, but don't you think those outfits might contribute to the lack of interest?"

"Why would you say that?" Ellie looked shocked.

"You wouldn't catch me wearing white tights and a black tunic. No sir."

Muriel wasn't adept at being humorous, but when every inch of her face seemed to scream, *please excuse this mess of a man who happens to be my husband*, Fern got to laughing so hard she got the hiccups.

"What's funny, Mommy?"

Fern gave June's shoulders a squeeze. "Your Uncle Leland. His hillbilly's just actin' up. He'll be all right in a minute." Fern's recovery might take a tad longer. While her brother glared, a spasm pinched her diaphragm and produced another *hic*.

"Since you don't care for my opinion, let me ask another question." Leland pouted before he turned his back to Muriel and Fern. He asked Ellie, "What do you call that fancy footwork Mr. Van Damme did when he jumped and did a little flutter with his feet?"

"A single tap of the feet is a *cabriole*. Two taps is a *double cabriole*."

"Well, I'm a-goin' to practice that one." Leland stood and extended his hand to Muriel. "Come on, partner."

Muriel took a gulp of coffee before she lowered her cup to the table. "No thank you, Mister Poet."

"Ask me, Uncle Leland." June was out of her seat before he could reply. "I'll be your partner."

"You'll be my forest elf?"

June's head bobbed like a yoyo.

"Hold on a minute. You need a fluffy white dress." Ellie put her fingers to her lips. "Any ideas, ladies?"

"I have one." Muriel donned the uncharacteristic mask of a rascal. "Follow me upstairs, June. You too, Mister Poet. Fern, will you give me a hand?"

Drawn by the hullabaloo, Percy, Nettie, and Becca inched

their way into the crowded kitchen. Becca, who'd arrived with her camera strap draped around her neck, walked to the back door. "Let's wait in the yard. They'll need a stage that's bigger than the kitchen."

After whipping up a costume, Muriel held the door open. June zipped outdoors, ready to perform. She wore a hastily trimmed, multi-layered petticoat Muriel used to wear with her western-style skirts. Fern followed, holding her hand over her mouth to conceal her uncontrollable hiccups.

Leland stuck his face past the doorframe, glancing in all directions.

"Come on," Muriel called out to him. "If you don't come now, I'll round up every last neighbor."

A red-faced Leland stepped outside, earning hoots and laughter from everyone. Percy clutched his belly and crumpled over. When he stood, tears streamed down the side of his face.

Leland tossed his head to the side, as if he were flinging long, European locks out of his eyes. He strode to the center of the lawn, exaggerating toe pointing in the process, and lifted his shoulders.

Fern had to hold her ribs while her big brother, clad in white long johns, a black shirt, and white socks, extended his hand to an enthralled, pink-cheeked forest sprite.

"You first, June. Show 'em your *boo-RAYS*, those tiny little tippy toe steps."

"Like this?" June stretched her arms and grabbed onto Leland's hands. "Hold me up." She didn't just raise herself onto her toes, she balanced herself on the toe-edge of her shoes.

Fern gritted her teeth while Leland pivoted the child in a circle. June's efforts to mimic a ballerina in toe shoes ended soon enough, but seconds later, Leland assumed the dancer's role.

"Okay, now it's time for my fancy cabaret jump. Hold me

steady while I flutter my feet, June."

Caberet? Fern reckoned that was close enough to *cabriole* for her brother, but if he wanted his good fortune to hold, he ought to mimic a clog dancer instead of Belgium's *danseur étoile*.

June shrieked when Leland wouldn't release his grip on her hands. "Don't fall on me, Uncle Leland."

After Leland pretended to jump—his feet didn't leave the ground—he faked a dramatic landing. He finished his fancy steps by rolling onto the ground, taking June with him, the girl flopping onto his chest, and Leland's feet flapping.

Roy and Wayne, who were old enough to stay home without supervision and determined to avoid any activity unrelated to sports or the outdoors, might have reconsidered passing up this trip to Charleston. Had they known about Leland and June's encore, they'd have camped out in the back yard.

From his down-on-the-ground view, Leland spied Becca, who'd hidden behind a bush. He scrambled to his feet. "Becca Bigler, gimme that camera!"

He started after her, but when his path veered toward the street, he stopped dead in his tracks. Leland, Fern's boastful, prideful brother, didn't want to prance around the neighborhood in his underwear. Do tell.

Chapter 35

Leland waited until Betty turned her back to him before he snuck across the lot line, his near-silent side-wheel lawnmower clipping a swath through the neighbor's grass. When he returned to the starting place of his trespassing, he spied the back yard and confirmed Betty was facing the other direction while she hung another sheet on the clothesline. He did an about-face and cut the rest of her front yard.

The game they played was silly, Betty pretending she didn't need help and ignoring Leland while he conducted his not-too-clandestine excursions onto her property for a wide assortment of tasks. On rare occasions she acknowledged Leland's work with a slight tip of her chin, but not once did she discard her scowl. It was sad to see that annoyance had carved permanent lines on her face. It seemed to have ruined her inner parts too.

Leland didn't mind heaping another kindness on Betty, not on a day filled with a sweet breeze and azure skies streaked with wispy cirrus clouds. The scent of fresh-mown grass soothed him, although not in the same manner as a morning spent along the banks of a creek. Those boyhood memories summoned a deep-seated longing, but grownups were supposed to find satisfaction in meeting expectations—mostly other people's—and on a job well done. As Leland measured the outcome of his yard work, he conceded that he'd done a splendid job. It wasn't the same as toting home a stringer of fresh-caught fish, but it inflated his city-dweller pride.

Back on his own turf, Leland chopped away at the unruly hedge. His nose curled when another neighbor, after a few false starts, fired up his gas-powered mower.

Since Leland's hillbilly heart was stuck in the city, it was appropriate to hum a song that blended rock with bluegrass. The upbeat rhythm of Gene Vincent's rockabilly tune, "Be-Bop-A-Lula," encouraged Leland to increase his hedge-trimming tempo and set his feet a-tappin'. He envisioned his own gray-eyed *baby* while he belted out the lyrics, and couldn't stop his noggin from bobbing as he leaned into his work.

"Ahem."

It was a woman's voice. It had to be Betty Hastings standing behind him, more'n likely holding a weapon. Maybe she'd taken offense when his swaying hips joined the rest of his body's appreciation of a lively tune. He stood, stretched his neck muscles, and turned around. The sight made him blink.

The *ahem* originated from an attractive brunette, probably in her early twenties. She wore a white dress with lilac-colored flowers strewn throughout the fabric. The scarf she tied around her ponytail matched the flower petals, and a narrow belt and full skirt drew attention to her curvy figure. She could have been one of those Avon ladies Muriel talked about, but she didn't carry anything that might have held a supply of cosmetics.

"Hello?" Her greeting sounded like a question.

"Can I help you?" Leland glanced down the street. Two doors down, a youngster peered at him from the back window of a sedan parked at the curb.

"I came to see Ellie Bigler. Is she here?"

"And, you are . . . ?"

"I'm Marjorie Greenwald."

"Is Ellie expecting you?"

"No, and she won't recognize my name. If I may, I'd like to introduce myself."

"Wait here."

Leland found Ellie upstairs, dusting furniture. After he described the visitor, Ellie started to reply. Instead, she went downstairs and walked onto the porch. Being the nosy uncle, Leland followed.

"Ellie?" Marjorie's face looked hopeful.

"You're the woman Martin brought to the diner."

"I am. Do you have a few minutes?"

Ellie gestured to the chairs sitting on the porch. Her second signal suggested Leland take himself elsewhere.

"Is that your boy waiting in the car?" Leland asked.

"Yes."

"You want me to go get him?"

"He'll be all right for a minute, but thanks for offering."

Leland resumed his hedge-clipping chore, but stepped around the side of the house to give the girls their privacy, which he interrupted with frequent pauses between snips. He caught bits and pieces of their conversation, which included the words, *scoundrel, ego, pride, possessive, grow up, respect,* and one that sounded mighty close to *salvation*. By the time the word *engaged* reached his hearing, the girls were laughing and carrying on as if they'd known each other for a long while.

If Marjorie had come a-callin' to commiserate with Ellie about the troublemaker known as Martin Hastings, Leland would have liked to add his opinion. It came as a surprise when he heard, not one, but two car doors slam, and two sets of feet strolling down the sidewalk.

The boy was about five years old. He had Marjorie's hair and eye coloring, and freckles on his cheeks and nose. His saunter, which resembled that of the man whose hand he held, was that of a prideful police officer. Leland bit his tongue, said hello to the child, and glowered at the man who knew he was an unwelcome visitor.

Since it was apparent that Ellie had motioned toward the car and invited the newcomers to join them on the porch, Leland moved on down the side of the house, his shears cutting the shrubbery at a ruthless pace. He minded his task until Danny, the boy who lived down the street, started hollering after that mutt of his.

"Princess!"

The mongrel roamed the streets more often than she spent time in her own yard. The sneaky terrier was a capable escape artist, and for reasons unknown, she made a habit of gravitating to Betty's yard. Today was no different, except for the line of laundry flapping in the breeze.

Princess zipped past Leland and tore into the neighbor's back yard. The pooch's timing was poor, in that Betty was wrestling with a sheet when Princess started nipping at the woman's ankles. She lost her footing when she tried to kick the dog, and as she landed, the sheet fluttered before it buried her.

Danny rounded the corner of the house and caught up with Princess, but couldn't grab her before she climbed aboard the neighbor's prostrate body and started dancing on the sheet. If not for the predictable tirade soon to follow, it might have been hilarious.

Martin came to assist, and when he and Danny crouched to corner Princess, Leland tried to snatch the dog. He missed, and that dang canine fled across the busy street, just as she had all those months ago. With Martin busy untangling his aunt from the laundry, Leland and Danny sped across the road. It took fancy footwork from both of them to squeeze Princess into a spot she couldn't escape.

Leland grabbed the dog by her collar, her feet still thrashing at escape speed. "Is your father ever going to fix your fence?"

Danny lowered his eyes. "He don't live there anymore."

"It's just you and your mom?"

"Yes."

"Ask your mom if she'd like me to fix the fence. If it's beyond fixing, maybe you and I can build a kennel for your pup."

Danny's eyes grew wide at the unexpected offer. Betty Hastings wasn't the only person on Truslow Street who could use a serving of kindness.

Leland and Danny waited for traffic to pass and walked back to the house. Martin stood in the yard, wiping dirt off his trousers. Ellie, Marjorie, and her son stood on the porch, watching. Leland transferred Princess to Danny's open arms.

"Keep your hand tight around her collar."

"I will. Thanks, Mr. Dugan."

"You're welcome." Leland's clippers sat on the ground, next to his lawnmower. He'd accomplished quite a bit already. "Tell you what, once I put away the mower and my tools, I'll mosey on over and figure out how to keep her in your yard."

"That'd be swell."

Betty's front door slammed, scaring Danny and everyone within a ten-mile radius. When Danny flinched, he loosened his grip on Princess, who hightailed it to Betty's back yard again.

"Get that dog away from my house," Betty yelled.

Martin rubbed his face with his hand, gave Leland a sympathetic scowl, and called back, "We'll get her. Just hold on."

"I'm tired of holding on. Stop this nonsense right now. Be a policeman."

Martin didn't bristle at the sarcasm. Growing up with Aunt Betty must have provided a lot of practice.

"We're trying to help. Give us a minute."

"Your minute is up." It wasn't until Betty stomped off the porch that Leland could see her hands. She pointed her revolver skyward and started hollering. "Get that blasted dog right now."

Martin set his jaw, lifted his hand, and strode over to Betty. "Give me that thing."

"No." When Betty redirected her aim to Martin's chest, panic seized Leland's form. He staggered as his lungs fought for air.

"Martin," he screamed. "No!"

Chapter 36

When Betty pulled the trigger, the blast was loud enough to pierce eardrums, and the tremor that shook Leland, real or imagined, threatened to take him to his knees. The first image to come into focus was Martin, who lay crumpled on the ground in the space between the two houses. Sunlight glistened against the wet grass, but unlike morning dew on emerald green, its rays reflected ruby red. The second image was Ellie ushering Marjorie's son into the house, horror written on her face and confusion framing his.

Leland scanned the back yard where Princess had backed into a corner, giving Danny a chance to catch her. Leland called out to him, "Take the back way home. Hurry up."

Marjorie rushed to Martin's side while Leland concentrated on Betty. The hand that gripped her revolver hung limply at her side. Her mouth hung partway open while her eyes drifted across the scene. When she peered at Martin, the right side of her face twitched, the expression one of puzzlement. She seemed unaware of the approaching sirens.

"Mrs. Hastings." Leland stood still while he waited for her to acknowledge him. He intended the use of a formal title to show respect. Maybe it would keep her from turning on him.

Betty's face was blank. She made no reply.

"I need you to put down the gun. Right there on the grass, by the hedge. Can you do that for me?"

If his request registered, she didn't show it.

"Mrs. Hastings? The dog's gone, so you don't need the gun. Why don't you put it on the ground?"

After a long wait, she bent over and lowered the revolver to the grass.

"That's good. Now, why don't you come with me? Let's go sit on your porch while help comes for Martin." He heard Marjorie weeping, begging Martin to hang on. Her anguish burned a hole in Leland's core that was as sharp and hot as a fire poker. He wanted to help her, but someone had to restrain Betty.

Betty didn't argue. She turned around, walked to her porch, and took a seat. In the confined area, the stink of booze grew heavy. Her bloodshot eyes added to her weary deportment, and her hands trembled as she lowered them to her lap.

The ambulance and the first of several patrol cars responding to the emergency arrived at the same time. When one of the officers recognized Martin as one of their own, his demeanor flipped faster than a light responded to a toggled switch. As he crossed Betty's yard, the policeman's stride and clenched fists suggested he was ready to exact street justice.

Leland descended the steps and met him in the yard. "Gun's over there."

"Johnson, come bag the gun," the officer yelled. He tried to sidestep Leland.

"Hold on. Let me tell you two things before you arrest her."

"We'll get statements from everyone. Right now, you need to get out of my way and let me do my job."

"That's Betty Hastings, Martin's aunt. They weren't feuding, so it wasn't like that. A while back, Martin made her hand over a cap gun that looked a lot like the gun sitting in the grass over there. When she walked out waving the thing, I think both of them forgot he'd confiscated the toy gun."

The officer didn't acknowledge Leland's comments, but he appeared more in control of his rage than he had just seconds earlier. In less time than it took Leland to walk over to Marjorie and put his arm around her shaking shoulders, the policeman shackled Betty's wrists and led her to his patrol car.

"How bad is it?" Leland asked.

"He's breathing." Marjorie stared at the bloodstained earth. "He's lost a lot of blood."

"What did the doctor say?"

"The intern? He was too busy to tell me anything."

The ambulance driver called out, "Miss? If you're coming along, you need to get in now."

Marjorie turned to Leland. "My son. Steven. Can I leave him with you?"

"Sure you can. When you're ready, I'll come get you and take both of you home." Leland rattled off his telephone number while Marjorie ran to the ambulance. As he watched the vehicle pull away, his shoulders drooped. Whatever the outcome, how could anyone endure what just happened? Marjorie's eyes were full of fear, her body in shock. Inside, a traumatized child sought refuge in the arms of an equally terrified young woman. Down the street, a young boy sat with his dog, seeking comfort from a woman who had no idea what her child had witnessed. Leland pressed his hand against his chest where the weight of the unspeakable scene pressed so hard that inhaling, an involuntary reflex, became a deliberate task.

The *what ifs* started at the back of his mind, but didn't wait long to try to suffocate him. *What if* he'd listened to Martin when he asked to visit Ellie all those weeks ago? *What if* he'd carried the dog home instead of handing her to Danny? *What if* he'd seen the gun before Betty fired it? All of the second-guessing made Leland moan. He walked to the side yard and retched.

He stood and wiped his mouth, drew in clean air. What about Marjorie? How many *what ifs* threatened to bury her? She shouldn't have to worry about remembering a telephone number, and she shouldn't have to sit alone in a hospital.

When one of the policemen approached, Leland asked, "Do you know where they're taking him?"

"Saint Francis Hospital."

"On Laidley Street?"

"Yes. Are you related to Martin Hastings?"

"No, sir."

"You'll need to give a statement to me before you go to the hospital."

"Fair enough." If Ellie could handle Steven, Leland would tend to the boy's mother. While the officer pulled out a pad of paper, Leland prayed for an extra portion of compassion and infinite mercy for all of them.

୰

Leland found Marjorie sitting alone in the corner of the waiting room. She shivered beneath a thin blanket someone had draped over her shoulders, and when Leland approached, she lowered her hands from her face, revealing tear-streaked cheeks and ashen skin. He settled into a nearby chair.

"Any news?"

"Nothing." She wiped her eyes and asked, "Is Steven all right?"

"He's pretty scared, but he's in good hands. My wife came home from work and between Ellie and Muriel, well, they'll take good care of him."

"Thank you."

Leland dipped his head, unwilling to give words to the ghastly stain that turned the lilac blooms on Marjorie's dress into a sordid display of violence. He extended the bag he held in his hand. "The girls thought these might fit you, supposing you'd like to change your clothes." Marjorie looked down, as if she'd been unaware.

While she changed into Muriel's skirt and blouse, Leland searched for a doctor or a nurse who could tend to Marjorie. During the war, he'd seen enough shell-shocked soldiers to know the woman needed more than a blanket. More than anything, she needed to know Martin's condition.

The woman at the registration desk gave Leland the same information she must have shared with Marjorie. "Go take a seat. The doctor will be with you soon."

After returning from the restroom, Marjorie took the cup of coffee Leland extended to her, but declined the sandwich. "I can't."

"Tell me about you and Martin," Leland said. "I'll admit to eavesdropping, but you and Ellie talked too quietly for me to catch much of your conversation."

Marjorie's high cheekbones lifted just a tad, along with the sides of her mouth. "We knew you were listening."

"I heard the word *engaged*."

She took a sip of coffee and closed her eyes for a moment. "We're getting married in October." Her body stiffened when someone strode through the double doors, but the physician who appeared turned away from the waiting room. "When I first met Martin, he swept me off my feet. He's quite the charmer, as I'm sure you've heard, and long before I should have, I let him meet Steven. Those two . . . well . . . it's so sweet to see them together.

I think Martin took everything he learned from his father, who was an abusive alcoholic, and did just the opposite with Steven."

That sounded fine, but that description did not fit the personality Martin exhibited when he spent time with Ellie. If Leland knew one thing about male egos, it was that they didn't change over night. It wasn't his place to impose his opinion, and this wasn't the time to insinuate he had one, so he'd let her talk.

"It was when Martin took me to Three Squares Diner that I got to worrying about him. Did Ellie tell you how awful he was that night?"

"She mentioned it."

"After that humiliating scene, I accused Martin of being a liar." Marjorie stared at the closed doors, her nose turning red and tears falling again. She accepted Leland's handkerchief and blotted her eyes. "I told him I didn't believe him when he told me he'd given his heart to the Savior. He defended himself, but was stunned when I told him that a man's actions were more telling than his words, and that his actions didn't reflect those of a true man of faith."

"I remember him making that claim when he talked about giving up booze."

"He did give it up, but he neglected to fix other things, like his pride."

"Muriel had to correct me on my share of defects," Leland replied. "Sometimes, more than once."

"When he insisted he was reformed and renewed, I told him that his actions needed to reflect his new being, his transformation. If he were truly a new creation, he wouldn't need to boast or to dominate a woman, treating her as something he owned instead of someone he cherished." Sorrow, like a shadow, fell across Marjorie's face.

"It's not as if he had any role models," Marjorie said. "I mean, his family is a mess. Every last one of them."

"What changed?"

"Martin did," Marjorie said with a pained smile. "When I turned his affections aside, he hit his knees, started reading the scriptures, and joined a men's group at church." The tension that enveloped her melted away at the recollection, and her brown eyes warmed when she said, "He wrote out a verse and taped copies to his bathroom mirror, to the front of his refrigerator, and to the back of his front door, so it's the last thing he sees before he leaves his house. 'Establish my footsteps by Your word, and let no wickedness have rule over me.' "

"That's a mighty powerful prayer."

Marjorie flinched when the double doors swung open again. The doctor stopped at the registration desk and let his gaze follow the clerk's finger as she pointed to Marjorie. Leland took Marjorie's hand.

"Miss Greenwald?"

Marjorie nodded.

"You're waiting for word on Martin Hastings?"

The dip of her chin was almost imperceptible.

The doctor put a hand on her shoulder. "I'm sorry, miss. We did—"

Marjorie didn't hear another word. Leland grabbed her shoulders as she slumped in the chair and started to slide to the floor.

Chapter 37

Leland walked onto the porch, intent on preparing his unofficial diagnosis. Like the good doctor who checked his patient's ticker, Leland closed his eyes and declared the temperature to be in the mid-sixties. Where blood pressure was another favorite of white-jacketed physicians, Leland's next test related to humidity. The early morning moisture was heavy, same as yesterday and a dozen days before. Next, instead of slapping the still-cold stethoscope on a patient's chest, listening to inhalations and exhalations, Leland stuck his finger into the air. No wind, not a hint of a breeze. His conclusion? Independence Day promised to be a scorcher.

His attention drifted toward Betty's empty house, an unintentional, yet predictable, action. The shooting was the first thing that came to mind whenever he stepped outside. Short of moving, would that ever change?

Ellie performed the same night Martin died. It was the occasion of the American Academy Ballet's annual recital at the Charleston High School auditorium. She participated because, if nothing else, she appreciated Mr. Van Damme's assertion that if the dancer could walk, she could dance. His remark had more to do with physical injuries than emotional turmoil, but he too, had danced during times of upheaval.

She was one of eighteen dancers, the renowned Julianne Kemp among them, who performed the *Largo Maestoso* portion of Hayden's Symphony no. 53. Later in the program, Ellie participated in *Andante*, a selection from Brahms' Double Concerto in A Minor.

It was more than a sense of duty that led her to the auditorium that dreadful day. Dancing soothed her wounded soul the same way lyrics, a smell, or a sight awakened a person's senses. Muriel found solace between the pages of a book while Leland strummed his guitar and hummed the melodies to countless folk songs. Many of the lyrics were reminiscent of lost yesterdays, and a fair number spoke of hopeful tomorrows. Mostly, the music left him in the present, and not quite as numb as he would have liked.

The following day, Leland introduced himself to Danny's mother and repaired the fence in her back yard. She'd heard the neighborhood gossip about Princess being involved in the altercation at Betty's house, and although Leland wanted to protect the woman from her own list of *what ifs*, he couldn't lie to her. One day, Danny would grasp the truth, and she needed to prepare herself for that. The boy hadn't seen the shooting, and Leland was certain he hadn't witnessed Martin's suffering, but given time, Danny would *know*.

One month after Betty Hasting's arrest, and following untold hours during which crews emptied and repaired her house, a realtor stuck a For Sale sign in the front yard. They mowed the lawn, uprooted dandelions—something akin to heresy for a country boy like Leland—trimmed the bushes, and attached flower boxes to the porch railing. If not for the negative publicity regarding the home, it might have sold already. More than likely, an unaware family would purchase the place and learn to deal with its history.

After Leland watered the blazing array of crimson geraniums that occupied large terra-cotta pots on either side of their porch, he dragged the hose to the back of the house. He could almost hear the tomato plants sigh when the water soaked into the dirt and soothed their thirsty roots. The chicken wire that protected the fruit from squirrels and other citified vermin wasn't particularly attractive, but it worked. He scooted the end aside, selected four plump beauties, and left them on the back stoop while he secured the wire and tamed the hose into a neat coil.

Before he retrieved the tomatoes, Leland pulled a handful of vibrant dandelion blooms and their spikey green leaves, and tucked the pretties into his shirt pocket. They'd add color to the salad.

The heat from the kitchen almost sent Leland back out the door. Company was coming soon, and Muriel had turned on the oven at the same time she brewed a pot of predawn coffee. If this were their house, he might have saved enough greenbacks to buy a window air conditioner. Most people who could only afford one unit put them in their bedroom, but in the Dugan household, the kitchen would be the wiser location. It was the hub. Give him a pillow, he'd sleep on the floor.

Leland put the tomatoes on the counter and pulled the dandelions out of his pocket. He waited until Muriel finished lifting a pie out of the oven before he placed a hand on each of her shoulders and spun her around so he could see her face. The humidity had tightened the natural curls in her hair, a fact of summer that annoyed her. Leland wouldn't have noticed the similarity between Muriel's summer locks and Shirley Temple's childhood curls, but since Muriel mentioned it, well, there it was. Despite the heat and dots of perspiration on her brow, her eyes maintained their cool, silvery tone and accentuated her rosy cheeks.

Muriel swatted her hot pad holder at the air as she pulled away. "It's too hot. Don't touch me."

"It'll never be too hot to give my girl a squeeze."

"Girl? I'm as wilted as a daylily long past sundown."

"Somehow you manage to be gorgeous and a wreck at the same time."

"*Pfft*. Either make yourself useful or get out of here."

"I'd rather be appreciated. What can I do?"

Muriel twisted sideways and directed his view to the sink, her expression offering a challenge. "I made a mess with the pies, but if that's too much trouble, you could set out the plates, glasses, and silverware, or you could make the salad."

A double dare. If he offered to make the salad, he'd have to do the dishes first.

"You just mosey on out to the front porch while I make haste with the sink and the salad. 'Bout the time you finish another cup of coffee, I'll be ready for a new assignment."

He didn't have to offer twice. Muriel tossed off her fruit-splotched apron, filled a cup, and fled. Leland was already warm, but his heart heated at her unspoken gratitude just the same.

The homestead in Elizabeth might have been a better place to gather for a picnic than the Truslow Street house. June, though, begged to see a big city parade, so everyone crammed into the tiny abode and miniscule yard that he, Muriel, and Ellie called home. Leland lost count of the number of people who joined the fun during the day, especially with Ellie's ballet friends coming and going.

Late in the afternoon, when Nettie, the clan's official matriarch, designated Percy, Wayne, and Roy as the cleanup crew, Leland counted himself among them. So it was that he found himself back in the kitchen, suds in the sink, passing dishes to

Roy, who would rinse them and hand them off to Wayne. Percy acted more like a supervisor than a cleaner-upper, although he did manage to hang up the last of the wet towels.

With the women lolling on the porch, Roy and Wayne went into the living room and turned on the television, and Percy and Leland retreated to the back yard. June squatted next to the stoop, her face pressed close to the pavement. Steven, Marjorie's boy and a frequent guest at the Dugan home, stood nearby, his heels rocking back and forth.

"What have you got there?" Percy asked.

June shrugged. "I dunno." Belly-up on the cement was a dark brown June bug. Back when Leland's family farmed, the critter was an unwelcome pest, gnawing on corn, strawberries, and potatoes. Here, the worst the beetle could do was chew flowers and damage the lawn or, in the case of a dead one, upset a little girl who thrilled at the wonder of all living things.

"Do you know what that's called?" Leland asked.

June didn't take her eyes off the insect. "No."

"That's a June bug."

She swung her head up, her face showing disbelief. "A June bug? June? Like me?"

"That's right," Leland said.

"Can you guess where the June bug got its name?" Percy asked.

"No."

"When's your birthday?"

"June nineteenth."

"Now can you guess?"

"They're born on my birthday?"

"They might be, but mostly they get their name because they start out as larvae, which are similar to caterpillars, and after they turn into beetles, like a caterpillar turns into a butterfly, they usually wake up during the month of June. That's why they're called June bugs."

That sounded like an awful lot of science for a child, but both June and Steven followed along with Percy's explanation.

"Can I touch him?" June asked.

"Why sure," Percy replied.

June used gentle fingers when she lifted the bug and turned it over so she could examine its wings. "How come it died?"

Steven offered his version of the obvious with nary a lost beat. "Because it's July. The Fourth of July."

June almost dropped the bug, and her eyes went wide with fright. "Is that true, Daddy?"

"I don't know why it died, but I don't think it had anything to do with Independence Day."

"What about me?"

"What about you?"

June lifted the bug toward Percy. "When it's July, am I . . ."

"Oh, no, no, no." Percy wrapped June in his arms, taking care not to dislodge the bug. "Your name has everything to do with the month you were born, a time full of sunshine and the goodness of summer, and nothing else. Do you hear me?"

The girl fastened her dark brown eyes on her father's face, examining his expression, mostly his hazel eyes. Percy didn't waver, and when June decided to believe him, she gave him a hug and pulled away. She turned around and handed the bug to Steven.

"Let's go show your mommy." Having discarded the temporary worry, June and Steven took off toward the front of the house.

Percy exhaled with enough force to move Charleston's stale air all the way to the Atlantic Ocean. "I didn't see that coming."

"Thought we'd have two children bawling," Leland replied.

"So did I." Percy pulled in another breath and let it out slowly, deliberately, as if the doctor in Leland's early morning analogy had issued the instruction. "It took me by surprise when Marjorie came back here for a visit, and when I heard she brought Steven along, I wondered at her wisdom."

"It took a lot of courage, but she and Ellie found friends in each other."

"I think you and Muriel have a lot to do with it too. You make folks feel at home."

"Funny thing about the places we call home. Never saw myself living here. I can't imagine how much you miss Ellie. Do you ever wish she'd go back to Elizabeth?"

"Wishing. That's all it would be. Ellie's never been happier, and it's not just the ballet. Don't repeat this to her mother, but I can see that Ellie belongs here. What about you?" Percy swung his hand from one side of the yard to the other. "Are you at home here?"

"You know me better than that. I was the one who whined the whole time we were in Nevada. The hills and hollows will always be home to me. We're in Charleston because we need to be."

"You ever think about coming back?"

"Don't know how we'd swing it."

"But, this place is all right for now?"

Leland regarded the yard, the staked tomato plants, and the yellow blooms poking through blades of grass. Just like always, when he closed his eyes, the persistent odor of chemicals and the incessant clamor that was inherent to the city fought with his determination to feel as if he belonged here. He turned toward Percy, who stood at an angle that pulled Betty's house into view.

"That place," Leland said as he jutted his chin in the direction of the house, "brings me down."

"Why don't you move?"

"Can't run from what happened."

"True, but although you can't do anything with the image you see in the mirror every day, you can change your surroundings."

Percy's observation held some truth, but . . . "Why would I want to change the image I see in the mirror?" Leland puffed out his chest, such as it was in his middle age, and hefted his shoulders. "I'll have you know that my wife still considers me a genuine Romeo."

"Romeo? Isn't that a variety of tomato?"

"That's Roma, wise guy. R-*o-m-a*. If you have to compare me to a tomato, I'd be more like one of those heirloom varieties. Perfection passed down. You probably fancy yourself a red beefsteak, which is appropriate, all things considered."

"All what things?" Percy said, his eyes narrowing.

"Go on inside and take a look in the mirror. See for yourself. Beefsteak tomatoes are a tad wide around the middle."

"Hey, now."

Fern peeked out the screen door. "What's going on out here?"

"Nothing," Leland said. "Just talking about gardening."

"I doubt that." Fern stepped onto the stoop, her eyes studying the men, both of whom straightened their posture.

"Your brother is challenging your husband's masculinity," Percy said as he made a feeble attempt to pump his biceps.

When Leland howled, Fern smacked his arm.

"Do that again."

All three of them turned toward Becca, who stood at the corner of the house, her face hidden behind her camera's viewfinder.

"Do what?" Fern asked.

"Dad. Do your muscleman interpretation for me."

"Hear that?" Leland asked, his voice saturated with amusement. "Your muscleman interpretation." He turned to Fern. "Not 'show me your muscles' but 'your muscleman interpretation.' What a hoot."

When Percy made a move, as if to cuff Leland in the chops, Leland bounced on his toes, an overt reminder to Percy that Leland "Ricochet" Dugan, the not-ever-famous CCC boxer, was fast on his feet.

"Come on, Methane, show me what you've got," Leland said.

"See what you started," Percy called out to Becca.

"I see. Y'all better settle down before the impressionable children see you."

"You mean June and Steven?" Leland asked.

"No, I mean Roy and Wayne."

"Another time then," Leland replied as he ran his eyes over Percy, pausing a tad when he reached the man's midsection, which earned an eyeball roll from his target. Leland hadn't had this much fun with Percy in a long time.

"Where'd you go?" Muriel asked as she stepped around Becca and walked toward Fern.

Muriel and Fern, different as they were from one another, were lovely to behold. Both were attractive in the physical sense, but it was their hearts that exposed their worth. Between the two of them, they had enough tenacity and determination to change the tilt of the earth's axis, traits that amazed Leland as much as they bewildered him.

"They distracted me," Fern said. "I came to invite you out front. June and Steven want to light sparklers, and Becca wants to take pictures." She waved her hand as if it held a lasso and she'd just captured Percy and Leland. "Let's go."

As the men followed the women to the front yard, Leland smacked his shoulder into Percy. "You ready to rumble?"

"Last time, things didn't turn out very well."

"Turned out all right for me. I won my girl."

Percy scowled. "Eventually, and in spite of yourself."

"I'll accept there's some truth in that."

"I believe you owe me an apology."

"After all this time?" Leland asked. "You're joking."

"Who's joking? You called me a wide-waisted wimp."

Leland couldn't hold his shoulders still. They shook in time with his horselaugh. "I did, although your words are a lot more creative than mine. You started it by calling my mug a tomato. Them's fighting words, Bigler."

Leland rammed his shoulder into Percy again, knocking both of them off balance. When they righted themselves, it was Fern Dugan Bigler's face burning holes in both of them that shut them right up. The tomato war was over. For now.

Chapter 38

"These are fabulous." Ellie studied the photograph before she lowered it to the countertop and lifted another one.

Despite Fern's frequent visits to Still Life Portrait Studio, every time she walked inside, her nose curled at the metallic odor emitted by the developing agent and the fixing bath. Aside from knowing the purpose of the chemicals used to process film, her understanding of photography was paltry. Ron, on the other hand, was proving to be a promising student, among other roles.

Fern leaned over Ellie's shoulder. "Is that your old roommate?"

"Sure is. I wonder if I should show this to Norma or let her boyfriend sneak a peek. I bet he'd like to buy one of these and frame it for her birthday."

"If you're asking for an opinion," Ron said, "I'd give the guy a chance to be a hero."

Fern turned around so she could rest her eyes on Ron, who scratched the back of his neck while he looked out the window. Heat scorched Becca's face, but Fern couldn't determine whether it was a reaction to Ron's reply or Fern's overt assessment of Becca's beau. Fern hadn't meant to embarrass either of them, but their quiet courtship reminded her of the sweet, unassuming manner Percy used when he wooed her. Like Percy, Ron displayed emotions that were both ardent and bashful.

Ron's focus came back inside, winding the long way around the room, deftly skirting Fern's appraisal, and landing on Ellie. "He ought to buy two. Keep one for himself."

"Her parents will want one," Fern said. "Her grandparents and aunts and uncles too."

"You're probably right," Ellie said. "So, how do you want to do this? Do you want me to take these to the studio and see who wants to place an order, or what?"

"Ron had a good suggestion," Becca said. "I'll let him explain."

"Well, like I told Becca, I think it might be more professional if she worked with Mr. Van Damme to schedule a time to display the pictures at the dance studio. He could invite the dancers and their parents, and Becca could take orders and collect money, both at the same time."

"Good idea," Ellie said. "I'd rather not be responsible for taking money or making mistakes with an order."

"If I can get away, I'll go along and give you a hand," Fern said.

Becca's blush warmed her cheeks again. "Thanks, but if you'd cover for Ron, I think he'd be more helpful." Becca's eyes widened. "He knows more about the studio."

"Yes, he does, and yes, I'll work around the schedule."

Ellie set another picture aside. She scanned the room, as if she were memorizing every detail. "You've got a mighty fine business here, Becca. Do you think I could do this some day?"

"You want to be a photographer?"

"No, but this makes me wonder if I could open a ballet school when I'm too old to perform."

"In Elizabeth?" Becca asked.

"Why not?"

"Do you think you'd have enough students to make it worthwhile? You know the population and their resources are limited."

"I could do the same thing Mr. Van Damme does. He teaches more than ballet, you know."

No, Fern wasn't aware. How Ellie's instructor fit one more thing into his schedule was inconceivable.

"In addition to dancing with the Royal Opera House of Brussels, he was a professor there. He also studied child psychology, so he knows more than dance steps and choreography. He believes dance promotes good health and instills discipline."

Fern ran her eyes down her own form. Granted, she didn't have a ballerina's sleek body, but she was fit as a fiddle, as the locals would say. "The way I see it, planting, weeding, and harvesting require flexibility, muscle, and endurance."

Ellie covered her mouth when she laughed aloud. "I've seen you do an impressive *grand jeté*—it's like doing splits in midair—when a snake sneaks up on you."

"Or a whole row of *pliés*, when it's weeding time." Becca demonstrated with a pair of deep knee bends, her hands yanking invisible weeds.

"I was going to say that my gymnastics lacked the artistic part, but according to you two, I'm already an accomplished performer." Fern swatted her hand at Ellie. "If you opened a dance studio in Elizabeth, I'd keep quiet about my healthy regimen. If word got out, you wouldn't see a single woman in your classroom, because everyone who lives here works a garden."

"I don't think I need to worry. Honestly, though, can you see me teaching children and adults how to dance, not just ballet, but folk dance and creative dancing?"

"I don't see why not," Fern replied. "We've all seen the way you interact with June. She loves to dance with you."

Ellie chewed the tip of her thumbnail, although her confidence increased with each positive response from her kin. "What about exercise classes meant to instill poise and grace? Do you think anyone would enroll in one of those?"

"I could probably use a few, especially when you consider how I *plié* my way through a row of tomatoes."

When Fern mimicked Becca's rendition of her weeding, Becca and Ellie broke into uncontrollable guffaws, but Ron, bless his mortified heart, feigned interest in the scene beyond the window again. He sure was a likeable young fella, respectful too.

※

Leland adjusted the drop cloth he'd stretched under the front door and stirred the can of ebony-tinted paint. He soaked in the fragrance of an early autumn day and dipped his brush into the lustrous solution. Muriel had a habit of singing softly while she did her housekeeping chores, and with the door ajar, she serenaded him, unaware.

Once he and Muriel agreed their futures rested in Charleston—he, with quiet acceptance and she, with unconcealed delight—they set out to find a home that hugged the Truslow neighborhood but put distance between them and Betty Hastings' place. A modest bungalow was the obvious choice, but Muriel had good reason to suggest Leland consider a larger house, not that she had visions of grandeur, but to make sure they were prepared to host any number of kin who might need to call Charleston home, whether long term or short. Once in a while, when Muriel caught a fever about something, it set her eyes to glowing like a child mesmerized by the wonder of a falling star. Where house shopping was concerned, she rearranged his thrifty mindset.

Some might consider their timing poor, what with the terms *Cold War* and *Atomic Age* capturing recent headlines. Just two months prior, the USSR sent shivers across the globe when it launched the world's first intercontinental ballistic missile. If that weren't enough, they sent up a satellite soon after, named it Sputnik. It seemed to Leland that the Russians carried out the act so they had reason to gloat, a personal affront to President Eisenhower, given the man's military credentials and expertise. Despite the disquieting threat, Leland had work to do. He'd trust the president to do his job, and he'd beseech the Giver and Sustainer of Life for whatever protection He might deem fit.

The words of a wise preacher tugged at Leland as he brushed paint over the surface of the wood. For centuries, the minister had said, people have speculated about the end times prophecy found in scripture, but the preacher suggested folks should recognize that the present represented their own "end times." Leland wiped a splotch of paint that snuck onto the window glass and assessed his own level of preparedness. People would make wiser choices if they heeded that message.

He and Muriel had taken care in their selection of a home. The two-story foursquare, with its traditional pyramid-shaped roof, needed a touch of general maintenance and spiffing up, but the home had good bones. It had four bedrooms and boasted a broad, covered front porch. Wide steps and a freshly painted railing tendered an invitation to passersby to stop and visit for a spell. And, they had. He and Muriel moved in less than a month earlier, and the visitors kept a-comin'. Overall, this relocation was right nice.

"Hey, mister. What'cha doing?" A little girl, about five or six years old, stood in front of the steps. She wore a wrinkled polka-dotted dress, anklet socks, and black patent leather shoes, not typical attire for October despite the unseasonably warm day. Her raven hair swirled into long ringlets as it fell past her shoulders, and her pale blue eyes captured the reflection of the morning sky. She rocked on her heels while she waited for a reply.

"Painting." Leland tilted his chin in her direction. "What are *you* doing?"

"Watching."

"What's your name?"

"Linda."

"Nice to meet you, Linda."

"What's your name?"

"Mr. Dugan."

Her face took on an expression that reminded Leland of Muriel, one part skeptical and the other part annoyed by a bothersome response. "What kind of name is that?"

"My kind of name."

"That's too hard. I'll forget."

"You could call me Mr. D."

"That's silly."

"Is not."

"Is too."

"How 'bout you call me Mr. Leland?"

Her face scrunched worse than before, but after obvious consternation, she had a breakthrough. "I know. You're Mr. Doody."

"Mr. Doody?"

"On account of your hair. It's red like Howdy Doody."

Well, *how do* to Leland's new nickname. Muriel would snigger, but if Percy got wind of the title, he'd wear out his welcome at the new Dugan abode in around eight seconds, maybe less.

Linda's tipped up nose suggested she'd won the debate. How could he argue? The tyke was cute as a button, epitome of the cliché, but it was her eyes that clinched the deal. They weren't the same color as Muriel's, but they emanated the same intensity. It was plain to see that Linda's personality, full of wonder, grace, and a generous serving of tenacity, like Muriel's, might require deliberation on his part. Mr. Doody, it was.

Muriel tapped on the doorframe. "Can I come out?" She held a book in one hand and a cup of coffee in the other. Leland opened the door wide while she slipped outside, settled her cup onto a little wrought iron table, and took a seat. "Thanks." She spied their visitor and smiled. "Hello."

"Who's she?"

"This is my wife, Mrs. Doody." Muriel's reaction was none too flattering.

"She's not Mrs. Doody."

"Why not?"

"Her hair's same as mine."

Muriel's jiggling shoulders told Leland she'd guessed the source of his new moniker.

"Muriel, this is my new friend Linda." Leland warmed at the sight of the girl, who beamed at Muriel. "I'll let you two figure out how she should address you."

Linda gathered her courage and ascended a single step. "Muriel's a pretty name. Can I call you Miss Muriel?"

"You sure can. Where do you live, Linda?"

"Down there. The yellow house." She climbed a second step.

"Does your mommy know you're here?"

Linda didn't answer the question, but advanced a third step. "What'cha reading?"

Muriel turned the book over. "It's a book about history."

"Can you read it to me?"

"I don't think you'd like this. It's pretty boring."

"Can you read a storybook to me instead?"

"I don't have any."

Linda looked as if Muriel had just committed a crime. "Why not? Don't you read to your babies?"

Muriel's face flushed. "I don't have any of those either."

"Oh." Linda turned around, climbed back down the steps, and walked toward the yellow house.

Leland stared at Muriel. She sat with her jaw hanging open, her expression bewildered. "What just happened?" she asked.

"I'm not sure." Leland set the paint can on the floor and balanced the brush on the rim before he walked over to Muriel. "She'll be back. The gal's curious. She's got spunk too. I like her." Leland kissed Muriel's cheek, retraced his steps, and bent to pick up his brush. "Y'already heard. She and I are friends."

A shadow fell over Muriel's face. "You're a lot better at that kind of thing than I am."

Leland turned his face away and squeezed his eyes. Would anything fill that void? Muriel had seasons in her life where she seemed content, but on occasion, something as simple as a giggle from one of Fern's brood reminded Muriel that, whereas Fern and Percy had made babies as easily and naturally as seasons change, Muriel and Leland had not. Certain folks considered childless couples failures, and during the times their empty arms believed the notion, they were in a heap of trouble. Preparing a defense for the self-abasement that materialized now and again was pert 'near impossible. What was Leland to say?

Before he turned back to Muriel, Leland heard Linda's feet skipping down the sidewalk. Muriel wiped her eyes and emitted a quiet puff of air. "What have you got there?"

"*Peter Rabbit*. Will you read it to me?" Linda, now wearing a sweater over her dress, held the book in front of her and swiveled her shoulders back and forth while she waited.

"Does your mommy know you're here?"

"No."

"You need to ask her permission first."

"I can't."

"Isn't she home?"

Linda turned around and waved. "That's my daddy."

When Leland stepped to the edge of the porch and saw a young man and a toddler walking toward the house, he joined them on the sidewalk. After a brief introduction to Alvin and his son Brett, and following a necessary chat, they shook hands.

Alvin called out to Linda. "Don't stay too long. You don't want to wear out your welcome."

Linda raced up the steps. She shoved her storybook into Muriel's hand, slid Leland's chair right next Muriel's, and plopped down in the seat.

When Muriel glanced at Leland, she'd shed her self-condemnation, stuffing it into the shadows where it would lurk until another untimely remark or memory would revive it. This instant, thankfulness draped itself over her form. She opened the book to the first page and tilted it so Linda could see the artwork.

"Ahem. Excuse me." Alvin stood at the base of the stairs, his face apologetic, and his son shifting his weight from one foot to the other. "Brett would like to join your story time. Could we impose more than we already have?"

Muriel handed the book to Linda, stepped to the edge of the porch, and extended her hand to the boy. "Hello, Brett. I'd love to read to you today. Why don't you sit right there while I meet your daddy?"

The dark-haired boy, who looked as much a scamp as his sister did, darted to Muriel's chair. As Alvin walked home, Muriel returned to her chair, put her hands on her hips, and said, "Hmm. Would you mind sitting on my lap so I don't have to sit on the floor?"

Brett hopped down and waited two seconds for Muriel to sit before he climbed aboard. Leland measured the joy in Muriel's face as she settled back, opened the book, and cleared her throat. Maybe he ought to talk to Becca about buying a camera. His mind might recall this scene in color, but it would do them both good to see a framed remembrance in black and white.

"Miss Muriel?" Linda's voice wavered. "Can you go to where my mommy left off?"

Muriel's face wore a question Leland dared not answer. Not with the children sitting right there. Linda had clambered to the porch before he could share Alvin's explanation.

"Sure." Muriel handed the book to Linda. "Just show me where I should pick up."

Linda thumbed through the pages. "Right here."

"Are you sure you don't want your mommy to read the rest?"

"She can't."

Leland couldn't see Linda's face, but Muriel had a hard time composing herself when Linda said, "My mommy doesn't live here anymore. She can't read to me again until I see her in heaven."

Chapter 39

Miss Muriel's story time took on a life of its own, a birthing of sorts. Alvin, embarrassed by his children's insistent begging, dropped off Linda and Brett the following week and stuck around to help Leland caulk window frames, pull off screens, and install storm windows.

Muriel baked gingerbread for the occasion, and when Linda asked if she could help next time, they adopted a new routine. Each week, a baking lesson preceded the book session. Whether it was the aroma of gingerbread, cookies, or cinnamon rolls wafting through the neighborhood, or Muriel's growing reputation as a fine storyteller, Leland couldn't guess, but her audience and her kitchen guests multiplied.

Wasn't long before a few boys started knocking on the door at the same time lessons started in the kitchen, but since they weren't interested in culinary arts—Muriel's terminology, not Leland's—he created projects for them. No question, they were downhill helpers. Since three-year-old Brett always came with Linda, he joined the ranks of the apprentice handymen. Alvin, a considerate neighbor and doting father, soon escorted his children each week and gave Leland a hand with the boys. Mostly, he helped Leland attend to the same kind of disaster Muriel faced in the kitchen, although the men dealt with heaps of nuts, bolts, and wood glue instead of cake batter, eggshells, and sticky countertops.

Today, Muriel had an able assistant. Fern and June arrived the day before, enjoyed a movie with Ellie, and spent the night so that they could join the neighborhood gathering.

Leland, the last of the woodworking warriors to clean up his mess, climbed the basement stairs and found Fern standing at the stove, stirring hot chocolate. Steam from the pot fogged the nearby window, while heat from the oven and the burner warmed the room.

"Something smells good. What did y'all bake today?"

Fern dipped the tip of her pinkie into the pot, checking the temperature. She turned up the heat on the burner before she answered. "Coffee cake."

"I smell more than cinnamon and vanilla."

"We thawed blueberries and tossed 'em into the batter."

"Whose idea was that?"

"June suggested it."

"Smart girl." Leland glanced around the kitchen and peered down the hallway. "Where is everybody?"

"Muriel and her bakers went outside to watch the boys coax birds to move into their new birdhouses."

"You're serious."

"They're pretty cute."

"Which? The boys or their birdhouses?"

"Both, but you might want to bring your carpenters inside and give them a short lesson about birds and their habitats, Mr. Doody."

Leland chewed on the nickname. "I'll do that while they're eating cake and drinking hot chocolate. Now, about the Mr.

Doody title, don't go telling your husband."

"He caught wind of it weeks ago. Fact is, I think he's trying to find a piece of wood big enough to make a sign for your porch that says, 'Welcome. Residence of Miss Muriel and Mr. Doody.'"

"You better count me out for Thanksgiving, then. Between working, repairing, and spiffing up the house, I'm too tired to tackle Percy and his wiseacre mouth."

"You ought to be grateful Linda dubbed you Mr. Doody. Percy would have a field day if she'd named you after Woody Woodpecker, especially with that beak of yours."

Leland pressed his hand against his nose. "What's wrong with my nose?"

"Nothing, Brother. I'm just grateful I take after my mother. That's all I'm saying."

"Now, see here . . ." Leland couldn't summon a retort, what with his curiosity resting on his nose.

Fern made wide circles with the spoon as she kept the hot chocolate from sticking to the bottom of the pot. She took on a thoughtful expression when she turned to face Leland. "It sounds odd coming from me, but I'm a mite jealous of you and Muriel."

"This house ain't any better than yours. Doesn't have land, woods, a stream nearby. You've got no reason to be jealous."

"I wasn't talking about the house."

"What, then?"

"Listen. What do you hear?"

It took a second, but Leland understood. "The same laughter and carrying on that you and Percy have enjoyed your whole married life."

"The laughter's thinning out in Elizabeth. Ellie's gone. Becca's always busy in her portrait studio or running off to a music session with Ron. Wayne's football schedule tore him away from the house since practice started in the summer, and now he wants to try out for the basketball team."

"You still have Roy and June underfoot."

"Roy wants to join the Rifle Club, but he's itching to finish school. He hasn't said as much, but I think he wants to enlist as soon as he graduates from high school."

"In what?"

"The Marine Corps."

"You think he wants to make a career out of soldiering?"

Fern bit her bottom lip, pride and fear warring across her furrowed brow. She answered with a reluctant nod. "You know, I used to think I understood how you and Muriel felt about wanting children of your own, but not having any. Now, while I prepare for an empty house, I understand how much I didn't grasp your situation. I'd like to apologize for every time I've spoken without realizing the effect my words have had on the two of you."

"You've got no reason to apologize."

"You're being kind. Those children outside? They've adopted you and Muriel, straight out. You've been a father to Danny after his own walked out. You've been Uncle Leland to Marjorie's boy, and you've cared for my children as if they were your own. I'm beholden, for sure, but you humble me, you and Muriel." Fern had to turn away from the stove so her tears didn't fall into the pan.

The Dugan men weren't huggers, but Leland couldn't help himself. He wrapped his arms around Fern's shoulders and pulled her face to his chest. "You get lonely, you just get in your car and come visit for a spell. Stay as long as you want." He released his arms and handed his handkerchief to her. Much as he tried to contain himself, he could not erase the naughty grin that forced up one side of his mouth.

"What's funny?"

"I'm just commiserating with you, Fern. That husband of yours? Well, it ain't no wonder you need encouragement now and again. I mean, Percy tries to be heroic and attentive and all of that, but like I've always said, you cannot expect Percy Bigler, the man of many words, to meet the high standards you witnessed when you grew up among the Dugan men." Leland stressed his assessment by stuffing his lungs with air, thrusting out his chest, and clenching his teeth so as to give his best toothsome comeback. He was ill prepared, however, for the spoonful of hot chocolate that she flicked all over the front of his favorite, worn-so-long-they-felt-like-pajamas overalls.

That night, after Fern went home, and hours after the house was empty of children, Muriel nestled next to Leland. His eyes bulged when she ran her icy toes along his calf. He should have purchased one of those electric blankets while Muriel still had her Diamond employee discount. When she reached over and ran her finger along his jaw, he gave thanks that her hands were warm.

"Leland?"

"Hmm?"

"Thank you for coming here."

"Why would you thank me? Your working helped us buy this house. It wasn't all me. Never has been."

"I'm not talking about the house. Thank you for leaving home, for working so hard, and for opening this house and the last one to kin and to strangers who have become friends. For heaping kindness without expecting anything in return."

"Why would you thank me for leaving home? I like Charleston just fine."

"I know your heart yearns for the hills and the hollows, for dawns that unfold while deer abandon their nighttime foraging and seek shelter in the woods. Where birdsong greets the sunrise and innumerable stars fill the nighttime skies. You hunger for those things."

She sounded like a poet who sat on a cabin's front porch, her back and forth motion in the rocking chair keeping time with the beat of life in the hills and hollows, and her senses giving verse to what Leland considered hallowed ground. The image and the recollections of that life brought a lump to his throat.

He rolled to his side and regarded Muriel. Moonlight washed her face and rested on the tips of her eyelashes. "I reckon I miss those things the same way you miss your mother, the way you miss Captain Levy." Habits stuck hard. Despite the time that elapsed after courting and marrying the captain's daughter, Leland couldn't bring himself to call him Gordon, or Pops, or anything else. "People come and go. People move around. You were right when you said home isn't a place. Remember?"

"Flinging my words back at me, are you?" Muriel's sigh was one of contentment, an emotion as elusive as joy, but nowadays, a frequent, welcome visitor.

"I am. 'No matter the location of the house, home is where you find the people you love.' Your words, exactly. Where you are is where I want to be. Do you believe me?"

Muriel leaned over and met Leland's lips with a kiss. "I do."

He ran his finger along her damp cheek. "I love you to pieces, Mrs. Dugan, and now that we've straightened out any misunderstandings, can we go back to your comment about flinging words back to you?"

"I guess. Why?"

"Well, speaking of flinging, did you see what Fern did to my overalls? Will that chocolate stain come out?"

Muriel patted Leland's hand, rolled over, and plumped her pillow. "Good night, Leland."

"Hey."

She shifted her warm foot away from him and snuged her

other set of ice cube toes against his leg.

"Hey!"

Epilogue

August 1968
Brussels, Belgium

Ellie's stomach was in knots, as queasy as it had been the night of her debut, the moment just before she passed beyond the wings and took her place on the stage. Tonight the sources of the churning were excitement, expectation, and exhilaration, all rolled up and ready to burst. She'd waited more than a decade for this, if dreaming counted among one's timetable. As vivid as her imagination had been, it didn't compare to the depth of emotion that set every cell of her body tingling.

Henri reached for her hand. In the dim light, his gaze, though intense, wrapped her in quietude. "You've no reason to be nervous, *mon papillon*." My butterfly. The term never failed to make Ellie blush. He ran his finger along her jaw and kissed her cheek, his composition serving a *crescendo* instead of his intended *diminuendo*.

Ellie's nerves were on edge for a host of reasons, the primary culprit being Brussels itself. Wonder upon wonder filled her senses as she devoured the capitol city's history, its beauty, and its elegance. The scenes, the people, the scents, and the food were as foreign to her as the language was. The city had its own rhythm, a European heartbeat, so different from the one that pulsed throughout West Virginia. Brussels invigorated her at the same time it intimidated her. If not for Henri's familiarity with the city and the language, she might not have exited the airplane. If not for Pan Am's blue-uniformed stewardesses, with their matching blue hats, their white-gloved hands, and their remarkable ability to calm a first-time passenger, Ellie might not have remained in her seat long enough for the pilot to guide the aircraft into the sky. But what a sight it was, inching upward, passing through clouds, and settling into another blue realm.

Ellie turned her face and pressed her lips against Henri's mouth. "*Mon trésor.*" Her pulse pitter-pattered as she said those words. In every respect, Henri was her treasure. If not for him, many of her dreams—the ones that counted—would have remained just that.

She pressed her hand near her waist where no one, as yet, could detect the secret she held. Aside from Henri, the only others who knew were Andre and Maggy Van Damme. If not for the trip to Belgium, Ellie would have shouted their news to the world, but rather than create worries where none were necessary, she and Henri decided to postpone the announcement until they returned to West Virginia.

This little one changed everything, all for the good. They'd waited five years, Ellie living out her passion and Henri content to put in a day's work at the Libbey-Owens-Ford Glass Company. Folks who believe the appearance or departure of people in their lives haphazard, fail to give the Maker His due. How much wiser to give credit to the One who determines the number of his days, the One who knows a man's coming and his going, his sleeping and his rising.

So, was it a coincidence when Uncle Leland invited the new Libbey employee to a family picnic? Did chance alter Ellie's schedule at Three Squares Diner so she could join the festivities? Did good fortune knit two like-minded souls together? Ellie scoffed at the thought. No, no, and no. It was He, the same omnipotent Elohim who breathed life into the tiny form that nestled in her womb. No doubt, no question, no argument. Not from Ellie. Not from Henri. Not from anyone who acknowledged the Creator, He who set the sun in the sky and choreographed the movement of the very same clouds the jet pierced as it soared upward. Ellie looked around her, awed by the path He placed before her.

Perhaps her reaction was due to the heightened levels of hormones coursing through her body, but when Henri studied her face, his serious expression transformed Ellie's awed state to one of uncontrollable glee. "I'm gobsmacked." She clapped her hand over her mouth, reigning in her laughter.

"You're what?"

"Gobsmacked. It's one of my father's favorite words. It just came to me. I'm gobsmacked."

"Ellie Dumont, you're a mystery." His wink was as much a tease as it was endearing.

Ellie Dumont. She loved her married name. It was part of His plan. Had to be. How else did she fall in love with the son of a Belgian glassblower who immigrated to West Virginia, and whose surname, Dumont, translated to *from the mountain*?

"We need to settle down before they throw us out of here," she said.

"Yes, we do."

"It's almost time. I still can't believe this." Ellie envisioned the program, *programme*, as it were. Tchaikowsky's *"Ni Fleurs, Ni Couronnes,"* *"Roméo et Juliette,"* *"Le Sacre du Printemps."* In her limited

French, she translated, "Neither Flowers, Nor Crowns," Romeo without the accent on the *e*, Juliet without the *te*, and the "Rites of Spring." It was *magnifique!*

When she had envisioned the Brussel's Royal Opera House, her perspective was from that of a dancer, off stage and waiting for her cue. Tonight, as the lights faded and the symphony's musicians played the first strains, Ellie pressed her shoulder against Henri, squeezed his hand, and watched the curtain rise. She gaped, mesmerized at the scene. Her heart, like a metronome, pounded at the tempo that directed the movements of the *danseuse* and the *danseur*. This was a preview of heaven, a moment of joy on earth.

Tomorrow, she and Henri would attend his cousin's wedding, the reason for their extravagant journey. When Henri read his father's note, translating from French to English as he shared it with Ellie, he stumbled part way through.

> *You know your mother cannot travel so far. Your aunt demanded you and Ellie go in our place. Use the enclosed gift for your travel. Enjoy the sights. Your lodging is free, of course. To encourage your bride to accompany you, I've already made arrangements for you to enjoy a night at the Opera House. With love and hopes for a bon voyage.*

How silly that her father-in-law thought he might have to bribe Ellie to go to Brussels. When they returned, Ellie's world would change. She would work with the academy's scholarship students, participants in a community program that introduced culturally disadvantaged children and their families to dance. The students bloomed into incredible artists along the way, stretching not just their bodies, but their existences. They soaked up discipline and instruction and discovered self-respect, better health, physical strength, and a sense of empowerment. Such an opportunity, as Ellie knew full well, was a rare gift.

Twelve years of ballet represented more than a good run. It was an extraordinary blessing. Would she perform again? Perhaps. Time and circumstances would tell. Would she keep dancing? Always.

As Ellie watched Romeo and Juliet portray the dance of lovers, contentment cradled her. The flit of a butterfly raced across her middle, an unexpected fluttering that almost made her gasp. The life within.

Henri, who still held her hand, must have detected her flinch. He turned his face to hers, a question in his eyes. She took her free hand and ran her fingers across her abdomen. When she mouthed, "baby," his expression changed to one of exultation.

His lips moved. "Baby?"

Ellie nodded. Their tiny miracle. Their *papillon*. Their *trésor*.

~

Elizabeth, West Virginia

"Fern? Are you all right?" Percy's anxious hazel eyes swept the room before they settled on Fern, who stood in front of a wall of framed photographs. With the door ajar, humid, warm air crept into Becca's shop where a window air conditioner fought an ongoing battle to keep the interior cool and dry, conditions favorable for the black and white collection that held Fern's attention. Unlike the other displays, filled with customer portraits that Becca changed with the seasons, the back wall was the Bigler memory wall, a testament to honor and love, from one generation to the next.

Fern pressed her lips together. "I came in here to remind myself of my blessings. Seemed like a good idea at the time, but . . ." She didn't need to finish. Percy understood.

"I thought this might help you today." Percy handed Fern a handwritten note.

> *I have learned to be content in whatever state I am. I know what it is to be humbled, and I know what it is to have in excess. In any and every situation I have learned both to be filled, and to be hungry, both to have in excess, and to be in need. I have strength to do all, through Messiah who empowers me.*

"Paul's words." Fern folded the paper and pressed it into her palm. "Thank you."

"I know you *know* that verse, but sometimes we have a hard time seeing things the way we should."

"Which is the reason I came here." Fern gestured to the photos. "To see clearly." Becca and Ron's twin boys peered down from their great-grandmother's lap, Nettie's eyes as mischievous as the conspiratorial expressions on the faces of three-year-old James and Jerry. "I miss your mom."

Percy put his arm around Fern's shoulder. "Me too. Every single day. I remember the words that came to me when she passed. 'Thankfulness softens the soft edges of sorrow.' They comfort me."

Nettie's passing left a void, but over time, the empty space healed. The photograph in the center of the array still held the power to make Fern fall apart. A hundred years could come and go, but nothing would ease the pain of losing a child. Roy hid his infectious smile for the solemn occasion of his United States Marine Corps photograph, exchanging it for an intense expression, one reflecting self-confidence and pride. More than anything, the image spoke of duty and his unwavering patriotism. It had been three years since he fought a battle in Vietnam, three years since the messenger knocked on their door, upending their lives and searing a hole in their souls. Fern wiped her eyes and stepped away. It was the best she could do. Step. Step through one day at a time.

The sixties. What would historians make of them in retrospect? Amateurish photographs kept in albums at the house memorialized the better parts of the decade, promises kept with outings to America's spectacular parks. Yellowstone was next on their list. Too often, however, recollections of their pleasant excursions faded beneath disturbing headlines. The country fumbled with the war in Vietnam at the same time news of a vicious nature originated within the borders of America. Sit-ins, riots, and marches for the sake of civil rights. Assassinations, first President Kennedy, and then Martin Luther King. A brief month later, Bobby Kennedy. The Cold War, the Space Race. In the midst of upheaval came Beatlemania, Batman and Robin, Johnny Carson. Next year, if plans materialized, the country would celebrate a launch that would send a man to the moon. Changing times. Many events were worth savoring, to be sure, but too many bore grief.

"This is one of my favorites." Percy stood in front of the portrait Becca took of Wayne's family. Elaine, Bonnie, and Louise looked ready to bolt right out of the picture frame. What a handful they were, and that was before Wayne's affable darling bore Lisa, daughter number four.

"Much as I wanted to hold a grudge against Shirley for luring Wayne to Parkersburg, I think they visit often enough to make up for it," Fern said.

"They wear me out. Haven't you noticed how my eyes are glazed over by the time they go home?" Percy wiped the side of his face, as if it were damp with sweat from running after the little hooligans. "Have you seen the mess those girls make of my barn?

One hour here and they undo a week's worth of chores."

Fern bumped his shoulder. "You love every second. Besides, their messes keep you busy while you pine for their next visit."

While Percy walked to a table at the corner of the room, Fern studied the photo Becca took of Ellie on her wedding day. The bride sat in front of a mirror, inspecting her image one last time before exchanging vows with her beloved. Even her father was at a loss to describe the innocence, the hope, and the cautious expectation reflected in her beautiful face.

Music from Becca's phonograph filled the room while Fern studied the image of June and her date, both bedecked in senior prom finery. Fern's baby, all grown up. Not so long ago, in mommy years anyway, she cradled the child in her arms. Today, grandbabies rested there, next to Fern's heart, a sacred place.

Percy extended his arms. "Dance with me?"

Fern rested her head on his shoulder as the soft music and lyrics of Patsy Cline's "Crazy" filled the air.

"You know the trouble with song lyrics?" Percy asked.

"What?"

"They all speak of unrequited love or lost love. Not too many speak of an I've-got-you-and-I-won't-let-go kind of love. If I could, I'd rewrite them, use more hopeful words."

"You already serenade me with language, Mr. B. You're an artist who knows how to woo me with words."

Percy's warm breath tickled Fern's neck. "Good to know. Maybe you'll let me practice later."

Fern nestled closer. "Maybe. You know, if you think about it, Ron woos Becca with his fiddle. Wayne gets Shirley's attention with his silly poems."

"At the end of the day, my father made a habit of inviting my mother to dance. I saw them swaying in the parlor countless times, nothing on their minds but each other." Percy pulled away, sending Fern into a gentle spin. When he retrieved her, he said, "We ought to do this more often."

"Yes, we should." Fern inhaled the scent of Percy, drank in the familiar touch of his hands, his arms. "I hadn't thought about it before, but I think Gordon captured your mother's affection and love with his laughter."

"I think the gift was mutual. No doubt, they had some good years together."

"What about Leland and Muriel?" Fern asked.

"I'll need a minute to think about it. Those two, put together, are as complex as a thousand-piece jigsaw puzzle."

"Mom? Dad?" Becca stepped into the shop.

Fern almost giggled. They wouldn't solve the Muriel and Leland conundrum today. Their union was . . . well . . . it just *was*.

"We've been searching for you. What are you doing over here?"

Percy paused mid step, keeping his arms around Fern. "Am I so bad on my feet that you can't tell I'm dancing with my girl?"

"Um, no. I see what you're doing, but June's waiting. She's ready."

Percy huffed, as if the interruption were a bother. "Guess we'll have to finish this later, Mrs. B."

Becca turned off the music and herded her parents outside. June stood on the porch, two boxes stacked to the left of her, a suitcase to her right, and a pair of *pointe* shoes, their satin ribbons tied together, draped over her shoulder.

"Are you ready?" Percy called out to June as they approached.

She looked ready. Mostly. "I wish," she replied.

Percy, attentive and tender father that he was, saw the worry in June's eyes. "Let's run down the list." Percy loved making lists, especially when he could emphasize his points by counting. He lifted his index finger. "One. Are you all packed?"

"Yes."

"Two. Are you ready to travel to Charleston?"

"Yes."

"Three. Are you prepared to move in with your gracious Aunt Muriel?"

Fern swatted Percy's arm. "Be nice."

The edges of June's mouth tipped upward. "Yes."

"Four. Are you confident you have the patience to spend time with your Uncle Leland, day after day after day?"

June's smile widened. "Yes."

"Five. Are you absolutely, undeniably, unquestionably, and totally gobsmacked about taking classes at the American Academy Ballet?"

"Yes."

"Are you sure?"

"Sure enough."

The shutter on Becca's camera emitted a soft click, capturing June's transformation from an insecure teenager to that of a spunky, confident young woman with a glorious agenda. A resplendent smile graced June's face, and her warm brown eyes glimmered with pleasure. Fern's heart leapt to her throat as she watched her daughter reach for her suitcase.

After Percy loaded the trunk, Becca walked to the car and gave June a hug.

"Wish me luck?" June asked as she opened the passenger door.

"Luck?" Becca asked. "We don't wish you luck, June Bigler. We wish you joy."

Author Notes

When the local PBS station aired the documentary, "Andre Van Damme and the Story of the Charleston Ballet," the program stunned me. Few may have considered that Charleston, West Virginia boasted a ballet company that was among the ten oldest in the nation. Aside from owning bragging rights related to their longevity, the company's creation intrigued me. As an author of historical fiction, I wanted to know more, and the storyteller in me wanted to make up more. Let me separate fact from fiction.

Andre Van Damme's history and the creation of the Academy and ballet company are, for the most part, factual. With the exception of Ellie's college visits to Glenville, Huntington, and Columbus, archived programs provided the musical works performed at recitals and ballets. Maggy Van Damme, the Hiersouxs, and Julianne Kemp made significant contributions to both organizations.

Dancers Kay and Norma, Ellie's roommates, are among my cast of fictional characters, as is Larry Tanner, the *Charleston Gazette* photographer who served as Becca's mentor.

If you'll travel with me to Elizabeth, I'll give you the rundown on reality versus imagination.

What fun it was to write about Wirt County High School's heroic Tiger football team, winners of the 1955-1956 Class B Championship. Coach Ray Watson, the team's opponents, and the game scores are matters of history and sources of hometown pride.

Bigler's General Store is a fictional shop based, somewhat, on the store my grandfather owned before the effects of the Great Depression forced him to close the doors. Percy's employer, Anders Oil, is an imaginary enterprise, as well.

I loved sharing the newspaper's description of the interior of the Theatre Restaurant, with its checkered floor, chrome trim, and red accessories. The article transported me to a time when poodle skirts and ponytails were in vogue. The restaurant, Stanley's Barber Shop, Huffman's Chevrolet, Elizabeth Theater, and far too many other establishments, are no longer in operation.

Although the number of residents and businesses in Elizabeth declined in recent decades, those who call the city home are proud of their roots. A few of the folks brag about their clannish ways and insist that they'd make Scotland proud. Elizabeth's townsfolk support their local businesses and are quick to help their neighbors. The citizens' wardrobes still contain plenty of items in orange and black, and if one were to drive through town on a football Friday night, he'd hear a host of "Go Tigers!" echo throughout the hillsides.

I'd like to share one more note about the Charleston Ballet. In the epilogue, Ellie envisioned her upcoming work with the scholarship students. The program, however, did not originate during my story's timeline. Because this is such an incredible community outreach undertaking, I advanced its existence in my narrative. Kim Pauley, who was Andre Van Damme's protégée and the company's principal ballerina, assumed the role of

Artistic Director following his passing in 1989. She breathed life into the scholarship program, and today she is actively involved in this incredible endeavor, one that alters and enriches the lives of the students, their families, and the community. Kim Pauley, the Charleston Ballet, the American Academy Ballet, their directors, and their supporters have earned a standing ovation.

Acknowledgments

Creating a novel requires a heap of dedicated solitude, but if not for the time and effort gifted to me by others, my stories wouldn't reach a reader's hands. The generosity of the women who review my manuscripts humbles me. Their comments, corrections, and suggestions improve my tales, and their encouragement keeps me focused. Just as an orchestra enriches the performance of a ballerina, my team is the symphony that accompanies my words. I am grateful to my mother, to Diana Wiley, and to Sue Copeland, my dear West Virginia friend and co-author of three West Virginia-themed novels. Y'all warm my heart.

It was an honor to receive an invitation from Kim Pauley to review documents held in the Charleston Ballet's library. I am grateful for her interest in this book and her willingness to review the text and offer suggestions and more than a few corrections related to my perception or assumptions regarding ballet. Any errors are my own. As Artistic Director and CEO of the Ballet, Ms. Pauley's responsibilities are many. When I asked how she kept up with the demands, she said she has a lot of energy. She also has a sweet, generous spirit. I appreciate her investment in my work.

I'd like to thank Jerry Waters, whose website, *mywvhome.com*, served as a 1950s travel guide through Charleston, West Virginia. His extensive photograph collection and anecdotes, which encompass decades, made my research hours enjoyable. His website is a modern-day method of time travel.

I found a phenomenal resource when I acquired a copy of *West Virginia, A Guide to the Mountain State*. The book, as detailed and expansive as an encyclopedia, is a literary treasure compiled by workers of the Writers' Program of the Work Projects Administration. The WPA, like the Civilian Conservation Corps, was one of Franklin D. Roosevelt's depression-era programs. The writers collected rich details of a multitude of subjects, including history, transportation, architecture, folklore, industry, the arts, and recreation, including a right nice description of Cacapon State Park.

Although last on my list of acknowledgements, He who gives the gift of life, the gift of story, and who guides my steps, comes first in all things. For every blessing, for every lesson learned, for every occasion in which He lifts me up and sets my feet a-dancin', I thank my Creator, Elohim.

About the Author

Valerie Banfield is a talespinner to the lost, the loved, and the found. She is the author of twelve novels, co-author of three West Virginia-themed tales, and recipient of the Cascade Award for Historical Fiction. In the course of writing about West Virginia, the hills and hollows beckoned her, so she uprooted her tent stakes and planted them in the Mountain State's red clay soil. Right now, she's pretty sure she's home. For more, visit www.valeriebanfield.com.

A Note to My Readers

I LEAVE YOU WITH A REQUEST. Every author wants and needs book reviews. If you've penned reviews for me, let me thank you. I would be grateful if you'd venture over to Amazon or Goodreads and leave a comment or two for *Wish Me Joy West Virginia*.

While you're there, you might want to take a gander at *Wish Me Home West Virginia*, *Playing Carnegie, While I Count the Stars*, or my other novels. Select one or two, sit back for a spell, and let some colorful characters take you on a captivating journey.

With more yarns on the horizon, I'd like to invite you to sign up for future newsletters at www.valeriebanfield.com.